Totally Bound Publishing books by C.J. Burright

Music, Love and Other Miseries
Every Kiss
Every Minute
Every Breath
Every Step

Hearts and Haunts
Now and Always

Hearts and Haunts

NOW AND ALWAYS

C.J. BURRIGHT

Now and Always
ISBN # 978-1-80250-508-5
©Copyright C.J. Burright 2023
Cover Art by Kelly Martin ©Copyright January 2023
Interior text design by Claire Siemaszkiewicz
Totally Bound Publishing

NOW AND ALWAYS

Dedication

To the Winchester boys, for encouraging my
fascination for all things supernatural.

Chapter One

"Isn't Halloween the best?" Karen grinned at the wrinkled face peering from a warped mirror hanging in the long hallway. Empty eyes gazed back at her. Beside her, Leo pressed closer, his powerful body already invading her personal space — not that she'd ever complain.

The image in the mirror lunged as if to escape the glass. Leo jerked and pushed Karen behind him, almost knocking her over to put himself between her and danger.

"Boo!" With a leer, the face in the mirror vanished.

"I loathe Halloween," Leo said, his voice strained. He steadied her with strong hands, but his face gleamed an unholy white in the gloom. "You know how much I hate it, and you still drag me to these things."

"Hearing you squeal is too much fun to resist."

"You're sick, Ren." He scowled but didn't move away.

The lights flickered, giving the hallway a strobe effect. Leo's black sweater and jeans turned an oily shade of jet. The red letters on her T-shirt reading *Be Very, Very Afraid* seemed to bleed. In a different section of the haunted house attraction, distant screams echoed like damaged sirens. Leo grabbed her hand in a death hold.

Her face hurting from a perpetual smile, she leaned into him and settled her free hand on his biceps for extra support. She wasn't completely heartless, after all, and she'd always take advantage of any reasonable excuse to grope his spectacular body without being obvious. It never failed to amaze her that the biggest, strongest, sexiest man she knew — a man who also happened to be her best friend and was therefore off limits — lost his courage when it came to anything Halloween.

He towed her at a quicker pace down the hallway, as if he could escape if he moved fast enough.

Her smile stretched wider. There was no escape.

A motor roared behind them and filled the corridor with noise. In one nimble move, Leo jumped and spun to face the new threat. For such a big man, he was shockingly quick. As she turned, Leo made a noise somewhere between a shriek and a howl.

A clown bearing a roaring chainsaw barreled toward them, his mouth opened wide. Two rows of sharp teeth gleamed like knives in the strobing lights.

Karen shivered. *Awesome.*

The thought hadn't even passed before Leo wrapped an arm around her waist, swept her off her feet and sprinted toward the exit sign at the end of the hall as if an army of hell hounds snapped at his heels. The walls closed in, the corridor narrowing with each of Leo's pounding steps. Hands reached from the walls and clawed at their clothes as they passed. The clown with the chainsaw kept on coming with a chittering laugh.

The exit turned out to be a locked door. Leo skidded to a stop and pounded with his free hand. When that proved ineffective, he switched to kicking and cursing. Not once did he put her down.

Karen cackled with delight the entire way.

As the demented clown came within reach and lunged, the door opened on a groan. Leo leaped out and slammed the door behind him. A heavy *thud* followed, and the door shuddered beneath the impact of the clown's failed pursuit. The chainsaw cut off, leaving them in silence and the crisp air of an early October night.

Leo didn't set her on the ground until he'd jumped over the back porch stairs, onto the lawn and made it past the crooked fence surrounding the staged haunted house. He leaned against the trunk of an oak tree and closed his eyes, his breath ragged.

"I need a moment," he gasped.

"Or two."

He cracked an eye to glare. "Give me three."

"So sad. A grown man scared of ghosties and goblins. The best way to overcome a fear is to face it full on."

"Or go the mature route and avoid it." He laid his head back and slumped. "That's how I roll when it comes to demons and small children demanding candy."

Laughing, Karen plopped onto the grass and stretched out her legs. She crossed her ankles and jiggled her boots, unable to contain the energy buzz still sliding through her. A bit of a fright — and watching Leo freak — had been exactly what she needed. "That was epic. Even better than the last two years. The clown at the end was a nice touch."

"Horrifying. All of it." Leo opened his eyes and inhaled. His broad chest expanded and stretched his black sweater taut in a delicious way that she pretended not to notice.

"You didn't have to come with me."

"You've had a crappy few weeks. If me being tortured cheers you up, I had to do it."

The mention of the last few weeks of her life took her adrenaline-high down a notch. Most people believed the source of said crappiness was Ian O'Connor, the out-of-her-league lawyer at Hamilton & Associates where she worked her accounting magic. She'd crush-lusted on him longer than she should have, a physical-only appreciation and shameless flirting that had never reached her heart. Hell, she'd known she didn't possess the necessary looks or charms to make more than a single blip on Ian's radar, and his staunch commitment to noncommitment made any interest harmless. He'd been an easy distraction from—

She toyed with a loose thread on her sleeve. It didn't matter. Now, Ian was engaged to her office friend Gia. And that was when the job situation had gone to Hades on a Harley.

The sting of rejection hadn't slowed her down. She never wasted a minute of beauty sleep on Ian. Even the twist of betrayal that Gia had hooked up with her current crush was nothing a pint of ice cream couldn't solve. But the sorry looks she caught too often from her coworkers, as if she hid her heartbreak behind a brave face?

Warmth invaded her cheeks. Those looks made her want to either stab them or slink away. That pity echoed too closely the memories she'd moved to

Graywood to escape, when the pain had been brutally real. With the Ian dilemma in her face Monday through Friday, the past returned to bite her...*hard.*

A flame-red leaf drifted from the canopy above and landed on her shoulder. Leo plucked it free. The leaf crackled as he twirled it between his long fingers, giving her time to process. He always knew what she needed in any given moment, one of the many reasons why she adored him. That adoration remained part of her own personal perdition, a fact he never needed to know. She sucked at romance and enjoyed his company too much to destroy it with a fling.

Fantasies made up for everything she missed.

"You only agreed to come with me tonight because you felt sorry for my pathetic life?" She swiped the leaf from his fingers and tossed it aside. "What's your excuse for last year?"

"Don't pretend you don't remember." He gave her a narrow look and tucked his hands into his jeans pockets. "Before I knew you well enough to understand you can't be trusted in certain situations, you recorded me at the same haunted house two years ago—without my knowledge, you terrible person—and threatened to show it to Liam. Handing any one of my brothers that information would have made my life a living hell, but Liam's the worst, which you also know." He shook his head, his mouth tight. "Not one of your finer moments, Ren."

"All a matter of perspective. Manipulation is a virtue." She gave him a sweet smile. "Come on, Hughes. Admit it. Wasn't this more fun than your usual Saturday nights, fighting off your brothers with light sabers?"

"No."

She laughed.

"Was it more fun than your usual Saturday night at Seven Devils?" he countered. His expression was calm, his voice steady, but his ocean-blue eyes glittered with an emotion she couldn't read. Maybe it was the remnants of blood-curdling fear.

She shrugged. "Depends on the night."

Leo looked away and straightened, apparently recovered from his near-death experience. "I need a drink."

"You're in luck." She jumped up and looped her arm through his. "There's a sports bar right down the block."

"Do they stream sword fighting?" he asked, hopeful, as if watching men swinging swords at one another was in high demand.

"Is that even a thing?"

He scowled. "What about ax throwing?"

"Unlikely." She grinned and patted his arm. "But I'll buy to compensate."

"Damn straight you'll buy," he grumbled, allowing her to guide him onto the sidewalk.

Brisk autumn air had her leaning closer to Leo, and she almost wished she'd brought a jacket. But that would leave her with no excuse to have her arms wrapped around his. Holy hell, the man was built, a toned body from hard years of construction work and combating the other members of the Hughes clan with all manners of weapons…for fun. And people said *she* was strange.

Maybe that was why they'd hit it off right away, two oddballs who'd given up trying to be normal. She tried not to think about his flexing muscles beneath her arms or how good he smelled, like cedar and perfect man, but it was useless. It was always useless.

Over the last two years, when it came to Leo, she'd become frickin' fantastic at the game of pretend and resist.

Their slow steps clicked on the pavement, the sidewalk empty of anyone but them. Stars shone in a clear, moonless sky. It was an ideal night for romance. She sighed, and her breath left a fleeting white cloud. If Leo weren't her best friend, she'd drag him to a stop and kiss him right here beneath the lamppost, the distant shrieks of terrified people in the background. He'd kiss her back, using that luscious mouth of his to set her skin aflame, and —

"I hate it when you sigh like that." Leo's soft, husky voice splintered her fantasy. "It means you're unhappy instead of plotting mischief." He bored his eyes into her.

She refused to squirm beneath the intensity, the sense that he saw straight through all her trappings and discerned the warp and weave of her soul. If he could read minds, he would have been scandalized by her thoughts long ago. "I've decided I need a change."

"What sort of change?"

"Scenery. I've been considering it for a while now, made a pro and con list, looked at my options from every angle. I woke up this morning with a clear answer."

Leo was always her go-to person who she ran everything by first. *Almost* everything. But saying this new plan aloud made it real, solid, and if she didn't follow through, she'd feel like a loser. Karen took a breath and blew it out. "I'm quitting Hamilton & Associates and applying for an accountant job at Cooper Homes. The posting showed up yesterday morning. Even though it doesn't pay as much as

Hamilton, the medical, dental and 401K plans are great."

The confession released a stab of exhilaration edged with scary. Accountant jobs in Graywood were rare. Her timing had been lucky with Hamilton & Associates. Another opening in her field might not come along for months, which would require a job search in other towns, maybe moving. She didn't want to leave the home she'd made here—worrying her bottom lip between her teeth, she glanced at Leo—or the friendships she'd forged.

He narrowed his eyes at some point in the distance, looking thoughtful. "If you want to switch to a construction company, work for me. I've been thinking about farming out the accounting side of my business, to free up some precious time to do more important things." He winked. "I'm the worst bookkeeper."

"No way." She shook her head. "Working for friends is a bad idea."

"Not if I'm the friend." His voice deepened an octave into a blood-warming rumble.

"Absolutely no." Leo was a great employer, generous and fair, his company always on the business bureaus' best list. But working for him would send her even deeper into the void with all her forbidden fantasies. Already she had trouble keeping them under control. And mixing business and friendship was almost as dangerous as combining best friends and physical desire. Nothing good ever emerged at the end. She wouldn't add Leo to her romantic wreckage.

She focused on the pub at the end of the block, the cheerful lights and hint of fried food, ignoring the weight of his steady stare. Changing her mind about this wasn't happening, not even with the power of Leo's super-scowl. Working for him would put pressure on their friendship, warp it into something else. Their relationship was far too important. *He* was too important.

Finally, he exhaled and swiped his fingers through his hair, leaving it rumpled and even more sexy. "Why do you always insist on being stubborn?"

She gave him an impish smile.

"Very well. Be that way. But I'll tell you this— The only way you're going to land the job at Cooper Homes is if you know at least a smidge of construction. Cooper expects all the staff, even office workers, to jump in and help out on site if they're short-handed. Construction crews aren't always the most reliable employees."

"That's not listed on the job announcement." She frowned up at him. His expression was serious, no sign of trickery, but he'd used his sexy voice on her, given her the scowl. He was up to something shady.

He shrugged. "I know Cooper."

"You know everyone." Graywood was a small town, and the Hughes family fingers were dipped in everything good, charitable and green. She'd been in Graywood for a couple of years, not enough to be trusted by the local residents. Even if no one admitted it, unless a soul was born and raised in Graywood, they were considered a permanent outsider.

Some things never changed. The one exception was Leo. Right away, he'd made her feel like she belonged. She couldn't lose that, not for anything.

Leo stopped and faced her. Karen braced herself. Here it was, his scheme.

"I have a proposal for you."

"Is it indecent?" Karen shut her mouth fast, heat rising to her neck. *Flirting level warning, code red.* "Kidding, of course."

"Actually," he said, drawing out the word. "The decency level depends on perspective."

He tugged on his ear lobe, a nervous tell. What—besides Halloween—could rattle the serious, steady, unshakable Leo Hughes?

"You've won my full attention." She poked him playfully in the chest. "Lay it on me."

One corner of his mouth curled up in a slow, lazy smile, and all hint of nervousness vanished as he met her gaze. That heat in her neck spread to her face. She hoped he assumed it to be the lamplight glow on her skin, not the tingling warmth curling through her veins.

"Remember the Granton estate a few miles out of town?" He didn't wait for her unnecessary answer. She'd been intrigued by the abandoned property since the moment she'd driven into Graywood job hunting, glimpses of the Gothic mansion and storybook landscape, full of secrets and gloom. "I bought it."

Karen gasped. "Without telling me?"

"Closed this afternoon. I was waiting for the right moment to share the news." His eyes gleamed with humor. "Now, back to my proposal."

"If it has anything to do with Granton, I'm in." She bounced in her boots, unable to keep still. Her best friend had bought Granton Hall. She couldn't wait to get inside.

"Always require full disclosure before making any binding agreements, Ren. As it happens, there is some fine print in this particular proposal."

That sounded ominous. She folded her arms and waited for him to continue.

"First, the background. There's a locals-only construction competition starting tomorrow. It involves renovating a single room by the end of the month. Whoever wins gets the bid to renovate town hall and a spread in *Renovation & Remodel*, the magazine every construction company aspires to be in. The publicity for that alone is worth the effort."

"Since when do you need extra attention or work?" Hughes & Sons Construction had been established by Leo's great-great-grandfather and passed down through the generations, growing in reputation and building an empire to fund all the Hughes' family good deeds. Leo had a few days over two years holding the reins. His father had passed right before Ren had met him, and he took the responsibilities of carrying on the family legacy very seriously.

"Since I bought Granton Hall." He tucked her arm through his again and strolled toward the pub. "The rules are simple. Must be a local company to enter. The owner must personally renovate their chosen room with the assistance of a single volunteer." He glanced at her. "Since you're in need of some construction experience and I need a reliable volunteer, it's a win-win."

Karen studied his unreadable expression. The opening for the position at Cooper Homes didn't close until the end of the month, enough of a window to gain some basic skills. Learning construction from Leo in her spare time would be perfect. But something about this proposal had made him nervous. "What's the catch?"

"I need you at least part-time."

She ignored how her blood heated at the words '*I need you*'. With all the personal days and vacation hours she'd built up at Hamilton & Associates, she could make it part-time. Escaping the cubicle and coworkers for half a day every day until she had the skills to land the job at Cooper Homes would be a definite bonus. Working only part-time with Leo, she could manage her fantasies, and Granton Hall would be the best distraction.

"No problem." She paused with him outside the pub entrance. Voices and laughter drifted out with delicious smells. A basket of garlic tots was about to meet its final destiny. "What else?"

"We have until Halloween to renovate one room at Granton Hall and impress the judges. Today was the last day to enter the competition, so the timing was perfect. Not going to lie— It will be a lot of hard labor."

She studied her stubby fingernails. "Guess I'll have to miss the manicurist for a month."

"Ready for the fine print?"

At his low, sultry voice, she lifted her gaze to his, and her breath caught. Behind the confident mask, another emotion flickered, banked and steaming. That heat in her veins rose a few degrees. Controlling her libido for a month was a small price to pay for the dream of walking the antique halls of Granton and learning a few construction skills on the side. *I can do this.*

"Go on."

"So that any spare minutes may be spent on the project, not wasting drive time, I'd require you to live at the mansion."

"Seriously, Leo?" For the first time in weeks, the excitement bubbling up erased all the shadows left by rejection reminders and dreams long lost. She fisted his sweater to keep from bouncing up and down like a pogo stick. "When do we start?"

"Not so fast. There's one last detail to my proposal."

She released his sweater and smoothed it out, one pat more than necessary of his firm chest. "Whatever it is, I'm in."

He gave her a lopsided smile, the one he used on only her. "Glad to hear it, but you won't be living at Granton alone."

"I won't?" The words tangled in her dry throat.

"No, Ren, darling." His eyes deepened to stormy seas, his voice to molten honey. He opened the pub door and motioned her inside. As the heat and chaos surrounded her, he leaned near her ear and whispered, "You'll be living with me."

Chapter Two

Leo ushered Karen into the pub. A group of men and women wearing team jerseys whooped it up in one corner, watching a soccer player score on a big screen. A glance at the other televisions throughout the open floorplan revealed popular sports and overpaid athletes, nothing to spark his interest. No blades or weapons, not worth his time.

The hostess motioned to him, and he settled a hand on the small of Ren's back, guiding her through the crowded tables and knots of laughing, talking people. The mere contact spiked his already-heightened awareness of her. All she had to do was breathe and all his senses zeroed in on her. Meanwhile, she relegated him to the best-friend sidelines.

Not for much longer.

She hadn't said a word since they'd walked in. He could count on one hand the number of times he'd rendered Karen speechless. That a spontaneous proposal to shack up—whether he intended to keep it purely professional or not—could tangle her tongue was a promising sign.

He'd need every advantage to persuade her to the dark side of Team Leo.

They stopped at a two-person table in a shadowed corner, perfect for his purposes. He pulled out Ren's chair for her and sat down as the waitress arrived. He ordered a beer, which gave him time to watch Ren look over the menu, biting her luscious lower lip as she decided.

Damn. He shifted in his seat and forced himself to watch the golf game happening on the screen before he did something irreparable, such as lean across the table, take her lip between his own teeth and find out if she tasted as delicious as she looked. *Not yet.* Not until she agreed to his proposal and gave him a month of her undivided attention. If he lost control now, all the progress he'd made in the last two years, earning her trust and creating a solid foundation of friendship, might be for nothing.

Speaking the truth into the space between them was long overdue. Miserable months he'd suffered in silence, pretended the simmering tension between them wasn't there. He'd stood on the sidelines as the best friend a girl could ever have while she dated men who were all wrong for her. *No more waiting.* His heart knew who it belonged to, no substitutes.

Convincing her wouldn't be easy, and winning the first wave was crucial to his cause. He'd have to use every tactic at his disposal to persuade her that living with him for a month was a deal she couldn't refuse.

Ren placed her order, and as soon as the waitress left, he girded his loins and stepped onto the battlefield.

"For the record, my proposal's level of indecency is under your complete control. I don't expect special favors while sharing space."

"Special favors?" She leaned back and folded her arms, one eyebrow arched.

"Such as doing my laundry or cooking." One side of his mouth twitched up. "But I'm open to other suggestions."

Her gaze flicked to his mouth then back to his eyes. "I believe you're fully aware of my cooking skills."

How could he forget? "You won't be allowed to touch any kitchen appliance other than the refrigerator. I have yet to extract the smoke from my favorite jacket after the one time you invited me over for dinner."

"Who knew cheese sandwiches could burn like that?" She batted her eyelashes.

"Hmm." He suspected she could cook well enough and simply preferred not to. "Granton Hall has been deserted for years, and while I haven't had time to inspect every floorboard for safety, a couple of bedrooms are habitable...*ish*. We'll be sleeping down the hall from each other. We can jog in the morning on Granton's trails." He gave her the smile that always added a flush to her pale skin. "Won't that be fun?"

"No." Karen shook her head and drummed her fingers on the table. "Absolutely nope, no way. We can't live together."

And the fight begins. "Why not? What happened to '*if it's anything to do with Granton, I'm in*'?"

"I'm considering the fine print."

The waitress brought their drinks and a basket of garlic tots, which Ren pulled close and looked like she might growl if he dared reach for one. Her fascination with Granton Hall was his mightiest weapon, and he had to keep her focus there, his best shot at getting the time and proximity he needed to win her heart. The fact that she wanted to switch jobs was a bit of unexpected serendipity. This chance would never come along again.

Leo sipped his beer and waited while the garlic tot fatality count rose. Ren was always more agreeable when food was involved. He counted five and renewed his assault.

"It would be only a month, and I promise you'll learn enough construction skills to land the job at Cooper Homes. What's the problem?"

"The problem?" She jabbed the tot between her fingers at him. "I —" She exhaled, whatever she'd been going to say gone. "Too much time together can kill the strongest relationship. No job is worth that."

Leo scowled, reading between the lines. *Hank.* Karen's childhood best friend farm boy, the idiot who had broken her heart, the driving force that had spurred her to move to Graywood... Some scars were easier to ignore and pretend they didn't exist rather than face on a daily basis.

It blew that some other guy had made her believe that friendship and romance couldn't mix. If he ruled the universe, *he* would have been the one to grow up with her, friends first, lovers later, soul mates forever. He'd break every bone in his body before causing the slightest hairline fracture in her beautiful heart. Her first love had severely altered her view, but he refused to believe the damage was irreversible.

"Hey there." A woman in a little black dress that left even less to the imagination set a drink in front of him. Smiling, she laid a hand on his shoulder, as if entitled to touch him. "Your glass is empty. I thought you might want another one. I'm Tianna, and while I'm here, I'll give you my number, too." She held out a business card.

She was gorgeous, her smile inviting, and his brother Liam would tell him he was an idgit for not taking her up on everything she offered. Funny how people always seemed to want what they couldn't have.

"Thank you for the kindness." He didn't take the business card and made a careful point not to smile. Any time he smiled at a woman, she seemed to interpret it as a neon welcome sign. "But my heart is otherwise engaged."

Tianna's gaze flicked to Karen, and in less than a heartbeat, she assessed and dismissed the competition.

Ren's responsive smile was sharp, and that single observation kept his hope alive for another day. Karen pretending not to be jealous was adorable.

"Sure about that?" Pushing her breasts out, Tianna dragged a finger along his shoulder.

He glanced at her hand now resting on his biceps. "Emphatically."

"Your loss." Flicking her long hair, she spun away.

"Tianna, wait."

Her face lit up as she pivoted. "Yes?"

"You forgot something." He handed her the glass she'd left on the table.

She stomped back, swiped the drink from his fingers and chugged its contents down. She *thunked* the empty glass on the table. "A-hole."

With a sniff, she strode off without a backward glance.

"Holy hell, Hughes." Karen leaned back in her chair and shook her head in mock disapproval. "You're rough on a girl's ego. I'm not sure Tianna is ever going to be the same."

"I didn't invite her to interrupt our conversation." And he hated how she'd sized up Ren and dismissed her as inconsequential. Anyone who made Karen feel anything less than invaluable didn't deserve his respect or time.

She studied him, a teasing curiosity sparkling in her eyes. "Why do you always use the same line, that garbage about your heart being engaged? As long as I've known you, you've never had a girlfriend. If you've dated, I haven't heard about it, and I *would* have heard." She cocked her head. "Are you keeping secrets from me?"

So many secrets. He maintained an impassive expression, practiced to perfection over the last years. "You have your fun. I have mine."

"But that's not fair. I share my fun." She bounced in her seat, clearly intrigued, and he made a point to keep his gaze on her face, not her perky assets. Karen didn't need to wear a slinky dress. In ripped jeans, a T-shirt, rocker belt and boots, she outshone all the women there. Her red hair, pixie short and styled at a choppy punk angle to still look professional enough for her accountant job, gleamed beneath the pub lights. He'd lost count of how many times he'd resisted brushing his fingers through it to test its softness.

"Not all fun includes public humiliation of your friends, more specifically me."

"Only the best fun." She smiled, showcasing the cutest dimple that he'd ever seen. He blamed that dimple for a lot of his less-than-rational decisions.

Taking a sip of her cinnamon-sweet cocktail — a Poison Apple, appropriate both for the season and the woman herself — Ren eyed him. Whatever schemes and speculations went on in her pretty head almost certainly had everything to do with him and nothing to do with the truth. He should probably be worried.

"You know you can tell me anything, right?" The sudden seriousness in her tone raised all sorts of suspicions. "That I'll never judge you?" She reached across the table and took his hand between both of hers.

His heart stuttered. Had she finally figured out his feelings for her ran far deeper than mere friendship? More importantly, was she at a point where she'd be open to discovering how much they could be to each other?

Ren leaned closer, as if ready to share an old secret, and he bent his head nearer so he wouldn't miss a word. "You're into men, aren't you?"

If not for the playful sparks in her eyes, he might have been insulted. He had enough of his own problems to keep him busy, and what another person chose to do in their romance life wasn't his business. But if Ren thought for even a moment that he was attracted to men, she was more oblivious to him than he believed.

His hand still trapped between hers, he caressed her palm with his thumb and held her gaze. "You're onto me." He sighed. "I've tried to switch teams, but all it takes is a pair of broad shoulders and strong arms to remind me of the truth—or a firm, muscled chest." With his free hand, he stroked his own chest over his sweater, slow and sensual. Her eyes tracked the movement, and he hid a smile when her throat worked. "Flat, washboard abs." Full of suggestion, he dragged his fingers along the plane of his stomach and lower, beneath the table and out of sight. "And all the other amenities, which I'm sure you can also appreciate."

She made a small noise that might have been affirmation and blinked a few times.

Before she recovered, he plucked the maraschino cherry from the rim of her glass and brought it to his lips. Holding it by the stem, Leo licked the cherry once and eased the fruit free with his teeth. He popped it into his mouth and chewed, Ren's full focus on his mouth, exactly where he wanted it.

Another nail of hope pounded into the framework of his heart. Longing had ignited the moment he'd first met her two years before in the toilet-plunger section of the hardware store, and she'd mistaken him for an employee. When it came to numbers, she was a wiz — not so much with simple household situations. If she wanted a job in construction, she needed him.

"Holy hell," she muttered. As if realizing she still held his hand, she pulled free and drained most of her drink. She set the glass down and pointed at him, accusing. "You're not gay."

"No?" He gave her a lazy smile.

"Jerk." The appearance of her dimple erased any annoyance.

Leo snapped his fingers. "I know what's preventing you from jumping on my generous, once-in-a-lifetime proposal. Our friendship is rock solid, so that's not a valid excuse." He leaned back in his chair as if he'd already won the argument. "You're afraid to spend a month with me at Granton Hall."

"*Pfft*." She stirred the ice in her glass with the straw. "I'm not afraid of anything."

"No need to be embarrassed of the truth." He stole a tot from her basket, narrowly avoiding her slap. "You're afraid that if you spend more than a few hours with me, you won't be able to resist my uncountable charms." He tossed the tot in his mouth and grinned.

"Grunting and making noises with your armpit are *not* charming."

"Are you saying I'm repulsive?" He softened his voice to a purr. "Want to look me straight in the baby blues and lie, Ren?"

Karen stared right back at him, but there was no hiding the twitch of her right eyelid.

"It's a yes or no question." And a question he'd never outright asked her, one he wanted her to answer aloud. He needed to hear her confess at least one tiny truth, some acknowledgment that unexplored layers waited beneath their friendship.

"Fine, since your ego needs assuaging after the clown and chainsaw incident." She wrinkled her nose, scrunching the scattering of cute freckles. "I'd have to be dead and bloodless not to appreciate your" — her gaze flicked over him and, whether or not she intended to, she licked her lips — "capital."

He managed to keep his expression cool and fought back a ridiculous smile. Only an accountant would compare his body to monetary assets, but the compliment was a start.

"Your repulsiveness or lack thereof has nothing to do with my decision. I like our friendship the way it is — fun, low-key, no drama. A month of close proximity might change that."

"There's no reason our friendship won't be stronger if we level it up." A growl of frustration rose into his throat, and he swallowed it. "Think of it as enhancing who we already are, a journey of discovery for further observation. It will be fun. Trust me. I promise to feed you."

She sighed. "Leo —"

Before she announced the final determination, he went for the kill. "Renovating Granton is more than winning the bid for the new city hall. I bought it with a vision, a charity project all my own in honor of my dad."

Palmer Hughes might not have been blood, but he was the only father he'd ever known. Leo's mom had been a struggling single parent of three small boys, deserted by her long-term boyfriend. She was barely scraping by, and more than a few times they'd slept in her car and lived off shelter food. When Palmer had found them, everything changed. He'd shown Leo what it meant to be a man of integrity.

"So, this is a personal charity project." By her flat tone, he wouldn't be surprised if she pictured his face as she jabbed her straw into the ice. He wasn't above using good deeds as a prybar of persuasion. Ren and her accounting skills would be an amazing asset to what he hoped to create.

"I want to turn Granton Hall into transitional housing for local, single mothers and their children who have fallen on hard times, to offer whatever support they need to get back on their feet — food and shelter, education, counseling, childcare, employment assistance. The recognition I'd get from the article in *Renovation & Remodel* would be huge in getting the word out."

"And for fundraising." Ren sounded grumpy, as he'd hoped. It was a sign her resistance crumbled. She knew his deep compassion for single mothers without a support system, colored by his own experiences.

"Correct. I poured a considerable portion of my finances into it. If I can't inspire public interest in the project, I'll have to move in with you instead." He winked. "Come on, Ren. You're perfect for this project — trustworthy, reliable, meticulous, smart — and there's no one I'd rather have working at Granton with me."

Her cheeks flushed. "Laying it on thick, Hughes."

"And all true. If it's not enough that you'll learn skills to work for Cooper, then do it for me. You'll save me precious time hunting down a dependable volunteer. Or do it for charity. Think of all the people you'll be helping while spending an entire month in the hallowed halls of Granton Hall, where mystery awaits around every corner."

"Using Granton *and* personal charity is a low blow, pure evil." Karen flicked her straw at him, scattering wet drops on his neck. "If I didn't know any better, I'd accuse you of buying it as part of a diabolical plot years in the making of convincing me to work with you."

He wasn't about to confirm that theory, not when she was so close to agreeing, offering him a real opportunity to charm her at all hours. So what if he'd watched the property ever since he'd learned of her fascination with it and maybe, possibly, made the owner an offer he couldn't refuse? The estate was a solid investment.

"That would take some serious scheming," he said carefully.

"Which you are totally capable of." She squeezed her eyes shut, as if he was the biggest pain in her butt. He had no intention of confirming that theory, either. "One month of sharing space and all my free time laboring with you within Granton walls?" She drained the last of her drink and stood. "And I'll come out of it with some killer construction experience, more than enough to impress Cooper?"

"You'll knock Cooper's overalls off." Leo held his breath, sensing how close she was to surrender. He'd take great pleasure in showing her the benefits of being both friends and lovers, partners and companions. Once she understood Hank was a brief stop along the way to her final destination—*him*—she'd recognize that she could have it all, scars notwithstanding.

"If I take you up on the offer—and I'm not saying I am—I'd have a condition of my own." She cocked her hip in that sassy, sexy way that drove him crazy. He couldn't wait to show her *how* crazy.

"Name it."

"One horror movie each weekend." Her auburn eyebrows lifted, a challenge.

"Animated?" he asked in a hopeful whisper.

"Not even." Her raspberry-stained lips curved into a wicked smile. "Sounds fun, doesn't it?"

"You can't use me to satisfy your sick need for a fear-induced adrenaline rush, hide your face in my shoulder when the beast leaps out and I'm left the victim, too scared senseless to close my eyes." He straightened from his chair and loomed over her. "This would be a legit mutual exchange of services. I will not be abused."

"It's a yes or no question, Hughes," she said sweetly.

Leo gave her a cool look. For a chance to win her heart, he'd already endured far more than a horror movie or two. He sucked in a long breath through his nose and released it. "You're an unfeeling monster."

"Some monsters are cuter than others." *Damn, that dimple.* "And most of them bite."

"Counting on it." He gave her a slow smirk.

Her humor faded, and the uncertainty in her lovely face made his heartbeat falter. If she didn't give him a chance now, with all the extra incentives, he'd be stuck in the friend zone forever.

"I'll sleep on it and let you know by Monday at the latest." She flipped some cash on the table. "That's all I can promise."

As she turned to go, he caught her wrist and gently pulled her close. Her vanilla perfume curled around him, drowning out the scents of fried food, sweet drinks and beer. He cupped her chin and held her gaze. "Just to be clear, you and me? We'll always be solid, no matter what you decide. Got it?"

"Got it." She patted his cheek. "And help yourself to the rest of my tots. I need some alone time to compile my pro and con list."

He glanced at the basket on the table. "There are only two left, Ren."

"You're welcome."

Leo watched the sexy sway of her hips until she disappeared from view. He sat down to finish his beer and plucked the last two tots from the basket. Before Ren, he'd never been in love. He'd thought gaining her friendship first would pave the way to her heart, show her the type of man he was, give her the time she'd need to realize he belonged to her, too. He had never imagined it would take years.

He drained his beer and watched the golf game streaming on the television screen a few tables away. Confessing that he wanted her was a risk, but if his genius plan couldn't break him out of the friendship prison she'd locked him in, nothing could.

A blonde woman sitting beneath the television stood, disrupting his view. She met his gaze, smiled and headed his way.

Dealing with another Tianna wasn't on the agenda. He stood and made his escape. One woman alone held his heart, and whatever reservations Ren had about living with him, she wouldn't deny a charitable cause or turn down a chance to spend a month at Granton Hall.

And he'd give her a Halloween she'd never forget.

Chapter Three

Monday morning in the breakroom at Hamilton & Associates, Karen poured herself a coffee and grabbed the sugar dispenser. *Living with Leo.* His condition to helping her land the job at Cooper's skated through her mind, stuck on repeat.

She aimed the sugar canister at her mug and watched a woman in the park across the street throw a frisbee for her poodle. The pro and con list she'd made had a ton of pros and a single con — the Leo temptation. Trapped between the same four walls with him for a month would be a serious challenge. What if, in a moment of weakness, she broke their sacred, unspoken rule by doing something stupid, such as sliding her hands under his shirt and exploring every inch of that velvet skin and hard muscle she'd dreamed about?

Her face heated at the mere memory of Saturday night, when he'd caressed his own chest over his sweater. Fairies had somersaulted in her stomach, and her overactive imagination had taken over. It hadn't been his hand stroking, but hers, the cashmere soft and sinful beneath her fingers, a taunting layer blocking her from the flesh she wanted. She'd dragged her fingertips over his taut stomach, lower, tracing the contours of each muscle as liquid fire burned her alive. And that cherry between his teeth? Her brain had blipped into dead air as sensation enslaved the rest of her body.

Her turtleneck seemed to shrink, strangling her, and she pushed the memory away. Leo had flirted with her before, but never with such intensity. She couldn't afford to think of him that way, at least not while he occupied the same room with her. If she tripped, there would be no going back. When romance between friends fizzled, no matter the best intentions, the relationship suffered...died.

Making the same mistake twice would *not* happen.

"Need a double extra sugar kick with your coffee to get you to the weekend?" Gia, her best friend at the office—and partly responsible for why she needed to switch scenery—leaned a hip against the counter and quirked an elegant eyebrow at the coffee spilling from Karen's overfull mug.

"Crappity-crap!" Karen set the sugar down and grabbed the paper towels. "I've committed the unforgivable act of negligent waste of caffeine and sugar."

"Just don't mess with the matcha." Reaching for a mug and tea from the cupboard, Gia looked at her askance. "Must be some deep thoughts."

"You have no idea, G." Karen finished cleaning up and bent to sip enough coffee so it wouldn't slosh over the rim. "My thoughts are more of an endless space, the final frontier. There's no escape."

Gia's eyes widened, and she hopped onto a dry spot of the counter, a glamor queen stopping to chat with the peasants. Smoothing her pin-striped skirt as she leaned in, she whispered, "What's his name, where did you meet him and when are you seeing him again?"

Karen took another stooped-over sip from her coffee. Usually, she'd spill any dirt on her latest fling, but Leo wasn't in the same universe, let alone the same class as the occasional guy she wound up with. Even talking about him in the same category felt like tiptoeing over thin ice, where a single crack would send her plummeting into frigid depths. But if she didn't tell someone, she might explode.

"His name is Leo Hughes, I met him at the hardware store two years ago and I'm sure I'll see him sooner rather than later."

"Leo?" A disappointed huff from Gia made the golden curl near her chin sway. "I'd hoped you met your hot HEA guy, not that Leo isn't hot." She narrowed her eyes and tilted her head. "Have you thought about it? You and Leo?"

Karen choked on her coffee. Did she have a neon sign on her forehead that read *showing now – naughty fantasies starring Leo Hughes, off-limits best friend*? "I'm not desperate enough to jump my best friend."

Yet.

"That's not an answer, Kar." Gia hopped off the counter and landed gracefully on her stilettos in a swirl of sweet perfume. "He's super-nice, super-gorgeous and super-rich." She slid Karen a sly look. "Besides, my spidey-senses say it wouldn't take much for you to go from friends to something smoking."

"Urgh." Karen hid her face in the coffee mug and took a long swallow. With any luck, Gia would assume steam caused the heat in her cheeks. "Leo and I are friends. Period. He isn't up for grabs."

"Which is odd for you to note, since you're usually the first to point out a man's most grabbable parts. And

Leo has so many yummy ones, all worth grabbing." Gia's grin edged on wicked.

She wiped her moist palms on her plaid wool skirt. If Leo was a bald, toothless blob, thinking of him beyond her BFF would be so much easier. If they hadn't hit it off right away, if he hadn't made her feel for the first time in forever, connected to another person, she *would* have had grabby hands. Leo always made her feel as if she was his favorite person in the world. A hard knot formed in her throat. She didn't want to lose that.

"Control yourself, Glitter Girl." Regaining her composure, she arched an eyebrow at Gia, leaned against the counter and crossed one booted ankle over the other. "You're engaged, which means you're only allowed to talk about Ian's parts."

"Not even. Engaged does not mean I go blind and mute. Speaking of engagements, I've been meaning to ask you something, and if you say 'no' it's okay." Gia fiddled with a pearl button on her cuff. "I won't be upset at all."

Karen paused, her cup halfway lifted. Anything that made the office glamor queen nervous couldn't be good for her. "Lay it on me."

A wide, brilliant smile lit up her angelic face, and Karen hid a stab of envy. If only she had the same power to shock a room with her beauty. No man would leave Gia Hellman unless the Grim Reaper took him. She'd commit some serious crimes to possess that skill, to never worry that she'd be abandoned by someone she trusted.

"Even though the wedding date hasn't been set, I'm planning ahead. With Ian's and my penchant for fashion?" Gia sighed, dreamy. "It's going to be the Graywood event of the millennium, guaranteed."

"I'm not much of a wedding kind of person, if that's what you're asking. Marriage, true love and happily ever after aren't on my list of life goals." A few years ago, it had been a different story, and she'd burned that book when she'd left home. "The only things I like about weddings are the open bar, fancy appetizers and recording all the hilarious dance moves that show up after a few too many free drinks."

Gia threw her head back and laughed, all bells and happiness. "I'll sign you up for the video crew, but I was hoping you'd agree to play a larger role and be in my wedding party."

She pasted on a smile. *Great.* Bearing the cross of a bridesmaid was not her idea of a good time.

"I promise the dresses won't be an ungodly color or have puffy sleeves." Gia watched her with big blue eyes. She was worse than a puppy begging for a treat.

"A promise that should be written in blood with a curse attached if broken, for the sake of all."

"True." Gia added a coax to her voice. "There will be lots of opportunities to mingle with groomsmen."

Karen snorted. "Ian has friends?"

"A couple." Gia grinned, unoffended.

"Besides your sister's boytoy Roman, and Garret, who's off the market?" She swirled her sugar coffee. "Not convincing."

"Oh, there will be opportunities." Gia winked. "Enough to make a bet on your future."

Dammit. She preferred to be the one meddling. It kept people on their toes, and she loved the distraction from her own lack of romance. In the two years she'd worked at Hamilton & Associates, she'd organized so many underground bets on office liaisons and shenanigans that she'd lost count. "I should've known betting on you and Ian would backfire in an unavoidable explosion someday."

"Yes, you should have." The devil himself—aka Ian O'Connor, Gia's fiancé—strolled in, looking sharp in a dark suit and blood-red tie.

Sleek and elegant with an edge of menace, Ian made many a woman want a bite of bad boy, and Karen hadn't been immune to that dangerous allure. The power suit represented his personality—polished, perfectly fitted, and a trap for the razor-sharp teeth waiting beneath the surface. While his courtroom track record was pristine, he needed improvement in the nice human department.

Her imagination had spun a fantasy or two around Ian, a fleeting fascination that she'd hoped would distract her from Leo. But beyond stunning masculine features, Leo was nothing like Ian. No matter where he was, what he did or wore, Leo never let the trappings define the man inside.

"Didn't you open your own office down the street?" Karen arched an eyebrow at Ian. "And yet you're still here, pirating Hamilton's coffee."

"That's not all I'm here for." His predatory gaze fixed on Gia, and he went straight for the kill. His prey didn't have the sense to run. A soft smile lighting her face, Gia lifted her mouth to Ian's for a kiss.

Bleck. Karen resumed pretending to study her coffee mug. If anyone deserved to have love again, it was Gia. She'd lost her first fiancé to cancer and had despaired of finding someone who might love her the same way again—deeply, madly, completely. No one, including Gia, had predicted Ian to be that person.

But beneath the happiness she had for her friend, she couldn't deny a thread of envy. In the pond of toads Gia had dated she'd found a shark, and despite the danger, there wasn't an ounce of doubt in their love. Beauty and the beast had found where they both belonged...with each other.

Alan, a newbie law clerk at Hamilton & Associates, stepped into the break room. His gaze flicked from Ian and Gia—the couple otherwise known as *Gian*—to Karen. Pity flashed in his eyes, echoed in the tight smile.

Sick to her stomach, Karen set her mug in the sink as Gia chirped a greeting to Alan, always Miss Friendly. Gia's engagement to Ian wasn't the reason her safe workspace had cracked. Dealing with *Gian* every so often didn't rip out the seams of her memories. It was the sorry expressions like Alan's that she needed to escape, the reminder that everyone knew she didn't measure up, wasn't enough for a lasting love. Pretending everything was copacetic wouldn't erase the souvenirs of a past she wanted to forget.

Pasting on a smile, she nodded at Alan and broke for the door before *Gian* disentangled into two separate individuals. "Gotta go. The numbers aren't going to crunch themselves."

"You can give me an answer later," Gia called after her. "No pink tulle, I promise!"

Around the hallway corner, Karen paused and pulled her cell phone from her skirt pocket. She hesitated another moment before texting Leo.

I'm in.

She shut her phone down and headed for human resources before sanity kicked back in and she considered the consequences of sharing living quarters with the best friend who already inspired too many fantasies that could never be fulfilled.

* * * *

Before the lunch hour had hit on Monday, Karen visited human resources, applied her saved vacation and personal time off so she could work part-time. She used Tuesday and Wednesday to finish up bookwork. Thursday at noon, she ditched the office and packed her suitcase. She made it to the gravel driveway leading to the Granton estate in time for afternoon cocktails. The mighty iron gate leading to the mansion, locked every time she'd driven by before, was opened wide in welcome.

Excitement shivered through her as she drove through the gate, and the crowding trees offered new glimpses of the building's pointed, Gothic gables. Diamond-paned windows flashed like waterfall spray in sunlight, liquid and magical. The woods opened up into a roundabout drive circling a cracked, dry fountain, and she got her first full look at the mysterious Granton Hall.

"Wowza." Karen parked her car beside Leo's motorcycle and got out for an unobstructed view. She knew Leo had some serious cash, but this must have cost most of his hard-earned fortune. The steep roof and killer gables made it seem taller than two stories high, not including the attic. Walls tangled with ivy and made of gray stone added a foreboding beauty. It would make the perfect horror movie setting. She couldn't hide a grin. Leo probably wouldn't appreciate the irony.

A fractured stone walkway, hardly more than a trail, led through weeds and overgrown grass to the mansion's front porch. An occasional sculpture weathered by years and negligence added a cemetery vibe. Matching faun statues flanked the entryway, lichen oozing from their eyes and leering mouths, ivy shackling their limbs.

She couldn't wait to see what hid inside.

Suitcase in hand, she stepped toward the walkway and paused as a tremor rolled down her back. Maybe it stemmed from delight at discovering Granton Hall's secrets. Maybe it came from taking a dive into the unknown.

Or maybe the man stepping from the porch and heading for her, his lopsided smile aimed at her, sparked her imagination to life.

Her pulse kicked into race-car speed. *Best friend. Not made for jumping.*

That was a total lie. There was no better specimen for a girl to jump on, grab ahold of and explore every wicked daydream with. Leo's collar-length hair would be perfect for her fingers to tangle in. Too many times to count she'd wondered if his mouth felt as soft as it looked. His body was sculpted from a foundation of sports and horseplay with four brothers, perfected by hard labor and the Hughes clan fighting with swords, light sabers or the weapon of the week. A few of those muscles tempted her from beneath his long-sleeved T-shirt and faded jeans. Had he been any other man, she'd be drooling.

But Leo wasn't any other man. She had to keep things cool…somehow.

"Hey, Ren." He took her suitcase and pivoted to face Granton Hall with her. "What do you think?"

Karen did her best to ignore the heat radiating from him, the scent of cedar and sawdust that always clung to his clothing and instead focused on the mansion before her. Shadows and secrets lurked in every corner, from the stained-glass windows frowning from the second floor to the moss-filled crevices in the stone walls. A black iron fence caged one side of the building, a subtle warning to keep out. No light glowed from within, as if Granton had already dismissed Leo's presence as a passing memory.

"It's everything I imagined—stark, arcane and breathtakingly Gothic...splendidly chilling. I'm shocked you went in there alone." She smirked sidelong at Leo. "Did you check under the stairs for demented clowns with chainsaws?"

"Yes," he said, utterly serious, "I did."

"Are you sure you're up for living here?"

"With you to protect me, I'm feeling pretty good about my odds." Hefting her suitcase as if it weighed no more than a goldfish, he led her past the statues guarding the entrance.

Karen followed, savoring each soft step of her boots on the moss-fuzzed pavestones. It was a true testament of her willpower that she managed to drag her gaze away from Leo's fine backside to the looming mansion. She slipped into the shadows cast by the gabled roof and shivered at the sudden cold. Dead leaves gathered in the corners of the covered porch, and dry husks of moths dangled from cobwebs in the rafters. A stand of pale toadstools crouched beside a faceless gargoyle.

"How long has it been since anyone lived here?" she asked, catching up with him as he reached the porch stairs.

"Decades. Careful of the steps." He frowned as the planks creaked under his boots.

"How much you want to bet someone died here?" The wooden steps groaned and threatened to buckle beneath her, and she jumped to the safety of the porch. "Or better, was murdered?"

"How is being murdered better?"

"You know, restless spirits. Secrets in the attic. Monsters in the basement."

"You watch too many horror flicks."

"Not possible. You're supplying popcorn, right?"

His lazy smile reappeared. "Movie buttered, caramel, chocolate dipped — I've got you covered."

"I knew there was a solid reason why we're friends."

"So many reasons." The blue of his eyes deepened. He held her gaze as he opened the front door wide. "After you, darling."

Her pulse quickened, and she forced herself to focus on the vines and roses carved into the door before her imagination took over. She slipped her hands into her coat pockets to prevent any touching mishaps as she passed by. That didn't prevent his heat from caressing her neck when her shoulder brushed his chest or the goosebumps on her arms. She crossed the threshold into the mansion, and electricity tingled through her, as if she'd shifted between one world to the next.

Inside the vestibule with its cathedral ceiling and missing tile floor, she took a moment to bask in the neglected glory of Granton Hall. The air smelled of dust, abandonment and years. Across the grungy stone floor disturbed only by Leo's footprints, a carved stairwell curved to the second floor. The openness gave the impression of a museum lobby, the first taste of grandeur beyond. An iron chandelier that reminded her of ancient, wicked kings hung overhead. Wide corridors filled with gloom stretched in each direction. The melancholy silence made her want to fill the void with laughter.

"Like I said, it needs some work." Leo's voice echoed in the emptiness. He set her suitcase down beside the stairwell and wiggled a loose banister rod. "Be careful where you step." He glanced at her, mischief sparkling in his eyes. "You signed the waiver, didn't you?"

"If I get hurt, I'm suing. I'm sure Ian will represent me."

His expression darkened. "He'd sue anyone for a buck."

"Lawyer," she said, no further explanation needed, and spun in a slow circle, taking in everything from the carved ceiling beams to the cracked floor tiles dull with decades of dust. She couldn't wait to explore every cupboard, closet and panel in search of secrets. "What is our first project?"

Leo flicked a light switch and frowned when nothing happened. "I'll find out why my quick-fix electrician skills have failed me. Go upstairs and pick whichever suite you want. The doors are open. The mattresses and bedding are new. Everything else is as old as the plumbing and wiring." A fine line appeared between his eyebrows as he tried the switch again with the same negative result. "I'll bring your suitcase up and give you a tour once I get the lights back on."

She made it halfway up the stairs before he'd even finished the sentence. Strolling the halls of Granton Hall after years of wondering what it was like inside felt like walking in a dream, surreal. "If you hear noises in the basement, run."

"Appreciate the image, Ren."

"You're welcome."

Beyond the landing, hallways extended in both directions, offering only shadows. Faded wallpaper in delicate lavender flowers covered the panels above wainscoting so dark that it verged on black. She kicked on her cell phone flashlight and shone it ahead. Dust motes sparkled like silver glitter. At the end of the hallway, two doors stood ajar, casting slices of light into the darkness. Karen stepped into the first open door and gasped.

The room was bigger than her entire pizza-box-sized apartment, with enough open space to dance a musical. In one corner, sheets draping stacked, furniture-shaped objects lay heavy and gray with age. Three Leo-sized windows, spaced evenly on one wall, offered a touch of warmth. A rug of vines and tiny lavender flowers matching the wallpaper rolled from the covered furniture to the giant bed on the other end.

Fit for a princess, worthy of any fairytale fantasy, the four-poster bed had vines carved into the wood and gauzy curtains pulled back at the headboard. A dozen pillows in her favorite forest-green matched the elegant, brocaded duvet. Leo had obviously cleaned this tiny section of the manor. She didn't need to see the other suite. This one was hers, love at first sight.

Knowing Leo had picked the decor and set up the bed for her made her all warm and fuzzy. She dragged her fingertips over the silken surface of the duvet. It wasn't hard to imagine him lounging in the pillows, wearing that lopsided smile he saved only for her, the blankets twisted around his sexy—

She squeezed her eyes shut. *Gah.* Less than an hour with him and already the fantasies she fought so hard to keep chained slipped free. How was she supposed to survive an entire month without cracking?

With the small job pool in Graywood, her options sucked. Unless she wanted to relocate, suffering would be required, either at Hamilton until another rare accountant opening popped up or temporarily with Leo to fluff her resume and nail the job at Cooper Homes. Moving was a last resort.

The mere thought of life without Leo formed a cold spot in her belly, hard and heavy. She picked up a pillow. Vanilla-scented air wafted from the material, the personal touch added by Leo squeezing her heart. Being best friends and lovers might work for some people but not her. *Been there, done that.*

She slumped. Keep her best friend and live in a fantasy world for the rest of her life or surrender to those fantasies and lose Leo. What a no-win situation.

A light scratching interrupted the useless thoughts. Karen set the pillow down, prickles stealing over the back of her neck. The sound came from the far wall, behind the stacked furniture, the slash of tiny claws digging.

Mice?

Give her a serial killer movie and she'd be amped. Urban legend monsters, tortured phantoms and demons hell-bent on possessing innocent souls? All stories she'd take on anytime. But if Leo learned of her fear for vermin, he'd use the knowledge against her mercilessly. She couldn't let that happen, not even if she had to face an entire nest of rabid, man-eating rats.

The can of pepper spray from her purse in hand, she crept toward the stacked furniture. The scratching continued, faint and weak, and scenes from some of her favorite films spun through her imagination. Granton Hall was old, and there had to be a reason why such an amazing house had remained empty for so long. Some of its secrets might lean toward sinister—such as a victim trapped inside a wall to die.

Maybe she should take up comedies for a while.

The scratching stopped at her approach. Dust stirred around her boots, glistening clouds in the light leaking from the windows. Shadows pooled in the windowless corner with the stacked furniture. Karen reactivated her cell phone flashlight and aimed it at the wall. Brocaded wallpaper, yellowed with age, curled at the edges as if in pain. Cracked and splintered plaster rested beneath one section, leaving a gap between boards.

Her heart hammered as she crouched. No wimping out. She leaned in with her light and put her eye to the crack in the wall.

Cobwebs and grit filled the space. She angled the light one way. No evidence of chewed insulation or vermin nests — or rusty lockboxes containing ancient scrolls, sadly. She released the breath she'd been holding. Whatever had been scratching had moved on to greener pastures, for now. Patching the wall skyrocketed to the top of her repair list, so nothing could —

Yellow flashed from deep within the wall, moist and iridescent...*alive*.

Definitely eyes.

Chapter Four

Karen yelped and scrambled away from the wall. Her cell phone flew from her fingers beneath the furniture.

"What are you doing, Ren?" Leo stood in the doorway, her suitcase in his hand.

She jumped up. Friendship lines be damned. She leaped onto him like a monkey climbing a tree to safety. "There's something in the wall."

"Not surprising." He dropped the suitcase and curled his arms around her, strong and sturdy, holding her in place. "Could be a cute raccoon or squirrel."

Karen buried her face in his neck. "That doesn't make it any better."

His laugh rumbled through her, and he brought his mouth close to her ear. "It's probably just rats."

Cold slithered down her back, and she did her best to ignore it. There was no way he knew about her secret phobia and no way she'd let him know how his warm breath at her ear sent a different sort of shiver down her spine. She lifted her head, hyperaware of the scrape of his stubble on her cheek, the powerful bands of his arms around her back and under her butt. When had she wrapped her legs around his hips?

Holy hell, it felt good being tight against him, close enough she could detail the delicious planes and ridges of his chest and abs. She inhaled deep of his cedar scent before regaining control.

"A rodent invasion should have been a disclaimer before any agreement." She forced herself to disentangle her legs from his lean hips. "Or did you omit that so I wouldn't change my mind? Shameful manipulation, Hughes."

Holding her gaze, Leo released her, letting her slide down his body in another round of torture. "I don't have to reveal all my secrets." He smirked, his blue eyes bright, hands on her hips keeping her lightly captive. "I told you Granton Hall needs heavy renovations. There's bound to be a surprise or two."

Karen couldn't look away from him, and the moment stretched into seconds. A mere inch separated them. His heat soaked through her sweater to tease her skin, and when his attention dropped to her mouth, her lips tingled in anticipation. A simple lift on tiptoes and she'd taste what she'd fantasized about since the moment he'd solemnly pointed out the differences in toilet plungers at the hardware store.

His smile faded into a different, more dangerous emotion, and her breath caught. Kissing him would ruin everything. She couldn't forget that.

Another scratch came from the wall, and they both froze.

"See?" she whispered, grabbing the distraction. She stepped out of his loose grasp and pointed at the crack in the wall. "You need to get rid of whatever that is. If I wake up to droppings of any kind in my hair, someone will get hurt."

"As you wish, my lady." He bowed at the waist, as if he was the lord of the manor attending to her every whim. The sarcastic tone ruined the effect. "Allow me to remedy the situation."

"My thanks, good sir." Sarcasm matched and trumped, the friendship boundary was safely back in place.

Leo strolled to the wall and crouched. Shining his flashlight inside, he eased close while she hovered behind him. "Hmm."

"What is it?" She wasn't sure why she whispered. "Mice? Possum?" She swallowed hard. "Rats?"

"It's worse than I thought." He clicked the flashlight off and stood with an unreadable expression. "Wait here. I'll be back in a second."

Karen kept a healthy distance between her and the wall in case something decided to break through before Leo returned. Whatever it was had claws. *Could be birds.* A chill swept through her. *Or bats.* As much as she loved all things dark and creepy, bats were too close to rats, and they frickin' flew. She backed up another step.

"This should do it." Wearing safety goggles and a determined expression, Leo strode to the wall, a sledgehammer in his grip. "You might want to stand aside. This could get messy."

Without waiting for her response, he slammed his weapon of choice into the wall a few feet from the broken portion. Wood splintered and plaster trailing tattered wallpaper fell to the rug. Leo gave another hard swing, leaving a ragged hole.

A cloud of grime filtered into the room, and Karen pulled her turtleneck sweater up to cover her nose and mouth. "Why did you do that? Now whatever is living in the walls can get out. I'm switching to the other suite."

"Too late. No takebacks." He waved the dust away and peeked into the hole he'd made. Frowning, he glanced over his shoulder at her. "You should wait outside until I take care of this."

That sounded sinister — and not in the way she preferred. Nightmares were only fun when they belonged to someone else.

Karen lurked in the hallway as Leo conducted his construction wizardry. Each thud of his hammer pounded the image of his muscles bunching beneath his T-shirt deeper into her brain. Holy hell the man was finely made, and when he moved with that natural, athletic grace, all the solid reasons why she couldn't cross the friend line with him wavered.

She released a breath and fanned her warm face. The imprint of his rock-hard arms around her, his chest against her breasts, lingered hot on her skin. He was right. Standing too close was dangerous.

Too much energy to stand still, she strolled the length of the corridor. Her boots tapped a slow beat on a hardwood floor in desperate need of a sweep, wax and shine. Past the stairwell banister, the hallway shrank in both height and width, marked by an ornate cornice that resembled a doorway. Wallpaper surrendered to panels of black wood, adding another layer of gloom. She had the sensation that she walked into a tunnel, the only light offered by the single arched window at the end of the corridor.

Doors lined one side — all locked, dammit. The other side held empty spaces waiting for artwork long lost, with one exception.

Karen paused before an old-time portrait the size of a museum painting. Faded colors reminded her of an old western photo shoot she'd done once with her sisters at a carnival with props and costumes, posing beside a wagon. The woman in the picture leaned against a tree, a rose in one hand, a sleeping kitten nestled in the crook of her other arm. A slight wind tousled her long, dark hair. She wore a turn-of-the-century gown, flowing and white, an ebony sash around her slender waist. Her smile was wistful, her eyes black holes.

Super-creepy. She couldn't wait to sneak into Leo's room, hang it on his wall and wait for him to freak out.

A prickle of awareness drifted over her back, as if someone watched her from one of the twenty or so rooms stretching in either direction. She remained still. If anyone else was in the mansion, Leo would have mentioned it.

Pretending to study the art, she searched the corridor and doorways in her peripheral vision for any movement. Leo must have finished his destruction of the wall. Silence stretched through the house, heavy and throbbing.

At the edge of light spilling in from the distant window, the shadows shifted. Maybe it was adrenaline or a trick of the dim light, but all the small hairs on her nape straightened as she faced that way. Under her full attention, nothing moved—of course—leaving her imagination to fill in the gaps.

"I have one question for you."

Leo's voice drew her around, and she dismissed any thoughts of moving shadows. "Yes, you're weird."

"That fact has already been well established." He strolled toward her, his hands behind his back, his expression grave. "Are you ready to meet the monstrosity dwelling for centuries in the darkest depths of Granton Hall?"

The mischief gleaming in his eyes was the first warning sign, his hidden hands the second. She should have kept her pepper spray as backup. Whatever he'd found was either so disgusting that he slavered to gross her out, or nothing at all and he wanted to trick her. "Keep your distance, Hughes. If you're intending to fling a dead squirrel at me, you'd better run now."

"Your choice." He shrugged, backpedaling, his hands out of sight. The lopsided smile that drove her crazy cracked his façade. "It's not my room. I won't be sleeping in there, alone and defenseless against unknown horrors."

She chased him, his teasing as irresistible as every other detail about him. "What are you hiding?" Spurred by his snicker, she caught up, cornering him against the banister. "Tell me, you son of a — "

Leo laughed as she scrambled uselessly to control one of his arms or look around him to see what he hid. The damn man was too agile and tall, his limbs too long.

But as his best friend, she knew his weaknesses. Giving up on trying to outmaneuver him, she went for the kill, straight to his most vulnerable point — his ticklish left armpit.

Two seconds and he gave up, wriggling to escape, breathless from laughing. "Mercy!" He somehow managed to keep the secret he held behind his back. "Promise to stop," he gasped, "and I'll show you."

Karen released him and batted her eyelashes, going for sweet and innocent.

He studied her with bright eyes. "Don't pretend you didn't enjoy that."

"What? Making you squeal like a wee piglet?" She smiled. "You know it."

"Ren, darling," he said, a new roughness in his voice. "Feel free to make me squeal anytime you want. No tickling required."

The sudden softness in his expression made her uncooperative heart flutter. Electricity prickled her skin. It would be so easy to take the single step separating them, slip her arms around his neck, press up to his solid body and kiss him. So easy, and so final. Their friendship would never be the same.

Never breaking her gaze, he lifted his hands in the air and wriggled his empty fingers.

"All that, and you don't even have anything?" She lunged for him. "I'm going to hurt you."

Laughing, he danced out of reach. Her fingertips grazed his T-shirt, too late, as the jerk slipped into her room.

"If I weren't wearing boots with heels, you'd already be dead, Hughes." Karen lurched into the bedroom and found him sitting on the edge of the bed. A dresser drawer rested beside him.

"I always account for what you wear before any attack, all part of the battle plan. I prefer to survive with my body parts intact." He glanced inside the drawer and looked at her, his eyebrows lifted. "Are you going to see what I found in the wall, or do you plan to stand there looking adorably peeved?"

He just had to slip 'adorably' in there, didn't he? She lifted her chin and marched forward. "I'll see what you found while retaining my state of peeved."

"Fair enough." He returned his attention to the drawer. "Prepare to be horrified."

She refused to show weakness, but whatever was in the drawer moved. It had black, sleek fur. If he'd put a rat on her bed, her earlier death threat would become reality.

Karen forced herself forward until a few feet separated her from the unknown creature on the very bed she'd planned to sleep in tonight. Nothing would stop her from relocating to a dusty couch in one of the numerous other rooms after Leo ventured to dreamland. He'd never know.

"Meet the terror of Granton, destroyer of walls." Cupping his hands, he lifted a tiny ball of black fur, whiskers and golden eyes. "I dub him Sir Snugglebottom, protector of the esteemed Lady Karen and captain of the new guard."

All the tightness in her shoulders disappeared and she sank onto the corner of the bed. She'd take a kitten over a rat any day. "You're such a nerd."

"Medieval enthusiast. There's a distinct difference."

She stroked the kitten's soft head with one finger, and its mouth opened in a silent meow. No wonder she hadn't heard anything besides scratching. "We should get him some milk. The poor thing could have been trapped for days. How did he even get in there?" She sucked in a breath. "What if his momma is still stuck? Brothers and sisters?"

"Before boarding up the hole in your wall tonight, I'll make a thorough inspection, I promise. First, let's raid the kitchen and get this little guy some sustenance." He cuddled the kitten close. It looked so small against his broad chest, protected by Leo's capable hands. "You're no longer lost, Sir Snugglebottom," he whispered in a silky voice. "I've got you now. You'll never be alone again."

Lazy butterflies fluttered to life in her stomach. She had to look away and blink back an absurd scald of tears before he noticed. She *never* cried. Day one living with Leo and already her common sense crumbled. There was only one way she'd survive a month with their friendship intact.

She needed to find a distraction of the male kind, fast.

Chapter Five

Karen called it quits early after assuring Sir Le Chat had all the supplies an abandoned kitten needed. Despite Leo's objections, she refused to accept the undignified title of Sir Snugglebottom.

Leo had fed her, too. With a belly full of sushi from her favorite Japanese restaurant, she settled into her new room. The abandoned furniture stacked in the corner included an old armoire that she'd convinced Leo to heave closer to the bed and private bathroom. A quick vacuum and dust job later, she emptied her suitcase, hung up her clothes and slid into bed. Burrowed into vanilla-scented sheets provided by Leo, she tried not to think about him being a mere shout away.

Hours later, midnight darkness lured Karen from some dream she couldn't remember. She sat up and scrubbed her fingers through her hair. Moonlight spilled through the windows and shimmered over walls, softening the boarded-up hole across the room.

The draped furniture slouched in the corner like fallen curtains. She'd left her door ajar after learning it didn't latch right, another project added to her learn-to-do list, and it remained open a wedge.

A silhouette darkened the doorway, and her pulse jumped. Leo eased past the door, shirtless in the shadows. He looked at her, and his burning gaze stole her breath.

"Leo?"

Without saying a word, he padded toward the bed, his bare feet silent on the rug, black boxers clinging to his muscular thighs.

With Leo, she never worried about appearances, but the silky tank top she'd worn to bed left zero to the imagination. Her face warmed. He'd have to be blind to miss how he affected her physically.

Something had to be wrong. He wouldn't enter a woman's bedroom without permission or knocking, not even if she happened to be his best friend. But the fire in his eyes erased all words from her brain, and when he crawled onto the bed on all fours, holding her gaze, she melted. Holy hell, he was a masterpiece, the powerful lines of his body hypnotic in the muted light.

As he approached with animal grace, she couldn't react, lulled by the skewed sanity of the darkness and fantasy coming to life before her eyes. Straddling her legs over the blankets, he didn't stop until he planted his palms on each side of her hips, caging her. Heat radiated from his bare skin, easing the chill of the air on her naked shoulders and arms. His breath brushed her lips.

"What are you doing, Leo?" The words hardly counted, more a rasp in her throat.

Leaning in, he bypassed her mouth and nuzzled her ear. "Tasting you." He nibbled her lobe and tugged with his teeth, then licked the sting away. "Hmm. Luscious."

A shiver trembled through her as the stubble on his cheek scraped her jaw and he pressed his lips to the sensitive spot beneath her ear. She fisted the sheet to keep from touching him. She should stop him, push him away, tell him to leave. But he trailed his lips to her shoulder, and the thought spun away, beyond her power. Her eyes closed of their own accord.

Denying the touch she'd dreamed of for so long was impossible. The fact that Leo was her best friend slithered out of reach. He rested his hot hand on her hip, and the magic of his mouth killed everything except desire.

"I've waited too long for you, Ren." He sat back on his heels, his knees spread on either side of her thighs, and cupped her face. "Far too long."

She could only watch as he bent his head, his gaze a hungry glitter. He brushed his mouth over hers with the softest friction, gently bit her bottom lip, and all her self-control shattered.

Releasing her lifeline of the blanket, Karen tangled her fingers in his hair and pulled him closer, her mouth desperate on his. His responsive groan told her everything she needed, that he wanted her, that she wasn't alone in her desire, that they were in this together. She ran her hand over his arm, savoring the shift of his muscles beneath her palm, the smooth skin she'd longed to discover.

"Ren," he murmured, and angled his head, deepening the kiss. His tongue was silken and coaxing on hers, a demand for more. "You're no longer lost."

"Umhuh." She traced a scar she'd never noticed before on his shoulder, every nerve singing. He needed to be closer, his heat wrapped around her tight.

He slid his hand along the curve of her hip to her waist in slow exploration. "I've got you now."

A sense of déjà vu sliced through her haze. Those words sounded so familiar.

"You'll never be alone again."

Hold up. Hadn't he said those exact words earlier? To a...cat? She leaned back.

His hooded eyes glowed, golden and iridescent, an animal's eyes.

All the blood left her head in a rush. She flailed and tried to scramble free from the blankets. A quick roll, and she landed hard on the floor, one ankle still snared in the bedding, the breath knocked from her lungs.

For a few seconds, she blinked at the ceiling, her heart playing ping-pong between the rug and her ribs.

"Ren?" A soft knock pushed the ajar door open wider. "Are you okay? I thought I heard a thump." After a pause, Leo poked his head in. When his gaze fell on her, still sprawled on the floor, his forehead creased. "Bed kick you out?"

She closed her eyes. *A dream*. It had all been a torturous dream inspired by strange events and her secret obsession.

When she opened her eyes again, Leo loomed over her, his hands braced on his knees. He wore blue-striped pajama pants, confirmation that the last few moments hadn't been real.

"I'll add some safety padding to the floor," he said. "Walls too. We'll rename this the Asylum Chamber."

"Hardy har." She pushed onto her elbows. "I had a vivid dream."

Curiosity sparkled in his eyes, and his attention drifted over her lace-trimmed shorts and silky tank top, one delicate strap fallen off her shoulder. "Was I in it?"

"Actually, yes." Her face hot, with a hard tug, she freed her foot from the blankets. "A terrible nightmare." She held out her hand, a silent command to help her stand.

Smirking, he hauled her up but didn't release her hand. "Did I save you from the monster?"

"You *were* the monster." Sure as hell she wasn't going to fess up that he'd been a total turn-on machine until the last few seconds of the dream. And if she ever met up with a monster, she'd take that version any time, any day.

"Lucky for me you've got a thing for monsters." He hit her with his lopsided smile.

Karen swallowed hard as his heat rolled over her. While he wore pajama bottoms instead of boxers, he was shirtless, like the dream. All the lovely muscles of his shoulders, chest and abs were on full display.

He brushed the hair from her eyes and cupped her chin. "Sure you're okay?"

The complete opposite. Forcing a smile, she ignored the delicious friction of his callused palm on her skin, how easy it would be to touch him and confirm every electrifying detail of the dream.

"Dandy." She pushed up the strap of her tank top, not missing how he tracked the movement. "Go back to sleep. I don't want a grumpy construction instructor tomorrow afternoon."

"I'm always grumpy." He headed for the door, taking his warmth with him. "Try not to hurt yourself — or dream about rats swarming the walls."

"Ugh." She trudged back to bed. "Stuff it somewhere dark, Hughes."

His low laughter drifted back to her, soft and seductive. "Love you, too, Ren, darling."

Tomorrow. She flung back the blankets and crawled into bed. Tomorrow night, after learning whatever fix-it tips Leo had in store for her, she'd begin hunting for a guy who could distract her for a month. And once safely in lust, she'd return to friendships and fantasies that had zero chance of becoming anything more.

* * * *

The aroma of cooking woke Karen before her alarm. Thankfully, the hole in her wall remained boarded up without any visible chew holes. A quick shower later, dressed in a black pleated skirt, olive-green sweater and a pair of boots with stomping heels, she trailed the smell downstairs.

Sizzling and clanking pans guided her through the vestibule, past the front door and a salon paneled in an ungodly shade of pink. A spacious room Leo had designated the archives chamber followed the next, block-long stretch of corridor. Apparently, the term 'library' didn't meet his archaic sensibilities.

The grand dining room came next, large enough to hold a high school cafeteria. A lone broken-legged chair kept company with a long table that looked like it belonged in ages past. Boards covered three of the four tall, diamond-paned windows, but enough morning light slanted through to shine on mahogany panels carved in a brocaded design.

Leo had given her a partial tour of the first floor before dinner yesterday evening, promising a more thorough show in daylight hours. She'd been too intent on putting much-needed space between them to protest at the time. Now, she regretted it. The small slice she'd seen so far held a distinct elegance, edged with an eccentricity that appealed to her basic nature. She suspected a month wouldn't be enough to explore every corner.

At last, the hallway emptied into a restaurant-sized kitchen. Why anyone would need such a huge space to microwave popcorn and the occasional dinner, she had no idea. The entirety of her cooking utensils could fit on the smallest shelf. Cupboards, drawers and counters stretched along three walls, and a deep sink the size of a watering trough rested beneath a window that looked over what might have once been an herb garden. The stove and refrigerator were new — bright, shiny and out of place. A kitchen island that looked more like a butcher's block sat as centerpiece with a couple of bar stools.

Her blue-ribbon, country-fair-pie-champion sisters would have drooled.

Karen leaned against the doorframe and crossed her arms. His back to her, Leo worked at the stove, cooking something that smelled delicious. He wore jeans and a long-sleeved T-shirt, hiding all his tempting muscles, which was a disappointment — er, a *relief*. She'd meant relief.

While self-torture had become her favorite pastime, she had to work on her control. She had to stay strong, find a quick-fix guy so she could retain a firm grip on her libido and keep their amazing relationship safe. She wasn't about to ruin their friendship with romance.

He turned for the refrigerator and spotted her. Sir Le Chat was perched on his shoulder as if he belonged there, all dark and fuzzy cuteness, melting her heart. Worse, that lopsided smile Leo saved only for her bloomed to life.

I'm in so much trouble.

"It lives. It rises from the deep in search of sustenance, a savage bloodlust in need of slaking, a hunt for souls." He pushed the coffee mug sitting on the island toward her. "Take it, I beg of you, and be satisfied with my humble offering."

She rolled her eyes and hid a grin. How could she not adore him? With a zombie groan, she shuffled around the island toward the waiting cup. "That will depend on the quality of your coffee, medievalist nerd."

"Compliment accepted." He plucked Sir from his shoulder and set him on the island counter. "Watch him. I'm afraid if he's on the floor, I'll squash him by mistake."

The kitten gave a pitiful, raspy meow, looking longingly at Leo as he returned to the stove to stir.

I completely understand. Karen pulled Sir near and rubbed his back. He squirmed free and scampered to the edge of the kitchen island, as close as he could get to Leo without falling off. *Snooty cat.*

Wrapping her hands around the warm mug, she breathed in the sweet scent of chocolate and cinnamon laced with coffee and sighed. "Is that French toast?"

"Plus eggs, sausage and blueberries." He rustled a bunch of green in her face. "And a spinach protein shake to wash it all down."

"Disgusting."

"Nourishing." He gave her a stern look. "Construction is hard labor, Ren. You'll need the energy. I'm going to work you." He planted his hands on the counter beside her and lowered his chin. "All. Day. Long."

Her body tightened at the suggestive words, and the way his eyes darkened to stormy seas didn't help her cause. What was his deal? He'd never flirted with her this hard. She took a swallow from her cup and moaned. Howling hounds of Hades, the man knew how to brew and prepare a proper Karen coffee. "Keep your green sludge. I'll take the rest."

"It'll balance out your sugar. Try it."

"Not ever."

He lifted his eyebrows. "You'll love it."

"I'll leave it a mystery, thanks."

"Ren." He used his low, honeyed voice meant to coax her to his will. "You'll never know what you're missing if you don't at least give it a chance." He held her gaze in challenge, but his words were soft and sober. "Don't be scared. I'll never let you down."

Mug lifted halfway to her mouth, she couldn't look away, her pulse ticking faster. While he took his protein shakes very seriously, she sensed that whatever he implied had nothing to do with food.

He still locked his stare on hers and eased forward, the breakfast sizzling in the pan behind him forgotten. The entire world narrowed to Leo, his dark lashes lowering as his attention drifted to her mouth. If she didn't know him better, if they weren't the best of friends, she'd swear he meant to kiss her.

Air rushed from her lungs, stealing any ability to form words. She should walk away right now, make up some excuse and head to work without breakfast. This was Leo—generous, admired, successful. He could have any woman he wanted, deserved the absolute best. Kissing him would start their temporary living situation with an awkward bang.

His warm breath brushed her lips, and last night's dream struck like lightning, echoing in her cells. The heat in his touch, the thrill of his body against hers, her heart soaring as he whispered words of longing in her ear. Nothing else mattered except his mouth close to hers.

A gong erupted, shaking the very rafters of the mansion, and they both jerked straight, guilty as teenagers caught in the act of stealing beer. The enchantment spun between them dissolved like delicate webs.

"No matter what part of the house you're in, you can't miss that doorbell." His expression pained, Leo waved the spinach greens. "I'll finish breakfast if you answer the door. It's the delivery guy. I'm expecting a package and left the gate open."

"Sure." Her voice rasped like a demon's. She cleared her throat, which did nothing for the bees thrumming and colliding in her bloodstream. As she stumbled out of the kitchen, she couldn't stop thinking about Leo's beautiful mouth only inches away from hers.

I'm so screwed.

Chapter Six

Karen left the kitchen and Leo behind on wobbling knees. Her mouth still tingled in anticipation of a kiss interrupted. What the hell was he doing, threatening to pop their sacred friendship bubble?

The doorbell gonged again as she passed the end of the archives chamber and hit the nauseating Pepto pink salon.

"Sheez. Patience is a virtue, people." She entered the vestibule and dismantled the deadbolt. The bell vibrated through her bones once more as she jerked the door open. "Seriously? Sorry I wasn't sitting by the door, waiting for you."

The words dried on her tongue as she looked up into eyes the deep green of peacock feathers. A man the same height as Leo and fifty pounds of muscle leaner stood on the porch. He held a box, but by his dress shirt and tie, the slacks and expensive loafers, she suspected he wasn't a delivery guy.

"My apologies." He had a lovely British accent. "A delivery truck was at the gate, and since I had hoped to speak to the owner, I agreed to carry the package up the drive. I hope that isn't an issue?"

"Oh, um, well. The owner is unavailable at the moment." She smoothed her skirt. "Is there anything I can help with?"

His inviting smile gleamed with white teeth.

A handsome new face in small town Graywood, and with that accent, he might be the perfect solution for her 'Resist Leo Campaign'.

"Are you the caretaker?" He cocked his head.

"Sure." Caretaker and volunteer novice construction worker weren't so far apart. She'd taken care of the sushi on her plate last night, supervised Leo boarding up her wall.

His smile widened, wolfish. "Then I'm certain we may assist each other." He tucked the large box beneath one arm and extended a hand. "Oliver Hunter."

"Karen Ives." She shook his hand, surprised at the chill of his skin. Late October leaned toward cold, but the morning sun warmed the front porch. "What can I do for you, Mr. Hunter?"

"Please, address me as Oliver." He held her fingers a second longer than necessary.

"Oliver," she amended with a little smile.

Before Oliver stated his business, a wall of warmth drifted over her back, joined by the scent of fresh French toast and cedar. Tingles scampered down her arms. She didn't need to look to know the source. Leo's presence always alerted all her senses.

He draped an arm around her shoulders and nodded at Oliver. "Need me to sign for that?"

Oliver studied the label on the box and handed it to Leo. "It doesn't seem to include any paperwork, but it's not my practice to perform delivery duties. I do, however, provide landscaping consulting and maintenance." He whipped a card from his blazer pocket. "Oliver Hunter at your service."

Karen nabbed the card, beating Leo to it as he juggled the box. The title read 'Hunter Horticulture and Garden Design. Let me add a touch of English charm to your life.'

"Not looking for a gardener at present." Leo hefted the box onto his shoulder and grabbed the door handle, a clear dismissal.

She frowned at the weeds choking the walkway, shrubs left free to become shapeless scrub and the lawn that was mostly field. "Even if the interior renovations are the subject of the competition, won't the exterior make an impact on the judges? Do the restrictions apply to outside work?"

"Hmm." Leo's favorite grunted response whenever he didn't like the question, the circumstances or anything in between. It was an indication that he suspected some manner of BSery.

"I'm new to the area, building my business. My prices are extremely competitive and quite honestly, I could use the work." Oliver slid his hands into his pockets and pivoted toward the grounds stretching from the porch. "I guarantee to perfect the immediate landscaping around the manor before your event."

"It couldn't hurt, and jobs are hard to come by in Graywood." She gave Leo a bright, innocent smile. "Think about all the people you'll be helping when you win, and you have the power to add Mr. Hunter to that list."

He narrowed his eyes, his mouth tight. She hadn't fooled him. No matter the man, he never approved of any guy she showed an interest in, always claimed that she could do better. At least she tried to find a slice of romance. He remained staunchly single.

Maybe she was going about her problem all wrong. There had to be a solid reason why Leo didn't date, why he sent beautiful, willing women away without so much as a smile. He'd made his sexual preferences clear, so whatever it was had to be dark, shameful or embarrassing. Nothing he shared could ever stain their friendship, a fact she'd assure him of while coaxing out the blackest corners of his heart. Maybe he'd buried something so disgusting that it had the power to kill her fantasies. As his best friend, it was her solemn duty to not let his secrets fester. If that failed, Oliver Hunter could be her backup plan.

"You could have an open house after the competition is over, and if the weather is nice, guests may want to explore the gardens." She elbowed Leo in the ribs. "Stroll along neat, pavestone paths lined by manicured plants, getting tipsy beneath the stars, loosening their donation pocketbooks? You want to impress any potential investors, right?"

He gave her a long, imperious look meant to make people squirm. It worked, but not in the way he probably intended. When Leo went from best-friendly to intimidating, the blood pumped harder through her veins and made her temperature rise a few degrees. When he went all domineering, her naughty side perked up and preened. It wasn't hard to picture a sword on his shoulder instead of the box, leather replacing every stitch of clothing. He could keep the boots.

So much for reining in my fantasies.

"I'll personally attend to your project." At Oliver's interruption, Leo's frosty gaze shifted to him. "I require no down payment or installments until the work is finished. If you're unsatisfied with my services in any manner, there will be no charge." His full smile was salesman smooth. "I'll put that in writing to negate any potential misunderstanding."

Leo studied Oliver for another long moment. "Send me a bid," he said at last, a snarl in his tone. "The email is on my website. Need a business card?"

"I may be new in town, but the reputation of Hughes & Sons Construction has rippled beyond city limits. I'll send you a proposal straight away." Oliver stuck out his hand and Leo took it. "Pleased to meet you, Mr. Hughes." He nodded at Karen and a spark warmed his eyes. "I hope to see you again soon, Miss Karen."

The second the door shut Leo's frown turned on her. "There's something shady about that guy."

"You say that about any person with a penis over the age of sixteen who happens to glance my way." Karen brushed past him, headed for the kitchen. "Unless you have a rational reason beyond your shady-guy-super-senses, you should take his offer. You know, keep with the Hughes family policy of helping people in need."

"Not if they're shady."

She snorted. "Everyone's a little shady."

Leo followed her into the kitchen, where two plates of food and two glasses of green sludge waited. He set the box on the island and whipped out the knife he always kept hidden. His fascination with sharp-edged things was sick — and, if she had to be honest, kinda sexy.

"Not drinking that." She jerked her chin at the protein shake.

"We'll see."

"Where's Sir Le Chat?" Leaning on the countertop, she grabbed a blueberry from one plate, fascinated by his long fingers slicing the box open.

"Safe in the laundry room with his breakfast. I got you a present." He lifted the cardboard flaps and removed some plastic bubble wrap. "Or two."

"Bribery? I approve." She tried to peek into the box, and he pushed the flaps back down with a warning frown. "Or is it appeasement for all the suffering I'm about to endure at your very capable hands?"

She had zero doubt he was superb with his hands, no matter what he chose to do with them, but the moment the suggestive words left her mouth, heat rolled through her. Focusing on the box, she pretended her face wasn't on fire.

"You'll have to wait and see until you get back from the office." He dragged out plastic packaging and shoved it at her while digging through the box contents. "This is the beginning of our grand adventure into the realm of creation and restoration." He paused, his expression serious. "I have one question for you, Ren."

Dammit. He used his sexy, coaxing voice, the one that talked her into almost anything. She threw the plastic at him. "Which is?"

He batted the packaging away. His slow smile was as wicked as the knife in his hand, and her pulse leaped. "Are you prepared to meet your destiny?"

* * * *

Friday morning blew by fast while Karen pumped out payroll, and she made it back to Granton Hall after lunch, ready to face her destiny and discover what surprises Leo had up his sexy sleeves.

She scanned the array of tools he'd laid out on a makeshift sawhorse and plywood table — in the annoying bubble-gum-pink room, as if he didn't know she loathed that color.

"If this is my destiny," she said, picking up a box of nails and shaking them, "I'm disappointed. I was hoping for a cape or at least some groovy tights to wear with my black mini skirt."

"A uniform can be arranged." Leo smirked, looking fine in his ratty jeans and faded Superman T-shirt, a tool belt around his lean waist. "Maybe something in carnation pink with embroidered butterflies."

"While I can't see my own destiny, one potential path of yours is crystal-clear, Hughes." She slid a finger across her throat in a slicing motion. "Put me in pink and you'll rue the day."

His smile widened, and the playful spark in his eyes promised a worthy challenger. "Shaking in my boots." He turned to the neat line of tools arranged in no particular order on the plywood. "Lesson of the day — basic construction tools."

Karen folded her arms across her Evanescence concert T-shirt and cocked her hip. "Bring it on, sunshine."

He lifted a purple-handled hammer and arched an eyebrow at her.

"Skull-crusher, also useful for pounding nails into coffins." She swiped it from his hand and flipped it around, aiming the prongs at him. "Or prying tombs open."

"One hundred percent so far." He lifted a screwdriver, also purple.

"For tightening torture devices." She pointed at the drill on the table. "And that's handy for an impromptu lobotomy."

"As one does from time to time." He lifted a knife with sharp teeth. "Drywall saw."

"For hacking through the bones of our enemies." She nodded.

His mouth turned down as he considered the tool in his hand. "Or drywall."

She picked up the measuring tape and flung the blade out. The flimsy tape wobbled and crackled before bending, doubling over. "I can't figure out what this is for," she said in her best airhead voice, retracting the tape with a flick of her wrist. "A garotte, maybe?"

"If you're short on rope and wire, it would suffice in a pinch." He snagged the measuring tape from her fingers. "It's imperative in construction to be precise. This will be your best friend in the days ahead."

"Aw, you know my best friend will always be you."

"Right back at you, Ren." His low voice rasped, and fire danced in his eyes.

Karen's mouth went dry. Friends did *not* look at other friends like that, as if he wanted to use the saw in his hand to slice away each article of clothing, bend her backward over the makeshift table and lick every inch of her along the way.

Shutting down the tingles before her imagination took over, she pointed at the last item on the plywood, a chop saw. "And that sucker is for getting rid of evidence."

"You're not ready for such power or responsibility." Leo gave her a steady, serious look. "I put it there with the other tools so you'll know not to mess with it."

"Trust issues, Hughes?"

"I prefer to keep my Ren in one lovely piece." He winked.

He just had to slip 'lovely' in there, didn't he? She picked up the hammer again, testing its weight. It felt perfect, as if custom made for her. "So what's the scoop with the competition? Who decides the winner?"

"There's a panel of judges — Mayor Evans, a member of the city council, an architect from Greenville, Ned the hardware store owner and a contributing writer for *Renovation & Remodel*."

"Nothing like small town favoritism to sway the scales, not that you need it." She gasped and spun, swinging the hammer. Leo leaned out of the way. "What about bribery? Cheating? This contract is a huge deal. Any one of your competitors could buy, schmooze or blackmail the judges. Owners are supposed to do the labor themselves with one volunteer, but what prevents an entire crew from working on the sly?"

"There's a final secret judge, hired by the chief editor of *Renovation & Remodel*." Leo plucked the hammer from her hand and set it on the table. "No one, not even the other judges, know who it is."

"Ooh, a mystery." She bounced and clapped her hands. "I love it."

"Thought you might. The secret judge could be anyone, from the pizza guy to the mailman, and could drop in at any site at any given hour. Anyone caught cheating is eliminated…with appropriate proof, of course." He shrugged. "With drones, cell phones and zoom power cameras, it's not difficult to spy on someone these days."

"Firsthand experience?" She grinned.

"Voyeurism isn't my thing."

"Whatever you say, Hughes."

He glanced at her sidelong from beneath his lashes. "The right woman might persuade me to change my ways, if that was her preference."

Is he flirting hard with me again? Her imagination took off, spinning a picture of Leo hiding in a closet, his blue eyes piercing as he watched her between the slats. Her face warmed and heat pooled in her belly. Voyeurism wasn't her thing either, but with Leo...

Stop. Best friend. Standing right in your face.

"Look what else I got for you." He lifted a smaller tool belt, and a pair of safety goggles hung from his index finger. "You're going to regret passing up the morning protein shake."

"I regret nothing." She released a long breath and snagged the tool belt from him. Their fingers brushed, and a shock zipped up her arm. "Did you feel that?"

As she met his gaze, desire spiked her straight in the gut. His eyes were electric blue, like she'd imagined only moments ago. He leaned into her personal space, and she couldn't muster enough brain cells to move.

Never breaking eye contact, he took the belt from her numb fingers and slid it around her waist. When he buckled it, his fingertips grazed the sliver of bare skin between her jeans and shirt, and her blood turned to lava.

"I felt it the second you walked through the door." He tightened the belt and slid the leather end through the buckle with agile fingers. "The moment you arrived yesterday. Two years ago when you mistook me for a hardware store employee." Finished with the belt, he stepped back. "Let's get to work."

Without another word, he strode into the corridor and out of sight.

Karen stared after him, hot, dazed and beyond bothered. *What. The. Hell?* Granton Hall had bewitched her best friend, and she had no idea what to do about it.

Chapter Seven

"The first step is to introduce you to the project." Leo glanced at Karen as she walked beside him through one of Granton Hall's many corridors. Adorable in her safety goggles, the tool belt he'd special-ordered for her bumped the sumptuous curve of her sexy hip, heavy with the new tools that he'd also ordered special.

Just for her. Always her.

"I thought the entire mansion was the project." She twirled the hammer with its custom-made purple handle, probably trying to hide her nerves. Any time Karen felt out of her element, she played it awkward-cool. The act never fooled him.

"I'd have to hire an army to renovate the entire mansion in a month. The east wing is mostly intact, which can't be said of the west wing." He glanced up to where the ceiling should be. A gaping hole opened to the rafters through a crumbled section of the second story. He'd cleared some of the rubble yesterday, but gashes remained in the floor, scars of abuse.

"Still waiting on the full tour."

"Did you sign the waiver? Besides, you're on the clock now."

"Volunteers don't clock in." She frowned at a portion of cracked drywall that exposed the house's skeleton beneath. "FYI, I refuse to be your scapegoat if you lose."

"I won't lose." He'd invested too much in Granton Hall and its future to lose. It represented his father's legacy, and a large portion of his assets were tied up in that dream. Losing would hurt him in more ways than one. "This is a mutually beneficial situation. I teach, you assist, but I'll hold you responsible for your handiwork. When it's all done, you'll look back and see how much you accomplished. Finishing in a timely manner will result in great rewards."

She quirked an eyebrow. "Such as?"

He could dream up all manners of rewards, none of which she'd appreciate until he convinced her to take a chance on him. "I thought you liked mysteries, Ren. Don't ruin the surprise by being pushy."

"But knowing the great reward is the best incentive."

"It's one you don't want to miss." He winked. "Trust me."

She stuck out her tongue as they entered the last leg of the hallway. Narrow, stained-glass windows lined one wall, their colors dulled by moss and mildew. Beyond the last window, the corridor opened into a dome-shaped foyer with glass doors leading into Granton Hall's formal ballroom.

Leo opened the doors and flicked the light switch. The only chandelier with lightbulbs cast a golden spotlight near the center of the room. One less thing to fix in the days ahead.

"What. Is. This?" Her voice all breathless and bedroom-sexy, Karen ambled down the four chipped-marble steps discolored by grime. She lifted her wide-eyed gaze to what remained of the ceiling, a section of it rubble on the floor. Most of the crystal chandeliers had survived, dull with decades of dust. "A freakin' ballroom? Are you kidding me? Is this what we're going to renovate?"

"You approve?" He followed her down the steps and somehow managed not to grin, her awe affecting him like a drug, generating a warm buzz.

"Oh yeah," she murmured. "It works."

All his blood rushed south. When she used that voice, his control fractured at the edges. Stuffing his hands into his pockets so he wouldn't touch her and lose all dignity, he joined her in surveying the once-upon-a-time-grand ballroom.

Bay windows rimmed by carved molding and separated by faded pilasters offered a full view of the wild gardens beyond. Glass doors led outside, an easy avenue for a breath of fresh air. An overgrown tree limb pressed against one cracked pane. *Hmm. Maybe it would be a good idea to hire that landscaper.* A board hid another window, too many storms too late to prevent water damage to the wall and section of parquet flooring. The remaining floor—what could be seen beneath the wreckage—required tender care to remove decades of disrepair. Some trim had warped and separated from walls. The section of ceiling that had fallen needed a new steel beam. Even the magnificent antique grandfather clock, abandoned by a former owner, had given up, its hands stuck at nine.

Compared to most other areas of the mansion, the ballroom wasn't a raving mad monster. The stage needed cleaning and a new banister. The balcony hadn't caved in. Renovating it in a month would be a challenge with plenty of projects to keep a beginner volunteer busy. He could already envision the before and after photos in *Renovation & Remodel*.

His chest tightened. This was the first charity project that he could call his own, his inspiration and idea. The entire risk laid on his shoulders, not his family's. Losing the money didn't bother him as much as the potential of failing.

"This is where the Granton family once entertained all of Graywood." He trailed a finger along a hairline crack spiderwebbing a patch of bare wall. "From what I read, although Arthur Granton was rumored to be miserly, he loved showing off Granton Hall. The doors opened wide, inviting anyone who wanted to spend a night in revelry and merriment."

"Well, yeah. It's not a real party unless there's some riffraff to gossip about behind extravagant fans." Ren spun, facing him, her eyes sparkling. "Is that the ultimate plan? To host a fancy, old-fashioned ball with long dresses, top hats and formal dancing?"

"Hmm." He pretended to consider the room as if he hadn't already spent hours studying, calculating, imagining. "I pictured more of a Dungeons and Dragons-themed event with suits of armor, banners and sword fighting."

"Big surprise." Her tone was an eye roll of its own.

He pivoted toward the stage. "In between battles, a trio of musicians will play — pipe, flute and fiddle. We'll set up long tables for guests with trenchers, whole roasted chickens and mead. Jugglers and acrobats during dinner. Dancing optional."

"Besides the Hughes family, who else in Graywood practices weekly with real weapons?"

"Suffocating my aspirations, Ren."

"Actually, I take that back." Karen navigated the rubble, following the length of the ballroom. She looked like an archeologist examining the hint of bones hidden in sand and depicting the entire skeleton beneath. "Rich people love having any reason to dress up. Not that I have any experience beyond watching Hamilton and his cronies from afar, and by that I mean preparing his taxes."

"You're a stronger person than me." Give him blueprints to build a house and he'd take it on, no hesitation. But taxes? He'd rather crawl beneath an old house into a spider nest. Karen had the patience of a saint. If she joined forces with him, they'd be unstoppable.

"True." She flashed him a grin before resuming her study of the ballroom. "I'm picturing rowan berries and ivy garlands in the rafters and wound around banisters. Candles and crystals everywhere to make the light dance."

He couldn't look away from her. While she surveyed the room like a queen weaving the details of a future festival, he imagined her in a belted, forest-green dress, her creamy skin glowing in the candlelight as they swirled across the dance floor. In a perfect world, a knife would be at her belt, but whether or not she possessed a weapon, her hands would be on him.

"Are you listening, Hughes?"

"Always." Leo hurriedly smiled. If she knew the direction of his thoughts, she'd back off, maybe leave him stuck forever in the realm of best friendship. He'd break out of that particular tower and expand the borders, but he had to be careful. "Ecstatic to hear we're on the same page with a medieval banquet charity event."

"We'll come up with a better title." Her eyes brightened, green and sparkling in the natural light. "Weapons will intrigue the men, renaissance gowns the women. You'll be golden." She patted his chest and froze with her hand above his heart, as if she hadn't intended to touch him, realized she had and couldn't figure out how to backpedal.

He held her hand in place with his. His pulse thrummed against her palm. "You're the only one I know who'd take my vision seriously and spin it with tangible features, bringing it one step closer to reality." He lowered his voice. "Thank you for agreeing to be here with me, Ren. There's no one else I'd rather have."

She licked her lips, and it was all he could do not to kiss her like he'd wanted to since the day they'd met. Sometimes he regretted being taught to be a gentleman, to not invade a woman's personal space unless invited. If he'd kissed Karen that first day instead of being patient and respectful, maybe he wouldn't be fighting to escape the friends-only pitfall he found himself in. This month, working close with her for hours at a time, that trap would be sprung.

One way or another.

Her gaze drifted to his mouth and lingered there. When she didn't pull away, he eased closer. His heart pounded faster. The slightest tilt of her head, a few inches, and he'd finally taste her.

"Hell-ooooo?" A husky female voice echoed from the corridor outside the ballroom, growing louder. "I found the gate open, the front door unlocked. Just a visit from your feisty rival."

Karen stepped back, the moment gone.

Leo swallowed a snarl. *Harlan Cooper*, his construction nemesis and strongest competitor. Worse, Harlan was the female version of a stereotypical construction worker. Of all the companies Karen wanted to work for, Cooper was last on his list. But whatever Ren chose to do, he'd support her.

Cooper strolled into the ballroom. Wearing a smug smile, she paused and planted a hand on her cocked hip. After a quick survey of the ballroom and dismissal of Karen, her focus landed on him. The smile took a dark turn toward a leer.

Harlan was an unexpected beauty in an unconventional career. Even in overalls and boots, her blonde hair up in a messy topknot, she captured male attention everywhere she went. But not from him, and his resistance seemed to incite her.

Why couldn't Karen be the woman chasing him? He'd resist long enough to make her crazy with need before satisfying every desire.

Scowling, he strode for the marble steps. If the planets were aligned, maybe he could get rid of Cooper fast. "Not all open doors are invitations."

Instead, she sauntered deeper into the ballroom, mischief glinting in her dark eyes. "I'd heard you bought Granton Hall, but choosing this monstrosity for the city hall competition?" She spread her arms, indicating the ruined ballroom. "You might as well give up now. Don't worry about losing your investment. I'll buy you out at a fair price after I win." She looked him up and down. "If you're real nice, I might keep the name. Cooper-Hughes Construction has a nice ring to it, don't you think? New motto? We nail them all."

Karen snorted, pretended to clear her throat and went about studying a cornice.

He turned his scowl on her. *Unhelpful volunteer assistant.* He folded his arms to prevent the urge to grab the back of Cooper's overalls and haul her out. "I never surrender, I don't do sweet and I'd rather frostbite my ass in the deepest pit of Hades than sell out."

"I love it when you get all moody," she purred.

"For future reference, the 'no trespassing' sign I'm putting up today applies to even you." He swept his hand toward the hallway and the direction of the front door. "I'm sure you can see yourself out."

"I'll try not to trip on the wreckage." Cooper laughed. "Go ahead and *erect* your sign. I was only checking to make sure you haven't been taken by the Granton curse before losing to me."

"Granton curse?" Ren asked. Her curiosity trumped watching him suffer.

"Oh, honey, you didn't know?" Cooper *tsk*ed. "I understand why you wouldn't turn down a job offer from Hughes. I mean, look at him. I'm tempted to work for him, too, but you should read the fine print before agreeing to any project, no matter the sexy scenery. Leo, I'm surprised at you, not informing your employees about the full job site particulars."

Before he snarled a response, Karen beat him to it. "I'd never pass up a cursed mansion, and I'm volunteering, no hiring required." She twirled her hammer once and almost dropped it. "Let the renovations begin!"

"My odds of winning get better all the time." The chuckle in Cooper's tone made Leo want to grind his teeth. "Did I miss the competition clause that required our volunteers to be rookies?"

"Don't you have a low-income apartment complex to slap together somewhere?" Leo gestured again toward the door. "We're busy here."

Cooper shrugged. "If you don't want to hear about the curse —"

"We don't," he said.

"We do!" Ignoring his glare, Karen stuffed her hammer in her belt, getting it right on the second try.

Cooper smiled. Anyone who didn't know her would think she was as sweet as cherry pie. She turned her full attention on Karen. "Only if you promise you'll get Leo to relax. He's so grumpy. Snuggle up and touch all those tasty, tempting muscles for me."

Crimson climbed into Karen's face, and a growl lodged deep in Leo's chest. He could handle being tested, was good with Karen teasing him and endured harassment from his brothers, but Cooper was neither friend nor family.

"Out, Cooper." That growl rose into his throat. He pointed at the door. "*Now.*"

"Before I even tell you how Granton's wife went missing, along with his riches? Or that he buried her bones in the walls?" Cooper's smile stretched wider. "Have it your way, but don't blame me when Granton's spirit sucks you dry. Or when that mold you thought you'd conquered returns the next day." She spun, patted his ass along the way and trotted up the ballroom stairs.

Leo pinched the bridge of his nose as her laughter floated back into the ballroom.

"So that's Cooper?" Karen asked, her tone neutral.

He'd hoped Ren wouldn't meet her potential employer so soon. Keeping her the entirety of the month was essential to his plan to win her heart. If she understood how challenging it would be working for Harlan Cooper, she might change her mind.

But first and always, Ren was his best friend. She wouldn't leave him in a lurch or do anything to undermine his chances in the competition. If she bailed, she'd do it now, when he still had time to find another volunteer. Hell, she'd probably help him find her replacement—and his best shot at seducing her into becoming more than friends would be lost forever.

Tension knotted his neck. *Please don't quit on me.*

He opened his eyes, found her watching him with an unreadable expression, and that knot tightened. Learning everything about Karen was his passion, and he hated being unable to decipher the thoughts stirring in her head. He hated when she shut him out.

"The offer to work for me instead of Cooper is always open." He watched for any sign of retreat.

"I think she might like you."

"She wants to get me into bed then destroy me, like a praying mantis."

He paused, a new twist on his plan sparking to life, thanks to Cooper's visit. Planting both hands on her shoulders, he looked her straight in the eye. "You don't understand the gravity of my situation. Ren, you have to save me. I can't endure another moment of being pawed and propositioned by her. It's insufferable."

"Says the man who wields swords and sabers for enjoyment?" She swiped her hand through the air. "If the flirting bothers you that much, threaten her with a sexual harassment suit."

"And become the laughingstock of the construction realm? My reputation would never recover." He shook his head. "Cooper will only respect my boundaries if she believes I'm otherwise involved with a sassy, possessive woman who isn't afraid to shut her down."

"Oh, is she immune to your usual line that your heart is otherwise engaged?" She batted her eyelashes, returning to the saccharine-sweet Ren he loved. "Grab a girlfriend from the willing masses. Problem solved."

"Excellent idea. Don't have the time." He gripped her shoulders harder as her eyes narrowed, wary. "Cooper doesn't need to know our living situation is temporary. If you accompany me, cling to my arm, gaze into my eyes a smidge longer than necessary, snarl at her if she gets too close, she'd be fooled."

She gave him a stern look. "Stop with the puppy-dog eyes."

"I'll throw in a pair of sexy boots with lots of buckles," he said in the low voice that always made her squirm.

Karen bit her lip.

"Come on, Ren. Be my Isabeau. At the very least, be my Phillipe." His pulse drummed fast against his ribs.

"I resent the very fact that I understand your *Ladyhawke* references." After a moment of returning his stare, she slumped. "Dammit."

His heart soared. A full month in close proximity with Ren, and now endless opportunities to woo her outside of Granton Hall.

"You're my hero." Grinning, he took her face between his hands. Without thinking, as if it was the most natural thing in the world, Leo kissed her.

Chapter Eight

As Leo pressed his mouth to hers, Karen couldn't move, tendrils of fire spinning through her veins. Not once since they'd been friends had he so much as given her a peck on the cheek. Casual touches? Fine. A playful bump with hip or shoulder? No problem. An occasional smack in the back of the head went without saying.

A kiss threatened the world as she knew it.

The kiss lingered, his lips soft on hers, and her heart made a slow barrel roll, shooting tingles through every nerve. It took all her strength not to lean into him and curl her arms around his neck in full claim.

It was exactly as she both fantasized and feared. Leo was like an addictive substance. The barest taste left her wanting more, more, more. The thrill of that single, sweet kiss scared her silly, left her utterly devastated.

"My apologies," he murmured, his big hands gently keeping her face captive. "I lost my head in the excitement of the moment." As he watched her with hooded eyes, a slow, half-smile curled to life. "Forgive me if I don't regret it."

Holding her ground took some serious effort but acting on her impulses would shatter the delicate balance between them. Whenever Leo flirted in that sober way of his, she resisted making any comeback overly sexual. Each time he sidled closer than friendship required, she told herself it meant nothing. Every heated look aimed her way was all her imagination. It *had* to be. Anything more could ignite an explosive spark that would destroy a friendship, leaving a trail of soot.

Granton Hall had bewitched Leo. It was the only rational explanation why, after two years of friendship, he'd kiss her.

She swallowed hard and managed to form words. "You need to get out more, Hughes."

"True."

Karen stepped out of his loose hold. She kept their friendship borders neat, clean and uncomplicated by pretending — pretending her so-much-more-than-friendly feelings would fade, pretending other women flirting with Leo didn't make her want to tear out some plucked and polished eyebrows, pretending her heart didn't flutter every time he walked into the room. She couldn't step off that path now, no matter how much she reeled from the briefest, tiniest taste of him.

"What's first?" She ignored the fake sunshine in her tone and pivoted. Looking anywhere but Leo was in her best interest. "I want to learn everything to impress Cooper."

He sighed. "You're not going to discuss it any further, are you?"

The kiss? No way in hell. She focused on the cracked and missing windows. "Maybe installing windows? Keeping animals and moisture out would be a solid start."

"Fair warning, Ren—I can't pretend it never happened. I won't forget how perfect your mouth felt on mine, but I'll let you cling to your delusions." He leaned close and his breath warmed the shell of her ear. "For now. Since you so generously agreed to save me from Cooper."

She could barely handle the Leo she knew, her friend who banked the heat between them. This man who tested the boundaries would destroy her. And she'd let her weakness for his puppy-dog eyes—his deep, blue, perceptive eyes that seemed to read her soul—sway her into playing occasional fake girlfriend. What had she been thinking? Maybe Granton Hall messed with her common sense, too.

"I think you've inhaled too much sawdust, Hughes."

"Or not enough." He folded his powerful arms. "So, Cooper... Not giving up the dream, even after meeting her?"

She ignored his heat brushing her arm, relieved to be discussing a safe subject again. Not that Cooper appeared harmless by any stretch. The woman clearly had layers, layers that could impact whether or not she landed the job. "A woman holding her own in a typically male environment is inspiring."

"As much as she vexes me, Cooper can keep up, no matter what gender she's challenging." He studied her sidelong, as if gauging whether or not she might ditch on day one.

Karen met his gaze and arched an eyebrow. He should know her better than that. Once she set her mind on something, she could be as stubborn as any Hughes.

One corner of his mouth curled up. "Grab your tools and gird your loins, Ren. The Leo Hughes' crash construction course begins right now."

* * * *

The sunlight slanting through the windows turned a molten gold before Leo allowed her to call it quits. Karen sat on her heels and scrubbed at a spot of dried spackle on her hand. Once Leo put his seductive self on the back burner and got down to business, he proved to be a strict taskmaster, and friendship entitled her to no special privileges. She'd labored for hours on one small section of the ballroom, clearing rubble, learning about wall repair, putting her putty knife to good use. Every time she'd thought she had it finished, he'd frown for a while, point out all the places she'd missed and send her back to work.

Perfectionist tyrant.

"Not too shabby for your first day." Leo extended a hand and hefted her to her feet. "You might decide to trade numbers for tools when this is over."

She winced and straightened, muscles she never knew she had sore and throbbing. "Don't count on it, Hughes. If I need work done on my future house, I'll crunch enough numbers to hire you."

That heat he'd kept chained all day returned to his eyes, darkening them to deep seas. "I'll always be free for you, Ren, darling." The workday over, he returned to his new favorite recreational activity — torturing her.

"Come on. I brought my grill from home. I'll cook, and we can summarize our progress."

"No dinner for me. I'm going out." If she had dinner with him, relaxed with a chilled beverage, she might lay her head on his shoulder. She might let him pull her close. Might decide kissing him more was a fantastic idea.

His forehead wrinkled and he gave her that soul-searching look that said he knew exactly where her thoughts went.

"A month of volunteering doesn't mean I surrender my evening hours." She sniffed. "I'm going out."

The forehead wrinkle morphed into a scowl. "I'll go with you."

"Impromptu girls' night, Hughes. Your boobs aren't big enough." She laughed and walked out before he read the lie on her face. It wasn't girls' night out, but if she didn't put some space between them, there wouldn't be any space left to squeeze in friendship.

After a shower, dressed in her favorite black and red plaid mini skirt, leather boots and a soft sweater that clung to her curves, Karen entered her favorite seedy hangout. Seven Devils had the best happy hour deals, bottomless fries and a pool table that made a great prop for showing off her long legs. The hour was earlier than her normal, most tables empty. She slid onto a bar stool and ordered some wings with a hard cider. Leo's grilled steak would have been better but not worth the price. She'd barely escaped intact.

She touched her mouth, the memory of his kiss branded on her skin. The harder she tried not to think about it, the more it took up space in her brain. How was she supposed to separate the man who had become her best friend from this new version who seemed intent on driving her crazy?

She'd thought it would pass, this desire for him, that friendship would overcome lust the better she got to know him. Instead, it morphed into a twisted ball of bands wound so tightly together that she had trouble distinguishing one from the other. She didn't want to lose her friend in there somewhere.

Jed, the Devils' regular evening bartender, slid her a bottle with a wink. He broke bartender protocol by not talking much, but no one seemed to mind. Sometimes a silent, sympathetic ear and the warm fuzz of a favorite brew made for the best catharsis.

She took a swig of her cider, the chilled glass making her lips tingle more. Working with Leo would be hard enough, but how would she manage to maintain her boundaries while pretending to be his devoted date? As much as it would be a new level of self-torture, the thought of being his hero for a few nights, stretching the limits of the fantasy without crossing the friendship line had been impossible to resist. She toppled into the Leo rabbit hole, no return.

Her heart couldn't afford to fall in love with—and lose—another best friend. Trusting someone on every level only to watch that bond crumble had nearly broken her once. It was why she kept her romance casual, easy to control and detached, not like rejection and heartache.

Not like Leo.

Jed set a basket of fries and wings in front of her, returning to the role of mixologist before she mumbled her gratitude for hot, greasy sustenance. She bit a fry in half, feeling better already. On the sunshine side, another afternoon of not enduring the whispers and looks at Hamilton & Associates had been bliss. She'd already learned some useful construction skills. Granton Hall still remained unexplored, and Cooper's mention of curses, hidden bones and spirits added to the thrill.

"Miss Karen?" The cultured English accent had her swiveling in her bar stool so fast that she nearly kicked Oliver Hunter in the shin with her boots. He stepped to the side, a flash of amusement in his eyes.

"Mr. Hunter, so sorry. You were closer than I expected."

"No need to apologize. Landscapers learn to be swift on their feet. One never knows when one might be required to dodge a stray shovel or rabid shrubbery."

She laughed, her shoulders relaxing. "Shrubberies can definitely be vicious."

He glanced at the empty stool next to her, the single serving of fries and wings on the counter. "May I join you?"

This was what she'd wanted, what she'd vowed to find to survive a month of sharing close quarters with Leo—a hot guy to distract her. So why did her stomach twist as if her heartstrings pulled?

At her hesitation, Oliver cocked his head and hooked his thumb into his jeans' pocket. "If you're expecting someone, I'll keep you company while you wait. I don't know many people in Graywood yet." A hint of vulnerability entered his tone. "It would be refreshing to not sit alone, even if for a moment."

"The garlic wings are delicious." Karen pushed out the bar stool beside her in invitation. She understood all about being lonely, feeling alone while surrounded by other people. Leo was the only person who never let her suffocate in that sensation. When he was with her, he never let her forget that he was there.

As Oliver settled in beside her and placed an order, those strings around her heart tightened.

"I didn't expect to find you here this evening." Oliver shifted, angling toward her. His eyes sparkled, bright against his gray Oxford button-down. He dressed much too classy for Seven Devils. "Has Granton Hall already driven you to drinking?"

She had no intention of sharing the real reason behind her outing. "What do you mean by 'already'?"

"Taking on such extensive renovations as required by a large property that has been abandoned for many years must be overwhelming."

"Oh." She couldn't hide her disappointment. "I was hoping you'd have some specific details about the curse."

Jed, fast and attentive as always, set a wine glass on the counter before Oliver and slipped away. Karen blinked in surprise. Seven Devils had a wine list? Who knew?

"You mean the curse Elizabeth Granton placed on her husband when he discovered her affair and killed her lover?" Oliver asked, all casual, as if such a history was commonplace. "Or the one cast after he murdered her and hid her bones in the walls?"

Karen dropped the wing in her fingers and swiveled on the bar stool, facing him. She leaned in. "Tell me *everything*."

Chapter Nine

After an hour of riding his motorcycle, hoping if he went fast enough the wind would loosen the barbed wire wrapped around his heart, Leo gave up. He rumbled to a stop in the Seven Devils' gravel parking lot and exhaled, long and slow.

His usual weekend evening agenda included any activity that might distract him from visualizing what Ren did without him, who she might be touching, kissing, wrapping her lovely legs around. Sword practice with one or more of his brothers usually worked. All his brothers at once? Exceptionally better. With the entire Hughes clan attacking from all sides, surviving required the entirety of his focus, leaving no room for imagination. By the time he dragged himself into bed, exhaustion erased everything but dreams of his favorite stubborn redhead.

He frowned at the dull black door leading into the pub and whatever horrors waited beyond. Seven Devils met the basic standards of a local dive. Stuck between a bowling alley and closed barbershop, its square windows needed a wash and the roof needed new shingles. Neon lights offering beer blinked blue and yellow.

His gloved grip on the handlebars ached, and he uncurled his fingers. When their friendship had been new, Karen had invited him out with her. He'd played the helpless bystander, the bewildered wingman while she seduced and slipped away with another guy. That was the moment he realized she'd friend-zoned him and vowed never to endure that torture again. She eventually stopped inviting him out on her weekend excursions but never asked why.

He removed his helmet, peeled off his leather gloves and raked his hair back. Maybe part of the problem was the simple, unconditional acceptance they afforded each other. Neither one of them pushed too hard, unwilling to do anything that might harm their friendship. He swung his leg over the bike and shoved his gloves into the helmet. But if a relationship couldn't withstand a few blows of honest truth, maybe it needed to man up and grow a pair.

Leo stalked toward the ominous black door and shouldered inside without slowing. Finding Karen took less than a heartbeat. She sat at the bar, her hair glowing blood-red in the dull lights, sexy black boots tucked beneath her as she leaned in close to…Oliver.

He clenched his jaw. What were the odds of the landscaper he'd hired hours ago to groom Granton's gardens—in big part due to Ren's persuasion—showing up at the watering hole she frequented on the weekends?

From her attentive pose, whatever line the Englishman spouted held her captive. Oliver's interest in her earlier at Granton had been obvious. If Karen wanted a hookup, contestant number one already played it hard.

Not this time, Ren. Too long he'd waited on the sidelines, pining after a woman who avoided testing the boundaries of friendship because of past pain. Too many days had already been wasted, keeping the truth to himself. He'd come here tonight to fight his demons and win. If she wanted to go home with someone, he'd use all the power tools in his possession to be the one she chose.

He made it halfway to the bar counter when Karen turned toward the door, as if sensing his presence. Her eyes lit up, and his heart lurched. Her dimpled smile was one of his favorite things in the world. When she aimed it at him, only he and Ren existed, and all was fine with the universe.

"Hughes!" She waved and patted the bar stool next to her. "You've got to hear this."

Hunter's mouth tightened before hiding behind the veneer of a plastic smile. The gardener hadn't expected competition tonight.

Sorry, not sorry.

Leo didn't bother holding back a smirk, and when Karen fisted the front of his flannel shirt and dragged him into the empty bar stool, he couldn't stop a rumble of laughter. "What has got you in such a tizzy?"

"You're just in time." She released his shirt as he steadied himself, planting his boots on the floor before the bar stool tipped. "Oliver was about to tell me about Granton's sordid history." Sparks glittered in her eyes, bright as stars. "You hit a gold mine of murder, hidden bones and curses when you bought Granton. Isn't that exciting?"

"Hmm."

"Hmm?" Her eyes narrowed. "Don't ruin my fun, Hughes."

"Never." He dropped his chin and lowered his voice. "Tonight, I'm in. Whatever you want, Ren."

She blinked several times and moistened her lips with the tip of her tongue as her gaze drifted to his mouth. She wrapped her fingers around the bottle as if needing a tether, her other hand clenched on her thigh.

Leo gave her his lazy half-smile, denying the savage need to drag her into his lap and kiss her until the lights blinked a last call. He'd almost messed up everything by that simple, thoughtless, nothing kiss earlier. The next time he kissed her, he'd make sure she couldn't dismiss it.

Hunter cleared his throat. "As I was saying…"

Karen swiveled toward Oliver, the moment gone, lost to the mere suggestion of curses.

He managed not to reach around Karen and erase Oliver's smug expression with a well-deserved fist-tap. He unclenched his fingers and forced them to relax on his thighs. Self-restraint wasn't nearly as fun as his imagination.

The bartender set a bottled beer that Karen must have ordered for him on the counter, and he nodded a thanks. The liquid cooled his throat and settled his temper enough to join the conversation without inflicting violence. He stole a fry from her basket.

"Don't keep us in suspense." Without looking, Ren slapped Leo's hand away when he reached for another fry.

He grinned. It was good to know Oliver didn't hold her entire focus, no matter how she pretended.

"What's the curse?" She bounced in her seat. "Where are the bones hidden? How did Mr. Granton get away with murder? Don't leave anything out."

"Including your sources." Leo leaned one elbow on the counter for a full view of his competition. "If there's research on my property that I don't know about, I want it."

"Of course." Oliver's voice was calm, verging on bored. "The information is available in the library archives. I always research a town before moving, investigate its history and people, the properties and landscaping opportunities." He lifted his wine glass in a semi-salute. "Which is how I happened upon your doorstep this morning."

Karen huffed, rustling her bangs. "If Leo wants boring details, you can hook up later. Get to the good stuff."

"I would never deny a lady's request." Oliver's teeth gleamed. "The Grantons were the wealthiest couple in Graywood and delighted in flaunting it. Their balls and parties were legendary, full of intrigue and merriment."

Merriment? Leo scowled. He didn't appreciate Oliver encroaching on his vintage vocabulary.

"Yet," Oliver continued, "Arthur Granton's wealth was not the sole source of gossip. His young wife Elizabeth held an unearthly beauty. Some say she never aged."

"You found that detail in the library archives?" Leo lifted his eyebrows.

"The rumor, yes."

"An alleged witch?" Karen wriggled in her seat, her eyes bright.

Oliver shrugged and swirled his wine. "The real trouble began when Elizabeth fell in love with the groundskeeper."

"Ooh, small town scandal, betrayal and forbidden love." Karen rubbed her hands together. "Tell me more."

"Reports say that business took Arthur away for long stretches, often months at a time. An outsider in a small town, Elizabeth had no experience being all alone with a huge estate to run. She loved her gardens and spent every available minute outside. The groundskeeper and his sister, who managed the housekeeping, were both childhood friends of Elizabeth. She insisted they move with her to Granton Hall when she married. The siblings resided in a small house across the woods on the property, within reach should they be needed." Oliver smirked. "For Elizabeth, that need went beyond the usual duties."

"Spare us the sordid details," Leo said.

"Speak for yourself." Karen elbowed him. "There's nothing better than an illicit affair gone bad to set the groundwork for a good curse."

Leo stole another fry and stuffed it in his mouth before she could swipe it back, a small act of vengeance for siding with the enemy. "Curses aren't real."

Oliver drained his wine glass and motioned for Jed to refill it. "Tell that to those who have died near Granton Hall over the decades."

"No way. Like guests falling down the stairs and breaking their necks? Drowning in bathtubs? Heart attacks in the cellar?" Karen bounced up and down in excitement. "How many people have kicked it at Granton? Or, to be more precise, how many restless spirits is Leo dealing with?"

A chill raced down his back. He hated how easily the supernatural unhinged him. He'd had more than enough teasing about it from his brothers over the years. Sometimes, honesty was more a nuisance than a virtue. "Morbid much, Ren?"

"You know it." She flashed him a grin.

"There are no ghosts haunting Granton." He ignored the growl in his voice. "No rattling chains or rocking chairs moving by themselves. The only open cupboard was the one you left ajar after putting the measuring tape away."

Karen swiveled in her seat to face him. "Ghosts don't always make their presence known to new owners right away, Hughes. Everyone knows that."

Oliver's chuckle did nothing to improve his temper. He swallowed the last of his beer and set the bottle on the counter louder than necessary. The bartender replaced it with a full one.

A gust of cool air brushed his neck as another patron entered the Seven Devils. Leo made the mistake of glancing at the door and cursed beneath his breath.

Harlan Cooper swept inside, dressed in tight jeans and even tighter T-shirt beneath a cropped denim jacket, her platinum hair loose and eyes lined a prowler-kohl black. Her predatory smile tripled the tension in his neck, and when she sauntered his way as if invited, he regretted not strapping his practice sword to his back. If Karen hadn't been here, he'd ditch out the back door. He wasn't too ashamed to flee if it meant survival.

"Leo Hughes," Cooper purred, hooking her claws on his shoulder for balance and sliding into the unfortunately empty bar stool beside him. "I thought you preferred exclusive clubs or posh resorts to spend your Friday nights. How lucky for me that you proved me wrong." She whispered close to his ear, "And how very lucky for you."

He peeled her fingers off his shoulder and pushed her hand away as politely as possible. "Don't you have some poor schmuck somewhere to bedazzle into signing an overpriced building contract?"

She removed her denim jacket and shimmied in her seat. "Not tonight." She traced a finger down his biceps. "Tonight, I'm all yours."

He did *not* appreciate how she echoed his earlier words to Karen.

"I don't believe we were introduced this morning." Ren leaned over him, her side brushing against his chest, and stuck out her hand. That particular touch, intentional or not, he didn't mind at all. "Karen Ives, temporary volunteer assistant at Hughes & Sons Construction." She hooked a thumb over her shoulder at Oliver. "Oliver Hunter, landscaper. He's new to town and looking for work."

Harlan shook Karen's hand and gave Oliver a cursory glance. Whatever attractive traits the Englishman possessed weren't enough to win her attention. She smiled at them both and rested a possessive hand on Leo's shoulder, her decision made. "Harlan Cooper, best construction contractor in Graywood, despite what the competition claims."

"Not all construction companies believe that fast and cheap are better than superior quality and craftmanship." Leo shrugged her hand off his shoulder with a little less courtesy than before. "Despite what the competition claims."

"Oh, but fast and cheap are so much more fun." Cooper laughed and motioned Jed over.

The night grew worse by the minute.

"We were discussing the Granton curse." Ren gave Harlan a sharp smile, that adorable hint of jealousy rising to the surface.

When another woman hit on him, she always played it cool, pretended she didn't care. There had been moments when her mildly possessive responses were all that kept his hope alive. Showing up tonight, it soothed all his jagged edges.

"*Alleged* curse," he said. With Karen's warmth against him, her green-eyed tiger growling right beneath the surface on his behalf, he couldn't resist resting a light hand on her back.

"Oh, the curse is real." Cooper gave Jed a wink as he set a tumbler down. "If you had done your homework before buying it, that wouldn't be a surprise. Sucks to be you."

Leo drew a breath in through his nose and released it before answering. He always did his homework before investing in any property, rumors of hauntings not included. Foundations and plumbing, signs of pest or dry rot, roof and electric? Those were the basics of what made a house profitable, not bad juju.

"If the curse isn't real," Oliver said, regaining control of the conversation, "explain why every fifty years, like clockwork, within a few days of Halloween, a tragedy occurs on Granton property?"

"What does Halloween have to do with it?" Karen pointed a French fry at Oliver. "Not that I'm questioning the facts."

Leo snorted. Any fact coming from Oliver or Cooper should be questioned from every angle, not taken as truth. He didn't trust either one of them.

"Halloween is the day Elizabeth Granton disappeared," Cooper said, resting her foot on his bar stool.

"Never to be seen again." Oliver saluted Cooper with his refilled wine glass. "Murdered by her husband, her bones hidden somewhere on Granton grounds."

"Allegedly," Leo repeated.

"So the curse began. Arthur died two years later." Oliver's last words were soft, and he stared into his glass, as if sobered by the sad history of Granton Hall's original owners.

Karen gripped Leo's forearm, her attention riveted on Oliver. "On Halloween?"

"Correct." Blinking away whatever road his thoughts had taken, Oliver looked up. "Every fifty years afterward, a death occurred—a hunting accident in the woods, an unknown illness, a car wreck in the drive— Every instance is documented in the town archives. The last one was a tragic fall down the stairs, forty-nine years ago."

"Which means another one is scheduled to occur this year." Ren's hold on his arm tightened.

"Confirmed." Cooper batted her fake eyelashes.

Oliver swirled his wine. "I feel relatively safe laboring outside."

"No spot on Granton property is safe." Jed tossed his rag beneath the counter, silencing them all with his unexpected response. He paused, as if he hadn't meant to intrude on their conversation or say anything aloud. Color stained his cheeks as he turned away. "My apologies."

"Nice try, Jed." Ren leaned across the counter and snagged his sleeve. "Tell us what you know or zero tips."

He grimaced, propped his elbows on the counter and lowered his chin, a conspirator spilling his secrets. "My mother told me stories about Granton," he said in a hushed voice. "She heard the same stories from her mother, who heard them from her mother and so on. My ancestor was a farrier for the Granton family back in the day."

Without meaning to, Leo found himself listening with the others, drawn by Jed's hypnotic voice.

"I never heard that Elizabeth Granton was a witch, but she did love the groundskeeper, Edwin. Their love blossomed in childhood, but their differences in social status made it impossible for them to be together. If you know where to look, their love is documented everywhere in the gardens by their initials. Every plant, statue and walkway declared adoration. The grounds are a lasting love letter from Edwin to Elizabeth."

"Sweet but not spine-tingling." Karen straightened, sounding disappointed.

Jed shrugged one shoulder. "When Edwin died — "

"Murdered," Cooper and Oliver said together.

"Elizabeth was inconsolable, mad with grief. A week later, on All Saints' Eve, she vanished."

"What does your mother say happened to her?" Leo asked.

"That she died of a broken heart, filled with regret."

"If true," Oliver said, his eyes narrowed, "her remains would have been found."

Cooper nodded. "No one has ever located her bones."

"My mother swears Elizabeth's restless spirit roams the grounds, searching for her Edwin." Jed slung his towel over his shoulder. "Anyone unlucky enough to see her befalls terrible tragedy...like Arthur."

"What happened to Arthur?" Ren whispered.

"Fell from the second story. Broke his neck. Just like my great-great-grandfather fifty years later." Jed straightened and turned to help a customer at the end of the bar, leaving them in silence.

"Lovely tale of tragedy." Oliver stood. "Excuse me for a moment." He headed for the restroom.

Karen finished her beer, set it down with a decisive *thunk* and rose as well. "I have to pee."

Leo tracked her journey to the bathroom corridor, a few steps behind Oliver. The first and only time he'd accompanied Ren to the Seven Devils, she'd left him behind for a meaningless tryst with another man. An icy snake coiled in his stomach, the sense that, like Elizabeth Granton, he'd lost someone precious and irreplaceable.

Chapter Ten

Karen patted her face with ice-cold water, leaned on the bathroom sink and considered dunking her head beneath the faucet to cool off. She gazed into the mirror and studied her reflection. Nothing wrong with her hair. No smears in her lipstick or mascara. The dim light hid the flush of her face. Maybe if she looked like everything was peachy, Leo wouldn't pick up the steel wire tightening her entire body, ready to snap with a single pluck of his long, capable fingers.

He wasn't supposed to be here tonight. He *never* came to Seven Devils, his distaste for the pub and its patrons clear after countless, refused invites out. He'd joined her once. *Once.* Why the hell was he here now? Ever since he'd bought Granton Hall, he seemed determined to demolish all their friendship safety precautions.

She blew out a breath and straightened. From the second Leo had walked in the door, she'd used every ounce of willpower to concentrate on the curse so she wouldn't think about how close he sat to her, his cedar scent, the warmth rolling off his powerful body, that tempting, lazy smile he aimed only at her.

Mission royally failed. As much as she loved all things supernatural, curses had nothing on the subtle, spellbinding magic of Leo Hughes. And when Cooper crashed the party, putting her hands on all over him?

"Hell." Karen jerked the faucet on and splashed her face again. Women hitting on Leo was nothing new, but when Harlan Cooper touched him, the gargoyle inside her sharpened its claws and growled. How was she supposed to ignore her attraction to her best friend when he was so damn irresistible and right in her space?

Before she decided to go with climbing out of the window, she exited the bathroom and strode through the shadowed corridor. At the doorway leading to the pub's open room, she jerked to a stop.

Oliver hadn't yet returned to his seat, leaving Leo and Harlan alone at the bar. As Karen watched, Harlan plopped onto Leo's lap and noosed her arms around his neck. He wore a cool expression and reached for her locked hands at his neck. Prying himself free resulted in a laughing Cooper pressing her boobs against him.

The heat recently tempered beneath the cold face splash rekindled, and all her goals, reasonings and barriers boiled to the surface in one defining moment. She could pretend like she always did, not risk her chance at being hired by Cooper, not put her heart in the line of fire — and let Leo down. Or she could rescue her best friend, go all in with the fake girlfriend act, and weather the emotional fallout sure to come her way.

He'd do it for her, no question.

Her pulse thumped faster, harder, a rhythm that had roused enough defiance and courage to leave everything familiar and land in Graywood on her own, to leave a good job even when it might be easier to stay and suffer in silence.

I can handle this. Confronting Harlan Cooper now might be a career curveball, but she'd perfect her construction skills at Granton Hall. When she applied for the accountant job at Cooper Homes, Harlan would be so wowed by her skills that she'd jump to hire her, girlfriend of Leo Hughes or not. Fake girlfriend. *Former* fake girlfriend. By that time, her friendship with Leo would be safely back to normal.

Getting her heart back to normal would be another horror story altogether.

Karen took a long, deep breath. Maybe Granton Hall dust already infected her brain too.

A warm hand settled on the small of her back, and she turned, bumping into Oliver's chest. Metal gleamed at his collar, a key hanging from a chain around his neck. It looked ancient, shaped of swirls. He shifted and it vanished beneath his shirt.

"Oof, sorry." She gripped his arm, the fine material of his Oxford soft beneath her fingers, his lean muscles firm. "I didn't know you were right behind me."

"No worries, love." He steadied her, his gaze lingering on her mouth before lifting to her eyes. "It appears our skeptical Mr. Hughes has found an eager companion. Perhaps we should leave them to it and sneak away ourselves?" His voice took a sultry turn, and the hold on her hip became a caress through her sweater. "Continue our discussion of curses in a more comfortable location with a bottle of wine?"

Handsome and charming, Oliver should have been enough of a distraction, maybe enough for her common sense to kick back in. But her blood didn't spark to life like when Leo smiled at her. No trip of her heart when he looked at her, reading her soul. No electric charge when he touched her.

And even if Oliver had some serious mojo going on, Leo needed her. His upbringing to hold the utmost respect for women left him vulnerable, and the very enemy he'd enlisted her to battle sat in his lap. If Leo couldn't be the sword-wielding badass who crushed his opponents in the ring, she had to do it for him.

"Raincheck." She stepped free of Oliver's light hold, not missing the flash of disappointment in his eyes. "Since you'll be working at Granton Hall, it'll be easy to track you down—if you manage to survive the ghosts and goblins." She gave him a wicked grin.

"I'm counting on it." He slipped his hands into his pockets. "See you in the morning, love. I'll be the one with the deadly pruners in the overgrown shrubbery, keeping spirits at bay." He brushed by her and headed for the door, leaving her alone to face the consequences of her choices.

Karen straightened her sweater and squared her shoulders. Pasting on her brightest smile, she forced herself to stroll to her seat rather than march to the death metal beat pounding in her head. She tapped Harlan on the shoulder.

Cooper twisted from her perch on Leo's lap and looked at Karen. "Oh." Her dark eyes sparkled with mischief. "I didn't expect you back for at least another ten, twelve minutes." She winked. "Is Oliver still recovering in the bathroom or closet or wherever you two went?"

The smile slid off Karen's face. She may occasionally distract herself with men, but she had enough class to refrain from any rendezvous in the Seven Devils' less-than-pristine bathroom. "Cookie, is it?"

Cooper's smirk didn't change. "My name is—"

"Don't care. Get the hell off my boyfriend. You're squishing him."

Leo blinked. His follow-up smile nearly blinded her.

"You and Hughes?" Harlan swung around and settled on Leo's thigh, her golden hair cascading over his arm. She swept an assessing look over Karen, from her heeled boots to her short-cropped hair. "Let me get this straight. You two, as a couple, chose to spend a romantic night at Seven Devils?"

"We like the atmosphere." So what if Seven Devils was one bum short of seedy? Jed was a great bartender and happy hour was affordable. The rowdy weekend night crowd offered options to a girl looking to forget—unless the man she came to forget showed up.

"What's not to like?" Leo stood in one fluid motion and stepped around the bar stool, away from Cooper. He slung an arm around Karen's shoulders and pulled her close.

Against his solid heat, the possessive arm holding her near, she couldn't deny a thrill.

Cooper grinned like a jackal. "Allow me to share the observations I made when I walked in, before y'all noticed me." She curled the end of her hair around her finger. "I saw a single woman who had sat down alone at the bar, was joined by a handsome newcomer and later gained a third wheel when Hughes showed up."

Leo stiffened. "I had an errand to run and arrived a few minutes late."

The subtle snarl in his voice caught Karen by surprise. Was that why, after the one time they'd gone out to Seven Devils, he never went again? Because he'd felt like her third wheel? Because she'd let him feel that way when he'd never, ever allow her to feel anything less than most important? Her face heated another degree. She was a jerk for not seeing it sooner, for being so involved in her own issues that she didn't notice the ripple effect on Leo.

"I've got an idea." Mischief shone in Cooper's eyes. "Kiss him."

Karen froze. "Excuse me?"

"Kiss him." Cooper licked her lips. "Convince me you're together and I'll be on my way. As much as I love the chase and a man who plays hard to get, I never encroach on another girl's territory." She tilted her head. "So convince me that Hughes hasn't recruited you in a misguided scheme to build the anticipation by making me jealous. Kiss him deep, long and like you mean it."

Her mouth went dry as she met Leo's gaze. He didn't seem to notice Cooper watching them as if her point had already been made. His focus burned on her. The barely-counted-as-a-kiss kiss from the morning remained a tingling imprint on her lips, impossible to forget. A longer kiss would drop her down the Leo black hole, no return.

But not following up with the required kiss — deep, long and like she meant it — would leave Leo plagued by Cooper. He'd suffer through it, too much of a gentleman to put a lady in her place, even when she deserved it.

Hell.

Leo faced her and lowered his head, his mouth a few inches from hers. He lifted his eyebrows, a question, a challenge.

Double hell. She tilted her chin up, unable to look away, pulled into his gravity. Her pulse pounded in her ears as he cupped her face between callused hands and caressed her cheek with his thumb. She would have welcomed his lazy, crooked smile, a promise that this was all a play that would end well, but his expressive mouth remained neutral, his eyes dark.

"Ah-ah-ah," Cooper *tsk*ed, shaking a finger. "It doesn't count unless Karen instigates the kiss. Even a ninety-year-old nun with one foot in the grave would respond to Leo making the moves on her. Hands off, Hughes."

When Leo dropped his hands to his sides, Karen fought the urge to leap over the bar stool and strangle the other woman. Allowing Leo to kiss her, knowing the reason behind it — she could manage that. But to be the one to kiss him? She might not be able to claw her way back.

"Don't be shy." Laughter laced Cooper's voice. "If you don't jump on him, I will. In five." Pause. "Four." A shorter pause. "Three."

Leo's eyes widened, a plea, the only sign he listened to Cooper at all. He dropped his chin, bringing his mouth closer to hers in silent invitation.

Cooper rested one arm against the back of a bar stool. "Two —"

Karen leaned into Leo, and all those delicious muscles flexed, as if he fought to hold himself still. Before she reconsidered, she fisted his shirt with one hand, slid her free arm around his lean waist and lifted on tippytoes.

The second their lips met, all her control crumbled to ash. Every sense sparked to full life with an energy that flamed through her blood. She intended to kiss him with a mild show of passion, but a fierce, howling hunger for him took her by storm and swept her out to sea.

The surrounding bar, scattered patrons, Cooper? All of it faded away, leaving only Leo and his hands in her hair, his hot, demanding mouth, the solid crush of his body. As his tongue touched hers, the silken thrust echoed between her thighs, aching. Legs wobbling, she anchored her arms around his powerful shoulders and held on for dear life.

Never had a kiss affected her like this, commanding all her focus, claiming every nuance of her being. A low, snarl of desire vibrated in his chest and rang through her bones in answer. Every inch of her responded to him, wanting more, needing more.

This was not the kiss she'd planned. This kiss was raw, urgent and absolutely real.

The crack of pool balls jolted Karen from her haze, and she opened her eyes. Cooper was gone. A new couple she hadn't even noticed enter Seven Devils lingered near the pool table in the corner. Her pulse throbbed, violent, trembling in every extremity.

She stepped out of Leo's embrace and didn't dare look at him, didn't dare reveal how his kiss had shaken her. Grabbing her jacket and keys, she hurried for the exit, his words drowned by the roaring blood in her head.

Autumn air cooled her hot skin and she gulped it in great breaths as she raced to her car and climbed in. She pulled out of the parking lot and refused to look back.

Kissing Leo had exceeded every one of her fantasies, even more destructive than she'd feared. Nothing would be the same again, and no amount of pretending could fix it.

Chapter Eleven

Sunday afternoon, Karen sat on her heels and laid the chisel beside her padded knees. Wood pieces of various sizes and types littered the dusty ballroom floor around her. Weak light brushed through the tall windows, dulled by rain. Every so often, a branch scratched against glass, pushed and pulled by a grumbling wind.

My poor palms. She examined the new collection of blisters. Leo had suggested gloves and she'd waved him off, anything to get him out of the door faster for his Sunday family fun with swords. Cooper had been right about one thing — working with Leo was a lesson in resisting temptation.

He hadn't pressed her about the Seven Devils incident when he'd returned to Granton Friday night. Saturday had passed in a blur, up at dawn for volunteer work. She'd been so exhausted from fevered Leo dreams and physical labor that she'd passed out on the couch two minutes into the mandated Saturday night horror movie. Leo's claim that he watched *Carnival of Souls* alone was subject to suspicion.

Sunday morning began with a bang and an electrical outage. Leo had tossed her a roll of tape, told her to mark the water-damaged section and promised a crash course on parquet flooring after he investigated the wiring mystery. An hour later, armored with kneepads and goggles, she began her delicate assault on the flooring with her purple-handled chisel. She'd passed on Leo's invitation to break and join him, needing alone time without distractions of the blue-eyed, muscled kind.

There hadn't been a single mention of fiery Friday night kisses.

Whatever his reasoning, she'd take it. She didn't want to know whether or not that fateful kiss had affected him like it had her — didn't want to know if his heart had stopped, if he'd forgotten where and who he was in that moment, if he'd felt like magic had rearranged his soul.

Maybe by the time Leo returned she'd have figured out how to go back to pretending that her BFF hadn't rocked her world off its axis.

She jerked the skulls and crossbones kerchief from her head and wiped the dust from her face. As much as she admired the intricate Celtic knot beauty of the parquet pattern, the task of measuring and arranging, replacing each piece of wood to replicate the existing floor would be murder. The part of her that loved puzzles and numbers was all over it. Her aching body? Violently protesting. She had a new appreciation for Leo and his job. Small wonder he had so many delicious muscles.

Heat shivered through her at the memory of pressing against him, the leashed strength of his arms around her. The taste of him lingered on her tongue. Hell, even when he wasn't present, Leo distracted her.

Karen stood and stretched. Her hands needed a break. She wandered toward the windows. The lonely echo of her steps rattled in the ceiling and crystal chandeliers, reminding her of all the secrets still waiting to be found. A branch scratched the window again, sounding like bones on granite. When surrounded by solitude and forgotten memories, the stories told about Granton Hall seemed entirely possible.

She paused near the end of the room. Cracks lined the wall, the surface swollen by moisture. A sliver of moss grew along one crooked seam, as if the wild gardens beyond searched for the lost remains of Elizabeth Granton within.

If Oliver was working, she hadn't seen him. She rubbed away a film of fog and grime with her handkerchief and peered through the sheets of rain. The wind sharpened to a howl, slicing at corners, and the glass panes shuddered beneath its claws. The chandeliers flickered several times before returning to full strength.

She blew out a breath. Leo was the king of preparation and had an industrial-strength generator, but she refused to creep around in the basement alone, searching for it. Loving all things supernatural had taught her not to do anything stupid, especially in the dark.

Goosebumps danced along her arms and down her neck as a sudden, undeniable awareness swept over her, as if someone—or something—watched her. A faint snuffle came from the doorway, and Karen whirled with a squeak.

A fluff of black fur stood on the marble steps and mewed.

"Sir Le Chat," she gasped, placing her hand over her thundering heart. "How did you get out? Did I not shut the laundry room door all the way?"

The kitten scrambled toward her faster than Leo running from a chainsaw wielding clown. His little claws ticked a frantic rhythm on the floor. When he tried to stop, he skidded right past her and into the gap of the flooring she'd torn up. Wood pieces clattered as his small body rolled through them.

Karen rushed to him and knelt, gathering him into her arms. He curled into her and mewled. "Poor thing. Are you okay?"

Beneath the dust hanging from his whiskers and fur, nothing appeared to be bloody or broken. She set him down, and he squirreled back up her knee to her thigh.

"I'm not a tree, kitty." His claws were cruel miniature needles, piercing her jeans and pricking her skin. She plucked him from her leg and settled him on her shoulder like he loved to do with Leo. A rattling purr tickled her ear, and soft fur brushed her cheek as she turned her face into him. "Happy now?"

His small, warm weight on her shoulder lightened her mood. Since she'd left home, she hadn't looked into adopting a pet. Growing up on a farm, she adamantly avoided cow pies and crack of dawn feeding duties. She rubbed Sir's head. But she missed the barn cats. They'd always find her when she hid in the hay loft to escape with her thoughts or cry in secret. With the magic of a purring cat snuggled close, loneliness lost its edge.

"When this project is done, I'm stealing you from Leo." She laughed as Sir's cold nose touched hers. "Bargain made, kitty."

Rain drummed harder and filled the ballroom with dull thunder as Karen gathered the collection of wood pieces she'd extracted, all different shapes, sizes and species. A triangle the size of her hand had fallen into the shallow hole in the floor, thanks to Sir Le Chat's enthusiastic greeting. It wedged in the corner, caught.

Karen plucked at the triangle. Leo had warned her not to break the pieces, and she wasn't about to ruin her perfect record on day two. The stubborn wood remained jammed. "Fine," she huffed. "You want to play? Let's dance."

Chisel in hand, she wriggled the blade into place and gave it some pressure. The lodged wood snapped, and she lost her balance, falling on her butt. Sir held on, with claws.

"Hell." She set the tool aside and crouched to inspect the damage. Not only had she shattered the triangle, which would be a painful task to replicate, the block of parquet where it had wedged had cracked. "Son of a wicked witch. Leo's going to fire me for sure now."

It would be so much easier not to love him if he did. She shook her head. Wrapping love and Leo in the same sentence after the kiss at Seven Devils was perilous to her health and sanity. Her fantasies were bad enough without adding an impossible happily ever after.

"I wonder what construction magic will fix this?" As she reached for the shattered fragments, silver glinted from the cracked floorboard, too large for a nail. She leaned nearer.

A hollow spot had been carved between parquet sections, and a tiny silver key lay within, as if it had been buried and rested in peace until she'd disturbed its grave.

A shiver stole through her. What secret did it lead to? Bones locked away in the basement? Stolen treasure in a lockbox? Whatever it was, she'd find it.

The hollow space was too narrow for her fingers. Luckily, Leo had bought her a pair of needle-nose pliers — with a purple handle, of course. How could she not adore him?

She kept a hand on Sir, retrieved the pliers from her tool belt that was hanging on a nearby sawhorse and returned to the hidey-hole. Feeling like a surgeon, she eased the tip of the pliers inside and pinched the very edge of the key. Carefully, she withdrew it.

In the hollow where the key had been, something moved. Long, black insect legs curled out of the hole, followed by the body of the biggest spider she'd ever seen.

"Oh, hell no." Holding on to Sir with one hand, she scrambled up. She swiped the key and dropped the pliers. Spiders were right beneath rats on her most not-wanted list, and she'd found the mama of all arachnids living beneath the floor. She shuddered. Such a massive spider living in so tiny a space defied logic.

The wind rose from a whimper to a sudden rage, snarling along the walls. The windows shook and rain whipped the glass. The chandelier lights flickered several times and surrendered to black, casting the ballroom in mist and shadows. While only mid-afternoon, with the clouds, rain and electricity dead, twilight took over.

Worse, so much worse, she couldn't find the spider.

Karen backed away. The flooring was dark enough in sections to camouflage an insect any shade between brown and black. Without direct light...that monster could be anywhere.

Sir hissed in her ear as lightning erupted, painting the ballroom in electric white. In that heartbeat-quick flash, the silhouette of a spider stretched across the floor, black and impossibly huge, skittering with terrible speed.

Straight at her.

She whipped Sir from her shoulder, tucked him in the crook of her arm like a football and sprinted toward the ballroom stairs. Thunder boomed, vibrating in the floor and up through the soles of her tennis shoes.

Looking back wasn't happening. Her rational mind whispered that the vision had been a reflection, a trick of muted light, but the fear thrumming through her didn't care. She refused to be a victim to some murderous ghost-spider that emerged every fifty years to feast on human flesh.

A few yards from the short stairwell leading out, lightning struck again, flaring hot and bright. The follow-up thunder crashed like a train wreck against the walls. Glass shattered, another window killed.

She flew up the three steps to the safety of the corridor, spun and shut the glass doors with a bang. Behind the safety of windows and wood, she dared to face what lurked within.

Shadows swathed the ballroom. Splintered glass glinted in the gloom near the hole in the floor. Lightning gleamed, farther away now, but close enough to illuminate the truth — only her imagination had chased her off. Karen exhaled, her pulse pounding hard at her throat.

Sir Le Chat squirmed, and as she returned him to his perch, the darkness where she'd found the key seemed to shift. It *had* been all her imagination, right?

Her hand trembling, she uncurled her fingers holding the key as lightning flickered again outside the windows. Eight miniscule black jewels sparkled in the bow of the key, centered within an etched image so worn and faded she hadn't noticed it earlier. Her mouth went dry.

A spider.

Chapter Twelve

Leo hunched through the rain toward the protection of the front porch. At the shift of his duffel bag and sword strap on his shoulder, every muscle complained. Sunday family fun day had been brutal, his brothers merciless, retaliation for missing Saturday night sword fights. But an evening with Ren curled up close on the couch, sleeping through the terrified screams blaring from the television had been worth every bruise.

Her kiss at Seven Devils colored his every dream, both awake and asleep. He'd expected a disciplined meeting of mouths, just enough to fool Cooper, not the wild, fervent touch that shot lightning through his blood and wrecked him with raw need. He'd loved Ren from the start. That kiss merely confirmed what his heart already knew.

He swiped raindrops from his eyes. When things got heavy, Ren deflected. Discussing serious topics over tea and crumpets wasn't how his girl operated, but some subjects were too important to avoid forever. She could pretend all she wanted that the kiss hadn't affected her. They both knew the truth, and he wouldn't let her off the hook any longer.

By the time he reached the porch, rain soaked through his shirt and trickled icy streams down his back. He climbed the steps and the planks beneath his boots groaned and shifted. He should barricade the stairs. The last thing he needed was someone like Cooper showing up unannounced, falling through and suing him blind.

Leo unlocked the front door and stepped into gloom. A flick of the light switch did nothing. Either the wind had knocked out the power or he had another wiring issue. He leaned his sword against the wall and tossed his duffel bag to the floor.

The air held a chill. How long had Ren been without heat and electricity? He hadn't wanted to leave her, but when she insisted with narrowed, dare-me eyes, he knew from experience that no argument would change her mind.

He grabbed the emergency flashlight he kept by the door and aimed the light at the second-floor landing. "Ren? You up there?"

No answer. She was probably still working, and in the farthest reaches of the mansion, she wouldn't hear him. As much as she loved to tease him, when it came to perfectionism, they were on equal ground. Ren's penchant for numbers made assigning her to the parquet floor an obvious choice. She wouldn't rest until every piece fit precisely in place, a delicate work of art, new blending seamlessly with old.

He hoped it took her until Halloween to finish, enough time for her to realize the inspiration of bringing out the beauty in the lost and forgotten. And, if all went as planned, she'd figure out that being with him was where she fit, too.

As he headed toward the ballroom, the flashlight beam flung shadows on the walls and ceiling, making the peeling wallpaper look like claw marks left by some raging beast. The temperature dropped a few more degrees, and goosebumps danced over his wet skin. A frail puff of white formed with his breath, there and gone.

Increasing his pace, Leo strode past a marble statue of a satyr left behind by a former owner. He ignored how its cracked eyes seemed to watch him pass and instead focused on what lay ahead — his future with Ren.

She was the one woman who invaded his thoughts, the one woman who liked him simply for the man he was, the one woman who drove him crazy with need. Before Ren, he'd been content with furthering his father's legacy and shining the family name. His world tilted the second he met her, as if recognizing a missing, necessary piece. Regaining balance without her was impossible.

He'd been training for the upcoming combat for months, gauging weaknesses and strengths, arming himself with facts, truths and fears in need of facing. He'd earned Ren's loyalty and friendship. Winning her heart, the last battleground, was a fight he wouldn't lose.

War face on, Leo stepped around the corner and into the line of fire.

Ren stood in the foyer outside the ballroom's glass doors. She stared at something small in her hand, Sir Snugglebottom perched on her shoulder. Her face, always pale, appeared paper-white in the gloom.

"Ren?" He kept his voice quiet, not wanting to startle her. Lightning forked the sky, momentarily painting the stained-glass windows in deep, rich colors. The tinted panes haloed Karen in an eerie red. Thunder rolled a few seconds later. She didn't seem to notice.

He made it within a few feet away before she looked up. Sheer relief filled her face. She launched straight at him and barreled into him with enough force to send him back a step. Shaking, she clung to him, Sir still attached to her shoulder.

Leo closed his eyes and held her slender form tight. He half-wondered if Liam had spiked his drink at family fun day. With Ren clutching him like she needed him more than air, he felt almost drunk. Whatever drove her into his arms, he'd take it.

"Your skin is icy," he murmured against her temple. "Not that I'm complaining."

"Your shirt is cold *and* wet." She sniffed, her cheek pressed against his chest. "Totally complaining here."

He huffed a laugh. "Don't be a whiner. I'll warm you up soon enough."

After a blissful moment, she released him, and he grudgingly loosened his hold. Sir jumped from her shoulder at him, and Leo caught him before the kitten left a trail of bloody pinpricks up his arm.

"Traitor," Karen muttered, giving the cat an evil eye.

Leo nestled the kitten on his shoulder. "Mind explaining why you look like me after watching *Carnival of Souls* alone last night?"

"Rattled and afraid of what might be hiding in the dark?" She glanced over her shoulder, through the glass of the closed ballroom doors. "Sounds about right." Lightning burst, revealing a surprising flash of fear in her eyes as she looked back at him.

Any thought of confronting her emotions vanished beneath a fierce need to protect her, even from a supernatural something — not because she was weak or unable to fight it herself, but because she was too important to risk. "What happened?"

"An overload of spooky stories, storms and spiders." Her smile was sickly. "Had a showdown in the ballroom with a disgruntled arachnid whose hidey-hole was disrupted. I let it win...this time."

"I thought you lived for dark and creepy stuff."

"Gothic-creepy, not creepy-crawly. Huge difference, Hughes."

"Since when are spiders a fear factor?"

"Since about two minutes ago." She hugged herself, as if cold. "With the lightning and thunder, no electricity, my imagination took over...I think." She pivoted and looked again into the ballroom.

Leo moved behind her and slipped an arm around her shoulders, drawing her back against his chest. When she relaxed into him, he brought his mouth close to her ear. "What aren't you telling me?"

Ren shivered. "I found this." She lifted a tiny key, not long enough to get a good look. "A space had been hollowed out inside a parquet piece, big enough for a spider and key to snuggle. When lightning struck, a trick of the light made the spider look a zillion times its already gigantic size." She spun and fisted his damp shirt, her eyes bright. "I know this sounds crazy, but maybe Elizabeth Granton's murderer wasn't human. Maybe that spider committed the dirty deed. Maybe it caught her in a web, fanged her with poison to keep her quiet and dragged her beneath the floor piece by piece until nothing remained to find."

"That sounds" — he tapped his chin, pretending to consider it — "completely rational."

"For your information, spiders can lift at least eight times their weight. That one could carry you off, no problem." She pinched his waist—hard, with a little twist.

"Ouch." He grunted and jumped beyond her reach. "Monster."

"Jerk." Her smile was wicked-sweet and shot a bolt of heat straight through him.

He didn't regret banishing her fear. That she looked to him for safety made every part of him that was a man and protector growl in satisfaction.

"Investigating the electricity issue can wait." He handed her Sir and his flashlight. "Give me a moment."

Before she stopped him, he dashed away, back to the front door where his sword waited against the wall. Weapon in hand, he returned to his lady, ready to fight dragons...or spiders.

Karen raised her eyebrows at his sword. "Unless that thing's iron, dipped in holy water and sprays salt with every swing, I don't think it's going to do much good."

Metal sang as he unsheathed it. He frowned at the pointy tip. "Sharp enough to skewer arachnids of all sizes. I'll take my chances."

"If you're going in"—she blew out a breath and squared her shoulders—"then I've got your back."

"Never doubted it." He gave her a lazy smile, which grew wider when she bit her lip before looking away.

Leo opened the glass doors and stepped onto the marble landing. Karen stuck close to his elbow, a warm, sweet-smelling phantom wielding the flashlight, Sir perched on her shoulder. The beam swept over the ballroom, revealing more destruction than he'd expected. Wind hissed through a blown window they'd replaced yesterday. Glass sparkled on the floor. Most of the damaged section of parquet had been extracted, leaving a dark gash. In the dim light, it resembled a hellish pit.

"You understand our goal is to fix up the place, right?" He kept his voice to a murmur, tightening his grip on the sword.

"You're hysterical, Hughes." She whispered, too, as if they'd stolen into a forbidden garden of graves and bones. "The wind shattered the window in perfect timing with the gigantic spider coming at me. Coincidence? I think not."

He didn't blink an eye at spiders, snakes or any flesh-and-blood beast. If it breathed, he could deal with it, no problem. Only the unseen and intangible pierced his armor and shredded his bravery.

He padded down the stairs and onto the ballroom floor. Tree limbs scraped the windowpanes, the shriek of fingernails. After spider hunting and fixing electrical boxes, he'd text the good gardener Oliver and direct him to the wild vegetation crowding the ballroom before another window met its doom.

Karen clutched his arm. Her fingers dug into his muscle, almost painfully. "Did you see that?" She pointed the flashlight beam at the broken flooring. The glow skimmed the surface, leaving the blackness beneath untouched. "Something moved in there."

"I got this. Keep the flashlight on it."

Raindrops gleamed on the floor and brushed wet on Leo's face as he approached the abandoned work. The light trembled with Ren's unsteady hand.

"I promise no spider will get through me to you." He brushed his fingers over hers.

"And I won't let your bones stay beneath the floor for centuries like Elizabeth's." She squeezed his arm tighter.

"Appreciate it."

A few steps from the hole, he halted. Ren aimed the flashlight into the darkness. No insects stirred inside. He crouched, and Karen pulled on his arm, as if to keep him with her. "I need a closer look."

"Careful. You don't want it leaping on your face. Trust me. *I* don't want it leaping on your face. I kind of like your face the way it is."

He couldn't stop a silly grin or the warmth spreading through his chest. An underhanded compliment, but from Ren? He'd hold it next to his heart.

"I found the key right there." She pointed the light at one parquet piece. The outer frame remained intact, but the interior appeared to have been carved out, leaving a space where a small item—such as a diary key—could be hidden. Or a spider burrow, depending on one's needs.

Leo laid his sword down and kneeled. Leaning closer, he reached blindly for the flashlight.

"I'd feel better if you're holding the sword." Ren surrendered the flashlight to him and rested her hand on his back as he shone the light into the hole.

No monstrous black spider lunged out, spitting venom. Silken threads glimmered deep within the hole, evidence that Karen's imagination hadn't entirely spun the spider from shadows and storms.

He settled the flashlight in the bottom of the hole and stacked a couple of wood pieces beneath it, angling the beam into the spider's nest. "Hand me my sword, Ren."

Poking his finger in there wasn't going to happen. With the blade tip, he hooked the thick web spilling from the hole like cotton and gingerly dragged it out.

Ren tapped him on the shoulder and offered her purple needle-nose pliers. "Not that your sword isn't good enough."

"I prefer a sword length between me and the enemy."

"These have grabby things." She clicked the pliers closed in demonstration.

"Fine." He traded his sword for the pliers, drew a long breath and inched closer to the hole. If hundreds of spiders poured out, he wouldn't be too ashamed to run for it. Steeling his nerves, he grasped the web with the pliers and pulled...and pulled. The silken threads were strong and not sticky, as if created to be a tunnel, and extended far beyond one parquet block. What worried him most, though, was the web's weight. Something clung to the end, dragging.

Karen picked up his sword with both hands and aimed it at the hole.

"If you want my sword, Ren, just ask. No trickery required."

"But trickery is so much more fun."

The web slipped free with a whispering sigh. The object tangled in its threads clattered to the floor.

A bone.

Karen jumped back with a blood-curling shriek, pointing his sword at the bone. Sir somehow kept his place on her shoulder. "I *told* you, Leo. A frickin' skeleton."

"We don't know for sure that it's human." He said that for himself as much as he did for her. Whether human or animal, he had no desire to cross paths with a spider that could take on a creature of that size and win.

A bang on the locked doors leading outside had him on his feet, sword plucked from Karen's hands and aiming at the new threat. Wearing a hooded raincoat an unfortunate shade of green, Oliver peered inside. He must have heard Ren's scream.

Leo willed his heart rate to slow and walked to the door. He released the locks. The wind pushed inside with a sheet of rain as Oliver hustled in, moisture dripping from his nose.

"What the hell are you doing out there?" Leo shut the door fast. "I don't expect you to work in weather like this."

"This mild April shower?" Oliver slipped his hood back. "You presented me with a deadline, and I shall do what I must to keep it." He arched an eyebrow at the sword in Leo's hand. "Fencing?"

"Does this look like a rapier?" He lifted his chin. Fencing was a far cry from the steel brawls he had with his brothers, and as much as he respected fencing and the sport's particular skills, it was not the same as swinging broadswords. "I don't waste my time with steel that bends."

"Ah." Oliver glanced at Karen, who kept a healthy distance from the spider's prize, still wrapped in webs and dust. "I heard a shout."

"Yeah, that was me." Karen swiped her fingers through her hair, leaving it sexy, bedroom-mussed. "We found Elizabeth Granton's bones — or at least one of them."

Oliver's eyes widened.

"We don't know that it's human, Ren." Leo shrugged at Oliver's questioning look. "If there's the slightest possibility of a murderous or supernatural element, she's all over it."

"Something wrong with that, Hughes?" Her eyes narrowed in accusation.

He gave her a lazy grin. "Just one of the many qualities I admire about you."

Her expression softened, and she stroked Sir, as if needing a distraction. But she didn't look away, and her eyes glittered in the dim light.

Oliver cleared his throat. "May I see it?"

"Feel free." Leo waved toward the silk strung on the parquet. He followed the other man and discreetly placed himself between Karen and the bone—and Oliver.

"You found this where?" Oliver crouched, pulled some pruners from a pocket in his raincoat, and nudged the web-covered bone.

"In a hollow piece of parquet wood." Karen shivered. "Found a giant spider, too, which is worryingly MIA."

"That would explain the webs." Oliver freed the bone with the point of his pruners.

"Patronize me more." Karen folded her arms beneath her breasts. "I love it."

Leo bit back a smile. Sassiness was another quality he adored, especially when she used its sharp edge to gut another man.

Wisely, Oliver kept any response to himself. He lifted the bone. "Hold the light on it, if you please."

Karen obliged. The bone gleamed a dull, ancient yellow. Leo didn't know much about skeletons, but it appeared the right size for a finger bone.

"Did you find more than this one?" Oliver's eyebrows bunched in concentration, and he trailed his pinkie finger down the length of the bone. His fully fleshed finger made the bone seem small.

"So far." Karen nodded, already convinced an entire graveyard lay hidden by the original flooring.

Oliver straightened with a serious expression. "I fear you very well might have an infestation." He wagged the bone. "A carnivorous species of arachnids dwelling within the floorboards. They are known for digging within wood and spinning endless tunnels to catch and devour prey. I would consult an exterminator as soon as possible."

Karen slipped her arm through Leo's and pressed close. Sir used her as a stepstool and curled up against his neck, warm and soft, a counter to the cold knot in his stomach. He couldn't afford extra surprises.

As Oliver looked between him and Karen, an oily smile came to life. "I'm teasing. This, my supernatural loving friends, belongs to the missing phalange of an unfortunate possum." He tossed the bone at Leo.

Leo caught it on instinct.

"Oh." Karen sounded disappointed. "But what sort of spider eats possums?"

"A large one." Oliver winked.

"Is it too late to fire him?" she asked Leo.

"Far too late, Miss Karen." Oliver's eyes glittered with laughter. "The contract has been signed."

She huffed. "Dammit."

"If you're through disrupting my work by shrieking and digging up animal bones, I must be on my way. I'll need every moment of daylight to complete this project by Halloween." Oliver lifted his hood. "Happy spider hunting."

After Oliver returned to the storm, Leo turned his attention to Ren. "You didn't tell him about the key."

She shrugged and looked away. Whatever had initially piqued her interest in Oliver seemed to have vanished, not that he was complaining.

"Did something happen between you two at Seven Devils? And I don't mean in the bathroom, as Cooper implied."

Her eyes narrowed and a flush darkened her cheeks, visible even in the gloom. "You know how much I hate being stereotyped."

"I do." Tossing an arm around her shoulders, careful not to disturb Sir, he led her toward the ballroom exit. "And I also know you're too classy to hook up in a bar bathroom for a few minutes of fun."

"Damn straight." She sniffed. "He pointed out that you and Cooper appeared to be getting it on and suggested we continue our discussion over a bottle of wine."

A tourniquet wrapped around his heart and squeezed, but he kept his voice casual. "Why didn't you?"

"I promised to save you from Cooper."

"Was that the only reason?"

They walked several steps in silence, long enough he thought she might bolt before answering. A few feet from the ballroom steps, she sighed. "The other reasons don't matter."

The hell they didn't.

"You're my best friend, and I'll always have your back." She curled an arm around his waist and squeezed. "Without you, I'd be lost."

A rollercoaster of emotions surged through him, but the best friend loop-de-loop only fueled his determination. "Ditto, but, Ren?"

"Yeah?"

He stopped and faced her. "You're having dinner with me tonight."

"Okay, bossy." She watched him, clearly waiting for the catch.

"And even if the entire mansion fills up with phantom, blood-sucking spiders, we *will* discuss the events at Seven Devils." He lowered his chin and held her gaze. "You, me, that kiss…all of it."

Chapter Thirteen

Karen wiped her moist palms on her plaid miniskirt and studied her reflection in the vanity mirror for the zillionth time. Usually, hanging out with Leo was a casual affair filled with easy conversation and fun. But tonight felt important...different. She couldn't dodge this discussion forever, and Leo had to know the truth.

No matter how much it hurt.

A dab of color on her lips, a final finger-comb to tousle her hair and she had nothing left to do but face her fate.

Glorious smells of garlic and cheese drifted from the first floor, and her stomach clenched. Why did this feel like the last supper? Her pulse thundered faster than it should as she straightened her shoulders and strode to the stairwell.

There was no reason to be nervous. When Leo asked about the kiss at Seven Devils—the ground-shaking, steal-her-senses kiss—she'd tell him that while trying to impress Cooper, she got lost in the moment. Leo couldn't argue such a rational, believable explanation.

Karen kept her steps quick and sure all the way to the kitchen. Dirty pots and pans filled the sink. Half-chopped vegetables littered the kitchen island and a delicious lasagne scent wafted from the oven...but no Leo.

Crimson splashed the tiles at the corner of the isle, and her throat tightened. Was that blood? She rushed to the other side of the cabinet. Red drops trailed to a door she'd never used, not blood but tiny, cinnamon hearts. Her favorite candy.

Dammit.

Fighting off the warm and fuzzies, she followed the come-hither trail. Why did Leo have to be so perfect? He embodied everything she wanted in a man—everything she couldn't have without ruining the most important relationship in her life. She could only keep their friendship safe by nursing her infatuation in secret and hope time erased it.

Cool air brushed through as she opened the door. The candy trail led along a steppingstone walkway through a sunroom. Clear panels veined with overgrown ivy and moss made up the roof and walls. A handful of lanterns illuminated the path and the red hearts leading to yet another doorway.

Leo had wasted a ton of candy on her.

Her boot heels clipped on stone as she continued. In all their years together, Hank had never put the same amount of effort into any date, gift or show of affection. True, they had both been young and inexperienced, but not once had Hank made her feel so...significant.

Leo did that for her every day.

At the next door, she paused in awestruck wonder. A dome of glass and iron large enough to encompass a city block stretched out like a great, crystal tent. On a clear night, starlight would spill inside and gild the plot of stonework and statues in silver. With the cloud cover, gloom veiled its secrets, brushed only by the glowing lanterns. Red candy hearts dotted the pea gravel and curved out of sight.

Her heart thrummed faster as she moved deeper into the statuary. Pebbles crunched with every step. Statues loomed on each side, hazy shapes observing her passage. One lantern rested beside a satyr sitting on a rock with a harp in his lap. Most of the instrument had crumbled, and time had molded the fairytale creature's smile into a leer. Devilish horns curled from the head and hollow eyes sent shivers of glee straight through her.

Leo, the sly dog, used her curiosity as a weapon. Her love for all things Gothic and delightfully creepy made the shadowed conservatory irresistible. He knew her too well.

The pathway roamed past dry fountains covered in moss and strangled by feral rosebushes, mythical beasts wrapped in vines, dark in the lantern's glow. Each new statue sharpened her questions about the legend surrounding Elizabeth Granton and the groundskeeper, Edwin. Had Elizabeth loved fairy tales, which had inspired Edwin to create this mystical indoor pocket of statues and woodland? Jed claimed Edwin had left evidence behind of his love. She'd have to return in daylight and explore.

Around another bend, Karen paused beneath a metal archway. The path ended at a wide, silver-veined marble terrace. Iron lampposts circled the nook, joined by a handful of wood nymphs and fauns mid-celebration, flutes in hand. A rusty birdcage hung from one statue's hand, the gate missing. Leo leaned against a lamppost, his hands in his pockets, staring out into the darkness.

Her heart squeezed as she drank in every detail, greedy. Dressed in black jeans and V-neck sweater, he seemed a part of the night, the somber, powerful lord overlooking his dancing subjects, aloof in his solitude. He was beautiful, from boots to crown, inside and out.

And he can never be mine.

He must have heard the pea gravel shift beneath her boots because he turned and straightened. His slow, lazy smile stirred butterflies in her ribcage. They fluttered, frantic, trying to escape. But there was no escape, not for her. No matter what choice she made, she lost.

"You didn't have to dress up for me." His gaze traveled down her legs, making her skin tingle. "But I appreciate it."

Whether he wore a ratty T-shirt and carpenter jeans or a black suit and tie, he always looked good. There was no need to confirm what all the other women already told him. *The witches.*

"I thought you might chicken out." He strolled toward her, his hands in his pockets, all coiled power and grace. "Glad you didn't. Saved me the trouble of tracking you down, throwing you over my shoulder and carting you here."

The image of him picking her up and tossing her on a bed to have his wicked way with her wasn't helpful to her resolve. She arched an eyebrow at him. "The attempt wouldn't have been beneficial to your health."

"Maybe not." He stopped a step away. "But whatever it takes to get you here is worth it."

And there went those butterflies again, wings flapping, trying to get to Leo. "Where's Sir?"

"Snoozing in the laundry basket. I left him there to chill. Cats sleep on an average of twenty hours per day, did you know that?"

"I do now." She pretended to study the statuary, anything to avoid looking at him. "Was this conservatory part of the original construction?"

He pivoted to stand beside her, his shoulder brushing hers. "No. It was built a year later, an anniversary gift to the missus."

"Sneaky man. I figured you were playing Oliver and Cooper, letting them think you didn't know what you were doing when you bought this place." She gave him an approving smirk, unsurprised. "Or that you might be in over your head."

"Arthur Granton imported most of these beauties while on business trips in different countries. He paid a fortune to ship them overseas." Leo pivoted toward a carving of a medieval lady in full, flowing gown. She wore a crown of lilies and ivy twined in her long hair. Half of her face was missing. "Every statue commemorates a moment in time when he was away from home."

"It's amazing."

"I thought you might appreciate it." He faced her again. "Are you through avoiding the subject?"

"Never."

"There's my girl." He slipped her arm through his, tugging her forward.

Warmth brushed the air as he led her inside the heat lamps circling the dais. A crystal bowl full of cinnamon heart candies rested beside a folded note and pen on the round granite table. Leo pulled one black iron chair out for her, always the gentleman. As she sat, he leaned close to her ear. "You'll survive tonight, Ren. I promise."

The seductive purr in his voice ignited her imagination. A picture of him came to life, leaning over her in the darkness. No sweater covered those delicious miles of muscles and smooth skin as he crawled up her body, his hands rough, his mouth hot on her skin. Electric tingles shot to all the best places, and she pressed her thighs together as he took his seat across from her. She bit her lip. That was a survival of the fittest test she could get on full board with.

If he wasn't her friend.

When she looked up, he gazed at her mouth, as if he imagined his own teeth nibbling her bottom lip.

Holy hell. She released her lip, wildfire heat spinning through her veins. She had to put a stop to this, right now.

"Leo—"

Before she said more, he pushed the note across the table to her with one finger.

She eyed the note with suspicion. "What's this?"

He cocked his head with that lazy smile, his blue eyes sparkling, and shrugged. The rat. Manipulating her curiosity again.

Holding his stare, she grabbed a handful of cinnamon hearts and popped one in her mouth. Once again, his gaze fixed on her lips, as if watching her crunch hearts was the most fascinating thing in the universe. All that primitive heat pooled in her belly with throbbing intensity. She swallowed harder than necessary. Letting him win one unimportant skirmish beat getting hot and bothered simply because he watched her scarf down her favorite candy.

"Fine." She swiped the paper and unfolded it. Inside, the words 'Do You Like Me?' were handwritten beside a single checkbox beneath a smiley-face and 'Yes'. She snorted, unable to hide a smile. "Where are the 'No' and 'Maybe' boxes? A girl needs choices."

"Tonight is about truth." His velvet voice curled over her skin like a physical caress, igniting all her senses. "No more pretending...not with me." He steepled his fingers and lowered his chin, casting his handsome face in shadows.

She sucked in a sharp breath, her heartbeat ricocheting all the way to her fingertips. Not once in all their friendship had they discussed the subtle flirting or underlying tension strung between them, an unspoken mutual agreement. That kiss at Seven Devils had changed everything. She hadn't been able to hide her feelings from him, not when his hands were in her hair, his mouth and tongue demanding her secrets. Leo deserved her honesty. If he wanted the truth, she had to give it to him.

This is going to be ugly.

"If you insist on an interrogation, I demand a drink." Her voice cracked beneath the pressure. She cleared her throat. "Please."

Leo didn't budge. "Check the box first."

"Seriously?"

He gave her his battle prep face, all cool, collected badass ready to meet and destroy any enemy in his path.

An electric thrill rolled through her. That look had never been aimed at her before, and while intimidating...she kinda liked it. She scribbled some words beside his, checked the box, and passed the note back to him.

His expression unchanged, he unfolded the note. One eyebrow twitched as he read it. "You only like me sometimes?"

"Remember when you tricked me into hiking before sunrise by convincing me there was a quaint new beanery with the best coffee? After sweating and panting my way for a mile up a grueling slope, I find that you're the barista, my much-needed caffeine the homemade sludge served from your thermos. No sugar. Didn't like you much then."

"But that sunrise?" He whistled. "Worth it." He lifted the six-pack from beside the table.

"I should have bailed." She huffed, rustling her bangs. "But I would have felt terrible if a rabid squirrel attacked and left you for dead."

"Love your compassionate side, Ren, darling." He passed her a chilled beer bottle. When she reached for it, he didn't let go. His fingers brushed hers. "I think you had ulterior motives for hiking with me up that mountain."

"Country-fresh air?"

"Besides that, even more than the ample opportunities to ogle my fine assets and bask in my sparkling personality." His expression remained unreadable.

"What else could there possibly be?"

"No pretending," he said in a soft growl.

"Since you seem to know already, enlighten me."

"Very well." He released his grip on the bottle and held her gaze. "You believe I'm safe."

"Aren't you?"

His stony expression threw her for a loop. Leo had always made her feel protected, important and comfortable, no matter what scenario they were in together. Tonight, he unsettled her.

He drew a long breath through his nose and stood so fast that the iron chair screeched across the marble. In two strides, he loomed over her and planted his hands on each of her armrests, caging her. "In the last two years, while gaining your trust, building our friendship, there have been uncountable moments that I heartily regret not doing this on the day I met you instead."

Before she set the beer bottle down or said a word, he took her face between his big, callused hands, cursed beneath his breath and kissed her.

Chapter Fourteen

Karen fumbled the beer bottle to the table as Leo kissed her senseless. Whatever protest she'd planned, all her arguments, rationality and boundaries disappeared into the ether of pure bliss.

His mouth wove pure magic, better than anything she'd ever tasted, his lips soft and sweetly demanding. The low hum of approval deep in his throat as he pulled her up against him set her skin aflame. She twisted her fingers in his hair, slid a hand beneath his sweater to the hot flesh beneath, needing direct contact. She couldn't touch him enough, couldn't get close enough. For so long, she'd dreamed what it would be like to kiss him, restrained to the safety of fantasies.

Safe. The word had the same effect as a plunge into ice water. Leo had been right about that. She *needed* to keep him in the safety zone.

"Wait," she gasped, breaking the kiss.

Ignoring the command, he trailed soft, silken nibbles along her jawline to her ear. Her knees went weak with pleasure. She didn't want him to stop, not when his hands felt so right on her hips, not when he spun a web of desire through every nerve.

Never had she needed to be touched and *not* touched simultaneously. Her mind warred with the sensations he awakened. She could admit in secret that she longed for Leo in every way, but at the cost of their friendship? Even if it meant an existence without his mouth inflaming her skin, his capable hands on her back, his arms capturing her against his solid strength, she couldn't lose him.

"Leo." She moaned as he nibbled her earlobe and ran a hand along her bare thigh to the hem of her short skirt. "We can't."

"Hmm." He bit harder, and pure heat struck her straight between the legs. "We can." He licked the sting away, which made the rest of her body ache more, desperate. "I've wanted you since the moment we met, Ren."

She clung to his powerful shoulders for support as he moved his wicked mouth to her neck. The chafe of his stubble made her eyelids flutter closed. Resistance was futile. How could she fight her private imaginings forging to full, dark life?

Because it was *Leo*. Living out her dreams, no matter how hot, wasn't worth the ultimate cost. This moment would fuel an entire year of fantasies, and their friendship could remain intact.

"Leo," she tried again. She forced her fingers to release his hair.

"Ren." The husky timbre of his voice, rough with need, demolished her determination again. In a smooth, effortless move, he pivoted them both and pushed her up against the table.

The stone surface offered the support Karen needed, not that Leo would let her fall. He circled her waist with one arm, crushing her against him. Once again, he silenced any protest with his mouth.

She slipped her arms around his neck and pulled him closer. He was like the worst drug. One taste made her an instant addict. She never should have agreed to pretend with him at Seven Devils, should have figured out a different way to get rid of Cooper.

But oh…she moaned as he maneuvered between her knees and trailed slow, hot kisses down her throat. Regret held no power in this moment, not with Leo encompassing every nuance, engaging all her rioting senses. Never had she felt so desired, adored, deliciously snared.

Lost in a haze of desire, it took her a moment to realize he'd stopped kissing her. He rested his big hands on her hips and eased back enough to study her, his blue eyes dark and watchful.

"What is it?" Even her voice had altered to his rhythm, all bedroom breathless.

"In anticipation of whatever argument you prepared to rationalize our very real kiss at Seven Devils, I'm saving you some time with the truth." He curled his hand around the back of her head, possessive. "We are far beyond mere friends, and I'm done letting you deny it. I'm done pretending friendship is all I want, done hoping you'll admit it of your own accord."

Without meaning to, she laid her palms on his chest, pushing him back. He moved a few inches away, not enough room to escape. Her pulse pounded in her ears and blood roared through her veins. This was it, the moment she'd hoped to avoid for eternity.

"I can't be more than your friend," she blurted. "I just...can't."

"That's not enough, especially after the last few moments. I need an explanation." He brushed his knuckles over her cheekbone, gently brutal. "Explain why you kissed me back with enough passion to make me believe that you want me in the same, deep, unstoppable, unchangeable way that I want you."

Holy hell. She drew a shaky breath. "I don't want to lose you. You're too important to me." Desperation made her words crack. "When I'm with you, I feel..."

"Like you're home? Grounded? Complete?" The lines on his forehead softened. "You can't lose me, darling. I'm yours, always, from the moment I met you."

The space in her heart, guarded for years, ached at his words. He'd described how she felt perfectly. What she wouldn't give to believe that adding romance to their relationship wouldn't damage the friendship. She knew he meant what he said, but time had a way of changing people, dulling love's flame until it fizzled and not even the best of friendships could withstand the burnout. Hank had taught her that, a hard lesson she hadn't wanted to learn.

Leo took her hand and kissed the inside of her wrist, right above her jackhammering pulse. "Your heart is safe in my care, I promise. When it comes to us, there's nothing to be afraid of."

Easy for him to say. He was the full package. If they were together, she'd be an idiot to dump him. There was no better man than Leo.

But along the way, he'd realize he could do far better than her, and it would be her heart that would get chopped into little pieces again. She was dead certain she couldn't survive having then losing Leo.

"Leo, I can't." She pulled free of his loose grasp, and his fingertips slid warm along her skin as he let her go.

"You don't trust me?" His jaw ticked.

"More than anyone else. That's not the issue."

"So explain." He straightened to his full, intimidating height and folded his arms, an immovable, thorny wall. "Use small words so I can understand why you'd prefer to be with someone else, anyone else, besides me."

"Don't get snarky." She glared at him through an unexpected burn of tears. Leo had never seen her cry, and she had no intention of starting that tradition. "No. How's that for a small word?"

Before she reacted, he grasped her wrist and twisted, sweeping her up with a squeak. The next second, he sat on the table with her on his lap, holding her hostage. Her legs slung over his knees, her butt planted on his muscled thighs.

"Allow me to reiterate." The threatening rumble in his low voice shocked her into stillness. "In whatever words you want, tell me." Unblinking, he lowered his chin, a wolf hypnotizing its prey. "No more evasion and playing, Ren. *Tell me.*"

Surrounded by his fire and strength, his scent invading every breath, those intense, soul-seeing blue eyes studying her, she couldn't deny him, not any longer. She exhaled, long and slow.

"Hank was the typical boy next door. We were babies together, had toddler playdates, attended the same school from preschool to graduation. He was the first boy to put a worm down my dress, the first boy I chased with a frog, the first boy I kissed." Sawdust gathered in her throat. She tried to swallow it down, but it caught her voice, made it rasp. "The first boy I loved."

Leo brushed away the wetness at the corner of her eye with his thumb, giving her a moment to gather herself, to muster her courage and continue. He always knew when to push or give her freedom, as if he sensed her emotional needs and reassembled his actions to fit into her color scheme.

"The childhood teasing turned to flirting in middle school. Hank and I held hands, snuck kisses beneath the bleachers." She shrugged. "We never talked about being boyfriend and girlfriend. It was just a given, a natural progression that I never questioned until everyone else did."

"What do you mean?" he asked softly, as if she might shut down. He wasn't entirely wrong, but he needed to hear about her past, to understand why they couldn't be more than friends.

"I was always the quirky girl who never fit anywhere. Even with my family I didn't quite mesh, polar opposite to my sisters who dreamed of being the local cherry pie champion and 4-H farm queen. My parents never knew what to do with me and my infatuation with mysterious things of a darker nature."

"Mmm…pie." Humor glittered in his eyes.

She snorted. "I sometimes wondered if the fae had left me as a changeling to replace the real Karen Ives, a girl so amazing they had to steal her away to live under the hill with them."

"Their loss." Leo scowled.

She couldn't hide a tiny smile. "Meanwhile, Hank grew up to be the local golden boy, captain of the football team, rodeo champion, yada. No one understood what he saw in the weird Goth girl, but every time I doubted, he reassured me that nothing could tear us apart. I was engaged at the age of sixteen. I didn't know anything—who I was, what future I wanted—but I never imagined it wouldn't include Hank."

Leo created a silent, comforting presence around her, calling her to relax. The shadows of the statuary soothed reality and made spilling the heartache she'd kept trapped inside, enduring its raw edges alone, possible.

"He was my best friend, the one person I trusted with every secret and dream, and despite all the promises, he walked away." Her voice sounded small and fragile. As much as she hated revealing this pathetic side of her, it had to be done. "He outgrew the quirky girl who preferred horror movies and books over parties. He wanted a partner who was his equal, someone who polished his image, not tarnished it. He wanted someone who...wasn't me." She didn't dare look at him, afraid of what she might find in his expression. She couldn't stand it if his opinion of her changed.

"Hmm." He paused. "I'll avenge your honor, challenge him to a duel. I vow to leave enough bruises with the flat of my blade that he won't take a single step or breath for weeks without regretting the pain he caused you."

By the flames in his eyes, he wasn't kidding. And she adored him all the more for it. "Not necessary."

He cocked his head with a hopeful look. "I could soften the punishment with a light saber instead. If wielded correctly, plastic can be painful."

"That's a match I'd love to watch. I'd be cheering for you all the way."

"So it's settled. I'll pay him a visit…in full gear."

A small, mean part of her would take an insane amount of pleasure witnessing Hank shaking in his boots as Leo, bearing a sword, dressed in black leathers and an even blacker scowl, showed up on his doorstep demanding satisfaction on her behalf — to watch as Hank realized that a man like Leo valued her so much that he'd go to extreme lengths for her.

Her heart squeezed, a reminder that Leo would do it if she asked him to, no questions, no hesitation. *Hell.* He wasn't being helpful in keeping their relationship to best friends without sexy benefits.

"You have no idea how happy you just made my imagination, but at least Hank recognized he didn't want me before we got hitched." She shrugged and plucked at her skirt hem. "I just…" Sighing, she surrendered her darkest wound to him, trusting him to understand, to accept her anyway. "I can't help believing that he's right, that I don't have the necessary ingredients to make anyone happy long-term, that I'm missing some important quality that makes me…enough."

"I loathe that he allowed you to feel even a smidgeon of pain, but he was correct to walk away. You weren't right for him."

The world seemed to crack at the edges, and she couldn't breathe. He must recognize the same truth Hank had — that who and what she was would never be quite enough, not for Hank and certainly not for someone as amazing as Leo.

With one finger, Leo lifted her chin, forcing her to meet his gaze. "Darling, listen to me very carefully.

There's absolutely nothing deficient in you. Anyone who implies otherwise is a self-indulgent ass incapable of seeing past the crap flying from his own piehole."

The laugh in her throat strangled beneath the fierce sincerity in his expression. He looked at her as if she were the moon to his stars, the only one who could collect all his pieces and hold them together.

"My sweet Ren." He kissed her, taking advantage of her temporary paralysis. "How could it be right to be with him when you belong with me?"

Chapter Fifteen

Karen froze on Leo's lap, and he tightened his hold, as if expecting a fight. Too staggered to even put up a mild struggle, she stared at him, his voice repeating in her brain.

"You belong with me."

She hadn't realized how starved she'd been to hear those words from him. Bittersweet yearning stormed through her, making her chest ache. Surrendering would be so sweet—and make the end-game pain worse. Would he still believe she belonged with him if she denied the heat between them?

Leo lifted his eyebrows. "Nothing to say?"

"I love you." Her voice croaked, strangled.

That lazy smile he spared only for her appeared. "I know."

"So you get why we can't level up our relationship."

"Because you believe that somewhere along the way our romance will sour and kill our friendship?" He held her gaze without flinching, his expression calm.

"Exactly." She slumped. Holy hell, he understood. The awkwardness could end.

"Was that what you were afraid of when Cooper challenged you at Seven Devils? That I'd fall desperately in lust with you, bewitched after one, fateful kiss, and thereby dooming our friendship for eternity?" He caressed her hand with his thumb, making small, soothing circles. "Or perhaps it was a case of you being overcome by raging jealousy?"

"Don't be ridiculous." She sniffed, her face heating, and focused on the faceless maiden statue nearby. If only the darkness beyond would swallow her and save her from this conversation.

"Or maybe you kissed me because I needed your help?"

That works. "Exactly."

"And even though that required an unexpected act beyond your comfort zone, you did it because you always have my back." He watched her, intent.

"Right." She dragged out the word. "Even when it requires uncomfortable public displays of fake affection." Why did it feel like a hidden trap closed its jaws?

"And you have my back because you know I'm worthy of your trust." A warning entered his tone. "Admit or deny, Ren."

"You know I trust you." Her pulse increased from a trot to a gallop. Nothing in her admissions felt incriminating, yet she couldn't shake the sensation that she stepped onto a one-way swing bridge across the Grand Canyon.

His eyes flashed. "The kiss at Seven Devils wasn't fake. Admit it."

"It was supposed to be." She huffed, the burn in her cheeks growing. "Then you and your tongue got involved and ruined everything."

"I believe you are the one who invited my tongue into the situation," he said, amusement vibrating in his voice.

"This isn't funny, Leo." She scrambled off his lap, relieved he let her go, and strode to one iron lamppost. Thinking straight was impossible while in direct contact. When she spun to face him, he stood right in front of her, a wall of heat, man and muscle.

"I'm not laughing at you. That kiss…" He closed his eyes briefly, and when he opened them again, they were an electric blue. "I have an idea that will put all your reservations to rest."

The last time he'd had a bright idea, she'd pledged a month of her life to learning construction while torturing herself with extra Leo hours. Going along with it had brought her right to this point, on the brink of disaster. "What is it?"

"Let's make a pact, right here, right now, that nothing will ever destroy our friendship. A vow that if, by some slim chance, we don't mesh as a couple, we'll always maintain best friend status. We'll work through whatever hurt that may occur until our relationship is mended. Fair enough?"

She rubbed her arms, the October chill creeping into her skin. If only it could be so easy.

"Ren," he said with soft frustration, "we can take it slow."

"Like that last kiss slow?" If that was his idea of slow, holy hell, she wasn't sure she could handle his version of fast.

"As slow as you wish. If you don't want me to kiss you, I won't." His attention drifted to her mouth, and her lips tingled in response. "If you don't want me to touch you, I'll restrain myself." He swept his gaze down her body, then back up. Every inch of her warmed beneath his stare. "All I want is a chance to prove how perfect we would be together."

Karen's breath came faster than she wanted as she recognized the trap he'd cleverly set for her. If she denied him now, it would be proof that she didn't trust him, that their friendship wasn't even real.

She gasped as he pulled out a knife from his pocket and flipped it open. "Seriously?"

"If it takes blood to demonstrate my sincerity, so be it." He placed the blade against the meat of his palm. "What could be stronger than a blood pact upon hallowed Granton ground between two best friends destined to be lovers?" His eyes sparkled, clear as a summer night. "The spirit of Elizabeth Granton herself shall bear witness to our sacred bargain."

A shiver skipped over her arms. "You don't believe in ghosts."

"What *you* believe is what matters right now." He lifted his eyebrows, the knife ready. "I, Leopold Henry Hughes, vow to defend, uphold and nurture my friendship with Karen Jora Ives to whatever end may come. I will allow no human scheme or power of hell to diminish my undying affection and deep love for her."

Before she fumbled through all the emotions swarming to life at his solemn words and formed a protest, he made a small, quick slice in his skin. Red flowed from the cut.

"Leo!"

He held his unwounded hand out for her, his eyes dark and intense. "Do you trust me?"

Hell. She couldn't back down now, not after he'd drawn his own blood. Her hands shook and her heart threatened to ricochet right out of her chest. Could she do this, step through the doorway with him into her fantasies where the consequences would be brutally real?

Karen placed her hand in his and steeled herself for the pain.

Leo pricked her palm so fast, the blade so sharp that she didn't feel it. A crimson drop welled up, and he clasped their palms together, mixing their blood.

"I, Karen Jora Ives—"

"Your vow isn't necessary. It's your fears that need soothed, not mine."

She exhaled noisily, and her breath clouded in the air. Even beneath the heat of the lamppost, her skin pebbled with sudden cold. The lights flickered. Leo's grip on her hand tightened to the point of almost painful. With an electrical buzz, the lights and heat went out. Only the dotted solar lanterns along the path left a dim glow.

"So much for my industrial-strength generator," Leo grumbled.

The hair on the back of her neck prickled. Among the statues and shadows, the night seemed to ripple, like leaves brushed by a distant wind. Focused on the darkness, she pressed their palms together and spoke into the aching silence. "I, Karen Jora Ives, vow to do everything in my power to ensure my friendship with Leopold Henry Hughes never dies."

The lights buzzed and flickered back on, revealing emptiness in the spaces between statues. Whether or not her imagination played a part, she knew, down to her bones, that completing the blood vow settled a jagged presence in the conservatory.

"Hmm." He squinted at the lights. "Looks like I'll have to investigate the electrical wiring in the basement yet again. But that can wait until tomorrow." He pulled a crisp, folded handkerchief from his pocket, set it on her bleeding palm and pressed their wounds together. "We have one important detail to finish — every true bargain must be sealed with a kiss."

Her fantasies had always been tempered by all the tomorrows. She had to face him in the morning and not reveal any hint of deeper emotions, speak to him like a normal person, keep the interaction platonic to preserve their endless tomorrow of friendship. Even with irreversible vows in place, knowing the gravity Leo gave to any promise he made, she couldn't just forget.

"Because I like you, I'll make it easier for you." His blue eyes twinkling, he stooped so they were eye level and puckered his lips.

Leo linked their fingers together and pulled her close. Tomorrow seemed out of reach and beyond her control. Losing him would kill her.

A crash erupted from the mansion, as if an asteroid had fallen through the roof, and they both jumped. Leo's wide-eyed gaze briefly found hers before he took off at a run toward the mansion.

Karen followed, her boots scattering pebbles as she hurried, too slow to keep up. Whatever had made that noise had been huge. She left the conservatory behind and burst into the kitchen. Nothing looked out of place. The lasagne still cooked, filling the room with the aroma of garlic. Leo's footsteps pounded down the corridor.

She rushed past the dining room and library, and as she neared the pink parlor, she spotted Leo in the front vestibule, looking up. She skidded to a stop beside him. Dust clouded the air. Plaster and splintered wood scattered the floor like the victims of an explosion. In the midst of it all, the giant iron chandelier lay askew, a fallen crown on a deadly battlefield.

"Hell," she murmured. She should be hot from the sprint, but cold iced her veins at the irrational sensation that the chandelier was somehow connected to a vow made with blood.

* * * *

Monday morning, Leo couldn't stop whistling as he set a drywall sheet down in the corridor between the guest side door and the ballroom. He'd seen Karen off to work with her favorite coffee, an egg muffin and a kiss to remember him by — hot and long enough that he had to steady her before she tackled the porch steps.

Finally, after years of waiting and wanting, Ren gave him a chance. Not even the chandelier inexplicably falling and damaging the vestibule floor could ruin his mood.

He made his way back to the front door where the rest of the drywall waited. Why hadn't he thought about a blood vow earlier? It would have saved him from the endless, restless nights where thoughts of Ren made it impossible to sleep. And even though he'd only managed a couple hours of sleep on the couch with her burrowed in his arms and Sir Snugglebottom curled up on his head, it was the best night he'd had in a long time — in forever, actually.

His face hurt from all the unaccustomed smiling.

Sunlight streamed in through the windows, all traces of yesterday's storm and its destruction forgiven and forgotten everywhere beyond the ballroom and chandelier. The mahogany woodwork of the stairwell railing and banister gleamed as if beneath a spotlight, every nick and scratch brought on by age and life deepened to scars. Someday, he'd sand them away and restore every inch of Granton Hall to its former glory for a far better purpose than a wealthy businessman's vanity.

As he reached the door, he paused and stopped whistling. The hair on his arms prickled. A distant violin drifted from the corridor, close to the kitchen, a faint, familiar melody that sent his heart into a gallop.

Danse Macabre.

Good God almighty, he hated that song.

He'd never told Ren the specifics behind why he hated Halloween and everything that went with it. It gave her a reason to tease him, which he'd always welcome. But he had a solid case for shunning the supernatural, and that tune unburied the memory in a flash of dread.

Leo drew a long breath through his nose and released it, the training exercise he used when facing his brothers in the ring. The familiar act lent him enough calm and focus to push fear back. There was a rational explanation for why music would be playing in a house where he was the sole human. There was a logical reason that the music happened to be *Danse Macabre*, the same tune that had haunted his nightmares until he'd wrestled with adolescent fear and overcome it with determination, sweat and swords.

After a few seconds, the melody repeated, some sort of recording rather than a radio or instrument. He needed to find where it came from. Letting fear take the lead wasn't an option.

The faint tune began again, and he hurried toward the kitchen, where it seemed to be coming from. As he passed the library, the song ended and began again as he reached the kitchen. It drifted from the basement. *Of course.*

He set his jaw. Ren would accuse him of being one of the too-stupid-to-live characters from her horror movies, the idiot who decided investigating a noise in the basement was a great idea. But fear lost its power if faced head on, and he wasn't about to surrender.

Leo jerked the basement door open, grabbed the flashlight he kept on the wall and thundered down the steps. By the time he reached the bottom, the music stopped. He swept the beam over shelves of junk abandoned behind by former owners, jars and boxes that he hadn't had time to look through. Moth-eaten furniture filled one corner, an old bicycle and rusted tools. The electrical box in the corner was open. He strode to it and shut it.

He aimed the light at the stacks and stacks of boxes, the scent of stone and mildew a permanent stain. The basement stretched beneath the dining room, library and parlor, ending at the door. Rows of garage sale rubbish filled the space. It was possible an old music box was stored somewhere in that mess. Searching for it wasn't on his priority list, not this month.

The music began again, and he jumped, his heart racing. The tune blasted from upstairs.

Not getting away this time. Leo raced up the basement stairs and rushed down the corridor toward the front door, brandishing the flashlight like a weapon.

The door opened and his youngest brother, Liam, peered inside. *Danse Macabre* replayed from the cell phone in his hand.

"You're a punk." Jaw set, Leo stalked straight for his annoying brother. "Why do you have that song as a ringtone?"

"Don't get your eyebrows in a twist. It's the ideal ringtone for you. And before you get all growly about how much you hate that song, since it plays when you call me, you're usually not around." He shrugged. "Not my fault you keep butt-dialing me, dude. Check your phone."

As *Danse Macabre* repeated, Leo jerked his cell phone from the back pocket of his worn jeans and shut it off. The music died with his phone. He folded his arms over his chest and scowled. "Why are you here?"

"You called me?" Liam gave him a look that said he was an imbecile. Intimidating him would be easier if Liam wasn't an inch taller than his own six foot four inches. "And you should fix those porch stairs. Lucky I didn't fall through."

Leo kept his scowl going.

"I can't believe you bought this place." Lifting his gaze from the suicidal chandelier to the new gash in the ceiling, Liam made a slow spin and whistled, long and low. "What a shipwreck."

Leo resisted the urge to drag his brother out by the back of his B-52s T-shirt. When it came to construction, Liam was the ultimate critic. He opened his mouth and observations of the worst kind spewed free. Leo suspected he did it so no one would ask for his help—

and he wouldn't have to try to fill their father's irreplaceable shoes and fail. "I was having a good day. If you can't be positive, shut your face or leave."

"So that *was* you I heard whistling." He glanced again at the chandelier. "Your definition of a good day scares me."

"Nothing, not even your unwelcome company, can ruin today." He grinned. "Ren's finally giving me a shot."

"You wily wolf." Liam whistled again. "How?"

"Blood vow."

Liam nodded as if vows incorporating blood were nothing out of the ordinary. Any woman other than Ren might have drawn concern, but it fit his Gothic-loving girl. All his family knew of her fascination with the supernatural and spooky, as they were aware of his love for her.

"Sounds about right." He slapped Leo on the shoulder. "Congrats. I never doubted you'd win her over to the dark side of the Hughes clan. When's the wedding?"

If Ren even heard the 'M' word, she'd run and never look back, blood vows and best friendships be damned. He gave his brother a stern look. "If you mention anything to do with marriage or commitment to Ren, I'll grind you to dust beneath my heel."

"You could try, old man." Liam lunged at him.

Leo danced out of the way at the last second. Liam smacked into the wall with barely enough time to lift his palms to cushion the impact. A hairline crack appeared in the paneling.

"You're fixing that before you leave." Leo pointed at the new damage.

"In exchange for a rematch in the ring tonight, one on one. My superior blue saber against your ungodly green."

"You're on. Right here. In the ballroom where there's enough space for me to kick your scrawny ass properly."

Liam grinned. "At dusk?"

"When else?" Leo turned to the drywall mess. "And you bring food — the price for bothering me."

"Dude." The grumble in his brother's groan made him smirk. "Not my fault your butt cheek called me."

And he couldn't deny he appreciated the company. Although Liam's cell phone somewhat explained the music, a cold rock remained in chest, like a grave cracked open, spilling the one moment in his life he'd battled to forget.

Chapter Sixteen

That evening, Karen relaxed on the marble ballroom steps and enjoyed the view. Both Leo and Liam were shirtless, barefoot, wearing loose, black pants and swinging light sabers at each other hard enough to sting. They sectioned off the unfinished floor to prevent any sprained ankles or falls — or unfair landscape advantage, according to Liam — and proceeded to try to kill one another.

It was sexy as hell, and a sweet sort of freedom to ogle Leo openly.

Leo nearly sliced his brother's head off with the glowing green saber in his grip. The weapon whirred over Liam's head as he ducked the vicious blow, leaving pink powder in his hair. One of the Hughes boys had invented special weapons — a mix between a light saber and padded SCA blade — and gifted them to all the brothers one year for Christmas. Wherever the sabers made contact, they left a glowing residue, along with the occasional welt to keep them all honest, even in the dark.

Men. She snorted.

She reached for another piece of pepperoni-and-pineapple pizza, courtesy of Liam. Pizza had nothing on Leo's lasagne from the previous night. After the spider mystery, blood vow and chilling chandelier tragedy, she couldn't have slept even if she'd wanted to. Instead, she'd devoured lasagne and garlic bread, curled up on the couch with Leo and talked about his dreams for Granton Hall into the night. True to his word, he'd left her in charge of the touching, the kissing. She still hadn't decided if she should be insulted or impressed by his self-control.

But as much as she trusted Leo, she'd agreed to this month with him to learn construction, not to be seduced. When she arrived at the office that morning, she'd made a beeline for Mr. Hamilton's office and submitted her official notice. She needed the incentive, a personal push to keep her focus on the goal—landing the job at Cooper Homes, not jumping Leo's bones.

The afternoon had blurred by learning all about hanging drywall. Before Liam had arrived, Leo had lectured her on the intricate ins and outs of a perfect parquet floor. She'd spent the last hour recouping what she could of the ruined wood and organizing them into boxes, after the assurance that a thorough investigation had detected no insect nests.

A sharp smack of plastic on flesh and a hiss brought her full attention back to the war. *Poor Liam.* He had slashes of pink on several important body parts. Leo had a single blue spot on his shoulder, a lucky blow. Almost an hour later and they were still going at it, sweating and panting.

She could think of a more personal way to make Leo sweat and pant, but watching him move with fierce, brutal efficiency was second best. As much as she fantasized about taking that next step in their relationship, going there would take her beyond any hope of return. She wasn't ready, no matter how delicious it had been the past night in his arms, only a barrier of clothes between them, except for his fingers beneath her sweater on her back, as if he'd needed direct contact.

I'm in so much trouble. Denying Leo was an uphill battle she'd never win. He was an irresistible force who never entertained the notion of retreat, as evidenced by the battle with his brother. She grimaced as Liam swiped at Leo and missed, earning another stripe on his back. The weapon made a wicked hiss against skin, as if it burned flesh like the real thing.

Setting the pizza down, she pulled the spider key from her hoodie's zippered pocket. She'd kept it with her all day, wondering how it had found its way beneath the floor, what it unlocked, who it had belonged to. She'd bet her first edition of *The Castle of Otranto* that the key had once belonged to Elizabeth. Every keyhole would be explored until she found some answers. A key with a spider etched on it had to be protecting juicy secrets.

Liam took a strike to the ribs and dropped to the floor with a loud thud, Leo's blade at his throat. He lifted his hands in surrender and his saber light winked out. "I give," he panted. "You win…this time."

"I'll allow you to cling to your dreams." Wearing an evil smile, Leo made two quick swipes, leaving a pink X of defeat on his brother's chest. "This time." He held out a hand and hefted Liam to his feet.

"Ow." Liam grimaced and limped beside Leo as they crossed the ballroom to her. "I think you cracked my ribs."

"Practice blocking with your sword, not your body," Leo said, merciless.

"Thanks for the tip. Never would've figured it out without your ancient wisdom."

"No problem."

Leo sprawled on the step beside her, grinning like a fool. Liam clung to the balustrade post for support and retrieved his water bottle from the floor. Instead of drinking, he poured it over his head, splashing her in the process.

"Watch it, loser." She pushed Liam back with her boot, beyond splash range.

"Aw, Ren, don't think less of me for caving to Leo." Liam slicked back his longish, golden-brown hair and gave her an innocent look. "I had to let him win. Taking a decrepit old man's pride in the only sport he's ever been mediocre at isn't worth my undying honor."

"Honor? Is that what you call that sad attempt to stab me in the nuggets right before I gave you that?" Leo poked his brother in the stomach with his saber, right where pink smudged, dead-center. "Punk."

"Geezer."

They smirked at each other.

"You two remind me of all the reasons why I don't miss my sisters."

"Sisters?" Liam sat on her other side, looking interested. "I had no idea, Ren. Older, younger? Equally gorgeous?" He wriggled his eyebrows. "Single?"

"None of your business." Leo reached around Karen and smacked his brother in the back of the head.

"Out of your league," she added, "in a backward way. They're both downhome farm girls. Their idea of a serious competition is the country-fair cherry pie bake off. Don't mess with those ladies and their pastries."

"Mm…pie and pastries." Liam rubbed his belly. "When are they visiting?"

"Not any time in the near future. Cows and chickens don't allow for many vacation days, and my parents rely on their help." Not that she'd ever invite her sisters Hannah or Iris, both loyal Hank fans, to Graywood. Texting her mom and fielding the occasional call from her dad were fine, but she avoided her sisters as much as possible.

That life had never been hers, even when she'd tried to fit into it, and none of her family had attempted to talk her out of moving away after Hank. But a small voice still sometimes whispered that she'd abandoned them to the particular hardships of farm life.

Leo nudged her shoulder with his and scooted closer, his thigh pressed to hers. "They can't be as tiresome as my family."

The reality of mixing Leo's family with hers sent an odd wave of panic and pride through her. Watching Leo charm her dad with his down-to-earth work ethics, her mom with his sincere nature and her sisters with nothing more than that crooked smile would be nothing short of epic. But the inevitable day Leo walked away? She couldn't endure her family's disappointment and sympathy again. *Wouldn't*…not for anything.

"Speak for yourself, dude. We're not all chained to our jobs and do-gooder endeavors." Liam swiped the last slice of pizza and stuffed it into his mouth.

"Since you brought it up, I could use help with the roof."

"And the siding, foundation, drywall, floors, for starters, but you bought this mess, not me. Don't drag me into the business, old man."

Leo scowled. "Graywood has a distinct lack of skilled construction workers, and with winter coming—"

"Nope." Liam jumped up, shoved his water bottle and saber into his duffel bag and leaned down to kiss Karen on the cheek. Barefoot, he headed into the hallway. "This slave is free and intends to keep it that way." He waggled his fingers in farewell.

"It seems he's heard the rumor that you're a perfectionist tyrant to work for." She planted her hand on her heart. "Not from me, of course. I happen to admire perfection."

"Clearly, since you chose me."

She arched an eyebrow. "I agreed to this arrangement for your arrogance, nothing else."

"Is that what this is?" Leo asked in a low, silken voice, his gaze settled on her mouth. "An *arrangement*?"

"I was referring to my volunteer position as newbie construction assistant." Her mouth tingled beneath his stare, anticipation of a kiss. "Of course."

"I was hoping you might volunteer for a different sort of position," he murmured, easing closer. The heat of his big body seeped through her hoodie and jeans. For so many months she'd dreamed about kissing him, and even though it was now something she could do whenever she wanted, it still felt taboo in a delicious sort of way.

"Cooking and cleaning aren't in my wheelhouse," she said, playing innocent. "Sorry. You'll have to tough it—eek!"

In one quick move, Leo hauled her onto his lap and leaned over her. Her booted feet flew up into the air, and she would have toppled right off if not for his arm beneath her back. He kissed her, long, sweet and possessive, and when he finally lifted her up, she gasped for air, all her limbs at his mercy.

"My apologies," he said. "You were saying?"

"I have no idea."

His crooked smile appeared "I believe we were discussing various positions."

She laid her palm on his chest. The steady beat of his heart vibrated beneath her hand, matching her thrumming pulse. He was in this arrangement with her, on equal ground, together for now. Maybe that was enough, to embrace what she could for now and not think about the future.

Karen looped her arms around his neck. "This might be my favorite position so far."

"Mine, too." He kissed the tip of her nose and his eyes darkened with heat. "So far."

Leo looked past her shoulder, out to the expanse of the ballroom. "We got a lot done today, most of the drywall up, the window repaired and you made excellent progress on the floor."

She snorted. "I still have to remove the original tar, diagram and measure, select and chop the various species of wood. I have to rip up every hint of the past, reassemble and reuse what I can and create new pieces that fit into the present complex puzzle. It's going to take me all month to finish, especially since I'm learning on the fly." She met his gaze, her throat tight.

"I know how much you've invested in this competition. I don't want to screw this up."

"Not possible. You didn't unearth more human-devouring spiders to delay the work, and you'll get faster each day." He brushed her bangs from her eyes, his touch gentle. "We'll meet the deadline. You'll be the best accountant with construction skills around."

"Speaking of accountants who want to land construction jobs, does Cooper specialize in any particular area? Is there a specific skill that would wow the smut right off her face?"

"Ren, darling." Damn, she loved the way he said her name, all rough with need. "The offer to work for me is open-ended." He nuzzled her ear, and she bit her lip. "I could use an accountant to set my books in order, and if that person is you, even better. Construction skills approved but not required."

And be financially dependent on him when he decided to end the romance? He'd feel obligated to keep her on, duty-bound to employ her, even when it would be awkward as hell. Hiding the pain from him would be impossible, then he'd be the one throwing her pitying looks. No way. It would be bad enough losing her best friend.

She gave him a stern look. "Still not working for you, Hughes."

"Still not giving up on you working for me, Ren. We've always made a great team. Admit it."

"I've spent my allotted time in the confessional this week already, thank you very much." She squirmed free of his hold and stood.

"Fine." He stood as well and rubbed the blue mark on his shoulder, grimacing. "Cooper happens to specialize in ornamental parquetry floor."

Oh, this man. Her heart clenched. Even though he preferred that she worked for him, not Cooper, he still had her back. "You're the best, you know that?"

He scowled.

"Come on. Let's go." She held out her hand.

He reached for her hand, willing to go with her without even knowing the destination, trusting her enough not to lead him astray. She loved that about him. It made it so easy to drag him to scary places, where he'd hover protectively close. It used to be a great excuse to cling to his arm and make physical contact.

"Where are we going, and should I put on a shirt and shoes first?"

She gave him a wicked grin. "We're going ghost hunting. Shoes suggested." She dragged her fingertips down the delicious plane of his chest. Needing no excuses was amazing. "Shirt optional."

Chapter Seventeen

Karen swung the lantern in a slow arc, making the silhouettes of trees and overgrown shrubs shiver in the darkness.

"I don't like this," Leo whispered near her ear for the tenth time.

"Don't be a whiner. I'll protect you from all the scary things in the dark waiting for you." She grinned at him and squeezed his fingers. "Big baby."

He ducked a low branch. A twig snapped beneath his boot, a sharp echo in the night. "You plan to save me from monstrous spiders that escaped the ballroom and thirst for new blood?"

She laughed. "That sounded like something I'd say. You're learning, Hughes. And yes, even from monstrous spiders. I'm wearing my heavy boots for that very reason."

Pine needles crunched with their steps as they followed the overgrown trail rambling through Granton property. Since finding the spider key, she'd spent hours considering what it might belong to and who might have hidden it in the floor. Arthur Granton would presumably have no reason to hide a key in such a strange location, and she doubted he knew which pieces of parquet flooring were loose.

She'd considered Elizabeth, too, but the lady of the house dabbling with parquet flooring was unlikely. If the key belonged to her and if she'd wanted it hidden, she'd assign the task to a trusted member of her staff.

Such as a beloved groundskeeper.

"What if we see Elizabeth's spirit? I, for one, have no desire to fall from the second floor and see what bones break." The shrubbery rustled, and he whipped his cell phone light toward the sound. A possum's eyes shone silver in the beam before it scurried away, its tail snaking through the leaves.

"If you don't believe in curses," she said in a sing-song voice, "neither do I."

"Lies. How do you even know there's a building out here? The realtor made no mention of outbuildings a mile away." He almost tripped on a fallen log fuzzed with moss and caught his balance before helping her over it. How could such a big, powerful man have the reflexes of an acrobat? Hell, he was beautiful without even trying.

Karen plucked a leaf from her shoulder, a thrill dancing through her at being in the woods at night, following the remains of a path to an abandoned building and all its ancient secrets.

"I caught up with Mr. Hamilton this morning and gave him my official notice."

Leo faced her, his eyebrows tented. "Why?"

"I already told you. I need a change of scenery." She gave him a bright smile and continued down the path.

"And now there's only one way to go—forward, with new construction skills and the accountant job at Cooper Homes."

"Hmm." He followed without further comment.

"Mr. Hamilton is nearly as old as the town itself and still sharp as a whip. I figured if there were any details about Granton Hall not included in newspaper or public records, he'd be the one to know. He loves crap like that—town history, rumors and reputations ruined. After all, local scandal and business gone bad is a healthy portion of what keeps Hamilton & Associates rich, rich and more rich."

"Lawyers." He made it sound like a curse word.

"Don't sound so warm and fuzzy. It's not Hamilton's fault that people screw themselves over or try to screw other people over."

"It's the preying on other people's misfortune that I don't like."

"It's business, not personal...usually." She could tell him how many clients Mr. Hamilton took on pro bono because of the soft heart beneath the shark suit, but that wasn't her secret to tell. Whatever she learned in the numbers as the firm's accountant remained as confidential as details spewed by clients behind closed doors.

"Work for me with a clear conscience." He gave her a sidelong look. "I never take advantage of people in need."

"Not happening."

"I didn't ask."

Karen blinked. Volunteering for only a few days and he already decided she wasn't up to snuff?

"This time." One corner of his mouth twitched up.

She hid her smile. If she set it free, he'd take it as a sign that she softened. "Mr. Hamilton assured me there once was a cottage out here used for occasional staff members who didn't have houses of their own. And you'll never guess the identity of the original cottage resident." A stand of mushrooms squished beneath her boots, and a draft rich with earth and decay swirled up from the ground.

"Freddy Krueger? Jason? Dracula?"

"You forgot Count Orlok."

He slid her an annoyed look. "Unfortunately, I haven't."

"I'll find a new monster or psycho for this weekend movie night, to take your mind off the others."

"Wonderful."

"All fine guesses, but no. Edwin lived here with his sister, the main housekeeper. According to Mr. Hamilton, just as we'd heard, both Edwin and his sister moved to Granton Hall with Elizabeth when she married."

"Convenient. Sounds like the beginning of one of your horror movies."

"One can only hope."

The path dipped into a sea of sharp-fronded ferns and trees thick with moss. It seemed no human had trespassed here for ages, and a strange sort of hush lingered.

"And why do we have to visit this rumor of ruins in the dark?" Leo sidled through two overgrown rowan trees blocking the path.

"Because I have accounting duties in the morning, you have a deadline to meet and now is the only time you're free to investigate where this spider key came from and to what it guards."

"Oh. And all this time I thought you just wanted to get me alone in the dark where you could have your way with me, no witnesses."

"We're the only ones living at Granton Hall."

"Excellent point." He pulled her to a stop, took the lantern from her and set it down. Wrapping a hand around the back of her neck, he slanted his mouth over hers.

The kiss began teasing, and while she intended to keep control, Leo stole it from her grip. He slid a hand beneath her sweater and, kissing her senseless, guided her backward until her spine pressed into a tree trunk. The solid support was more than welcome as her knees wobbled.

Holy hell the man could kiss, sweet and sinful, silken tongue and soft lips. He kissed her as if she were the last drop of chilled water in a desert and he was a man dying of thirst. A low, possessive growl rumbled in his throat as he pressed his warm, delicious body into hers.

With the night surrounding them, the quiet presence of the forest keeping watch, this could be one of her fantasies spun to life. She pushed the hem of his T-shirt up, needing to touch his skin. The dips and planes of his torso were hot beneath her exploring fingers. She couldn't get enough. She wasn't sure she'd ever get enough of him.

With a husky, rueful laugh, Leo broke the kiss and trapped her hands with his. "Ren, darling, as tempting as you are and as much as I want you — and I do want you, so badly it aches — our first time together won't be on the cold ground at the mercy of insects and pine needles in unfortunate crevices."

Karen caught her breath and leaned her forehead against his chest. "I knew it. You're a romance killer."

"What, because I want our first time to be as special as you are?" He cupped her face and lifted her gaze to his, worry lines on his forehead.

Her heart skipped a hard beat. He was so sweet and sexy she could barely stand it. No other man she knew would be so concerned about an uncomfortable location or pleasant memories that he'd wait. She shook her head and stepped back, afraid she might lose control again. "I was referring to locations a pine needle might wind up, not your romantic sense of place or making a girl feel special."

"Not *a* girl, Ren," he said softly. "You...just you."

She had to look away. If he realized how close she was crumbling, he'd be relentless. "While we might have all night, I get grumpy when I don't get enough sleep." She grabbed the lantern. "Let's go."

"Do we have to?"

"You can go back, if you want." She shrugged. "Alone through the dark, creepy woods with uncountable unknown creatures that haven't been disturbed in eons waiting for you—hidden, watching."

He scowled. "It's not nice to manipulate me."

"When have I ever claimed to be nice?" She grinned.

"The only reason I'm doing this is because I adore you, Ren."

"I know."

They almost walked right by the cottage and would have if Leo hadn't spotted the wink of glass in the beam from his cell phone. Ivy had clawed its way over the walls and twined through broken windows. Moss invaded the sagging roof, and the overgrown trees crowding the structure made it seem as if the forest had claimed it for its own.

Karen struggled with a screen of vines and peeked into the gaping hole of the doorway.

"Looks empty," Leo whispered from behind her. "A dead end, not to mention a hazard zone. That roof might collapse at any moment. We should go."

She pushed through the ivy with her lantern. After a mumbled curse, Leo shouldered inside with a loud rustle of vegetation.

Vandals had left their mark on the brick walls, words and abstract symbols in faded black paint, nearly obliterated by moss and age. It seemed even the local hoodlums had forgotten the place existed. Within the walls and suffocating greenery, it seemed as though they'd walked into a pocket of silence...or a tomb.

"Great. We're not alone." Leo pointed to the skull of some large animal lying crooked in the corner. "This is probably some wild beast's lair and we bumbled right in, saving it the trouble of going hunting."

"I think you're safe, Hughes. No other bones or fur." She kicked through a layer of dried leaves that had piled in the corner.

"I should've brought my sword." Leo peeked into the dark hallway.

She decided not to tell him about the smaller animal bones among the leaves. "If some beastie shows up, run. You're in better shape than me, and by the time it's through snacking on my delectable flesh, you'll be at Granton Hall, safe and sound."

He looked over his shoulder, and his gaze raked her up and down, slow and sensual. "I have no intention of sharing any of my delicacies, Ren, darling."

A shiver rippled through her. How was she supposed to keep her heart safe when he melted her with only a look and a few words? "If you want to sacrifice yourself so I can escape, who am I to argue?"

"I made no mention of sacrifice." He lifted his chin. "I'd slay the beast with my bare hands."

"Never doubted it."

His lazy smile doubled the heat in her blood, and she focused on Edwin's former cottage. Rain from the earlier storm had filtered through the bower of limbs and rotten shingles, leaving small puddles on the cement floor. It was impossible to determine what portions of the cottage were original.

Karen crouched and shone the lantern in a crevice between two bricks. "I wonder if this building is as old as the mansion?"

Leo assumed his scrutinizing face, his eyes narrowed, assessing details she never saw unless he pointed them out. His father had dragged him along to work and taught him with a lifetime of hands-on experience. He'd died before she arrived on the scene. He scuffed the toe of his boot on the foundation. "Brick buildings weren't uncommon in that period. They require little maintenance and aren't prone to mold or insects. Perfect for this climate." He dragged a fingertip along the crumbling seam between two crooked bricks. "It's the mortar that tells more of a tale."

Karen moved beside him, close to his heat, and examined the space he touched. "And what does this particular mortar say?"

"Help me." He grinned.

"I think that's the building you hear. It's the last, dying gasp of ancient bones."

He scowled. "Did you have to mention bones and death?"

"Only for you." She gave him a sweet smile. Shining the lamp at a seam between bricks, she knelt on the gritty floor. The mortar had crumbled to dust, leaving a gap. She scanned the wall in search of loose bricks. "Is it possible that when the brick was laid, a pocket was created, small enough for a jewelry box?"

"Possible, not probable." Leo frowned at the doorway between rooms. "The walls aren't thick and I'm not seeing any disparities in width."

"Hmm," she said, disappointed.

He turned and examined corner shelves built into the brickwork. His grin faded as he crouched and aimed his cell phone light at the lowest shelf. "This doesn't seem right."

"What is it?" She left her search behind and kneeled beside him.

"It appears the foundation shifted, which isn't uncommon, but usually more than the space of a few bricks are affected."

A shiver of excitement rolled down her back as she handed him her purple-handled chisel. "Get to work, Hughes."

"Do you know how proud I am of you right now?" He traded her chisel for his phone, his eyes sparkling. "My construction queen in the making, already prepared for anything."

"Not anything." She fought off a ridiculous smile. "Just potential hidey-holes in ruined cottages of groundskeepers who have illicit affairs with the lady of the manor."

Leo shifted onto his stomach as she shone the light inside the shelving. "The entire place will probably fall down when I remove these bricks. You know that, right?"

"Worth the risk."

"I may be opening a spider nest that has been here for centuries, undisturbed."

She poked him in the shoulder. "Stop procrastinating."

He *hmph*ed and reached into the shelves. After a few jabs and a bit of prying with the chisel, he handed the tool back to her. A brick came next, then another.

"What the—?" His voice strained as he struggled with something beneath the shelf.

Karen scrambled onto her stomach beside him. "What is it?"

"Not sure." His features set in concentration, he reached elbow-deep into the hole left behind by the removed bricks. He grunted. "Got it."

Coated in spider webs, dust and mold, he deposited a leather pouch on the floor.

Karen gasped. "A hex bag." She gripped his arm. "Open it."

"Nope." He sat up and dusted off his jacket. "I would have up to the point you called it a hex bag."

"Wimp." Still on her stomach, she loosened the stiff, leather drawstrings. One end broke off. Carefully, she opened the mouth and dumped the contents. A smoking pipe and small wooden box tumbled out. "I stand corrected—not a hex bag." She picked up the box and turned it over. "No locks."

"Don't open it." Leo hovered near, protective. "Could hold spiders."

"Prepare to run." She set it down and opened it.

Another smaller, leather pouch rested inside. "No spiderwebs. It's safe."

"So it seems."

She dumped that pouch, too. A few dried tobacco leaves drifted free, followed by a matchbox with the name 'Lucifers' stamped on it.

Leo frowned and pointed at the matchbox. "I don't like that."

"Lucifers. Do you know how old these things are?" She opened the matchbox. A single matchstick rested inside. "That's what these types of matches were called back in the day. They're toxic, but I'm relatively certain they don't belong to the devil."

"We'll let Liam open the box next time he's over. He'll be thrilled."

"*I'm* thrilled." She sat back on her heels. "Bummed that there's nothing here connected to the spider key, but still... This is an awesome find."

"A pipe belonging to some rotten-toothed Granton employee and matches belonging to Satan." His eyebrow quirked. "At least it's not a finger."

"Or a possum bone." She put everything back in the leather pouch and stuffed it into her coat pocket.

Leo helped her to her feet. His fingers were warm and strong around hers. "Cross the dilapidated shack in the back forty off your paranormal investigation list. If there are more forgotten buildings on my property, I prefer not to know." He plucked some moss from her hair and met her gaze. "May we go home now?"

Home. Without warning, yearning rose. She hadn't felt homesick for years, but she suddenly very much wanted to be home, and somewhere along the way, home and Leo had become intertwined. *Hell.* With fantasy and reality weaving together, she fell harder with every second. The fall, she could handle. The end crash, she dreaded with every ounce of her soul.

Locking her fingers with his, she gave him a smile. "Let's get you home, Hughes."

Chapter Eighteen

With Ren's hand in his, Leo restrained himself the entire walk back to Granton Hall through the night woods. The innocent touch strengthened the ever-present need to protect her. At the same time, the mere contact of her skin on his made his blood simmer. When he'd called Granton Hall *their* home, he hadn't missed the flash of longing in her eyes, the vulnerability there and gone so fast he might have missed it if he hadn't been paying attention.

When it came to Ren, he noticed everything. He would follow her to the ends of the earth, no questions asked, as long as she let him stay beside her every step. Wherever she landed, no matter how long or far, his home was with her. It was about time she understood that.

Granton Hall loomed up from the dark, its gables stabbing the clear sky. Some people might see the shape as menacing, a silent warning to keep out. To him, it felt like a welcome sign.

They followed the unkempt path to the front door beneath the watchful gazes of the statues. Before Ren made the rickety porch steps, he swept her off the ground.

"Hey!" She flung her arms around his neck.

"Hold on." He grinned, and before she asked why, launched onto the porch, skipping all the questionable steps in the process. Her squeak of surprise was adorable, and even though he'd vowed to control himself, as he set her back on her feet, he couldn't deny the urge to kiss her.

Leo grasped both lapels of her wool coat, pulled her close and brushed his mouth over hers. He kept the kiss to a lazy taste, savoring the sweet friction, how she pressed against him with a little purr, her eyelids fluttering shut. He could spend the rest of his life kissing her. For now, he banked the fire in his blood and contented himself with a slow, lulling kiss. Ren needed to know he wanted her for all she was, not what she'd give.

A savage sound came from Ren, and she locked her arms around his neck, slamming him back against the door with unexpected strength. The latch opened at the impact, and they stumbled inside, tripping over the giant chandelier still on the floor. He caught her as they fell, and they tumbled to the floor, Ren on top of him.

She grinned down at him, her eyes sparkling. "I totally meant to do that."

"I'm at your mercy." He brushed her bangs from her eyes. "Whatever are you going to do with me now?"

She bit her lip.

The door slammed, kicked shut by a sudden wind. At the same moment, a small, black fuzzball darted past them into the corridor.

Sir had escaped the laundry room. There were still too many dangerous places in Granton Hall for a tiny kitten to run free. If he got into the wall again or went beneath the house, they might not be able to get him out.

"Did you forget to shut the laundry room door before we left?" Leo sat up as Ren scrambled off him.

"Nope." Ren shed her coat as he jumped to his feet. Together, they hurried after the kitten. "I thought that yesterday when he got out, but I'm positive I shut the door tonight. He must have found an escape tunnel."

They turned into the next hallway, and Sir flashed around another corner, his tail three sizes bigger than usual. He headed in the direction of the ballroom.

"Something scared him."

"Most likely us making a racket outside." Karen gave him a teasing look, her irresistible dimple on display. "I bet we sounded like some soul-slurping kitten collector at the door, trying to get in."

"How is it you always see a monster in even the most pleasant of situations?"

"Skills." Her gaze drifted over him, slow and seductive. "But you on the floor beneath me was one of the better situations I've been in recently."

"Only recently?" When he kissed her next, he'd make sure it superseded any other kiss from every other man.

"The last guy I kissed was six months ago. He was about as inspiring as a senior citizen golf tournament." Her smile widened to wicked proportions. "I think you've got him beat."

"Thanks for the vote of confidence, *friend*." He scowled but couldn't deny a flare of relief. She hadn't been with anyone else in the past six months. All the

Saturday nights that he had let his brothers thrash him while battling visions of Ren with another man had been empty fears. Even though he'd earned enough bruises to color a map, he'd take it knowing that she hadn't been with anyone else — that maybe she'd been thinking about him all those Saturday nights, too.

They passed the ballroom guest door and entered the section of corridor mended that morning. Reflecting the night beyond, the stained-glass windows offered no light. The corridor opened into the ballroom foyer, and Leo cursed beneath his breath.

The glass doors leading into the ballroom were flung open wide.

Sir launched into the ballroom and down the marble steps. Like a furry black pinball, he tumbled onto the floor, rolled upright and slid a good dozen feet. He stopped halfway across the ballroom floor, his back arched, his tail a black bottlebrush bigger than his body, a cartoon silhouette against the windows.

"I thought we closed these doors after Liam left," Leo murmured, a chill prickling the back of his neck.

"We did." Ren led him inside and closed the doors, trapping them in with Sir. "Do you smell that?" She paused and sniffed the air, her head tilted at a thoughtful angle. "I think it's pipe smoke, cloves."

He flicked on the lights and went still. Sir stood near the section of floor Ren had been working on. Before they'd quit for the day, she'd organized the salvageable wood in boxes. Now, those boxes were tipped, wood bits scattered, splintered and broken.

"How — ? What...? Who?" Her eyes wide and sparking with fury, Ren walked toward Sir and her ruined work. "There's no way Sir did this — he's too little—but I'm going to destroy whoever did. It took me forever to inspect and separate those pieces."

"Hold up, Ren." Leo caught her sleeve, his skin icing over as he studied the loose parquet littering the floor. "Are you seeing what I'm seeing?"

"Yeah." Her voice strained through gritted teeth. "My afternoon of labor up in smoke."

"That's not what I mean." He shook his head and held on to her sleeve, his throat dry. "Do you see a particular pattern in the wood?" The chill on his neck spread down his arms as his brain confirmed what his eyes processed. The pieces weren't randomly strewn at all. They'd been laid out in precise arrangement, an undeniable shape.

"Hell." Ren's whisper barely held any noise, and she sidled closer to him.

Just as meticulously as Ren had removed the parquet and organized the remnants, someone had taken all the wood and formed them into a specific image.

Of a giant spider.

* * * *

At Ren's insistence, Leo had defied the need to take up his sword and search the entire premises, no matter that they weren't in a horror movie and no spirits haunted Granton Hall. If she asked him to avoid being the victim who searched for the psychopathic killer alone, he'd acquiesce.

For her.

He raked his fingers through his hair and paced the length of the porch while Ren leaned against the railing, her gaze on the woods beyond. They'd stowed Sir and all his necessities in his bedroom and waited for the authorities to show up. He should be doing something productive, not waiting for a rescue. Some jerkhole had not only broken into Granton Hall and set their work back a day, but also dared to scare the bejuju out of them with the damn spider image.

Flashing blue and red lights reflected on the windows and a Graywood police car pulled into the driveway. Katerina Hellman, the newest member of the local force climbed from the car, her eyes narrowed, already assessing her surroundings with sharp scrutiny.

Tall and slender in an athletic way, Katerina strode up the walk with the fierce confidence of a champion gladiator stepping into the arena. He immediately liked her. With a light saber in her hands, she might offer some hefty competition.

"Kat!" Ren brushed past him to meet Officer Hellman at the bottom of the porch steps. "I thought you were on school resource officer duty."

"Still am. School's out for the day and another officer left for a larger agency, so the chief asked me to fill the position. I can handle both. There's not a lot of crime in Graywood." She flicked a dark glance at Leo. "Usually."

"How's Roman? Vicki?"

Katerina's stern expression softened, making her appear younger, more carefree. "Great. Roman's got Vick in the cadet program now. They make a terrifying team. They gang up on me at card games." She glowered. "Cheaters. So what's this about a break-in?"

Ren swiped her bangs from her eyes. The flashing lights gave her hair an otherworldly sheen, bright and bloody. "While we were out, something pulled up the floor in the ballroom and arranged all the pieces into the shape of a spider."

"Something?" Katerina's eyebrows lifted.

Both sensible and skeptical. Leo liked her even more.

Nodding, Ren pivoted and led Kat up the porch steps. "We'll show you."

The stairs groaned and sagged beneath their combined weight. Kat leaped to the safety of the porch. "You should repair those steps before someone falls through and sues you."

"They're on the long, long list of repairs to get to." Ren shrugged.

Kat frowned down at the half-rotten wooden planks. "Might want to bump it up to the top of that list."

"I intend to put up caution tape tomorrow morning." Leo extended his hand. "Leo Hughes." Kat's handshake was as firm as he expected. "We had an intruder. I would have searched for him or her —"

"Or it," Ren said, solemn.

"But I didn't want to endanger Ren by leaving her alone."

"Or yourself." Katerina arched an eyebrow and pinned him with a stern look. "A civilian searching for a perpetrator alone after a criminal act is not advised."

Ren choked on a laugh and pretended to clear her throat.

Maybe his first impression of Officer Hellman had been too hasty. He sniffed. "I have a sword."

She gave him a flat stare. "I'm sure you do."

He held her gaze, unflinching, one warrior unyielding before another. His brothers spoke the same language — surrender once was ground forever lost.

"Come on." Ren waved her through the door. "You have to see it for yourself."

If Katerina was surprised by the giant chandelier lying dead in the vestibule, the scarred corridors and floors or what awaited in the ballroom, she didn't show it. With all the lights on and setting the entire space ablaze, the wreckage seemed sharper, more real. She circled the ruined section of floor and pattern created from its rescued wood.

"Any idea who would do this?" she asked, clicking pictures with her phone.

"Oliver Hunter." Leo didn't hesitate.

"Elizabeth Granton," Ren said at the same time. She met Leo's frown with one of her own. "Why would Oliver do this?"

"I can't answer that, but no one else knew about the spider's nest or the bone." He folded his arms over his chest. "It's too much of a coincidence."

"Bone?" Kat turned, her dark eyes alight with new interest.

"An animal bone, sadly." Ren crouched near the damaged floor and shone her cell phone light at where the spider's nest had been. "We found it in there when I removed the flooring. The spider escaped." Her slender shoulders shuddered. "It was monster-sized."

"Then again, Oliver is the one who claimed the bone belonged to a possum." For the first time, he wondered if the bone had belonged to an animal — or a species closer to home. But he couldn't think of a reason why Oliver would lie about it, sabotage Ren's efforts or leave a warning spider sign when it would all point to him.

"Who's Oliver?" Kat held a small notebook and pen, going old school with her investigation, another point in her favor to counter her earlier challenge of his manhood and skills.

"The innocent-until-proven-guilty gardener." Ren flashed him an annoyed look. "If we had to point fingers at a human, I'd aim all ten at Cooper."

"And Cooper is?" Kat asked, without looking up from scribbling her notes.

"Harlan Cooper of Cooper Homes, my heaviest competition in the construction bid for renovating the new city hall. But she wouldn't do anything like this." He shook his head. "She isn't that desperate...or stupid."

"Why are you sticking up for her?" Ren planted a hand on her cocked hip, her lovely mouth pressed in a thin line. "She'd do something like this to get your attention. Even better if it helped her win."

"I might agree with you except that Cooper didn't know about the spider. She wouldn't risk being cut from the competition" — he let a trace of his lazy smile free — "no matter how delicious I may be."

Ren narrowed her eyes at him. "Hmm."

Kat looked between him and Ren, her eyebrows raised. "And where were you two when this happened? Specific time frame."

"We went to a corner of the property to inspect an old building about an hour ago." Leo figured Kat wouldn't care about the reason behind the inspection.

"At night?"

"We took a lantern" — Ren lifted her chin, defensive — "and a chisel."

"With less than a month to complete the ballroom, every hour of daylight is spent working," Leo added. "All the doors were locked and closed when we left. I always secure the premises."

Kat nodded her approval. "I'll check for any points of entry before I leave." She tucked her phone in the side pocket of her duty pants. "It's good you didn't investigate on your own." She gave him a disdainful glance. "A civilian's interference almost always ruins evidence."

He assumed his war face. And he had just been starting to like her again.

"You're not going to find anything. It was Elizabeth Granton's ghost, making her presence known." Ren fumbled in her coat pocket and lifted the spider key. "I found this key in the spider's nest. Coincidence?" She sniffed. "I think not."

"May I?" Kat held out her hand, and Ren passed her the key. She frowned as she turned it over. "Looks old." Her gaze flicked to the formation on the floor and back to the key. "Interesting. You found it beneath the floor?"

"In the floor." Ren waved at the arranged parquet blocks as Kat took a photo of the key. "If you're okay with me messing with evidence, I can find the piece I found it in. It was hollowed out, as if someone meant to use it as a hiding spot. Or do you need to dust for fingerprints?"

Katerina snorted and handed the key back to Ren. "You watch too many crime shows."

"Horror, actually," Leo added.

"Even worse."

He nodded, his opinion of Kat readjusted once more to positive.

"The odds of lifting a fingerprint are minimal, and with a mere break-in and prank, not worth the expense."

"I doubt ghosts have fingerprints, anyway." Ren smiled sweetly.

Kat snapped her notebook shut. "Mr. Hughes, with your permission, I'll search the premises. There's not much I can do after the fact other than document the crime." She lifted her gaze to the heights of the ballroom, the balcony, rows of windows and wide doors leading out to the gardens. "You might consider a security system. Such a large house and surrounding acreage make it difficult to keep a determined intruder out."

Leo nodded. A security system was already on his long, long list of improvements. While he hoped Kat might find some evidence besides the destruction in the ballroom, he hadn't noticed any signs of missing items or other mischief. This was a personal attack, plain and simple. But against him? Or Ren?

"Do you intend to interview Oliver Hunter?" He held Katerina's narrowed gaze, not backing down from her death stare.

"My investigations are always thorough, Mr. Hughes." She looked down her nose at him with the dignity of a queen offended by the presence of odious riffraff.

"Never doubted it."

"I'll grab his business card from the kitchen. I'm sure he has nothing to hide." With a meaningful glance his way, Karen marched up the ballroom stairs.

Apparently, tonight was for inadvertently offending the female population. He should escape to his room with Sir Snugglebottom, who appreciated every word out of his mouth—as long as scritches were happening.

After Ren had slipped around the corner, Kat turned back to him. "What's your take on the ghost theory?"

"Ren loves any hint of the supernatural. If there's a creep factor, she'll find it." He turned his attention to the spider image on the floor, hesitating. He had to back up Ren, even if he hated the subject. "I'm not one to entertain woo-woo for the unexplained, but there have been some…strange happenings."

"Such as?"

Dammit. He hadn't wanted to go into detail. "Lights blinking on and off when the wiring is fine. The chandelier falling for no apparent reason. Music that has no definite source."

"You did know it's haunted before buying it, didn't you?" Her radio buzzed, static and broken. "Even I knew that, and I'm not from Graywood." She hooked a thumb over her shoulder. "There's an old asylum down the road, if you're wanting to increase your haunted property portfolio."

"Appreciate the suggestion." He managed to keep his tone civil. "Buying Granton nearly tapped me out. The renovations will take what's left."

Her eyes narrowed. "So you *need* the city hall contract?"

"'Need' is a strong word." He gave her a cool look, his turn to be offended. "If you're suggesting I'm sabotaging myself for financial gain or sympathy points in the competition, I would never do that. If I fall, I take the breaks and bruises, no complaints. But I won't stand for someone destroying Ren's hard work. If you don't find who did this, I promise I will."

"So, you're saying you don't suspect a ghost committed this criminal activity?" Her mouth twitched in the merest hint at a smile.

He scowled. "Is that all, Officer Hellman?"

"For now." Her dark eyes glittered. "I'll take a look around before leaving. Don't investigate on your own. I'll find the culprit. You focus on installing a security system." She tucked her notepad and pen into her back pocket. As she strode away, she called over her shoulder, "And fix your damn front stairs before someone breaks their neck and sticks around to haunt you."

Leo pinched his nose and waited until the rapid clop of her boots faded away. All he'd wanted was a month filled with Ren, the joy of bringing out Granton's beauty and ending with the love of his life as his, a charity to call his own.

He looked back at the image created by Ren's damaged floor. Alone in the ballroom, with night closing in on all sides, it wasn't hard to imagine someone watching him from the dark.

As he turned his back on the wall of windows and crossed the floor, the hair on his nape prickled. He switched the lights off and secured the doors. In the sudden gloom, it seemed the shadows stirred among the parquetry, phantoms dancing, barely seen.

Chapter Nineteen

By the time Kat—aka Officer Hellman—had inspected Granton Hall and the outlying premises to her satisfaction, Karen couldn't stop yawning. Leo insisted upon making his own determination that the property was empty of any spider-building-block maniacs, so she waited on the couch, snuggled with Sir, Leo's sword handy in case she needed it.

She didn't know why he bothered. Unless Elizabeth decided to show herself, he wouldn't find any clues, and steel wouldn't stop a ghost. Eventually, she drifted off to sleep, a kitten's happy purr lulling her into oblivion.

"Coast is clear."

At Leo's voice close to her ear, Karen sat up with a gasp, almost conking him in the nose with her head. Only his fast reflexes saved him. She held a hand over her pattering heart. "Why would you do that?"

"Revenge." He gazed down at her, his eyes twinkling like stars, as Sir stretched and jumped onto the back of the couch to get closer to his true love.

"I can't even argue that." She grabbed his outstretched hand and let him pull her up. "No eerie groaning or rattling chains out there?"

"Not even a whisper." His expression darkened. "Or any other sign of mischief. I have an endless list of questions and suspicions."

"Me, too." She stifled another yawn. "Which I'll address tomorrow."

"Tomorrow." He guided her toward the vestibule, around the chandelier to the stairwell beyond. Sir followed him, a tiny black shadow dancing on his heels. "Every door, window and any potential points of entrance are either locked, blocked or booby-trapped."

"Booby-trapped. I heartily approve." She doubted the traps Leo set were aimed at ghosts. Why would anyone arrange her precious parquet pieces into a spider? The list of human suspects was tiny, and Leo was right—Oliver alone knew about the spider. He could have told someone else he'd met in Graywood, maybe Cooper or Jed. Cooper had motive. Jed didn't. Unless…

Halfway up the stairs, she grabbed Leo by the arm, pulling him to a stop. "What if the parquet mystery was a ploy, an excuse for the secret judge to make an appearance without tipping us off? Do you think Kat could be the secret judge?"

"No." He continued up the steps. "Sabotage isn't part of the competition, and none of the sponsors possess your capacity for imaginative schemes." He paused at the landing. "My bet is on the lumber delivery guy. He insisted on helping me take all the supplies to the ballroom instead of dropping it off outside. Quite suspicious."

"Quite boring, you mean." She sniffed.

"Ren, are you sure you're okay?" He stepped closer and ran his hands down her shoulders to her arms, awakening tingles. "I'll stand guard outside your room, if it helps you sleep better." His eyes darkened, and heat swirled low in her belly. "Or stay with you, if you promise to behave yourself."

"Quite boring," she repeated with a grin.

"Get some sleep, Ren."

As he turned for his own bedroom, she grabbed his hand and pulled him close, unable to deny a shiver of heat as his hard, lean body brushed hers. "I have a question."

"Hmm?"

"Why would you go anywhere with me from country fairs to indie band concerts, knitting lessons at the senior center or the haunted corn maze to be gloriously terrified, but not Seven Devils? And don't blame your sword practice, because you've stood up your brothers for me before on a Saturday."

"Good to know uncomfortable subjects are on the table now." He brushed her bangs from her forehead with his free hand. "I couldn't bear watching you ditch me for another man again." He released a long breath, and his blue eyes turned fierce, a contrast to the smooth lull of his voice. "Do you know the hell I've gone through the last two years?"

Her chest squeezed. She'd walked out on him, not realizing she'd hurt him. All this time, rather than putting pressure on their friendship, he'd stayed away, while she'd been trying to squash the desperate wanting he brought to life in her.

"You know what I think, Ren, darling?" He didn't give her a chance to respond. "I think you go to Seven Devils on Saturday nights to find a guy you have no problem walking away from, a man who holds no power to affect you or get under your skin, nothing more than a speed bump beneath your tires, easily forgotten."

Karen's back hit the wall, startling her. Trapped in his furious gaze, caught off guard by his vehemence, she hadn't even realized she'd taken a step backward. *Uh-oh.* His war face was on at full level. She'd set him off. The thrill coursing through her was of excitement, not the alarm it should be.

Leo planted his palms against the wall on either side of her shoulders and leaned down so they were eye level.

"You crush on guys like Ian O'Connor because you know men like him will never give you what you need." His heat curled around her, possessive, sinking into her skin and staking a claim. "What you're afraid to admit you need."

"Space?" she asked, trying for humor.

His expression darkened even more. "You want someone who won't ever let you go, someone who will never give up on you or let you down. Someone who will accept you unconditionally and love you eternally."

Her breath came faster. Of course, she wanted that. Who didn't? But to hear him say it and apply it to her felt as if he'd bared her soul without permission.

"It's easy to dream." His voice remained calm, ruthlessly sincere. "Dreams are safe and have no power to hurt you, but how long do you want to remain stagnant, trapped by the past?"

Annoyance flared, quick and hot. She hadn't asked for his opinion on her avoidance issues. "So I'm a stubborn unrealist *and* stagnant?" Karen poked him in the chest with one finger. He didn't budge, the brute. "At least I don't waste my Saturday nights playing knights in armor with sabers."

Faster than she could blink, he grabbed her wrist and trapped it above her head. His eyes flashed, lightning in a stormy sky. "Do you know why I spend my Saturday nights beating back my brothers with swords?"

"Because you have a sick need to be the best." She made a half-hearted effort to free herself, her heart dancing fast. He was too near, sucking the air from her lungs, his body heat a furnace blast. "And you accuse me of being a dreamer. At least I'm not stuck in the Middle Ages, wishing I was born in another time."

Leo bared his teeth in a scary smile. "Says the Goth girl who's always searching for the merest hint of magic in a mundane world because she's so afraid that this disappointing life might be all there is."

She notched her chin. "I'm not ashamed of that."

"Never said you should be," he snarled. *Snarled*, as if he was truly angry. Leo had never been angry at her. "Swords and the physical toll of practicing battle are the only way I can get any semblance of peace on Saturday nights. Letting my brothers drive me into the ground until I'm too exhausted to think, because if I have the energy to think too much, I'll go insane — wondering who you're with, what you might be doing, when all I long to do is be with you."

A flash of vulnerability softened his expression, sharp enough to pierce her heart and deflate her ire. While she'd been out, distracting herself however she could, confining herself to fantasies, he'd been giving her freedom while he suffered in silence. It was too much. *He* was too much.

With a force close to violence, Karen wrapped her free arm around his neck. She jerked him to her and kissed him as if she might imprint him over her scarred heart if she could get close enough.

Leo groaned into her mouth and pressed the full length of his lean body against her, crushing her between the wall and his strength. She didn't care anymore about blending fantasies with reality, blurring the boundaries between friendship and romance. All she wanted was him sealed around her, infusing the cold spot inside her with his undying warmth.

He slipped his fingers under the hem of her sweater. The calluses on his fingertips caused a delicious friction on her skin as his touch drifted up her ribs and the edge of her bra, driving her crazy with the slowness.

Needing more, she fumbled beneath his T-shirt and laid her hand on his hot skin. The contact sent a zing through her nerve endings, and she dug her fingernails into his back. Smooth skin layered over muscle — she couldn't get enough…needed more.

"Off," she commanded, pushing his shirt up to his shoulders.

Without missing a beat or releasing her from the wall, he pulled his shirt off, tossed it over his shoulder and resumed kissing her, hot, mind-blowing kisses that made her forget her own name. But she always remembered his. *Leo, Leo, Leo.*

How have I lived so long without this? She twined her fingers in his hair and held on for dear life. Never had a kiss consumed her this way, reached through every inch of her body to brush her soul, a deep magic of its own. With each glide of his hot, silken tongue, each nibble of his soft lips, each scrape of his callused fingertips on her sensitive skin, the yearning that she'd tried so hard to deny branded another acre of her heart.

Leo kissed her with gentle savagery, a demand that she admit the passion burning between them. He buried his hands in her hair and tilted her head back, deepening the kiss, and when he pressed his hips against her, there was no denying his arousal. Every sense growled with pleasure, and desire shuddered through her with such force that she moaned.

As if triggered by the sound, Leo quieted. He caressed her face with a trembling hand and cradled her jaw, tender. He broke from her mouth and brushed light kisses over her nose, her eyelids and forehead.

"I'm not like Ian O'Connor." He nuzzled her ear, his stubble a delicious scrape on her neck. "I'm not like any guy you'd meet at Seven Devils."

"I know," she gasped, sucking much-needed air. "I've always known that."

"Good. So we're on the same page." He turned away, leaving her panting and wilted against the wall.

"Where are you going?"

"To bed...alone."

She managed to straighten, still needing the wall for support. "What the hell, Leo?"

He stooped and picked up his shirt from the floor. "I'm not willing to be friends with benefits." Pausing, he released a shaky breath. "I know what it's like to be afraid of losing someone. Before Mom married Palmer, there were times I waited in the car alone, terrified, sometimes for hours, praying she'd come back for me."

Karen swallowed hard. It was difficult to reconcile that image of a homeless boy with the strong, competent man standing within reach.

"I get the fear, but I refuse to mold my life around it or accept less to avoid the possibility of being hurt." His eyes bored into hers, a fierce, electric blue. "I don't want only your friendship. I want all of you. Neither one of us should settle for less than we deserve. And, Ren, whether or not you believe it, you deserve it all, too."

Stunned speechless, she watched him stroll to his bedroom, the muscles in his back on full, tempting display.

Leo paused at the doorway and looked at her. "When you decide you're all in, let me know. Until then, I'll be waiting."

The door shut behind him without a sound, leaving her hot, bothered and alone in the silent, watchful darkness.

Chapter Twenty

The air smelled like cloves and tobacco again. Carrying two planks of lumber on his shoulder, Leo paused outside the ballroom and inhaled. *So strange.* Ever since the spider incident a week before, he'd swear someone smoked a pipe in various rooms of Granton Hall. He caught a lingering whiff of it every morning in the kitchen while making breakfast for Ren, as if he'd narrowly missed a visitor.

Every so often, both he and Ren smelled it in the ballroom, close to the dead grandfather clock on the landing. But there was never any evidence of ash, leaves or even a wisp of smoke. Ren wasn't shy about her thoughts on the matter, that some phantom made itself known. He preferred to keep Granton Hall open only to the living.

He stepped through the open ballroom doors and stopped, his body tightening at the scene before him. Ren lay on her stomach near the area of damaged floor, a pencil in her hand, graph paper spread before her and dozens of pieces of various wood types scattered around her. Her feet were in the air, ankles crossed, and every so often one of her ankle boots absently flexed, back and forth. She frowned as she crafted lines and made notes in the margins, so engrossed in her calculations that she didn't seem to notice him.

He set his burden down as quietly as he could, never taking his gaze from her. Good lord, she inspired his imagination in wicked ways. Her T-shirt had ridden up, revealing a tempting inch of pale skin at her lower back. He wanted to crawl to her and lick the dip of her spine to discover if she was sensitive there. Lying prone accentuated the delectable curves of her hips and ass, and his fingers twitched with the urge to touch, squeeze and hold on tight. His fingers weren't the only appendages responding.

More than her body had his blood humming. The way she focused, measuring sections, graphing sizes and shapes to fit the puzzle pieces in perfect order? *Irresistible. Provocative.* She had no idea what her nerdy side did to him.

Two years he'd known her, and each day he wanted her more. He'd made it very clear where he stood, that he wanted all of her and refused to warm her bed if she couldn't commit. That had been a full week ago.

He'd taken a card from her deck and played it cool this last week, pretended he didn't want to drag her into his arms at every second — pretended he could forget the way her mouth moved sweetly beneath his, pretended his every moment wasn't colored by the memory of her elegant hands in his hair, on his body, driving him mad with need.

He still wasn't sure how he'd found the strength to walk away from her. The motive was strong enough, sincere enough. He'd meant every word, that they both deserved a love that could withstand any fear, that he wouldn't settle for anything less than her entire heart. A dozen cold showers hadn't doused the fire still torching his veins.

And since Ren stubbornly hedged, he took it upon himself to remind her what she was missing at every opportunity. Even though October's chill laced the halls, it wasn't his fault that construction worked up a sweat or that he used every occasion possible to lose his shirt. He doubted he'd ever get tired of how she bit her lower lip every time he showed up half-naked or how her breath caught when he leaned near to whisper in her ear for even the most mundane question.

With her, being the flirt was damn fun. He took every chance to torment her, but if she refused to shift the boundaries of their relationship soon, he might not make it out alive. But he had no intention of letting her know that particular truth.

Keeping his steps quiet, he padded toward her. Not once did she look up from her sketches, even when he loomed over her and studied her neat handwriting and diagram. She'd sketched the parquet design, shading the various species of wood, noting details in the margins.

Leo dove to the floor on his stomach beside her, and the pencil flew from her hand.

"Dammit!" Gasping, she glared at him. "Are you trying to scare me?"

"Ren, darling." He gave her an innocent look and retrieved her pencil. "Scaring people is *your* gig, not mine." He scooted close to her, his arm touching hers. "We barely have two weeks before the final judging.

While I appreciate perfectionism, finishing the project requires action."

So near, her mint shampoo infused the air, and it took an ungodly amount of control not to pull her on top of him and kiss her senseless.

"Don't rush me, Hughes." She jabbed her pencil at him. "This floor is going to be exceptional, even if I have to spend the rest of my two weeks working on it. Besides, you still won't let me near any of your precious saws. I have dozens of pieces to cut and sand. If you teach me how to use the saw, you won't have to waste time doing it."

He leaned near her ear and said in a low voice, "You're not getting anywhere near my jigsaw."

Ren swallowed but didn't move away. Her gaze drifted to his mouth and jerked back to his eyes. "How am I supposed to convince Cooper that I'm worth my construction salt if I can't even use a saw?"

"I'll let you watch." He gave her a slow, lazy smile, anticipating where her thoughts would stray.

"You're not playing fair." She jabbed him in the shoulder with the pencil eraser before slipping it behind her ear. He supposed he should be thankful she didn't use the pointy end. "You don't want to be just friends. You don't even want to be friends with benefits."

"True. I want it all—friendship, your heart and all the benefits that go with it."

"Friends don't torture friends."

"Don't they?" He focused on her raspberry-stained mouth. "You know how to end it." He leaned near, a mere breath between them. "Say you're mine...all of you. Say you want me...all of me."

Her expression was pained. "Making our relationship official is a death wish. I don't —"

He cut her off with a brush of her lips with his, sweet friction, the barest of kisses. When she moaned and reached for him, he jumped to his feet.

"Give me the specs. I'll let you watch me use the saw." He stripped off his shirt and tossed it over his shoulder. "Why is it so unbearably hot in here? I should check the heating system." With a wink, he sauntered away.

"I hate you, Hughes."

He chuckled. "Love you, too, Ren."

* * * *

Karen yawned for the zillionth time that morning and rubbed her tired eyes. Working was useless. Her brain was fried from restless nights and her body ached in frustration. Leo was playing her hard, and every day she slid closer to the breaking point of surrender.

If the man had been anyone other than Leo, she wouldn't hesitate to try him out, say it didn't work later and call it quits — no refunds, no returns. But she couldn't do that to him, and she couldn't let him go. She abandoned her desk and headed for the breakroom. If she didn't get another coffee, she might hurt someone.

The thought of coffee brought her right back to this morning as she'd left for work. Leo always had breakfast ready and waiting with her favorite coffee to go. This particular morning, as she'd stepped out of her bedroom, he'd strolled down the hallway with nothing on but his black workout pants, his hair wet from a shower, droplets of water glistening on his delectable, bare chest.

He'd smirked a greeting as he passed by, casually brushing her hand, and all she could do was stare. *The sneaky bastard.*

"Karen!" Gia's sunshine voice carried through the building. "Wait up!"

The drill of hurrying stilettos on thick rug heralded Gia's appearance. She whipped around the corner, her pearls crooked on her neck, white against her robin-egg-blue cardigan. Her smile brightened as her gaze landed on Karen.

"Miss me, G?" Karen grinned. For the first time in weeks, seeing her best work friend didn't inspire the urge to slink away.

"Of course, I've missed you." Gia flung her arms around her and squeezed as Karen winced. "The number of office pranks has dropped to a horrifyingly low level with you gone." She eased back and studied Karen's face. "But I have to say, working part-time with Leo Hughes on the side looks good on you."

Her face heated, killing any attempt to play it cool before she even tried. *Damn red hair and vampire skin.* That didn't mean she couldn't deflect.

"Granton Hall is a Gothic girl's dream come true—an iron chandelier that fell for no apparent reason, a conservatory with awesome-creepy statues and an unnatural chill, an old, abandoned cottage in the woods with hidey-holes in the wall." She left out the bone and the spider since it was still under investigation. "Parts of it are too dangerous from disrepair to explore, so I haven't seen it all." She grinned wickedly. "Yet."

"I plan to see it in person after Hughes & Sons Construction wins." Gia looped her arm through hers and towed her toward the break room. "You heading for coffee? I need more details about Granton and its new owner. Leo has such capable hands, doesn't he?"

Some battles were lost before they even started. "Yeah." She sighed, dreamy. "He really does."

"I knew it!" Gia pogo-sticked the rest of the way into the break room, which was thankfully empty. "I *knew* you two would get together."

"We're not *together*, just…" She trailed off, not ready to give the boundaries of her relationship with Leo a label. She hoped their friendship would be repairable when the renovation dust settled.

"Best friends with steamy benefits?" Gia pulled a mug from the cupboard and handed it to her.

"I'm trying my best to cool any steam, to keep it chill between us." She poured half a cup of coffee, leaving lots of room for the substances that made coffee drinkable, sugar and sweet caramel creamer. "He isn't making it easy, which is why I have to keep my focus on the finish line and what's important."

"What finish line? And what is more important than steamy times with Leo? Who are you and what have you done with my pal Karen, who never runs from a steamy situation?" Gia batted her eyelashes, a failed attempt to look innocent. "You can't tell me Leo doesn't make your blood sing, Kar. I'm head over heels for Ian, and I still have to look twice when Leo's around. He's the entire reason there's always an uptick of women walking into poles near any Hughes & Sons Construction site."

On her first sip, Karen choked at the image of a Tianna clone colliding with a lamppost, not watching where she walked while ogling Leo hard at work. Leo wouldn't even notice, and that was sexy as hell. She set the mug on the counter before she spilled sugared coffee all over her sweater.

"Having hot thoughts about Leo isn't the problem. It's the taming of them. First and foremost, he's my best friend. I shouldn't be having hot thoughts about him at all."

"Why not? Leo's the very epitome of hot male fantasy material."

"True. But chaining that side of him to my fantasies kept our friendship easy, uncomplicated. I love just being with him, hanging out. He gets me, and I can be myself with him, no apologies." She stared into her coffee, trying to find the right words without giving too much away. "He's pretty much perfect."

"And that's a problem?"

"For those of us who aren't even close to pretty much perfect? Yeah." She blew out a breath and met Gia's gaze. "I'm at Granton to help out my BFF and learn a bit of construction skills along the way, period. I refuse to be another bimbo who runs into a lamppost every time Leo Hughes smiles at me or looks at me like I'm his favorite holiday dessert."

"Mmm. So, we're talking fresh apple pie a la mode?"

"More like molten chocolate lava cake with hot caramel sauce that he wants to spend hours licking."

"Holy crap. *Stop*." Gia waved a hand near her face. "I'm overheating."

"Exactly. Focusing has been difficult with him purposely fueling my fantasies. I'll never admit it to Leo, but I'm enjoying what I've learned so far." She spread her hands and examined the blisters on her palms. "For the most part. If I can manage to keep my libido in check long enough for Leo to figure out we're better off as friends, I'll be frickin' ecstatic."

"Good luck with that, girl." Gia grinned and tapped their mugs together. "My vote is you ride that pony for all its worth and stay in the saddle until the last sunset. Leo's smart enough to know when he's found the woman who's pretty much perfect for him."

Karen sipped her coffee and hid her face in her mug until an unexpected burn of tears faded. *If only that were true.*

Chapter Twenty-One

After an afternoon on hands and knees arranging her measured parquet pieces, Karen stood and stretched her back. The sun had set hours ago, leaving darkness beyond the ballroom windows. The rhythmic pounding of Leo's hammer echoed from the hallway. He probably wasn't wearing a shirt, the rat.

The last week had been a living fantasy hell. He'd given her the barest taste, knowing she'd get addicted and couldn't resist coming back for more. Now, he invaded every moment, both waking and sleeping — teasing her, tormenting her.

Over the last two years, he'd clearly saved up every one of his sexy moves and now shot them all at her in a barrage. She wasn't going to make it out alive. She wasn't sure she *wanted* to make it out alive. Leo made a future sound as simple as a first-grade math problem. One plus one equals two. He seemed to forget the possibility of subtraction and a sum total of zero.

Instead of surrendering to the urge to check if Leo wasn't wearing his shirt, she wandered to the grandfather clock on the landing. It hadn't worked since she'd been at Granton, but even beneath the layer of dust, its magnificent craftmanship lured her.

She cleaned a section of the woodwork with the hem of her already-dirty T-shirt. Carved vines and roses came to life, delicate and lifelike, so much that the rose stems included sharp-as-sin thorns. The structure towered at least a foot taller than Leo, and the head-sized clock face boasted slender silver arms molded into cruelly pointed daggers. *Awesome.* If a few random teardrop rubies to resemble blood had been added, the masterpiece would be absolute perfection.

She eased open the glass protecting the clock face. Her grandmother used to have an old, quirky clock that would make her jump every time it gonged the hour. It had needed a good wind every few days or it quit. Maybe this one required the same thing.

Three small winding points at even intervals set below the clock face, cleverly woven into the design of black, brocaded vines. She traced the dagger-shaped minute hand with a fingertip. While delicate in appearance, the silver metal didn't so much as bend beneath her touch.

Roses and vines wove into the dagger handle as well. In the center of the clock face, nestled in the circle between the numbers, lines indicated a tiny split door, like that of a cuckoo clock. What sort of creature would pop its head out at every hour in such a clock? With the fine craftmanship and attention to detail, it couldn't be anything so mundane as a squawking bird. *What a priceless piece of ancient art.* If she couldn't get the clock working, it would be tragic.

Her grandmother always kept a key with her clock so she wouldn't lose it, tucked on a corner ledge. Crouching, Karen searched for a winding key inside the cabinet. Dust and cobwebs—no spiders, thank God—draped the woodwork. The exquisite detail continued even within the cabinet. An entire forest had been carved into the wood, a three-dimensional scene of trees veined with vines and roses.

Silver glinted from the very bottom of the cabinet beneath the hanging weights and pendulums, a small winding key. She picked it up and straightened. The key fit into the first winding point. She cranked the key clockwise until it stopped—thirteen times. Same for the second, then the third. Holding her breath, she adjusted the minute hand until it pointed to the correct time—eight fifty-nine.

As if by magic, a steady tick-tick-tick came from deep within, and Karen bounced on her feet, too excited to keep still. "Leo! I fixed the clock!"

The hammering in the corridor ceased, and his soft footfalls joined the rhythmic clicking of new time. He appeared between the open ballroom doors as the minute hand moved to straight up nine.

A deep, tolling gong struck the hour, resonating through the ballroom like a sonic boom, and Leo halted, his eyes wide. The sound rolled, filling every space and corner in a series of nine. As the last gong faded, the miniature doors in the clock clicked and parted like window shutters after a long, cold winter.

Karen caught her breath. A quick, classical tune cut through the lingering echoes of the tolling bells, sounding small and innocent after the thunder. An underlying mechanical whirr heralded a plank emerging through the doors. One by one, nine miniature skeletons bearing rose-entwined daggers slid out of the clock, spinning in time to the tune.

"Turn it off," Leo choked from his stalled position at the ballroom doorway. His face had turned paper-pale, and he grasped the doorjamb in a white-knuckled hold. "Make it stop."

Seeing him so off-kilter for no apparent reason fired a bolt of shock through her. Never, not even in the haunted house attractions she'd dragged him to, had he looked so lost, so terrified.

"Ren, *please*."

The brokenness in his voice shattered the ice of her trance. As skeletons twirled and danced to the song, she scrambled to shut off the noise. There didn't seem to be a music switch, so she grabbed the pendulum and held it still. The song and rhythmic ticking died. Skeletons froze mid-waltz. Only Leo's harsh breaths disrupted the sudden silence. His shoulders heaving, he dropped his head, hiding his face.

"Leo?" Karen didn't dare let go of the pendulum. "Are you okay?"

For a long moment, he didn't answer. He clung to the doorjamb as if it alone kept him upright. With everything in her, she wanted to go to him, wrap her arms around him and be his support beam, but that would require leaving the clock. Whatever had freaked him out—*truly* freaked him out—might resume and make matters worse.

She kept her voice soft. "Talk to me, Hughes."

He looked up, and the shadows in his gorgeous eyes twisted her heart. "I need a drink."

With that, he disappeared down the corridor.

Karen waited until his footfalls had faded before releasing the pendulum. The clock remained fixed on nine o'clock, the pendulum unmoving. The nine skeletons with their swords remained trapped in time, the doors to their tomb open, waiting for their return. Only the music could call them back.

She blew out a breath and wiped her shaking hands on her jeans. It had been the song that had sent Leo into an unexpected spiral. But why?

Securing the ballroom doors behind her to muffle any wayward musical clocks, she hunted Leo down. It wasn't hard. The library lights were on full blaze, creating a warm pool of light that stretched into the hallway. She paused in the entrance. Leo sat on the couch, contemplating the half-full glass of whiskey dangling in his fingers. He didn't look up as she entered.

Not saying anything, she eased the glass from his loose grip and set it on the end table. She settled onto his lap and slipped her arms around his neck. When he dropped his forehead onto her shoulder, wrapping his arms around her as if she alone was his anchor to sanity, she kissed his temple and held on tight.

"I hate that song," he mumbled against her shirt.

"Do you?" She ran her fingers through the hair at his nape in a slow, soothing rhythm. "I couldn't tell."

He huffed a strangled laugh and lifted his head from her shoulder. "With the burning force of a million hell fires."

"Not a classical music fan, then." She stroked his face and scraped her fingernails along the stubble of his jaw. "New, fun facts to learn about my Leo."

"*My Leo.*" A hint of his lopsided smile appeared, and he settled his hands on her waist. "I like it when you say that." He skimmed his thumbs beneath her sweater and stroked her bare skin.

"Distracting me won't work," she warned, even as her temperature rose. She fought the urge to melt into him, to take his mouth with hers and let him avoid what had happened in the ballroom for a few moments more.

"No?" He pressed a kiss to the sensitive spot on her throat, the one he'd discovered by tricking her, and she couldn't resist baring her neck to give him better access.

"Absolutely not." A moan slipped free, and she tangled her fingers in his hair, pulling his head back and looking him in the eyes instead of surrendering, not that it helped. His blue eyes flamed with need, need for *her*. Yeah, maybe he could distract her.

She closed her eyes, took a deep breath and pretended the hard press of his arousal beneath her butt wasn't there. Nope, no side mission this time. Whatever had made her strong, brave, fight-the-enemy Leo run couldn't wait.

"Business first." She booped his nose. "Treats after."

"Unfair. I give you dessert first whenever you ask."

"You're a better person than me." She shifted on his lap and planted her knees on either side of his hips, giving the illusion she trapped him. They both knew how easily he could regain control. If he wanted, she'd be flipped on her back, his heavy, delicious body pressing her into the couch cushions. Her face heated. *Back, fantasies. Not the time.*

She settled on his thighs and gave him her best Leo Hughes war face stare down. "What happened back there? And don't sugarcoat or minimize or I'll tickle you, no mercy."

"I might prefer the tickling." His mouth tightened.

Karen cupped his face and kissed him once, erasing the tension. "What memories are tied to that song to make you hate it so much?"

Leo leaned his head back and rested his hands on the outside of her thighs. He ran his thumb along the rip in her jeans, teasing her skin, more as a stall method than sexual diversion. His chest expanded on a big inhale, and he released the breath. "I need my drink."

She leaned over and grabbed his glass from the end table. Before she handed it to him, she took a sip. The liquid burned a trail down her throat and melted the icy ball in her stomach that had been there since the clock had struck nine.

Leo drained the rest of the glass and set it on the couch arm. "I was thirteen," he said in a low voice. "It was Halloween. A bunch of us decided a visit to the cemetery would be an epic place to take stock of our candy stash."

Usually, she'd agree with that assessment, but his slow, careful cadence kept her mouth shut. Whatever he was about to tell her had left a scar deep enough to make him freak fifteen years later.

"We'd dumped all our candy out on the grass between graves. A couple of my friends were grab-assing, trading treasures. Others were making scary faces with their flashlights and messing around." He shrugged. "You know, being stupid kids."

Karen twined her fingers with his in silent support.

He lifted her fingers to his mouth and kissed them. "I was sitting on a stone cross, a jawbreaker in my mouth, watching my friends being idiots when…" He squeezed his eyes shut and his big body trembled beneath her.

"I'm right here, Leo."

He opened his eyes. "Stay with me, Ren." He searched her face for some answer to a question she didn't know. "Don't ever go."

"I won't."

His shoulders relaxed a degree and he nodded. "As I sat there on that headstone, I was pushed in the chest, hard enough to make me fall backward. None of my friends could have done it. They were all right there in front of me, a dozen feet away. I landed on my back in the grass and choked on the jawbreaker. I rolled over, coughing, and spit the candy out." He paused and his mouth tightened. "When I got up, my friends were gone, their flashlights and laughter, all the candy. It was like they hadn't been there at all."

A shiver slid through her as he held her gaze. Shadows of his past flitted through the blue, dark and sharp. As much as the supernatural thrilled her, she couldn't let that excitement be at Leo's expense, not when his graveyard experience still haunted him. In silence, she waited for him to continue, making small circles with her thumb on the pulse at his wrist.

His powerful throat worked as he swallowed. "It was then, while alone in the darkness, that I heard it—*Danse Macabre*, echoing from deeper within the cemetery. It seemed to ricochet off the gravestones and made it impossible to determine which direction it came from. I knew it had to be my friends tricking me somehow, even though I couldn't explain how they had disappeared. But my rational brain refused to consider the alternative, and I wasn't about to let them know I was terrified."

"Oh no." Karen shook her head, all the horror movies she loved spinning through her head, and the too-stupid-to-live characters who always had to investigate the noise in the basement instead of run. "You didn't, did you?"

"I was an idiot. If I'd met you when I was thirteen, I would have known better."

"If I'd met you then, we probably wouldn't have been friends. I was a nerd."

"Was?" The corner of his mouth curled up. "Kindred spirits, Ren."

"So you headed toward the music." She needed him to finish the story, both for her own curiosity and so he could purge. Sharing fear with another made it easier to bear, to face and overcome. Sometimes, confessing it was enough.

"The song grew louder and louder until I couldn't hear my footsteps on the grass or my breathing. I called my friends by name, but if they answered, I never heard them." His voice strengthened, carrying his words faster. "There was this huge oak tree that separated from the gloom ahead. The music seemed to be coming from inside it. A light glowed from behind its trunk, but not like a flashlight, more of a...silver."

Karen kept her mouth shut, his cold hand in hers. All this time, Leo had a ghost story to share, so terrifying that he'd never told her. She couldn't press him about it, not tonight, anyway. Later, maybe weeks from now, maybe years when he could speak about it without shaking, she'd find out every detail.

"It had to be my friends. Even though my heart pounded so hard it threatened to tear out of my chest and my instincts told me to turn and run fast and far, I couldn't. And it wasn't due to my pride. I...*couldn't*. Some force pulled me forward to that light, in time with the music, and I couldn't resist." He released a shaky breath.

"Hold on." Karen slid off his lap, refilled his glass with the bottle of whiskey on the sideboard and handed it back to him.

"Thanks, darling." He gave her a grateful smile and took a sip. Then another, staring into the dead space of some decades-old memory.

She snuggled up beside him and tucked her feet under her. When she looped her arm through his, he blinked and looked at her, as if a spell had been broken. The rest of his story came out in a rush.

"The light wasn't my friends trying to trick me. When I peeked around the trunk, a man in a period costume sat there, his back against the tree. I saw straight *through* him. He held a music box in his hands, the source of the tune. He sat still, staring at the box as the music played for what seemed hours. Then he looked up at me, as if he'd chosen that moment to reveal he'd known I'd been watching him all that time. His eyes weren't human. They were nothing but a black, endless void."

Icy fingers tapped down her spine, and she shivered.

"When I looked into his eyes, an overwhelming sense of despair and loneliness hit me. I was alone in the darkness, without friends or family. No one would come for me. I'd die there, forgotten."

Holy crap.

"The terror must have been enough to snap me out of whatever held me there," Leo continued, his voice rough and raw. "I didn't stop running until I reached the cemetery fence and vaulted over it. My friends were in the parking lot. They'd been looking for me. I didn't wait for them. I ran all the way home and locked myself in my room. I never breathed a word about it, too afraid that *thing* might hear and follow me. And that's why I can't bear that song."

"Hell," she murmured, her throat dry. All this time, she'd believed his fear of Halloween was rooted in childhood fireside tales, easily overcome by Leo's rationality and no-nonsense practicality. He was truly frightened of what hid in the dark—and had indulged her anyway.

"I picked up sword fighting and weightlifting the next day. I needed an enemy of flesh and blood, solid and real, one I could defeat. Weapons and weights kept me sane, and I started paying a lot more attention in church." A ghost of a smile flickered on his mouth. "I decided the way to deal was to never say a word about it and pray to God nothing similar ever happened again."

Karen blew out a long breath. "Wowza."

"I haven't told anyone about that night, not even Liam." He pulled her back onto his lap and buried his face in her hair. "You're the only one who knows."

The fact that he trusted her with such a powerful, perspective-altering, life-warping memory made her heart squeeze. Some secrets were sacred, too deeply rooted to the heart, meant to be kept safe. Joking about it would be a betrayal.

She slipped her arms around his neck and kissed his ear. "That explains so much, and I get it. Fear comes in all shapes and sizes and has the ability to immobilize even the bravest, strongest, sword-swinging badass."

"Even you?" He brushed her bangs back, such naked vulnerability in his eyes that she couldn't play it cool.

"It's not ghosts that claw beneath my skin and trigger my inner-bunny."

"Spiders?" he guessed.

She shook her head, tried to smile. Her throat felt swollen, battling the words she didn't want to confess, not to anyone, certainly not to him. Her opinion of him remained diamond-solid. Nothing he did or said could ever change her love for him. That might not be true from his end, but her best friend had shared his darkest childhood secret. She couldn't let him hang suspended in that void alone.

"You okay?" he murmured.

She took his face between her hands. "How can you ask me that after what you just told me, Leo? You kill me sometimes."

"The proper term, I believe, is 'slay'."

Her heart ached. How could she not love this man when he shoved his pain and deep-seated fear behind him the very second she showed a smidge of emotion and dedicated himself to making her smile? How was she ever to get through the rest of this month wrapped up in him with the cage protecting her heart intact? It would be rough, but she could handle losing his touch, the hot kisses, the way he brought her body to full life. She *could* lose all those parts of him and still survive. But it was this sweet, fun, devoted best friend in the form of the sexiest man on the planet who she'd stumbled into at a hardware shop that she couldn't do without.

"I'm terrified that you'll get over me," she said in a small voice.

He went still and watched her in the way that skipped right through flesh and bones and went straight into the soul.

She had to look away, unable to stand the thought that he saw into her core, all the flaws and failures, all the reasons why he shouldn't ever settle, even temporarily, for less than he deserved. He deserved a sweet, nice girl to be the perfect wife and mother to a tribe of kids, a girl who wasn't fascinated by unexplained things that sparked a hope of magic in a mundane world and was more into action movies than horror.

"I'm afraid that I'll lose my best friend when you figure out that I don't live up to the hype, that I'm not really what you want and you need someone more suitable." She let her shoulders slump. There, she'd said it, let the ugliness out, no more secrets. Figuring he needed some quiet time to process, she made to stand up.

Before she shifted a single centimeter, Leo squeezed her hip with one strong hand, holding her in place. He lifted her chin with his knuckles, forcing her to meet his gaze.

His eyes were blue fire, sharp and blazing, all shadows of hair-raising cemetery tales gone. "Hello. I'm Leopold Hughes. I believe we've met before, but you seem to have forgotten who I am, so let's discuss our past, shall we?" He didn't give her time to respond. "Name one time I've hurt you, made you cry or feel anything less than important to me."

"Never," she muttered.

"If you would be so kind, please explain an incident in which I have caused you to distrust me. In detail, so we'll both be certain to recall it."

Her throat went dry at his formal speech, a simmering testament to his fury, all aimed at her.

Leo cocked an eyebrow, waiting for her answer, his hold on her hip unyielding. He wasn't letting her off the hook...again. *Dammit, anyway.*

Karen wracked her brain, hoping to find something, anything that might save her. Giving in now, admitting she had no reason not to trust him, meant there was no reason not to take their relationship further, deeper, past the point of no return.

"I trusted Hank, too." She hated the crack in her voice, how her hands trembled.

"I am *not* him." His tone remained furious, but his hand skimming up her ribs was gentle. "I will *never* be him, Ren."

"I know you're not." And dammit, she hated the tears burning her eyes. She blinked them away before they spilled. "But knowing that doesn't erase the fear."

"You're the one who said the way to conquer fear is to face it." Faster than she could squeak, he had her off his lap and standing, her hand gripped tight in his. He tugged her through the library and into the corridor, his drink left behind.

"Where are we going?"

He glanced at her without slowing. His war face gave him a fierce edge and shot a thrill straight into her gut. "To conquer our fears."

Chapter Twenty-Two

Leo focused on breathing slow and steady as he opened the ballroom doors and flung them wide before he reconsidered — no turning back, no running, not this time. If having Ren permanently in his life the way he wanted — friend, lover, forever — required listening to *Danse Macabre* until he could whistle it through his nose, he'd do it. And if he survived this with her at his side, witnessing his weakness firsthand, maybe she'd face her fear, too.

And entrust her heart to his safekeeping, where it belonged.

Her slender fingers curled around his hand as they stepped onto the ballroom landing, igniting every protective, alpha instinct. That she believed for even a moment he'd ever hurt her, stop loving her or walk away, fueled a combustible ball of emotions — frustration that she doubted him after all this time, determination to show her, once and for all, that he couldn't be compared to any other man, past, present or future and grief that she'd been wounded so badly that she reflected the past on the incomparable magic they had together.

"Did you growl at me?" Ren studied him, her green eyes wary.

"Maybe."

They stopped before the giant grandfather clock, and he was still enough of the cowardly teenager to admit that he was relieved it remained quiet, the hour hand stuck on nine, the miniature skeletons trapped in mid-dance. When it came to life this time, he'd be ready.

"Are you able to get it going again?" He ignored the gruffness in his voice and fixed his glare on the clock face, the skeletons and their knives in a half-circle as if preparing for a ritual. *You. Are. Going. Down.*

"Leo." She sighed. "You don't have to do this."

He growled again.

"Fine." Ren tugged on her hand, still caught tight in his. "A girl needs her paws."

He released his grip, and his fingers ached as blood rushed back in.

As she fiddled with the clock pendulum, he held his shoulders straight, his gaze steady. He wasn't a scrawny, stupid teenager anymore. No song or spirit would break him. His empty fingers twitched. He should have grabbed his sword along the way. It wouldn't do any good, but it would have made him feel better.

Whatever Ren did to the clock parts worked. A hidden mechanism inside clicked and the skeletons resumed their circling dance. The spine-tingling, music box notes of *Danse Macabre* resumed mid-chorus.

Leo concentrated on his breathing as the music swirled around him, calling, calling him back to that cemetery, to the darkness and those endless, dead eyes.

His heart pounded too fast, and no matter his intentions, he couldn't breathe, an invisible hand choking him.

The music played on and on, growing louder, more distorted. The lights in the ballroom dimmed until only the skeletons remained, dancing, dancing to the nightmare tune.

"Hughes." Ren stepped in front of him, filling his vision. Her rich, vibrant presence disrupted the darkness, and he clung to it with everything he had. "I'm right here. If a spirit shows up, I'll go all ghostbuster on it, okay?" Her voice was a lighthouse in the storm of music and memories. "But if an army of spiders rises from the flooring, it's all you."

The coiling fear inside him eased a knot, enough to separate the present from the past, and he took a gulping breath. He wasn't hiding by himself in a car for hours, waiting for his mother to return. He wasn't alone in some cemetery, lost and forgotten to die.

"Ren." He pulled her against his chest and held on to her like a life buoy. "If an army of spiders swarm, I may need my sword."

"There you are." She laughed into his shirt and slipped her arms around his waist. "Welcome back to the real world."

The music no longer sounded as if it filled the room like the thunder of a thousand dancing cloven hooves. Lively and quick, the last few notes curled through the air and ended on a quiet echo.

Leo released a shaky breath. "Again. Make it play again."

"Not necessary. You proved your point."

He gazed down at her. "You sure about that? Because I'm still feeling it, the terror of what might happen. There's no magic or overnight cure, but if given enough time, maybe my heart will understand what my head is saying — that hearing the song can't do anything to me."

Ren stepped away, averting her gaze, and he suspected she understood that he referred to her fear as much as his own. He'd thought two years of demonstrating his character would be enough, showing her he was there for the long haul, no matter what. If she needed a lifetime of demonstration, he was down with that as long as she stayed in his arms.

"You could play it on your phone over and over." She crossed her arms and turned toward the clock. "Hey, it jammed up again."

The minute hand remained on twelve, the hour hand on nine. The pendulum had stopped swinging, silencing the clock. All nine skeletons lined up on the platform in a half-circle, the doors to their tomb stuck open and waiting. Within the shadows of the doors, a dull, metallic gleam caught the chandelier lights.

"Something's in there." He pulled his phone from his pocket.

Ren squeezed his arm. "A spider?"

Maybe it was wrong that he enjoyed her clinging to him while he got to play the courageous warrior, but he couldn't deny a flash of masculine pride that she looked to him for protection — or that he was the brave one for the moment.

"Let's find out." He shone the light from his phone into the clock doorway.

"No. Way." Ren's words were hardly more than a breath, and he didn't have to ask why. It was, indeed, a spider. Past the ring of skeletons and deep inside the doors, etched into the back of the clock, the same arachnid emblem as on the key she'd discovered in the flooring stared back, as if waiting to be found. This spider, however, protected a lock between its fangs.

"Where do you keep the —"

"Right here." She pulled the spider key from her bra.

He gave her a sidelong look. "Hmm."

"What?" She sniffed. "It's too mysterious to lose, so I keep it close. If someone or some*thing* comes looking for it and wants to steal it, they'll have to pry it from my cold, dead fingers…or boobs."

"Too soon, Ren. I'm barely recovered from my brush with the supernatural over a decade ago."

She grinned, impish, showing off that irresistible dimple. "Lift me, Hughes." She bounced on her toes, her eyes bright. "Your hand is too big to fit in there. I'll have to do the honors."

Any chance to touch her, especially at her request, would never be denied. He stepped behind her and wrapped an arm around her waist, pulling her back in alignment with his body. The slight catch of her breath fanned the flames in his blood. He'd never get enough of her luscious curves pressing against him.

He lowered his mouth to her ear and whispered, "Ready?"

"In so many different ways."

He lifted her within reach of the open maw of the cuckoo doors. Maybe he held her tighter, closer than he needed to, but he wasn't one to waste an opportunity. She wiggled her butt against him.

"Don't be cheeky, Ren."

She huffed a laugh. "Too late."

The space inside the clock had been made to fit the hand of a woman or a child, far too small for a man's. Karen squeezed her slender fingers inside, filling up the entire doorway. Without the benefit of his cell phone light to guide her, she fumbled to fit the key into the lock.

She made a frustrated noise. "Lift me higher."

"As you command." In one easy move, he hefted her up. Her delighted shriek ricocheted to the ballroom rafters as he settled her on his shoulders, snug behind his head. With her shapely legs dangling on either side of him, her fingers in his hair, her heat on his neck, he fought the urge to take her upstairs and discover what hid within the clock later…much later.

"This is perfect." The purr in her voice suggested they were on the same train of thought. She leaned toward the clock, and her breasts pressed into his scalp. "A little closer."

Damn, if she got any closer, he might combust on the spot. Holding her knees, he took a half-step nearer. His elbow grazed the clock's smooth oak surface, and the skeletons were right at eye level. Every one of them faced him, as if watching with their black, empty sockets. He swallowed hard. It had to be a coincidence, the similarity of the skeletons to the cemetery nightmare.

"Got it, I think." Gripping his scalp with one hand, Ren wriggled against his neck, straining to fit the key into the lock. "There!"

A sharp click marked her success. Machinery whirred to life, and she jerked her hand free. At the same time, Leo stepped away from the clock, all his senses on alert. He kept a firm grip on her legs. Both his breath and Ren's sounded harsh amid the muted rasp of wheels and cogs rolling from deep inside the clog.

"I feel like I'm in the pages of a Gothic mystery novel," she whispered, an unhealthy amount of enthusiasm in her voice. Her fingers clutching his hair verged on painful.

It would have been marvelous if the previous owners of Granton had left a normal grandfather clock instead of a wicked half-working timepiece holding nightmares and secrets.

The clock face itself split in half and yawned open, tick by tick. Ren hunched over his head, straining for a closer look, while he had the urge to step back and keep moving until the entire city of Graywood separated him from the clock. If she didn't love it so much, he'd drag it into the back forty and burn every cog, wheel and pendulum to ash — or at least a puddle of brass that he could toss into the river or bury in a different country.

As the clock face finished opening like window shutters to the morning light, the mechanical whirring stopped. Shadows hid whatever lived inside.

"Put me down." Ren gripped his ears and swung one leg off his shoulder. He helped her slide down his back before she leaped off and hurt herself — or ripped his ear off in her excitement to get to the clock. The heat of her hands on his shoulders and hips as she climbed down seeped through his shirt, leaving imprints on his skin. Once on the floor, she gave his butt a playful pat before darting around him.

At least he wasn't entirely forgotten. He trailed her as she peered inside the clock cavity with her cell phone light.

"Holy crap." She jammed her phone into her back pocket then reached inside the clock.

"Ren, wait—" Before he pulled her out of harm's way, she'd already grabbed whatever had caught her interest and turned to him.

"Leo, look!" She dusted off a rectangular wooden box, secured with a lock. "What do you think is inside?"

"Haven't you read the story about Pandora's box? It's not too late to return it, pretend we never saw anything weird hidden within a clock that plays the *Dance of Death* and hides its secrets with spider keys."

"Oh, it's far too late to go back." She plopped onto the floor, cross-legged, the box perched on her knees, the spider key in her hand. "Wouldn't you wonder for the rest of your life what's inside?"

"I'm really, really good at *not* wondering," he muttered and sat beside her. He bent one knee up and used it as an elbow rest, nowhere near relaxed. "Do what you must."

"Already planned on it." She gave him a teasing smile that told him she wasn't kidding. She'd never culled her curiosity for his sake, dragging him into whatever viper nest she happened upon in her quest to find magic in a mundane world. It was just another quality that he loved. She flashed that adorable dimple and dazzled him right out of his comfort zone, no apology.

Ren never apologized for who she was, even when she harbored uncertainties. He hated that she ever doubted the woman she was might not be enough. All her flaws and interests, weaknesses and strengths made her exactly who she was supposed to be, and he'd do everything in his power to protect that precious combination.

"Watch out for arachnid nests and possum bones."

"Hilarious, Hughes." Ren slid the spider key into the lock of the wooden box. It fit, of course. She looked at him once, her eyebrows raised, and turned the key. The lock *snicked* open and she lifted the hinged top, a crack first, then wider.

Danse Macabre began, and a single skeleton matching the ones in the clock spun in time with the tune, his dagger lifted in salute. Ren wrapped her fingers around the figurine, holding it fast, and the tune died. She glanced at him, her eyes worried.

"I can take it, now that I know the source."

She nodded and released the skeleton, allowing the music to play as she peeked into the music box.

Leo leaned over her shoulder. A bundle of yellowed paper rested inside, tied together with a faded pink ribbon, and there was no question the material was some sort of linen, not the modern white paper found in stores. The top, folded note appeared brittle, as if it might crumble to dust if touched.

"Love letters," Ren breathed.

"How do you know?"

She lifted a lock of blonde hair tied by another pale pink, velvet ribbon. "Who else besides a mother or a lover would keep a hunk of someone else's hair?"

"That's...creepy. For the record, I like your hair right where it is on your head, and if I want to touch your hair, I prefer to do it while you're beside me." He gave her a lazy smile. "So I can touch other parts of you, too."

A flush stained her cheeks. "I think the idea is romantic, that you love someone so much that you need a part of them with you at all times."

"All you have to do is ask and I'll be there."

Her gaze dropped to his mouth and lingered there, doing witchy things to his pulse. She straightened, her eyes wide. "I bet these are letters documenting a secret affair. Why else would they be kept locked inside a clock, the key hidden in the floor? Why else would someone need strands of their lover's hair unless they couldn't be together?"

"Why not burn the letters after reading instead of hiding them? No evidence that way."

"And no romantic mementos to moon over while alone?" She shook her head at him, her mouth twisted in disappointment. "You need to read more Gothic romance. Part of the thrill of an illicit affair is the danger of being caught." She frowned at the letters. "Unless it wasn't about the excitement at all. Maybe it was for protection." Ren brushed her fingertip over the top note, testing the weakness of the paper. "We should read them."

Disturbing the past, unearthing personal secrets someone who once lived in Granton Hall wanted kept hidden sounded like a terrible idea. "For what purpose?"

"Curiosity?" She snorted. "Besides, don't you think all these pieces are entangled too tight to be pure coincidence? Your experience in the cemetery with the song, the one section of damaged flooring where the key happened to be, the clock and music box? There's no way it's not all connected."

His stomach clenched, and he somehow kept his voice even. "You're saying a spirit knew I'd buy Granton Hall over a dozen years in the future, that you'd be here with me, find the key and harass me into figuring out the mysteries?"

She grinned, temptingly mischievous. "Let's find out."

Chapter Twenty-Three

Back in the library, Karen perched on the couch beside Leo with the music box. Sir sniffed the treasure once, dismissed it and curled up on Leo's lap.

"Ready to do this?" She studied his face, the weariness around his eyes. Tonight had been hard for him, confessing dark secrets, revealing his weakness, dealing with his deepest fears. She should be easy on him. "Just one letter. We'll save the rest for tomorrow."

He sighed, his long fingers stroking Sir's silky black fur. "One, then I'm going to bed."

At the mention of bed, an image of him tangled in sheets, his hair mussed by her fingers took over her brain. "Alone?"

His eyes darkened. "That's up to you."

The low, sensual tone pooled hot in her belly, and she swallowed hard. *Right.* With Leo, it had to be all or nothing. She opened the music box.

Danse Macabre trilled as the skeleton spun. Karen lifted the stack of letters tied together by a faded pink ribbon. The matchbox hidden beneath them made her breath catch. "Hughes, check this out." She wiggled the matchbox under his nose. "Another pack of Lucifers."

He frowned. "Still don't like it."

Chilled air drifted from the corridor, carrying a faint whiff of pipe smoke and cloves. Ever since she'd brought back the tobacco pouch, pipe and matchbox they'd unearthed in Edwin's cottage, the scent of pipe smoke and cloves had randomly appeared. What were the odds of the same matches being found both at the cottage and the mysterious music box? Or that pipe smoke showed up now? Instead of pointing out the coincidences to Leo, she kept her observations to herself.

Karen closed the lid, killing the music. The letters felt like they might crumble beneath her touch as she untied the ribbon. The movement caught Sir's attention, and he pawed at the end of the silk. Leo caught him before he pounced.

"Might want to make this quick, Ren." He grimaced as Sir made good use of his claws.

She put all but the first letter back in the music box and set the ribbon aside. "Here, fiend."

Leo released the kitten, who leapt at the ribbon and tossed it into the air. "So much for buying all those expensive cat toys."

"His taste in toys doesn't affect his cuteness."

"I can say the same for other people I know."

She paused, the letter in her hand. "Are you saying I'm cute?"

His lazy grin appeared. "Especially when you're flustered. That blush when you're trying to pretend that you're not checking me out? Adorable."

Her face warmed. *Dammit.* Carefully, she unfolded the letter and read the faded black ink. "*My dearest Elizabeth.*" Without looking away from the letter, she gripped Leo's arm. "*Night upon night I lie awake and ponder if you lie in bed across the wood at the great hall, awake as well, thinking of me. My musings are not to inspire guilt or shame. I understand your position, the fear that keeps us apart. Fate has not deigned to allow you the freedom to love me, but we are together, friends eternal, and that is enough.*"

Karen paused and met Leo's gaze. "Holy. Hell."

"Is that it?" he asked, his voice tight.

"One more paragraph." She drew a breath and continued. "*I completed the conservatory rose garden. Every flower I plant, every stone I place, I do for you, my love immortal.*"

She leaned back, her heart thumping faster. "It's initialed 'E'. Jed was right. Edwin created the gardens for Elizabeth, a lasting testament of his love, the one way he could express it."

"Loving someone, the power it has to destroy you, is terrifying. But not being with the person you love when they're right there in your face? That's so much worse. Good to know they were friends eternal." Leo abruptly stood and stalked for the hallway, his back stiff and straight. "See you in the morning."

"What—?" The letter forgotten in her lap, she twisted on the couch to watch him go, but he was already beyond sight. The empty space where he'd been left a sinking sensation in her stomach. Sir abandoned his ribbon and raced after Leo, leaving her alone in the quiet.

Friends eternal. It was what she wanted with Leo, but could she be like the Elizabeth that Edwin portrayed? Knowing how Leo felt about her, too afraid to take it deeper? Love had nothing to do with it. She'd been in love with Leo for months.

But she couldn't deny the fear.

How many nights had she lain awake thinking about Leo, not knowing he'd been doing the same? The obstacles that stood between Elizabeth and Edwin — Elizabeth's marriage, being the obvious one — had been solid, formidable in a society where divorce was unheard of and women lesser citizens, dependent in every way on their husbands.

Her excuses paled in comparison, weak and shallow, shadows of 'maybes'. She hated that her decision, even if she believed it was best, hurt Leo.

She refolded the letter and returned it to the music box. Leo's half-full whiskey glass sat on the end table. She drained it, refilled it again and stared out of the window into the night...alone.

* * * *

Karen awoke with a start, her pulse on a racetrack, speeding toward the finish line. Tears wetted her cheeks and a gnawing, aching emptiness threatened to swallow her hole. The dream remained out of reach, but it curled inside her, whispering that she'd lost something both cherished and irreplaceable.

Or someone.

Only a dream. With shaking hands, she wiped at her face. She'd fallen asleep on the couch in the library. Darkness filled the room. Wind howled around the corners and hissed in the cracks of Granton Hall. She switched on the lamp by the couch and received a dead *click*. The wind must have knocked out the power again. Patting around for her cell phone, she came up empty handed.

Hell.

Granton Hall was always drafty, and while it might have been her imagination, a deeper chill slithered in the air. The scent of cloves and smoke lifted the hairs on her arms. *I'm not alone.*

Loving the supernatural from afar, safely beyond reach, was far different than waking up in the middle of someone else's ghost story. And after Leo's confession of his graveyard experience, lingering alone in the blackness of Granton Hall—she wasn't going down like a horror movie victim.

Karen fumbled through the dark and around the couch without crashing—a slight miracle with whiskey fuzzing her senses. She held her hands out in front of her, bumped into the wall and found the doorway. The wind heaved against the windows, snarling over the roof, a rabid beast trying to gain entrance.

Guided by the solid line of walls, she made it to the vestibule. She stubbed her toe on the fallen chandelier, tripped and grabbed the stairwell post before an awkward face plant. Why the hell was the room spinning so fast? She hadn't drunk *that* much.

A shadow in the gloom, the stairs rose above and she stumbled up, clutching the banister for support. The cold from the library seemed to follow her, as did the sweet-laced odor of pipe smoke. The stairs went on forever, and she swore a breath brushed the back of her neck. She reached the second-floor landing and spun. If something followed her, the night hid it. A shudder rolled through her. If that giant spider from the ballroom watched her, waiting to pounce, she preferred not to know.

A flashlight beam from below blinded her, and she shielded her eyes.

"Ren?" Leo's voice cut through the storm outside, the best sound in the world. "I was just checking on the generator. It's out again. Shocking, I know. Why are you wandering around in the dark?"

"Leo." His name came out as a sob.

Bounding up the steps two at a time, he made it to her in a heartbeat. He wrapped her in his arms and held her close.

She clung to him, shaking. Had something chased her up the stairs or had it been her imagination on high? Nothing—and everything—seemed real. In the dark, tethered to dreams that seemed like memories, she couldn't separate what was and wasn't. She only knew for certain that Leo was warm and solid, all that anchored her to the present.

"The power is out everywhere, and my generator quit." He rubbed her back in slow, soothing circles as she leaned into him, safe in his arms. "You okay?"

She hiccupped. "Am now."

"Have you been drinking?" He eased back, angled the flashlight to reflect off the ceiling, and frowned at her.

"Only a little."

He brushed his thumb over the corner of her eye, and his expression softened. "Darling, why were you crying?"

The emotions sharpened by her dream clawed up her throat, unstoppable. "I don't want to lie awake night after night thinking about you while you're doing the same." She dropped her forehead to his chest and lowered her voice to a whisper. "Even if it breaks me, I don't want you to feel alone when you're not."

He stroked her hair, holding her against his pounding heart. "I'll never break anything in you. I love you exactly as you are, flaws, strengths and every detail in between. Nothing has the power to change that."

"I hope so." She lifted her head and met his gaze, all the tangled emotions weaving together into a frame of clarity. "I'm in...all of you, all of me."

He went utterly still and for a full thirty seconds he didn't breathe as he studied her beneath the flashlight's glow. "Be absolutely certain. Once I have you, I won't let you go without a battle to the death."

The sincerity in his words, the fierceness in his expression killed the laugh bubbling up. Only Leo would bring up battle at a time like this. "Your expensive whiskey isn't affecting my decision making, if that's what you're implying." She cleared the gravel in her throat. "In, Hughes, all the way."

He closed his eyes and muttered what sounded to be a prayer.

"But there's one tiny thing."

"Hmm." His jaw clenched, as if he knew any easy concession was too good to be true.

"We never finalized our blood vow in the conservatory. The chandelier fell before the kiss sealing the bargain. If I'm going to risk our friendship, that vow better be binding."

His slow, lazy smile made her toes curl. "We better fix that, fast."

The fear clinging to her like webs dissolved into tatters, and she could suddenly breathe again. If Leo was her doom, at least she'd fall into the black with real memories to cherish years later. "Close your eyes."

Her pulse tripped as he obeyed, waiting for his kiss, stooped over. Holy hell, he was so beautiful that her heart hurt. Losing him would destroy her.

He slitted one eye and growled. "No takebacks, Ren."

"No takebacks." *God help me.* She slipped her free arm around his neck and pressed her mouth to his, light and sweet, a farewell to their past, a cherished friendship that would never be—could never be—the same. And when he curled his fingers in her hair and deepened the kiss, she surrendered to the inevitable fall.

Chapter Twenty-Four

Between one kiss and the next, Karen found herself swept off the floor. She flung her arms around Leo's neck as he carried her down the hallway, setting her aflame with his mouth and tongue. He passed by her bedroom door, headed to his.

Leo's bedroom had been off limits, the territory too dangerous to her boundaries. She broke from his kiss as he shouldered past the ajar door. The bobbing flashlight beam left most of the room in shadows, the silhouettes of a chair, dresser and desk. A big bed draped in navy took up one corner. His scent of cedar, outdoors and Leo infused the air. Rain pelted the windowpanes in a ferocious beat.

She had the distinct sensation that she'd been brought to the dragon's lair to be sacrificed and couldn't bring herself to care.

Leo set the flashlight on the dresser, bulb up. The reflection off the ceiling added a candlelight glow to the room. A few feet from the bed, he let her slide down his body, making it impossible to miss every hard, amazing inch of him. Holding her gaze, he pulled his T-shirt off and dropped it to the floor at his feet, leaving his loose, black pajama pants.

Her blood roared hot in her veins, loud in her ears. The gloom made him look like some dark lord from the shadows, freed by the violence of the storm until dawn. An element of magic twisted the night into a fateful blend of wishes and dreams, where tomorrow felt a world away. Only now mattered.

He trailed his fingers under her shirt and brushed the flesh beneath. The flames in his eyes contradicted the tender touch. She couldn't move or look away, hypnotized by all that was Leo. He lowered his head and pressed a lingering kiss to the curve of her neck. "My sweet Ren." His breath warmed her ear. "I've waited for you so long."

His callused fingertips scraped a delicious friction as he skimmed up her ribs and pushed her T-shirt over her head. He tossed her shirt next to his and simply stared at her.

Chilled air brushed her exposed skin. Her bra, decorated with black skulls and crossbones, left little to the imagination. The wind moaned beyond the window and her pounding pulse joined the storm, the intensity of Leo's focus rattling her confidence. She wavered between punching him for making her feel vulnerable while so exposed or —

"So beautiful," he murmured. His lazy grin appeared. "I should've known you wouldn't wear anything lacy or pink."

Her shoulders relaxed. "I have some lace in my closet, definitely not pink."

"What you wear doesn't matter." He cupped her chin, his gaze reverent. "You're the only woman I ever see." He nibbled her bottom lip. "The only one I want." Through the silken material, he rubbed a thumb over her nipple. She sucked in a breath as sparks shot through every nerve. "At the moment, I'm more interested in your clothes being off."

Her heart swelled. She didn't deserve him, this man who made her feel wanted, transcendent and alive. Someday, he'd understand that, too, but she couldn't stop the desperate need for more—more of his words, his touch. A sudden, frenzied need took over, to experience everything he offered, no matter the fallout. It was the one way she'd know whether or not this moment was real or a dream.

Karen kicked off her shoes and ankle socks. She unclasped her bra and tossed it into the clothing pile. His sharp inhalation was everything she'd ever wanted. When she slithered out of her jeans, his low growl of approval made every fantasy pale. In nothing but her skimpy, silk underwear of matching skulls and crossbones, she lifted her chin.

Hunger glittered in his eyes as he studied her body from crown to bare feet, lingering on every slope and curve, a caress she could almost feel. The heat scorched her, pooling low, sending moisture straight to her core.

"Leo." Her voice rasped, a plea.

In one, quick move, he had her on the bed. The next moment, he braced his elbows on each side of her, his hard, heavy body a delicious pressure, his mouth poised above hers. His breath tickled her lips, warm and teasing. He trailed a finger down her face, tracing her mouth as if she were the most delicate treasure, and every nerve ending lit up in anticipation. Never had she felt more seen, more cherished.

"Kiss me again." She tangled her fingers in his hair and pulled his head down to her. "Or is this your idea of vengeance, a torture-teasing session?"

"I've suffered patiently for years and now you want to hurry?" He laughed, low and sensual, his eyes dark. But he obeyed, exploring her mouth with his tongue in slow, hedonistic strokes, as if coaxing all her secrets free, one by one. He slid a hand in a tormenting journey down her body, caressing the side of her breast, skating over her ribs and landing on her hip.

She was a fireworks display on the verge of explosion. The craving that she'd tried so hard to suppress over the last two years broke free of its cage and took possession of her, uncontrollable and savage. Karen wrapped her legs around his waist, and his heat between her thighs made all her best parts clench with need.

"Leo." She didn't care that her tone verged on begging. Every reason why she'd avoided being in this position scattered like sand in a desert wind. All she cared about was this moment with Leo, losing track of where she began and he ended. "*Please.*"

"Do you need me, Ren?" He traced her hip bone and dipped a finger into the fragile waistband of her underwear. He flicked the tiny black bow at the center with his thumb, but when his gaze found hers, a hint of vulnerability softened the fire.

"Always," she breathed, unable to deny him that truth, even if it cost her dearly later. "I always need you, Leo."

I always need you. Ren's confession rang with soft sincerity, sucked the air from his lungs and left him breathless. Leo closed his eyes, nailing those words on the doorpost of his heart.

"I've waited an entire lifetime to hear that from you." He peppered kisses over her face, probably not the sort of kiss she wanted at the moment, but he couldn't help himself. When she curled her arms around his neck, he figured she didn't mind.

"You haven't known me an entire lifetime." She tweaked his nipple and he hissed. With her legs around his waist, her heat against his hardness, she had to feel him throb in response.

"But I've waited for you my entire life."

Ren's coy dimple faded, and emotions tangled in her green eyes. Instead of letting her overthink it and make her usual retreat, he nuzzled the sensitive, whimper-inducing spot on her throat. He slipped his hand between them, beneath the thin silk barrier, all that remained of her clothing, to the heated flesh beneath. They both moaned, and when she squirmed against him, biting her full lower lip, he nearly lost control. She felt so perfect, so right beneath him, her legs curled around him, claiming him as hers.

"I need you right now." Her breath frantic, Ren pushed his pajama pants down his hips as far as she could. She reached for his neck, pulling his mouth back to hers. "More. I need all of you."

Panting, Leo pressed his forehead into the crook of her neck. The wind clawed at the ancient stones and howled its frustration, echoing the storm inside him. He wanted to take his time with her, but a primal urge to feel, touch, taste every inch of her drove him onward. He hadn't been exaggerating when he told her this was the point of no return. The line she'd fought to keep stable had been crossed, no turning back, whether she regretted tonight in the morning or not. No matter how she pretended, they'd never been just friends, and he'd use every possible angle to remind her of it.

Ren dug her fingernails into his back, a silent plea, and he shuddered beneath her touch. He'd never been any good at denying her anything.

Needing his skin against hers, he slid down her body, leaving kisses along the way, every gasp from her lips threatening to undo him. He freed himself of his pants and kicked them aside.

Her gaze raked every inch of him with such open desire, all the blood that still remained in his head flooded south. Women admired him all the time, and he never let it affect his ego. Appearances were little more than a God-given peel that didn't always reflect what hid beneath the flesh.

But Ren was different. She saw *him*. She didn't care about what she could get from him, not his money or reputation, not even what pleasure he could provide with his body. She simply wanted to be with him, had pushed aside attraction and romance rather than endanger that. She knew the man beneath the trappings, adored all his eccentricities, had witnessed his weakness, heard his greatest fear — his best friend, always. He'd protect that gift to the bitter end and, in the process, show her friendship could make love even better.

"You're so damn bewitching, Ren." He crawled back up her long, lovely legs and paused at the delicate black ribbon resting a few inches beneath her cute belly button. He traced one skull and crossbones with his tongue, leaving the silk wet, and her breath caught. Using his teeth, he bit the bow and tugged. Ren lifted her hips, and he slid the scrap of silk down her legs, adding it to the scattered clothes on the floor.

As he unabashedly gazed upon every beautiful inch of her, a quiver ran through the firm flesh of her thighs. The sound she made—part whimper, part growl—demolished all his restraint. He returned to her, needing to touch her, kiss her, feel her body beneath his. She knotted her fingers in his hair and twisted her legs around him again, warm, demanding and absolute perfection.

With a groan, Leo nipped the column of her throat and settled against her heat. "No matter how many times I kiss or touch or taste you, Ren, I'll never get enough."

"Hughes, talk later." She bit his shoulder, hard enough to sting, and licked the same spot, her tongue warm and wet. Her hips lift beneath him. "Don't stop."

"Never." He twined her fingers with his and met her gaze. "I'll never stop showing you how much I need you with me." With a slow, powerful thrust, he slid into her, and she sighed. He leaned his mouth close to her ear. "I'll never let you go."

And they moved together, in sync, a rhythm to match pounding hearts and racing blood. When she groaned his name like a raw, desperate prayer, dug her fingernails into his flesh and shattered around him, he fed himself to her fire. So close to losing control, he thrusted harder, faster and, with a low growl, followed her over the edge into eternity.

Chapter Twenty-Five

Daylight woke Leo from the best night's sleep he'd ever had. Even though his arm was numb, he kept still, listening to Ren breathing. A trace of her mint shampoo infused his sheets and teased his nose. Her head rested on his shoulder. She'd slung one arm over his chest, a leg over his knees, as if he were her own personal teddy bear.

Whatever she needed him to be, he was all over it, especially if it included her touching him, loving him. Last night—and into the wee hours of the morning—she'd taken all his imaginings and blown them to smithereens. Being as close to her as humanly possible, allowed into her heart, felt like soaring, free and weightless.

She'd probably claim it was nothing but a moment's weakness, that they couldn't let sex ruin their friendship, try to push him back. He laced his fingers with hers. *Not this time*. She'd finally trusted him enough to cross that boundary. He wouldn't surrender any ground.

Ren's eyelashes fluttered, and she looked at him, remnants of dreams in her eyes. "Hmm."

He smiled, her teasing a promising sign to the new place they found themselves. "Good morning to you, too."

"Oh, is that what it is? Morning?" She squinted at the barely-there dawn gleaming in the window. "I have no intention of getting up until the very last snooze alarm." She snuggled closer. "This is the best dream ever. You're too comfy to be real."

"Oh, I'm very much real." He caressed her hip, light and teasing, enjoying her responsive shiver. "Do you need proof?"

She faked a yawn. "I may be convinced, depending on your skills of persuasion."

He flipped her onto her back and stretched over her, laughing at her surprised squeak. The lovely curves and planes of her body molded to his, as if they were two pieces of a matched set. She gazed up at him, mischief in her smile.

God, how he loved her.

"Prepare, my fair lady, to be thoroughly wooed."

"Wooed?" One auburn eyebrow twitched up. "Is that what kids are calling it nowadays?"

"I have no idea." He nuzzled her neck and pressed a kiss beneath her ear. Her sigh heated his blood another degree. "The name doesn't matter, as long as you enjoy it."

"Well said, sir." Ren moaned as he bit the cord between her neck and shoulder. She gave an impatient buck of her hips. "And do, I beg of you, get to it before I smite you."

"So impatient. I love it when you get rough with me, darling."

Her eyes sparked like new stars, and she dug her fingernails into his back. "Ditto."

The conversation ended in a tangle of tongues and teeth, and the only intelligible word that came from her lips for quite some time was his name, first and last, separate and together. He didn't care what she called him as long as she didn't stop calling him, needing him, running to him. As long as they were together.

* * * *

The morning at the office dragged by, and after staring at her computer screen for an hour without seeing any of the numbers, Karen gave up. Her chair squeaked as she leaned back and spun from her desk. How could she focus on anything after last night with Leo? Her face heated. *And this morning…* Her body still ached in the best of ways. Holy hell, the man knew how to make a girl want to trade her fantasies for the real thing.

"That's the biggest, most wistful sigh I've heard since my sister decided to ditch my couch after her divorce."

At Gia's voice, Karen swiveled to face the doorway. As always, she looked like a glamor queen in a cashmere pink sweater, pin-striped, gray pencil skirt and four-inch stilettos. Their mutual love for killer shoes had made them instant friends.

She waved Gia off. "Must have been one of the windbags in suits down the hall."

"Maybe." She perched on the edge of the desk and dangled her feet. "I can't believe you didn't tell me, though."

Karen blinked. How the hell had Gia already found out about her and Leo? Mere hours had passed since she'd left his bed. Mentally, she was *still* there, wrapped up in him like the best, most decadent package.

"I get it." Gia crossed her ankles and toyed with her ridiculous pink diamond engagement ring. "It's not like I can judge you at all for your decisions."

"No judging, no regrets." That mutual understanding was another reason they'd become fast friends. When it came to playing it loose and easy with men, Gia had been worlds beyond Karen's own occasional distractions at Seven Devils. Then along had come Ian, and everything had changed.

Just like Leo and his Granton Hall project proposition... What if, while she and Gia had been flirting and calling the shots with their independence, the men in their lives had been playing them all along, waiting for the right time to strike?

Scary thought.

"But I believed we were friends," Gia said in a sad voice as she examined her polished fingernails. "I thought you could talk to me about anything."

She hadn't had the time or brain cells to process her new stage with Leo, definitely wasn't ready to discuss it. "Well, it's all brand spankin' new, even for me."

"How long have you known?" Gia glanced up from beneath her long eyelashes.

How long had she known the wall she kept strong and mighty to protect the relationship with her best friend would crumble? *Never.* She'd never wanted to believe it was possible, that he'd destroy her barricade so easily, but he'd kissed her and kept kissing her. Tempted and teased her until she couldn't think, bared his soul and woven her dreams with reality so she couldn't tell the two apart. Beneath the spell of his mouth and hands — and all his other hard, persuasive, delicious parts — resistance had been futile.

And a bit of whiskey, storms and supernatural hadn't helped her decision.

She collapsed back in her chair. "I didn't know."

"Lies!" Gia jerked to her feet and pointed an accusing finger in her face. "Mr. Hamilton told me everything."

"Hamilton?" How did Mr. Hamilton know about her and Leo? "I'm not lying. I never intended to erase the lines between friendship and lovers. It's all Leo's fault. He refuses to listen to reason. The stubborn man doesn't know the meaning of surrender."

Gia squinted at her. "Are we talking about the same thing?"

"Isn't it the usual subject? Men and all the things they do to drive us insane?"

All the hurt in Gia's expression drained away, replaced by glittering curiosity. "What happened between you and Leo?"

Hell. Now she'd never escape this conversation unscathed. "What were *you* talking about?"

"You leaving Hamilton & Associates. Mr. Hamilton mentioned it in the break room today, that you'd filed your official notice. What is Hamilton going to do without either one of us?"

"Drown in the sea of sharks he's surrounded himself with." They shared an evil smile. "I love that you're going to law school, G. You'll be a fantastic advocate for domestic violence victims. You should talk to Leo about his plans for Granton Hall, share ideas, work together."

Gia cocked her head, her golden curls sliding over her shoulder. "Everyone knows my reason for leaving Hamilton, but yours is a mystery. I thought you were happy working the books here."

"It's not that I'm *un*happy." She drummed her fingertips on the desk. Hedging wasn't lying, right? "I need a change, a challenge, a new adventure. Lawyers are so boring."

Her sunshine dimmed to a shade beneath brilliant. "You're not leaving because of me and Ian, are you?"

Karen plucked the extra pencil she always kept behind her ear and fiddled with it. "I'm glad that you found the man you want in Ian, honest. I hope with all my twisted soul that he doesn't screw you over, but if he does, the vengeance we'll plot will be epic."

"If he does, you're the first person I'll call." Gia's voice softened. "But he won't."

"How do you know?" Tapping the pencil in a quick beat, she studied Gia's expression. "He's broken tons of hearts before you."

"But not yours, right?" Worry lines appeared on her forehead. "Please tell me your heart wasn't invested in Ian, that your feelings for him weren't deep."

Karen wanted to roll her eyes. This discussion hadn't been part of her game plan today. Or ever. "Ian doesn't have the power to break anything in me." She tossed the pencil on the desk, and it clattered against her computer before rolling to a stop, leaving a wedge of silence. "What stung me is that I had no idea *you* had feelings for Ian, so when you wound up together, it was a shock. And yeah, it hurt a little, felt too close to a betrayal not to."

Tears shone in Gia's eyes. "Kar, I'm sorry."

She waved the apology away, itching to escape this topic. "I know you didn't intend to hurt my pride, and I appreciate that you care enough to harass me about it. I *am* happy for you. I'd love for things to go back to normal for us."

"Me, too. I miss our shenanigans."

Karen let her wicked smile slide free. "Even when you're the subject of the bet?"

"As long as it doesn't include Ian, how long we'll last, who will break up with who, before or after the wedding."

"I don't control the wagers," she said sweetly. "And I already handed over the underground office bet reins to Chuck. You'll need to talk to him about it."

"Dammit." She stomped a stiletto, but her eyes gleamed with humor.

Karen's smile faded at the edges, and since the bandage had been ripped off, she wanted to claw the scab away, too, get the wound aired out and healed. "Initially, seeing you and Ian together was rough, and not for the reasons you think. I'm fine, but everyone looks at me as if I'm pretending. That's part of the reason I'm leaving Hamilton, but honestly?" She shrugged. "As much as I love working here, I need different scenery."

"Such as the hunk renovating Granton Hall?" Gia wriggled her eyebrows. "You mentioned friends and lovers, and I do hope it has everything to do with one Leo Hughes."

Heat crept up her neck and into her face, making it impossible to play it cool. Hiding her steamy night— and morning—with Leo wasn't going to work with Gia.

Clapping, Gia did a little jig. She grabbed Karen's hands, dragged her out of the chair and spun her around. The woman was stronger than she looked.

"I think I liked you better when you weren't madly in love," Karen grumbled, wrestling free.

Gia's eyes sparkled, her joy impossible to resist. "Girl, tell me *everything*."

Instead of spilling the details on Leo, she went a different direction. "You didn't answer me. How do you know that Ian won't walk out on you?"

"If he walks out, he knows Kat will murder him and hide the body." A hint of melancholy touched Gia's smile. "I can't know for sure. No one can. But there comes a point where you have to decide that the risk is worth it."

"Even after losing Joey?" She usually avoided the subject of Joey, Gia's first fiancé. Joey's death had sent the Glitter Girl into a dark spiral of too many drinks and useless men who weren't worthy to kiss the soles of her sparkling stilettos.

"*Especially* after losing Joey. My love for him will always be with me. It never goes away, and even though a part of me died when he did, I'd never give up a single moment with him." Only peace reflected in her eyes, a painful past set to rest.

A twist of both envy and hope clenched her stomach. If it were possible for Queen Gia to believe in second chances after the hell she'd been through, maybe a peasant could wish for a happy ending, too.

"If I'd never met Joey, I might not have understood how to appreciate being truly and deeply loved." Gia studied her, as if she read more into the question than Karen intended. "That it's not something to be found with any random guy, but with another person who understands you, appreciates all that you are — both the good and bad — and will always want you anyway."

Her throat tightened. Leo was all that, but Ian hadn't been Gia's best friend, or a friend at all, before they'd fallen in love. It wasn't the same. But a fated love who refused to walk away, who'd fight any monster to keep her? That sounded nice.

Friends eternal. She shivered.

"I'll never waste a second with Ian. Second-guessing his love for me would be an insult to Joey. When he died, I missed out on a lifetime together, love and laughter and memories. I'll treasure every single breath with Ian, even if he decides he wants something or someone else one day." She shrugged. "I have no power to prevent that, but if he does choose that path, it won't be because he ever doubted I love him."

The words struck her like arrows to her chest, cracking open memories and stealing her breath. Other than Leo, she'd never told anyone else in Graywood about Hank. It was as if Gia read her past and dared her to confront it. "I saw you after Joey died, G. How can you be okay with the prospect of returning to that place? How can you trust Ian enough not to send you there?"

"The way I see it, there are two choices — trust that no matter what happens, love is worth whatever pain that comes along with it." Compassion quieted her voice. "Or don't trust, and miss out on all of it, including the joy."

Easy for Gia to say. Ian would be a fool to ever leave her. Everyone loved her. Karen, meanwhile, had been a regular guest on the easily forgotten chart, never hitting the 'forever girl' list. She walked away before it got serious and remained in the open and accepting arms of her fantasies. With Leo, there was no going back to fantasies.

"Kar." Recapturing her full attention, Gia crossed her arms and frowned. "If the mere mention of Leo Hughes brings up this heavy topic, something significant definitely happened between you."

Groaning, Karen laid her head on the desk with a *thunk*. "I might have kissed him. And kept kissing him until this morning when I woke up in his arms."

"Nekkid?" she asked hopefully.

"Not a stitch." Karen lifted her head and wailed, "I don't know what to do! He's my best friend, and he wants more."

"I'd say he got more."

"Not helpful." She slumped. "Leo is perfect. He's everything I'd want in a boyfriend. He's sweet, sexy, we're both geeks in different ways and we make each other laugh. We get each other. But if I make it official like I know he wants, everyone gets involved, families and friends—which for the Hughes family includes the majority of Graywood."

"That's generally how relationships work." Gia grinned, impish.

"What if he decides that the more isn't as great as he thinks? I'll lose my best friend." And an entire town of pitying looks for the girl who got dumped by her best friend would be hell. "He's my lifeboat. Without him, I'll sink."

"So let him be your lifeboat in both sides of the relationship. Leo has been googly-eyed over you for as long as I've seen you together." Her sunshine smile showed up. "And I don't mean as just friends."

Leo had said as much last night, but in a way that made her toes curl and her heart sing the *Hallelujah Chorus*.

"Karen." Gia grasped both her arms and looked her straight in the eyes. "Leo's a smart chocolate chip cookie. He got to know you first, built a foundation of friendship, took his sweet, sweet time to learn every detail about you before making his move. Instead of dating you and possibly getting dumped early on, he made sure to keep the woman he loves close by being her best friend."

She sucked in a breath. Dammit, how did she have two friends who seemed to see everything? "That sneaky bastard."

"If Leo is who you want, don't let any 'what if's' hold you back, sugar." Gia released her grip and smoothed the wrinkle in Karen's sweater. "Now I'm off to see Chuck and make a big, fat wager that you'll make a go for it with Leo." She winked and turned for the door. "Don't let me lose."

"That's not how betting works," she grumbled as Gia floated into the corridor and out of sight. "You can't hedge the odds!"

"Wanna bet?" Her happy-as-bells laughter drifted back.

Karen plopped into her chair and held her head in her hands. *I'm so screwed.*

Chapter Twenty-Six

Music echoed into the ballroom from the corridor where Leo ripped out carpet, and Karen hummed along to the rock beat. She adjusted a sliver of walnut wood and eyeballed it for the fifth time before easing a mahogany piece beside it.

She stood and circled the design, studying it from every angle. Parquetry, she'd discovered, was a lot like life. All damaged fragments had to be removed and examined to determine which ones would be useful to keep. The hard, resistant goop beneath the destruction had to be scraped out, tough — and essential — labor that had left her sore.

There might still be some goop clinging to her heart corners that she'd need to deal with to stretch her Leo relationship further. For now, the water felt amazing.

Beside the wall of windows, she paused to watch Oliver trimming the boxwood hedge bordering the walkway. The strides he'd made on the landscape almost equaled the progress in the ballroom itself.

Trees closest to the windows had been conquered, any dangerous limbs removed. Weeds had been vanquished. Every shrub, plant and flower within view of the windows had been tamed and tailored to perfection.

He hadn't been kidding about being killer with his shears.

Oliver looked up, smiled and waved. She wriggled her fingers at him and turned back to her work before it got awkward. Since Seven Devils, she'd exchanged only a handful of words with him. Each time, he mentioned that glass of wine she'd promised. And each time, she found an excuse—all valid, but still... She hadn't told him about her and Leo. Doing that made their romance official, on record. She wasn't ready to curse it.

Karen faced the ballroom. Every bit of debris had been cleared away, the dance floor clean but still in need of a good waxing. Leo had repaired the fallen ceiling beam, and although the antique crystal chandeliers all needed to be polished, they all functioned now. The last slice of evening light glittered through the replaced windows and bathed the new brocaded wallpaper in gold. After a heated argument against Leo's choice in pink-flowered paper, she'd convinced him to let her decide. He hadn't fooled her. The only reason he'd picked pink in the first place was to torment her.

A smile broke free, an uncontrollable echo to the warmth bubbling in her chest. He'd made it up to her that night—long, slow and all sorts of steamy. Her body throbbed at the memory. And if she thought on that too long, she'd never get done with her floor.

Karen examined the trial run parquet square she'd put together, a thrill of pride rolling through her. It blended into the original floor set centuries ago. She'd spent hours sorting through the pried-up pieces, more hours comparing wood, grain and colors to get an exact match.

After the wood acclimated to the temperature and humidity of the ballroom, Leo had performed all the sawing. It had taken him over half a day to cut all the pieces to her specifications. She didn't miss that he started in the morning while she was at Hamilton's. He couldn't keep her from his saw forever.

But she'd watched him while he'd finished, the expert way his big, capable hands operated the equipment, how he handled even the smallest pieces of wood. *Almost as sexy as his swordplay.*

Less than a week stood between them and the competition deadline, the end of her volunteer term. Her stomach twisted. The path her life would take after that point remained a mystery.

Leo trotted down the marble stairs and headed her way, his gaze locked on her. The splintered light softened the splotches on his black T-shirt and jeans, the dust on his boots. He looked like a fey lord ready to shed his human shape and slip off into the twilight. "Looking good."

"Thanks." She folded her arms and squinted at her parquet again, searching for any flaw.

"I was talking about you, but the floor looks damn fine, too." He winked and stopped beside her.

She rolled her eyes, but warmth bloomed in her face. "It should, after how many times you made me arrange each block…tyrant."

"I thought that was what you loved most about me."

"I admit nothing." She lifted on tiptoes and kissed him. "Unless you want to teach me how to use your jigsaw?"

"Not happening."

"Isn't that part of being an expert parquetry person?" She fisted his shirt and aimed a sweet, shameless smile at him.

"Hmm. Our agreement was to teach you basic construction skills, not mold you into Graywood's next parquet flooring expert. Nice try."

"What if I promise not to chop you into little pieces anytime soon?" She batted her eyelashes.

"Stay away from my saw, Ren."

"Fine." She released his shirt and smoothed the material, enjoying the hard planes of his chest beneath her palm. Suggestively, she dragged her fingers down the ridges of his stomach.

He caught her wrist, his eyes aflame, and lifted her hand to his mouth. One by one, he kissed her fingertips, shooting tendrils of heat through every nerve. "As much as I'd love you to keep touching me, I only have a few minutes."

"That'll do." She gave him a wicked grin.

"Not even close." His voice lowered, rough and raw. "With you, I need to take my time and properly worship every lovely inch."

Leo released her and slipped his hands into his pockets, as if he might lose all control if he touched her a second longer. The fact that she could threaten his restraint was a powerful, wonderful feeling.

Her smile widened. "You say the best things, Hughes."

"Sucking up won't change my mind about the saw." He pivoted, facing the ballroom. "We're getting there.

Deadline's next week. Tight, but doable. I'm having trouble finding the sander I'll need to finish the floor, but a rental place in Greenville promises to have one available this weekend. Think you'll be finished by then?"

"Yep. I'll arrange all the blocks on kraft paper, make sure I'm not missing any pieces. Saturday morning, I'm up at dawn to glue it all in perfect order. That should leave enough time for it to set up." She elbowed him in the ribs. "Sunday, it will be all you."

"It better be all me every day." His eyes sparkled, belying his growl. "The paneling is scheduled to arrive Monday morning. Finally. I placed the order the same day I bought Granton. Want me to panic? Delay my specialty orders when I have a deadline."

"You, panic?" She snorted. With the exception of Halloween-inspired entertainment and a certain, macabre tune, Leo never lost his cool.

"Occasionally." His mouth curled in a half-smile. "I'll finish the walls between the windows while you seal the floor. Might be a long night."

"Cleaning and polishing every detail to an immaculate shine for the final judging on Tuesday?"

Leo nodded. "And Wednesday we'll win."

"On Halloween, my favorite day of the year." She bounced on her feet. "There will be tricks and most definitely treats."

His slow, lazy grin came to life, steaming her blood. "Count on it."

"Until then, you might as well give up trying to freak me out." She shook her head and gave him a sad look. "Sneaking out of bed to plant the tobacco pouch on my dresser every morning isn't worth the effort."

"I haven't touched that nasty pouch, unlike you." He narrowed his eyes at her. "I'll attend Halloween events that scare the crap out of me to humor you, but pranking me here, after what I told you? Not cool, Ren."

She laughed. "Not fooling me, Hughes."

"Right back at you." He leaned down and kissed her, sweet and slow, long enough to scatter her thoughts. "Have I told you what that dimple of yours does to me?"

"I believe you showed me last night." *And this morning*. Not that she was counting so much as savoring, absorbing, memorizing every second with him. "But feel free to tell me again."

"We'll see what transpires in the wee hours tonight, after I finish up. Lots of work, limited time to do it and ravish you properly, too, as you deserve." He kissed her nose and smirked as he slid beyond range of her grabby hands. "No rest for the wicked."

"No prob." She added a brightness to her voice and studied her ruined fingernails. Parquetry was a bitch on the manicure. "I'm busy anyway."

"Girls' night out at Seven Devils?" His expression turned border-line scary.

"Even better. Tonight, after I'm done with the volunteer slavery tasks you've assigned, I'm reading more Edwin letters."

He groaned and walked backward toward the corridor, his expression of such forced affliction she had to laugh. "I don't want to hear more about his fascination with insects."

"And spiders in particular." When she'd read that detail, sandwiched between descriptions of the glowing morning sunrise and his sister's nagging, she'd jumped off the couch in excitement, scaring Sir in the process. How could Leo be so nonchalant about it after the grandfather clock? "Coincidence? I think not."

"Don't care, not about that, what he planted in Elizabeth's honor or how his every deed revolves around ensuring her everlasting felicity."

"If we don't read them all, how are we supposed to discover any clues about Elizabeth's fate?" Leo wasn't wrong. So far, Edwin's letters had been a snoozefest, nothing incriminating beyond loving the girl he'd grown up with, a girl so far out of his league he never had a chance.

"Expecting to find a murder confession in a love letter will lead to disappointment."

"You don't read the right kind of books or watch the right shows, obviously."

"Damn straight."

She waved at the windows. "Oliver's doing a fantastic job outside, don't you think?"

He paused, and as his gaze flicked to the landscape beyond, his expression turned thunderous. "To throw off any suspicion. Officer Hellman hasn't reported her findings yet. Until then, I'm avoiding him as much as possible. I've never been good at hiding my opinion, especially when I know someone's guilty."

"Still no motive there, Hughes."

"Not that we know of. I don't trust him." He pivoted and climbed the marble stairs. "No matter how great my hedges look."

* * * *

Karen stared into the darkness clinging to the bedroom rafters and gave up trying to sleep. After an hour of listening to Leo's steady breaths, she eased free from the arm he'd slung over her waist, careful not to wake him. Snuggled up with Leo had become her favorite place in the world, second best to just being with him. But they didn't both have to be zombies in the morning.

Surrendering Leo's warmth for the perpetual chill of Granton, she slipped out of bed, grabbed her cell phone from the nightstand and sat on the floor. Three-thirteen a.m. *Ergh*. Tomorrow would be ugly. Her brain didn't operate at full capacity without her eight hours of snooze time.

In the glow of her cell phone, the music box with its onion-skin letters gleamed. An open letter rested askew beside it. Earlier, she'd barely got through the opening before Leo had attacked her, taking no prisoners. After that, everything had blurred away into bliss.

Holy hell, the man knew how to make a girl want to believe in forever.

She flicked on her cell phone light and picked up the letter.

My dearest Elizabeth...

"Ren?"

At Leo's sleep-roughened voice, she twisted to face him. "Sorry," she whispered, leaning her forearm on the mattress. Even half-awake he was smoking hot, his head resting on the bulge of his biceps, blue eyes dreamy, hair temptingly mussed. "Couldn't sleep. Didn't mean to wake you."

"'Sokay." He stretched his hand out for her and she twined her fingers with his, her heart squeezing. How could one man be so sexy-sweet that all her defenses crumbled to ash? "May I ask you something?"

She rested her chin on her arm. "Sure."

"What was the deciding factor that made you put me in the friends-only category?" His expression was so open she wondered if he was truly awake. "I wasn't witty enough? Chatty or fun enough? Too grotesque, wimpy, unsuccessful?"

Ren wanted to roll her eyes, but the vulnerability in his gaze stopped her. She rubbed her thumb along the ridge of his knuckles and decided to go with brutal honesty. Odds were he wouldn't remember what she said in the morning.

"When I first met you, I wondered what sort of Greek deity would dabble in the plunger section of the hardware store wearing jeans, work boots, T-shirt and black beanie." She sighed. "With the most mesmerizing blue eyes. I thought I might be hallucinating."

"Hmm." A corner of his mouth twitched up.

"Then when you pretended to be an employee and proceeded to give specific details on the pros and cons of each type of plunger with a completely straight face, I knew you were special." The darkness softened the room into a midnight fantasy, lending the impression that her confession, the very moment, stemmed from magic and dreams where words could only be whispered. "If you had asked me out for a drink that night, I would have gone with you and on to whatever might have come after that."

"We went to the renaissance faire outside of town instead." He smiled, as if the memory were one of his best. "That was epic. Sword fighting, jousts, so many fine weapons to be had."

"And that was the problem."

He blinked slowly, half-asleep. "My interest in blades turned you off?"

"Try the opposite. You, swinging a sword, shirtless?" She blew out a breath, her blood heating at the mere memory of him battling Liam in the ballroom. "A girl can only take so much heat without combusting. Don't let it go to your head."

"Too late."

She let her grin fade, holding his gaze. "The problem was I liked you right away, too much, too soon. I knew if I let the fun go beyond friends — even though you're the sexiest man I've ever met — that I'd be sacrificing future days like that one."

"I didn't want to mess up what we had, either." His voice blended with the gloom, hushed and velvet. "I thought you just needed time to get to know me, so I practiced everything my mother taught me about being a gentleman" — a hint of his scowl showed up — "while the woman I'd fallen irrevocably in love with planted her gorgeous mouth on other guys instead of me. Do you know how crazy that made me?"

Her ribs squeezed, her heart pulsing for every time she'd unknowingly hurt him, soaring for every one of his words. "You've never once seemed crazy."

"Ask my brothers. They were my victims every Saturday night in the ring. They're lucky to have survived." His eyelids drifted shut and his fingers went limp in hers. "Love you, Ren."

They'd spoken those words hundreds of times over the years, usually after some friendly squabble, insult or prank. This time, their meaning rooted deeper, tendrils curling around her soul. The tightness in her throat strangled her voice. "Love you, too, Hughes."

His soft snore broke the quiet.

She freed a soft, shuddering breath, her heart seams stretched to full capacity. Maybe, like his brothers, she'd be lucky enough to survive Leo too. Shining her cell phone light on the letter, she continued reading.

Dearest Elizabeth,

Your words have haunted my steps these past weeks. The joy I once found in my gardens has paled to ash. I long for a single glance of you, a smile, your laugh, yet even those simple favors have been denied me. I was a fool to express the deepest desire of my heart, to put you in such a precarious position that you had no choice but to reject even our friendship.

I know a simple, lowborn gardener will never be worthy of your affection. All the love I possess, as deep as the churning sea, cannot provide the future you deserve. Please forgive me. I cannot bear it if you no longer see me, at the very least, as your friend.

E

Karen dropped the letter, a cold pit opening in her stomach. All the warmth drained into it and left her on empty. Edwin's rejection felt like her own, stirring up memories she preferred to forget. Memories that, in the last few weeks, she nearly *had* forgotten. Edwin and Elizabeth had been friends, and in the end, he hadn't been enough for her.

The sweet scent of cloves and pipe smoke drifted on the air. Her hands shaking, she folded up the letter and set it on the music box. As her cell phone light faded, she wondered if, centuries later, Edwin still regretted exposing his heart.

Chapter Twenty-Seven

Karen's right butt cheek vibrated for the tenth time in the last half hour. Growling, she set her trowel aside and slipped her protective mask down. With her teeth, she pulled her glove off her right hand and fumbled for the cell phone in her jeans' back pocket. Whoever dared disturb her concentration while she was laying her parquet masterpiece better be prepared for a tongue lashing.

Leo strode into the ballroom, his brow furrowed. "Have you seen my cordless drill, Ren? I swore it was sitting on the sawhorse, but now it's not. And the screws I needed? Gone."

"Nope, sorry. I..." She stared at the cell phone screen, not sure she read the name right. *Hannah.* Ten missed calls from her younger sister, who she'd talked to on the phone maybe twice since leaving Graywood. Her stomach knotted at all the possible reasons Hannah might call her multiple times within minutes. None of them were good.

He crouched beside her. "Something wrong?"

"Not sure. Hannah keeps calling me."

"Your sister?"

"The very one." She stuffed the phone back in her pocket. "I'll call her after I'm done." She made sure her smile was bright. The chemical scent of the parquet adhesive burned the air, and she pulled her mask back up. "Don't want to mess with the mojo. I'm on a roll. Can't let the adhesive dry."

"Ren." His low tone made it clear that she hadn't fooled him. "It might be important."

Whatever news Hannah had might derail her focus, and they couldn't afford that. Three short days separated them from the final judging. Her parquetry came first. She shook her head. "Later."

He plucked the other glove off her hand. "Hey, I wasn't done with —"

He hefted her up and over his shoulder and trapped her legs with one arm. "Mandatory ten-minute volunteer break." With a determined gait, he strode toward the ballroom doors leading out into the garden. Wherever Oliver worked his landscaping voodoo, he did it out of sight.

"Put me down, you insufferable neanderthal!" Unable to keep a laugh out of her voice, she pounded his derriere with her fists. It took some effort to punch rather than squeeze. "I'm capable of conducting my own work schedule."

"This work-volunteer environment follows established rules. I'm sure you read the fine print before volunteering, including the consequences of insubordination." If her hits even stung, he didn't show it. He opened the glass doors, and cool October air snaked through her jeans to nip her backside. "Breaks make volunteers happy. Happy volunteers work harder. Known fact."

She ripped off her mask as he set her down on a stone bench surrounded by holly. "Who are you to decide whether or not I want to be a happy volunteer? Maybe I prefer to be disgruntled and overworked."

He leaned over her, wearing his war face. "Call your sister."

"Bully."

That lopsided smile she loved twitched at the corner of his mouth. "The fine print also provided full warning about the overbearing boss on this project." His blue eyes softened. "Want me to stay?"

Since she'd read Edwin's forlorn letter, while irrational, she knew she'd projected a tepid knot of emotions at Leo the last couple of days. Hard not to do when Edwin's words had hit so close to home, but Leo didn't deserve to juggle all her baggage.

She patted the bench next to her, and when he sat, his welcome warmth eased the chill on her skin and in her heart. When he curled his fingers around hers, she found the strength to drag out her phone and return Hannah's call. She put the call on speaker phone.

Hannah picked up on the second ring. "Karen. Finally!"

"Hello to you, too." She snorted. "What's so important that you had to blow up my phone?"

"No 'how are Mom and Dad?' 'What's been going on at home?' 'How the hell are you, Hannah?'"

"I talk to Mom all the time. She tells me all I need to know."

"Texting doesn't count as talking, and there's something I know that she doesn't—something that you need to know."

Karen made a crazy face at Leo before answering. "What does that even mean, Hannah?"

Hannah paused and paused, and with each passing second her heart pummeled faster, harder. Anything that made her callus-hearted sister hesitate had to be bad.

"Hannah?" She could barely hear through the roaring waterfall in her head. "You still there?"

"I don't know how to say this in a way that will lessen the impact, so I'm just going to rip off the Band-Aid." She drew a deep breath and let it out with a hissing whoosh. "Hank and I eloped."

The second Hank's name blared from Ren's cell phone speaker, Leo tuned every ounce of his focus on her. Her fingers went limp, still in his. Any flush the autumn air had added to her cheeks faded. She stared ahead at the ballroom windows, as if becoming another Granton statue, lost and alone in a world abandoned.

He wanted to drag her onto his lap, wrap her in his arms until she understood that the past only had the power to hurt her if she allowed it. He'd be more than willing to kick anyone's ass to help her come to that realization. If he had it his way, Hank would be first to face him in the ring. Then he'd take on Hannah with his expression and words sharper than any blade.

But as much as he longed to protect Ren in whatever way she'd let him, she wanted to fight her own battles. And this particular war was one she had to choose to fight. All he could do was remain by her side and support her.

"Karen?" Hannah's voice held a hint of worry. "You still there? You're not crying, are you?"

Leo clenched his teeth against the urge to reach through time and space to slap his hand over Hannah's mouth. Ren had told him her family leaned toward the insensitive side, but he had no idea. Before he could steal her cell phone and tell Hannah to shut her piehole — politely enough to make his mother proud — Karen snapped out of her daze.

"Why would I be crying? *Pssht*. Guess it's been so long since I've been home that you forgot who I am. I shed tears over people like Frankenstein and Dracula, not simple country folk finding true love in the haybarn." The twang she added to her words made an effective mirror to her expression.

"Your sickness for monsters." Hannah sniffed. "Yeah, we haven't forgotten."

Leo valued family, but right then and there, he decided if he never met her siblings, he could live with that.

"So, you and Hank?" Ren's tone was calm and smooth, but her smile was brittle, on the verge of shattering. "That's an unexpected development. When did this monumental occasion occur?"

"We got back from Vegas today and haven't told anyone yet. Hank insisted that we call you first."

"Lucky me."

"Don't act the scorned woman," Hannah snapped. "What happened between you and Hank is well in the past. There's no going back, so get over it."

Leo swallowed a growl and curled his fingers into a tight fist on the bench. What was wrong with these people?

"I'm so far over it I can't even remember what we're discussing." Karen still focused on the ballroom, her sharp smile a permanent tattoo on her face. "Something about cowpies, rocky mountain oysters and carnival princesses gone to the dark side?"

"Stop being a witch when I'm trying to be civil." Hannah paused and her tone softened. "This is more than a courtesy call. Family is important, and we don't want to create any more tension than necessary. We haven't told everyone else yet because we want your blessing first."

Leo made soothing circles on Ren's wrist with his thumb, but if she noticed him beside her at all, he couldn't tell. She remained stiff, the phone clenched tight in her white-knuckled fingers. He knew she was over Hank. The scars she bore came from her own self-doubts, reinforced by people like Hannah, who believed if she didn't conform to a man-made box that she wasn't enough. The very people closest to her, the people who should have shielded her as much as possible and helped her heal, had instead left her wounded and alone.

He wanted to destroy them all and keep her safe from their poisoned arrows, but he'd entered her life too late to prevent the venom already infecting her heart. He could only stand beside her as she fought her way through the pain of the past and back to the present.

Back to him.

"Asking for my blessing after you've done the dirty deed lessens the impact, but whatever. You want my approval? You've got it. One hundred percent, no reservations. I hope your marriage lasts into eternity, Hannah. You and Hank absolutely deserve each other."

The sincerity in Ren's tone sounded so real that Leo would have believed her if not for the betrayal darkening her bright eyes, the frozen smile that seemed to be the one crooked hinge holding her intact. His chest ached for her.

"Thanks, Karen. That's such a relief. You've made us so happy."

"And now my life is complete."

"Don't ruin the moment."

The vise clamped around Leo's chest eased a notch at the return of Karen's sarcasm. Already, she bounced back from the blow of Hannah's call. An extra caramel latte, a snuggle and a few dizzying kisses to reset her focus on the present, and she'd be on the fast lane to recovery.

"Hannah's right," a deep voice said into the speaker. "Your approval means the world to us."

Leo tensed. That voice could only belong to one man.

For a heartbeat, Karen shrunk into herself and jerked straight as if pulled up by strings. "Hey, Hank."

"Hi, Kar-Kar."

Kar-Kar. What a half-witted nickname. Leo scowled, and as much as his possessive side demanded that he tell both Hank and Hannah what they could do with their selfishness, he couldn't surrender to his own whims when Ren needed his strength. Behind the disguise she'd slipped into the moment Hannah had spouted her news, that lost, lonely girl who believed she didn't belong anywhere with anyone curled in the corner.

"Anyway." Ren cleared her throat and said too brightly, "Congrats, you two. I'm in the middle of a time-sensitive project that I need to get back to. Chat later."

Ren ended the call, cutting off any response from Hannah or Hank. She turned the cell off and stared at the blank screen.

"You okay?" When she didn't answer him, he turned her chin his way, guiding her gaze to his.

She blinked and looked at him, really looked at him, as if she'd forgotten he was there at all. That sharp, frozen smile returned. "Why wouldn't I be okay?" She stood, pulling her hand from his. "Come on, Hughes. My parquet isn't going to lay itself."

Leo snagged her wrist before she escaped to the ballroom. "You don't have to pretend with me. You know that." He studied her face, hating the mask she'd donned to hide her hurt, hating the space she planted between them. That worrisome barrier had showed up a couple days ago, creeping between them. "Talk to me, Ren."

"What is there to say? My childhood sweetheart, ex-fiancé got hitched to my little sister." She shrugged. "Good for them."

He arched an eyebrow. "That's interesting, because I barely refrained from swiping your phone from your hand and smashing it so I wouldn't have to listen to the pile of crap that flew from their pieholes."

Briefly, her smile hinted at sincere, erased too soon. "I'm fine. Honest. We have less than three days to finish Granton, and I'm not going to let a little thing like Hannah and Hank taking the plunge slow us down."

She wasn't anywhere close to fine but pushing her right now would get nowhere. He brushed his knuckles over her cheekbone.

Instead of snuggling into him, she walked away, leaving him standing by the bench, alone. An icy nail formed in his stomach, small and sharp, as if the door she'd opened had just closed, locking him out.

Chapter Twenty-Eight

Leo scowled at his missing drill lying on the front porch railing as if he'd left it there. How the hell had it wound up outside? And what had happened to the caution tape he'd tied to the porch?

A ragged remnant of crime-scene yellow fluttered in the wind, all that was left of his warning to keep people off the rotten stairs. The tense knot in his neck tightened.

Someone was messing with him. Usually, he'd set some traps, wait in the shadows for his prey, but with the competition deadline looming large, he didn't have time. And he wasn't going to delay his work, as he believed the culprit—his main suspect, Oliver Hunter—hoped.

He grabbed his drill and stomped back inside. No matter the lack of proof or motive, Oliver was the only person on the premises besides him and Ren. There was no other explanation. If the landscape around the ballroom didn't look as if Granton's original gardener,

Edwin, had been resurrected, he'd fire the Englishman on the spot.

Damn shady horticulture skills.

Circumnavigating the fallen chandelier, he headed for the ballroom. The oddball sabotage over the last couple of days wasn't all that had him on edge. He'd thought he and Ren were on the same page, that she had trusted him with her heart, no more reservations or walls. They'd made a sacred blood vow, after all.

But something subtle had changed between them. No matter how Ren deflected or denied it, Hannah's elopement with Hank had ripped open an old wound that had festered after reading Edwin's letters. She'd spent the last two nights in her own bed, blaming exhaustion and deadlines. Excuses, each one, but pushing her wouldn't end well. When Ren needed space, all he could do was give it to her and wait for her to return to him.

Hope she returned to him.

He frowned at a new stain on the corridor carpet, shook his head and kept going. After Hannah's call, the hairline crevice between them cracked wider with each day. He hated when she shut him out, hated when she stuffed him into categories where he didn't fit. Hated when she wasn't running into his arms where she belonged.

And the final creampuff on his Mount Doom of tension? Little things falling apart for no apparent reason at the eleventh hour. He didn't have the time to fix a crack in the wall that hadn't been there the day before or repaint a rosette that had yellowed overnight. None of the repairs were major or difficult, but with an already-cramped deadline, he couldn't keep up. The judges would notice every detail, both good and bad, big and small.

At the open glass doors of the ballroom, he paused, his heart tripping. An early morning blush crept over the clean floor, highlighting the slivers of oak and ash in the parquetry. The myriad of colors had nothing on Ren. A small paintbrush in hand, she stroked delicate bristles over a pilaster, adding a brightness to paint long faded. She wore jeans with a rip in one thigh and a T-shirt knotted at her waist that revealed strips of pale, tempting skin. The light caught in her hair, making it shimmer like bronze. She looked as if she belonged to dawn and all its glory.

He cleared his throat, and the sound echoed in the quiet, impossible not to notice. "Ren?"

"Yeahuh?" She didn't pause or even look at him, focused on her painting.

He got that she wanted to keep the paint in its duly appointed place, but not even a smile thrown his way wasn't like her. His chest squeezed. "Headed out to Greenville to grab the sander, then to the hardware store. Need another caramel sugar coffee concoction to keep you going?"

"Nope. I'm good."

He waited another heartbeat for her irresistible dimple to show up, for a flippant comment about ogling her from afar. Hell, he would have settled for a sassy middle finger to send him off.

The nothing she gave him left a hollow cavity between his ribs that ached with every step out of the door. The ballroom would be done in a couple of days, and he had the sinking sensation that Ren had decided to be done with him, too.

* * * *

Two hours later, Leo stormed into the hardware store and glared as he passed Steve, the owner's pimple-infested teenage son manning the counter. He didn't care if he wore his scary face. The trip to Greenville had been a waste of time that wrenched his tension to throttle proportions. The special sander he'd reserved — the only one available in the area and required to finish the parquet floor in time for the final judging on Tuesday — hadn't been returned by the previous renter. It wasn't the rental store's fault, and to their credit, they'd apologized and tried to contact the company that hadn't returned the sander, without success. Exorbitant late fees and threats couldn't help him meet his deadline.

Sanding the parquet by hand would be meticulous, time-stealing work, time he didn't have. Ren had no experience, and he had no spare seconds left to teach her. A mistake would be impossible to fix before the judging.

He raked his fingers through his hair and strode down another aisle. Wasting more minutes on a trip to the hardware store to purchase supplies he'd already bought once, supplies that had mysteriously gone missing like his drill, didn't help his bad mood.

If he couldn't meet the deadline, the odds of losing the competition skyrocketed. He might lose every penny he'd invested, the future of his company and poison his dream for Granton Hall. Leo clenched his jaw. He wouldn't let that happen.

He grabbed a box of screws from the shelf, turned, and bumped straight into Harlan Cooper. From the looks of it, she'd been stalking him, waiting to strike when he least expected it. She wore a sneaky smile and paint-splattered overalls, her golden hair tucked up in a ball cap. Steve gawked at her from the cash register up front.

"I've been accused of a variety of offenses over my lifetime but never personally sabotaging my competition's handiwork." She hooked her thumbs in her pockets and rocked on her heels, her dark eyes twinkling. "You must be feeling the pressure if you'd sink so low as to sic the police on me, Leo."

Leo resisted pinching his nose. Officer Hellman's version of interviewing a person of interest probably leaned more toward a Spanish inquisition than a few casual questions. Any information Hellman provided during her interview, Cooper would turn to her advantage — hard.

He schooled his expression into nonchalance. Allowing Cooper to detect any emotion would only encourage whatever notion she'd taken up as her banner. "I didn't accuse you of anything. We were the unfortunate victims of some specific vandalization. I'm sure Officer Hellman was merely being thorough in her investigation and interviewing any possible witnesses."

"Or suspects." She winked. "Hellman was thorough, all right. I have no illusions that I'm at the top of her potential criminal list, which is super-fun. She's quite the feisty beauty, almost makes me want to switch teams. And I've always dreamed about having my own wanted poster hanging on the post office wall."

"Hmm." He folded his arms and didn't miss how her attention drifted brazenly over his chest, along his biceps, dropping all the way to the tips of his work boots. He'd be forever grateful to Ren for kissing him at Seven Devils—and he had to give Cooper some credit for pushing her. Without Cooper blending her concoction of jealousy and coercion, he might still be trapped in the 'friend' box.

"I may not be above an occasional double-cross or sketchy deal to beat out my competitors, cutting a few, unimportant corners to get the job done. But assembling ancient parquet into the shape of an arachnid ain't my style." She shuddered and adjusted her ball cap. "Spiders are the worst."

"Uninterested in your hobbies, Harlan. Too busy winning the competition honestly. See you at the final decision." Before he stepped past her, she blocked the way.

"As further proof of my innocence—and because I'm in a fanfrickintastic mood—I'll let you in on a tiny secret." She cupped her mouth and lowered her voice, leaning in. "The judges are randomly dropping by all the sites today." She winked and straightened. "I'm feeling fine about their responses to my schoolyard cleanup. All that's left are the brass wall plates for the electrical outlets. Super-fancy impressive, if I do say so myself."

That knot in his neck gave birth to two more. Cooper had chosen to turn an abandoned school into business offices for the competition. When she decided to put her personal stamp on a project, the work was quality. He had no doubt the judges had been impressed, especially if the renovation had been completed ahead of schedule.

An early finish might give her a slim advantage, enough to bump her ahead of the pack. A single glance at the ballroom and the judges would know he pushed the deadline.

Harlan grinned, as if she'd read his thoughts and picked out every seed of doubt. "Since your confidence is unshakable and we've always been friendly competitors, you won't mind helping out a local construction girl."

He narrowed his eyes. Cooper's innocent expression made every warning bell shriek. "What is it?"

"You don't happen to know where I might find a tri-planetary sander, do you? A customer wanted some parquetry redone, and wouldn't you know it? The floor is all laid, and no sander. Sanding all that different wood species by hand is such a bitch, but I'm sure you know that." She batted her eyelashes.

It took every ounce of his considerable self-control and upbringing as a gentleman not to hogtie her, stuff her in a crate and ship her off to Antarctica. So that was why he couldn't find the sander he needed anywhere within a hundred miles in any direction. Cooper had rented all of them. Sabotage without officially cheating.

"Good day, Cooper. I'm busy." He somehow managed to keep his voice civil.

"All work and no play… No wonder you're grumpy." Her grin turned malicious. "How's your girlfriend slash inexperienced volunteer?"

The implication that Ren might not be making him happy brought a growl to his throat. He pushed it down and plastered on his war face, all cold menace. No answer required.

Harlan lifted her hands and pivoted. "No need to get prickly over an innocent question. If you ever want to discuss the latest trends with a peer or have an itch that won't go away" — another wink — "my door's always open."

Fixing his gaze on the front counter, he stepped around her.

"And don't worry," she called after him, laughter in her voice, "I won't bring up the police report when I win. If I were you, I'd be more concerned about stirring up Granton ghosts and goblins. Who knows what a murderous ancestral spirit might do when the veil between our world and the spirit realm is at its thinnest?"

How had Cooper learned about his aversion to all things Halloween? Leo set his jaw and dropped the box of screws on the counter. He'd been an idiot to hope that Officer Hellman would be subtle and not tip off Cooper. He could do without her being aware of his setbacks. Then again, with her despicable sander interference, she already knew he scrambled to meet the competition deadline.

He paid for the screws, thanked Steve, who still watched Cooper while she shopped, and went to his truck. Cooper had proven her capability for shady doings, but he doubted she'd sneak into a competitor's site and vandalize their work. She'd grown up in Graywood, too, and was well-known in the community. She'd have to be beyond desperate to risk being caught, damaging her reputation and business.

Leo climbed into the truck, tossed the bag of screws on the seat and shut the door with a bang. Cooper shouldn't even be on the suspect list. Only one other person knew about Ren's situation with the spider, had been present when they'd found that bone and on site daily since the beginning.

Oliver.

The engine roared to life, and he pulled out of the parking lot. It was time to confront Granton's current groundskeeper.

Chapter Twenty-Nine

Karen set the paintbrush down and stretched her back, done coloring one pilaster a fresh shade of pale moon. Smoked cloves teased the air. No matter what room she wandered into the past few days, the aroma trailed her like a memory.

After two sleepless nights in her own bed, wool filled her head and every muscle ached. She could have barfed her opinion about the Hannah and Hank situation on Leo, but it seemed too much like retracing ground she'd already covered with him weeks ago. Backtracking through that swamp wasn't happening.

But Hannah's call had sparked every bad memory to violent life, and she couldn't shake the echoes of her past, the sense that something terrible crouched around the corner, ready to strike. To Hank, her sister possessed all the elements she didn't. And bonus, now at every family event she'd be reminded of all the ways she didn't measure up. Christmas would be a blast.

Karen rubbed her throbbing temples. Even Leo's coffee had lost its magic, powerless against the fuzz clouding her brain—not that she wanted to think. Thinking led to pondering the future, Leo and what waited after the competition. Her heart felt as if it split, tugged apart by sharp teeth. Leaving Granton Hall symbolized leaving Leo. Staying meant a full investment in Granton, in him, in them. She had the distinct impression that no matter what decision she made, she'd wind up the loser.

She needed a break, needed to escape the four walls, clear the paint fumes and pipe smoke from her head.

"I'm going out." She faced the ballroom and narrowed her eyes at the emptiness. "Don't follow me. While I'm gone, consider a different tobacco every now and then. Cloves twenty-four seven gets frickin' old."

Not waiting for a response and positive she didn't want one, she pivoted and pushed open the glass doors leading to the garden.

Clouds scudded across the sullen sky and the breeze carried a chill. Autumn, her favorite season. She zipped up her hoodie and breathed deep. The musky-sweet odor of fallen leaves made a welcome change. Rain whispered on the air. More than once, she'd imagined curling up in a chair beside the library window with a cup of tea and a thick book. In every one of those imaginings, Leo had been there, too.

She wanted that future. The deep ache of that wanting—and what tragedy might wait for her at the end—terrified the red right out of her hair. All the 'what-ifs' tangled her up, kept her frozen at the crossroads.

From behind the boxwood hedge, the scuff of a shovel indicated Oliver worked away. She stuffed her hands into her hoodie pockets and strolled toward the sound. A white moth drifted near her tennis shoe and fluttered past a stand of pale mushrooms. Lavender skirted the pea gravel trail she followed, popping with tiny purple blooms. Their subtle scent blended with the sweetness of a trellised honeysuckle beside a cracked deer statue that was missing one ear.

Oliver focused his landscaping wizardry on the immediate gardens outside the ballroom. He'd single-handedly transformed a jungle into a botanical marvel. She could only imagine how beautiful the grounds had been while Edwin had been their creator and caretaker.

The moment she stepped around the hedge and into view, Oliver paused. He drove the shovel blade into the earth and frowned. "Do you believe I'm capable of so sinister a deed as to despoil your handiwork and arrange it to resemble a spider?" He leaned on the handle and gave her a clear-eyed, guilt-free look. "I apologize if I misled you regarding my expertise, but it encompasses gardening, not woodwork."

She smiled at his disgruntled tone. "Let me guess. You met Katerina Hellman."

"Hellman. Appropriate name." He pushed up the sleeves of his Henley, exposing lean, corded forearms dusted with dark hair. Dirt stained his jeans and boots, evidence of his morning labor.

"So true. Kat can be relentless." Karen sat on the stone bench rescued from two overgrown holly shrubs. "She didn't seem interested in exploring my notion that Elizabeth Granton's spirit is to blame."

"Why would Mrs. Granton's ghost wish to deface the parquet flooring and frighten you in the process?" Ivy that had reigned the rose garden for years rustled as he resumed digging.

Karen resisted touching the spider key tucked in her bra, resting cool and hard against her skin. The letters were locked in the music box to read later when her head space was less preoccupied. Even though Oliver had no apparent ulterior motives, that didn't mean she wanted him knowing about the key, the clock or the letters. Those were sacred secrets shared with Leo alone.

"Maybe she's trying to tell us something." She shrugged.

"That she's deeply insulted at the disruption of her pet spider, and she remains quite unimpressed with your parquet workmanship?" Oliver flashed a teasing grin.

Her stomach dropped. With all the recent happenings, her ego was too raw to let the joke slide off, harmless. She hid it behind a disdainful sniff. "Don't disrespect my new skills. Do you know how tough it was to get the present to fit with the past? One stubborn piece took hours and a lot of cursing to get right."

"I'm simply pestering you, love." Oliver wedged the shovel blade into the ground with his heel and the soil made a hushed sigh, as if he dug up a grave. "I wish I had been around to catch the culprit—provided he or she *is* catchable." He winked and heaved a tangle of ivy roots and dirt next to the bench. The roots writhed like snakes before going still.

Hiding a shiver, Karen looked away. A sliver of the ballroom peeked between the hedge row, a window view from the bench. It was easy to imagine the swirl of colorful gowns passing by, gleaming beneath the candlelight chandeliers. An iron archway transitioned the main pathway to a pocket of roses, a few which still bore red blooms.

"Are you some sort of garden druid?" She twisted to face Oliver. "I can't believe how much progress you've made on your lonesome. The grounds look great."

"I only practice safe vegetation voodoo." He paused and examined the calluses on his hands. "And perspiration. Copious amounts of perspiration. My morning soap and shower wore off hours ago. Perhaps you should reconsider sitting so close."

"I must be downwind. All I smell are the roses."

"Count yourself fortunate." He chuckled and resumed battling the ivy. "The offer to discuss curses and phantoms in more detail over wine remains open, Miss Karen. We may add spiders and debauched flooring to the topics, if you desire. I promise I shall be scrubbed clean and smell better than any withered roses. All dangerous pruners will be placed safely out of reach."

What was it with men wanting to keep sharp objects away from her? "Appreciate the offer, but with the competition deadline on Tuesday, I'll be lucky if I have time to pee." She stretched out her legs and gazed up at the brooding sky. "Do you know the sacrifices I've made for this project? Halloween is this week, and I've been to only one haunted house. One! All the corn mazes, cemetery tours, ghost hunting I've missed? It's tragic. Not even kidding."

"Halloween night then. Prior to the partaking of wine—or after, if you wish—we shall add a haunted location of your choice to the agenda." He paused and cocked his head, studying her. "Unless Mr. Hughes requires your assistance past the competition?"

Oliver was funny, handsome, interesting and not her best friend. It would be easy to say yes, to push Leo back into the just-friends box and secure it with five layers of duct tape. But she'd never betray Leo that way.

"Leo might need me. Probably will. Definitely." She huffed a strained laugh. "My foreseeable free time will be used to sleep, provided I *can* sleep. Lately, drifting off to dreamland has proven almost as hairy as laying parquet flooring."

"I understand." Oliver resumed digging. "However, should you find yourself unable to find your dreams, reconsider my invitation. I often find it difficult to sleep and would welcome the company at any hour."

"Careful, Oliver." She arched an eyebrow at him, going for casual. "You make it sound like I'd bore you into snoring."

"Not at all." He glanced up at her from beneath his dark eyelashes. His gaze flicked over her, heating. "I'm certain you have methods to keep me awake." His obvious interest in her did nothing, not a spark or twitch. Leo had ruined her for anyone else.

"I won't be getting any sleep at all if I don't get back to the grindstone." She stood and faced the ballroom, where her future — whatever direction it led — waited. "I just wanted you to know I never believed you were responsible for any trouble."

"My sincere thanks." Oliver wiped his brow and flashed a stunning smile, all white, gleaming teeth. "I appreciate your confidence in me."

"I should get back to it before the grouchy boss returns. Wouldn't want him to think I'm slacking while he's out."

"Too late." Leo appeared around the corner of trimmed boxwood, scowling, his phone in his hand. "Got a text from Officer Hellman. The results of her investigation are inconclusive, no solid suspects." His chilled gaze landed on Oliver. "Anyone with a motive had a fail-proof alibi. Without any leads, she has nothing."

Made sense. Ghosts were difficult to nail down and interview. "Even Cooper?"

"Cooper didn't have anything to do with it." The growl in his words took her aback. He was *definitely* grumpy.

"How do you know?" Oliver paused, one elbow leaned on the spade handle, his boot propped on the head.

"For one, she had no information about the spider." Leo crossed his arms, intimidating. "Unlike you."

Karen arched an eyebrow. Leo could put on a scary face, but it wasn't like him to accuse innocent people without solid proof. "Leo—"

"Second," he said, continuing over her protest, his focus trained on Oliver, "Cooper wouldn't risk her reputation by sabotaging me in an effort to win the city hall contract. She'd have to be desperate to do something like that."

"Are you certain she isn't desperate?" Oliver asked in a low, careful voice, his eyes flashing.

Were the planets aligned to bring out the worst in hard-headed men? How the hell had this escalated so hard, so fast? "Oliver would never do anything like that."

At last, Leo looked at her. "Hmm."

She narrowed her eyes at him.

"I would never undermine my employer or my first contract in Graywood, Mr. Hughes." Oliver left the spade implanted in the earth and straightened. He met Leo's stare, his green eyes sincere. "My resolve to make a brilliant first impression on this town hasn't changed in the least."

"I haven't paid you yet."

"Hughes." Karen softened her voice. "Maybe the suspects are too obvious and we're overlooking other possibilities."

"Ghosts?" he asked, his tone flat.

"Or teenagers bent on mischief." Even after sharing his cemetery experience, he still chose to explore every rational, scientific explanation before giving credit to any supernatural possibility. Pointing that out wouldn't help her cause. "Until a few weeks ago, Granton used to be open territory, right? If we left any doors unlocked, anyone could have got in. And nothing like that has happened since you installed the security system, right?"

The expression on Leo's face was enough of a 'hmm' that he didn't need to say it aloud.

"Mr. Hughes, I assure you that I took no part in the ballroom happenings. I would never do that to either of you." Oliver laid a hand over his heart, smudging his shirt. "I vow it."

Leo lowered his arms, which had no effect on his scowl. "I won't tolerate any more pranks."

"Tell that to Elizabeth Granton." *Or Edwin.* Karen gave him a bright smile, which he didn't return. What the hell was wrong with her Leo, who always softened for her and only her?

Without another word, he pivoted and stalked toward the ballroom. She trailed after him and threw an apologetic smile over her shoulder at Oliver, who gouged the dirt, leaves and clods flying. His dark expression matched Leo's.

"What," she asked Leo, once they were inside the ballroom, the doors closed behind them, "was that prickly ball of hostility about? Do you honestly believe Oliver made that parquet spider?"

"I don't know what to believe anymore." Leo raked his fingers through his hair and took a deep breath before facing her. "I had the misfortune of running into Cooper at the hardware store."

"Ah." They both avoided discussing the fact that she hadn't changed her mind about applying for the accountant job at Cooper Homes. Tomorrow was her last day at Hamilton & Associates, the point of no return. If nothing else, working with Harlan Cooper would be an adventure.

"She insinuated I got the police involved to manipulate the competition." He shook his head, his beautiful mouth in a tight line. "Slipping that detail to the judges is a given."

"Anyone who knows you would never believe that." She couldn't decide if she should admire Cooper for the sneaky move. Had Cooper pulled it on anyone other than Leo, it wouldn't even be a question.

"Not all the judges are local or know me from Cooper. That's not even the worst of it. When I went to pick up the sander I reserved, it wasn't there." He exhaled roughly. "I suspect Cooper's behind it, not to mention the delightful fact that every tri-planetary sander within a hundred-mile radius is out of stock, on rent or in the shop."

"What does that mean?"

"That means I have to drive across state lines and hope I find a sander in the next few hours. That means I'm toast if I don't." His words were quick and hard, like bullets. "That means when the judges show up for a random site check—which should be any minute now—they'll form their own opinions of both my character and skills."

"Oh, crap." She swallowed the sand in her throat. Leo freaking out freaked *her* out. "The judges are coming *now*?"

"Another Cooper helpful hint. She was too smug to be lying about it." He glanced around the ballroom, at the unstained, half-erected banister separating the stage from the dance floor, the remaining unpainted pilasters, the bare section of wall and the hole with wiring poking out like twisted snakes. His focus lingered on the section of parquet flooring in need of sanding and polish, a dull spot among the elegance, impossible to miss.

"But only the finished product gets judged, right?" Her voice sounded weak in the quiet.

"The judges can base their decisions on whatever they want—craftmanship, economy, personal taste, maintaining deadlines..." Leo hefted a piece of plywood leaning against the wall. "At least when they show up, it'll look like I'm doing something."

"Need my help?" She had an undeniable sense that he blamed her in some way for the disaster.

"Why don't you clean up what you can of the sawdust? Who knows? Maybe we'll get mercy points for cleanliness." Without looking at her, he climbed the stairs and disappeared into the hallway with the plywood.

As Karen grabbed the broom, the ballroom doorbell chimed like Christmas bells. She shoved the sawdust into a heap as voices grew closer. Leo returned to the ballroom, looking grim. The half-dozen judges trailed him, cell phones and tablets at the ready. After an initial greeting, they traded off making notes and taking photos, no telling comments to reveal their opinions.

But she studied their expressions, the narrowed eyes, a sniff or subtle shake of a head. When one judge paused at her parquet flooring and stared down between his polished shoes, her heart stopped.

He circled her handiwork, frowning. With each picture he took, each note scribbled on his tablet, that frown deepened.

She had the distinct sensation of falling from an airplane, helpless, watching the ground get closer. Leo had invested everything in Granton Hall. If he lost this competition, he'd be fighting for years, maybe decades, to recover. What had he done, choosing her as his assistant on this project? She'd been minimal help. Allowing romance into their friendship had undermined his focus. Now, he paid the price.

Because of her. Because of a ridiculous notion that they could be more than best friends. Because he thought she was something *more*. If Leo lost, he'd always be reminded that she had been the reason.

She kept her smile plastered on tight and stared straight ahead until the sting of tears burned away. No matter what they called their relationship, there would be no coming back from this loss.

For either of them.

Chapter Thirty

Monday afternoon, Ren parked in Granton Hall's drive, turned the engine off and sat in the silence, numb. After the judge's unenthusiastic reaction to her parquet, the writing was on the wall. Scribbled, actually, with a neon pink permanent marker.

If Leo lost the contract—a huge probability after the day before—everyone would know why. Leo and his company owned a solid, pristine reputation. No one would blame the local renovation king, which left the newbie volunteer to blame. Cooper would hear the details. The odds of landing the accountant job with Cooper Homes were zilch, minus a few.

All her hopeful plans, smoked to bones and ash.

She dropped her forehead on the steering wheel with a *thunk* and closed her eyes. This morning, her last day at Hamilton & Associates, she'd marched into Mr. Hamilton's office, prepared to perform whatever groveling necessary to get her job back. Instead, she'd come face to face with the new accountant, all friendly smiles and smart questions.

Replaced, faster than a finger snap. No one had even thrown her a going-away party.

Her backup plan had failed, too. She free-fell, nothing beneath her but empty space and the inevitable crash to earth.

Shit.

At a tap on the window, she squeaked and straightened. Leo studied her, his face close to the glass. A line of concern appeared between his eyebrows. She smiled to throw him off.

"Got the sander." He jerked his chin at the house. "Let's move."

Karen blew out a long breath through her teeth and nodded. "Shit."

* * * *

In the wee hours between midnight and dawn, Karen slumped on the ballroom steps. Every muscle ached, even the ones she didn't know she had. Her feet throbbed, her fingers were dead and she could use a few toothpicks to keep her eyelids from drooping. Curling up on the cold marble and taking a long snooze sounded like the best idea she'd had in forever.

"We pulled it off." Leo sat beside her with a weary sigh. He held up his hand for a high five.

"Yay us." She mustered up enough energy to flop her palm against his and slid sideways. Luckily, her head landed on his shoulder.

"Look at what we did, Ren."

"Can't move," she mumbled. He leaned away, and the removal of her headrest forced her to straighten. "Jerk."

He grinned and looked out over the ballroom, finished at last. "Can't you see it? The glory of the past blending with the present?" His whisper melted into the lingering hush as he leaned near. "People will swarm through the open doors to bask in the elegance that is and was Granton Hall. Ready to dance and laugh, forget the outside world for an evening, they'll arrive in colorful gowns and grand suits, their eyes bright."

Karen's weariness slipped into the background as his low, hypnotic voice coaxed her deeper into the image he conjured.

"There will be food and wine, crystal glasses and sparkling light." His focus drifted to the recessed stage with its new, polished banister stained to match the oak pieces in the floor. "Musicians will entertain guests from the stage, playing merry folk tunes for dancing — a flute, piano, fiddle."

In the distance, far beyond the walls and windows, she swore the muted strain of a violin drifted from the night, calling from another time.

"People will linger on the balcony, talking, smiling, gossiping," Leo continued in a murmur. "Some will watch the dancers below. Others will be struck by the glamor above them, the cornices and crystal chandeliers, the delicate artwork of the plaster ceiling."

Karen nodded and lifted her gaze to the ballroom heights. More than a few times she'd gawped at the same ceiling, the intricate details etched into a place where most people wouldn't think to look, let alone find beauty.

"The dancers will be dazzled from every direction as they spin to the music — the frieze of roses and vines stretching above the entrance, the white marble steps, the moonlit garden beyond the windows to the gleaming floor beneath their feet. They'll wonder if they've fallen into a fairy tale."

For a moment, the picture he painted came to full life. Vibrant silk swished and gleamed as dancers passed, circling to the music's rhythm. The darkness beyond the windows softened into waiting mystery and magic. Light and glass glittered. Laughter echoed from the corners, as if sleeping memories stirred awake.

She blinked, and the vision slipped away like morning mist.

"We should celebrate." Before she objected, Leo dragged her into his lap and his lips found hers.

For a breath, two, she drowned in him, tattooing every detail on her heart—how his clothes always smelled of cedar, the silken slide of his tongue on hers, his callused fingertips, the sweet friction on her skin, the leashed power of his arms and the rumble of desire in his throat, fire that he alone ignited in her veins, weaving fantasies of belonging and family and home.

Karen gasped and broke the kiss. She scrambled free before she lost herself completely in him and couldn't find her way back. "Celebrating early is bad luck, Hughes. Everyone knows that. Besides, I barely have enough strength to zombie-lurch to my bed."

Hurt flashed in his gaze. "I don't mind carrying you."

"Manhandled again?" She sniffed, ignoring the pang in her chest. "A girl needs to maintain some semblance of self-respect. And if you want me there when Liam shows up at the butt-crack of morning for a final nitpick session, I need to crash alone for the next three hours."

"Ren." He gave her *the look,* the one that saw right through her.

She hadn't told him about asking for her job back or her thoughts on his odds of winning, couldn't confess that every doubt and fear had slithered beneath her defenses, choking. Pretending was the only way she'd get through the next hour, next day, next week, and she didn't have the willpower while wrapped in his arms. Sleep-deprivation already unraveled the edges of her act. If she lost another button, she'd fall apart.

"Tomorrow's the big day, Hughes." Backpedaling toward the corridor, she mustered up her wicked smile. "See you at dawn, my least favorite hour. Expect snarls and teeth."

Before she buckled, she fled for her room, the scent of cloves and smoke trailing after.

* * * *

Gray light shadowed the hallway as Karen slouched out of her bedroom in yoga pants and a hoodie. She rubbed her grainy eyes and finger-combed her hair. Spending the last hours alone instead of letting Leo distract her with his magic had been a wasted effort. She hadn't slept at all.

She trudged down the stairs in her slip-ons and zipped up her hoodie against the chill. There should be a law about leaving bed before the sun showed up. Why Leo had insisted that she attend Liam's last-minute critique session of the ballroom seemed above and beyond her volunteer pay grade, but the joke was on them. She hadn't put on any makeup.

Her favorite travel mug waited at the bottom of the stairs. Poe's quote of 'Nevermore' beneath the raven felt appropriate for the day. The sweetness of caramel and coffee rising to her nose tightened the gnarls in her stomach, and she left it behind. While she appreciated Leo's thoughtfulness, not even the superpower of caffeine and sugar could help today.

The great iron chandelier still lay askew in the vestibule, and she skirted it. She wouldn't be surprised if Leo hoisted it back into place this afternoon, after the judges made their final visit in a few hours. Her pulse fluttered in her throat.

Hands stuffed in her pockets, she pushed onward into the corridor, past cracked wainscoting and peeling wallpaper, the occasional debris piled to one side, wreckage the judges would never see. Guests would enter through the ballroom door and the renovated corridor leading into the ballroom. She felt as if she floated between the rooms of her own life, some damaged almost to the point of no repair, others recently restored, a few in need of new wiring and a good polish. If only she knew which one she'd find herself in tomorrow.

Muffled voices drifted from the ballroom — Leo and Liam. Putting on the bright and shiny act today would be tough with two members of the Hughes clan on watch. With any luck, Liam would distract Leo enough to keep his attention off her. It would be a temporary delay of the inevitable interrogation waiting for her, but she could only handle one crisis at a time.

Morning strained through the stained-glass windows heralding the ballroom, and as she stepped into the first stream of dull, red light, Liam's words became clear.

"Dude, this is terrible. You expect to win with this renovation tragedy? I'd suggest you quit before you stain the Hughes name beyond repair."

Karen stopped in her tracks, her heart pulsing madly. Both Leo and Liam had learned construction beneath the tutelage of their father, but Liam had refused to join the legacy for reasons she never learned. When it came to details, Liam put Leo's perfectionism to shame. Still, she hadn't expected so harsh a criticism from Leo's otherwise-carefree brother.

"Is that what you call fixing the ceiling?" Disgust turned Liam's voice into a sneer. "It looks like you slapped some clay on and called it good. Maybe you should make an eye appointment, old man. Those cornices with that plaster design are like trying to breed zebras and giraffes." A low, disapproving whistle followed. "What is the name for the ungodly color staining the stage banister, Applesauce Baby Crap? If you're going to stray from the classics, at least make it a natural shade."

Her hands trembled. She'd picked that color because it matched the oak slivers in the floor. Leo had presented her with two options, oak or mahogany, but if Liam mentioned it, she'd chosen wrong, led him astray. What else had she messed up for Leo?

"There's a crack in the second window molding and I guarantee every single judge will hate your tacky choice of wallpaper," Liam continued. "Did you even look at the wainscoting between the windows? It's all wrong, doesn't mesh right with the floor. And speaking of floors, I spotted the repaired section of parquet from outside, no binoculars required. It's like a patch of plaid slapped into a Monet. I adore Ren, you know that, but with so much at stake, was she the best choice for this project? You'd be lucky to get a participation ribbon with this."

All the blood rushed from her head, and Leo's response drowned in the roar filling her ears. The past collided with the present in a twisted train wreck. Every dark emotion burrowed deep in her heart clawed to the surface, doubts inspired by the quirky girl dating the golden boy, the shock of being loved one day by her best friend and rejected the next, the merciless 'I-told-you-so's' from her family, the pitying looks, reminding her over and over how she wasn't enough.

Liam was one hundred percent right. Leo had offered her the volunteer position to humor her need to learn skills for another job. Out of his endless kindness, he'd sacrificed the efficient assistance of an experienced worker for her.

The hall seemed to shrink, suffocating. Allowing romance into the friendship had distracted them both. That wouldn't have any impact on her nonexistent skills, but Leo might have been too preoccupied to notice details a nitpicking judge would detect. She'd been the worst choice possible in a volunteer, and because of her ineptitude — because she wasn't who he needed in so many ways — Leo would lose everything.

Their relationship wouldn't survive. How could it? Leo couldn't deny the truth. Whatever admiration he held for her would disintegrate until he realized she'd been right. Friendship never survived romance. She'd be the reminder of his lapse in judgment, and that reminder would erode whatever remained of their relationship.

She planted a palm against the wall to steady herself and focused on taking one breath after another. The best thing she could do for them both was to break away now, when he still had a chance to recover. A few hours alone without her around to slow him down with 'construction for dummies' would be enough to fix some of her mistakes and still have a shot at winning the competition. He might not be willing to admit it now, but she'd already lost him.

Holy hell, her heart hurt.

Straightening, she forced her chin up. She had to do this now, while she had enough strength, before Leo understood he had to do the dirty deed himself. She could at least spare him that. Karen took a deep breath and crossed the last few feet to the ballroom entrance.

The glass doors were flung open wide. Leo stood beside Liam, his arms folded over his chest, war face on full display. Liam crouched near the short stairwell and frowned at where the banister met the marble.

Leo looked at her. His instant smile melted into a furrowed brow and concerned eyes. Before he spoke, she beat him to it.

"Liam's right. You should have chosen a volunteer who'd give you the best chance at winning. All my obvious novice work will be hard for the judges to overlook."

Leo eased his arms to his sides. He watched her as if she was a bird ready to take flight. His intuition had always been spot on. "Liam's an ass, Ren. You know that."

"Rude," Liam muttered.

"I distracted you with ghost stories and mysteries"—*and wasn't strong enough to resist your magical kisses when it was in both of our best interests*—"when we should have been focusing on the work. Granton is your dream, Leo, a tribute to your father, and I—"

"I don't regret a single minute," he growled. He took a step toward her, and when she backpedaled, he stopped. "I know what you're implying, Ren." His blue eyes pierced her soul. "Don't. It's not true."

"Even if you can't bring yourself to believe the truth, that doesn't mean it's not real."

"Right back at you, darling." He stuffed his hands into his jeans' pockets, going for casual. The tension in his jaw betrayed him.

"I'm leaving. Without me here, you'll at least have a few hours to fix what you can of my screwups before the judges arrive."

"Ren—"

She spun on her heel and hurried into the corridor. Whatever possessions were upstairs in her room could be collected later. Right now, she needed to escape Granton Hall.

And Leo.

"Ren, wait." Leo's footsteps pounded the floor, getting closer. Outrunning him was impossible. She should've known he wouldn't let her leave without a fight, without trying to soften the blow of Liam's statements. That's what he did—held on stubbornly to his convictions even when they were a bomb waiting to be detonated.

Karen didn't slow, didn't look at him as he came abreast of her and matched her pace. "I have to go. Quit following me and get back to the ballroom, Hughes. The floor isn't going to fix itself."

"There's nothing wrong with the floor." He cursed beneath his breath, and as she entered the vestibule, he grabbed her arm, dragging her to a stop. He pulled her around to face him, and she had no choice but to look at him. The hurt in his gaze felt like a fiery blade skinning her heart.

"Don't do this, Ren. I invited Liam this morning as a second pair of eyes because he doesn't miss anything. That doesn't mean I agree with his assessments. He points out ridiculously small, unimportant details. He finds flaws in everything because he takes great joy in being a construction critic a-hole. You can't take anything he said to heart."

Too late. "Liam is right. You deserve a woman who is at your level in every way. I'm destined to disappoint you."

"Not true." His expression hardened. "Liam is an idgit, and you've never disappointed me."

"Give it until tomorrow." She managed a small smile, hating that the admiration he'd always held for her would never be the same. If only he was right and no matter what she did, he'd always respect her, treasure her.

Love her.

He cupped her face. "You could only disappoint me by leaving now, like this, without working it out."

"Then I guess you'll be disappointed even sooner than tomorrow." She pulled away from his hold before she gave into the urge to lean into his strength and let him try to fix everything. This couldn't be fixed. Their relationship was a dilapidated mansion on the verge of crumbling to dust. She grabbed her keys hanging by the door. "I need to go."

"I need you to stay." A growl of frustration entered his voice.

"Focus, Hughes." All her emotions gathered into a vibrating ball of razor blades, and she glared up at him. She couldn't take much more of his stubborn denial without shattering. "What you need is to grab your tools and put them to use in fixing the ballroom as best as you can."

"Not without you." He folded his arms across his chest, his eyes narrowed and glittering with fury.

"Stop it," she snapped. "Do what you can to salvage your dream for Granton, because you sure as hell can't renovate me." Once again, she pivoted for the door.

He snagged her wrist. "I wouldn't change a thing about you, Ren." The roughness in his voice threatened to undo her. "I love you exactly as you are. There's nothing beneath the sun, in the depths of the earth or the heights of the stars that has the power to alter how I feel about you. *Nothing*."

Karen kept her gaze on her fingers gripping the doorknob. If she looked at him, she'd break into jagged pieces. "Let me go, Leo."

"You're really just going to walk away?"

"I have to." She swallowed hard. "For both our sakes."

He hesitated, then dropped his hand. "I'll always be here, Ren. Never forget that."

No, you won't.

She flew out of the front door and ducked under the first line of caution tape strung between the porch pillars. Launching over the dangerous steps, she cleared the second barrier of tape and hit the ground running before he reconsidered and gave chase. If he caught her again, told her that he loved her, she'd crack. A sob escaped as she stumbled to her car. She flung herself inside and floundered with the keys. As she took off down the driveway, she looked once at Granton in her rearview mirror, the mansion warped through her tears.

I love you, too, Leo.

Chapter Thirty-One

Leo remained frozen, too stunned to do more than watch Ren disappear through the front door. It felt as if she'd taken a sledgehammer to his ribs, ripped open his heart and left him to deal with the destruction alone. How could she walk away as if they were nothing, neither lovers nor friends? They'd made a blood vow, for God's sake. That, at least, she should hold sacred.

Yet, she'd turned her back on him, on *them*.

He raked his fingers through his hair. Ever since reading Edwin's letters, she hadn't been herself. Hannah's call had strengthened whatever storm brewed inside her. She'd tried to hide it in typical Ren fashion, but her smiles had been forced, the usual fire in her eyes clouded. Topped by Liam's tactless comments, the lost girl who still doubted her value rose from the grave.

Leo kicked the iron chandelier, and the clang echoed to the ceiling. He thought he'd gotten through to her, that she trusted him enough to always choose her, always love her. If she couldn't put the past behind her enough to do that, what hope did he have of the future he wanted with the only woman he needed beside him?

"What was that all about?" Liam strolled in from the corridor, idly scratching his stomach, one thumb hooked in his Bermuda shorts pocket. He wore innocence like armor, as if he hadn't played a part in bringing down the woman Leo loved, fracturing the fragile chance he had at winning her heart forever.

Before he even thought to act, his fist connected with Liam's jaw. His brother stumbled and toppled on his keister beside the giant chandelier, his blue eyes wide.

"What was that for?" Sprawled on the floor, Liam rubbed his jaw, looking sour.

"For being an insensitive ass. Be thankful I didn't break your nose."

Liam's eyebrows rose. "Um, thank you?"

"You're welcome." Leo held out a hand and hauled Liam to his feet. "Sorry."

"Any time you need to use me as a punchbag, dude, I'm there for you." Despite his brave words, he stepped beyond reach. "Next time, give me a warning...or a weapon to defend myself with."

Slumping, Leo wandered to the stairs and sank onto the second step. He stared at his clasped hands rather than his brother. "Ren left."

"To get celebratory donuts?" Liam asked hopefully.

"No, moron. She left *me*."

"Oh." Liam draped his arms over the banister, studying him. "Bummer."

"Yeah." Leo squeezed his eyes shut, his chest aching.

"If it's any consolation, I'm still here, gracing you with my glorious presence."

He cracked one eye and glared at his brother. "It's not."

"Want to play it out in the ring? Sabers, swords, name it. I'll run home and grab mine."

As much as he needed an hour or four in the ring to plow through the frustration, the pain, the helplessness — the fear that he'd lost Ren forever — he shook his head. Ren believed she'd ruined the competition for him. While total crap, he understood the roots of that belief. The one chance he had at convincing her that their relationship would survive whatever the world threw at them was to prove her wrong. She wouldn't listen unless they beat the competition.

"Thanks for the non-help." Leo stood and shoved Liam toward the door. "Out. I need to work."

"No need to be pushy, big brother." Liam opened the front door and glanced over his shoulder. "And, dude, replace the steps before someone sues you."

"Tomorrow," he growled. At least the bright yellow warning tape hadn't vanished again.

"There's no working tomorrow. After you win, it's a free for all in the ballroom until you drop." Liam wriggled his eyebrows. "I'll bring the beer."

Until he had Ren back in his arms where she belonged, he couldn't promise anything. Leo assumed his war face. "We'll see what tomorrow brings."

* * * *

Instead of going to her apartment where Leo would expect her to be, Karen drove for hours. Leo always knew when to give her space, but the way she'd left had been different than any other time, echoing the finality of a breakup. He wouldn't miss that detail, and she had no idea how he might deal with new territory.

The tepid sun dropped toward the horizon when she circled back to Graywood, nowhere else to go. She hoped Leo hadn't planted his butt outside her apartment door, waiting for her to return rather than focusing on fixing the ballroom. The thought made her stomach twist. Like the brave shield-maiden she was, she headed for Seven Devils, where she could drown her sorrows for an hour or two before facing her doom.

As Karen stepped inside the pub, a green-eyed witch with wild black hair dropped from the ceiling and cackled. She swung her broom around before going silent and mechanically returning to the shadowed eaves. Lines of dancing red devils with horns, tails and pitchforks decorated the walls. Cobwebs filled the corners and rubber bats dangled from the ceiling. A lone skeleton wearing a blood-red tie hunched in a bar stool beside a jack-o-lantern with a wide, wicked grin.

Halloween. For the first time ever, she had no desire to join in the revelry of her favorite holiday.

Besides the decorations, Seven Devils hadn't changed. It felt like a lifetime ago that she'd had her first real Leo kiss here, the pivotal point that led to losing her best friend. She headed straight for the bar, where Jed stood as if waiting for her.

"Hey, Jed. Long time no see." Karen slid onto a bar stool and breathed in the aroma of fried food and beer. When everything else in her life had been smashed like an abandoned pumpkin, at least Seven Devils remained the same.

Jed popped the cap of her favorite dark beer and set it before her.

"You're the best." She gave him a small smile. "Chicken wings and garlic tots."

"And a witch's heart?"

Not even her favorite Halloween cocktail, all blackberries and purple shimmers, sparked her interest. "Maybe later."

He winked and headed off to place her order.

"What's a pretty girl like you doing drinking alone at four in the afternoon?" Harlan Cooper hopped onto the next bar stool and shimmied out of her denim jacket. Her grin was wide, sly, much too close to a hyena's. "Shouldn't you be crossing your fingers, praying or rubbing some dead animal's severed foot with Hughes at Granton Hall in hopes of the big win tomorrow?"

"Shouldn't you be doing the same?" As much as she respected Cooper's bravery for her choice in careers, standing by while she made insinuations about Leo wasn't happening. "Leo rocks. He doesn't need any of that to win."

"Time will tell. And I'd rub anything Hughes asked me to, lucky charm or not." Cooper motioned at Jed, the rhinestones on her shirt winking like demented stars. The forked tail on the last letter of the glittering word 'Angel' seemed fitting. "Whiskey sour, please, honey."

A drink with Harlan instead of moping alone made for proper punishment. At least *Monster Mash* blared from the jukebox, not a tear-jerking country song about family and loss.

Cooper pivoted in the stool, facing her. "I don't mean to pry—ha, kidding. Why isn't your scrumptiously moody renovation partner aka boyfriend here with you?"

"Because I suck at construction." She snorted and slid her finger through the condensation on the beer bottle. "I volunteered to learn some basic skills and land the open accountant job with—wait for it—Cooper Homes." She glanced at Harlan. "Quite the twist, isn't it?"

"You're an accountant? Why didn't you say so earlier?" Harlan studied her, and for a moment, the brash pretense vanished. Shrewdness flashed in her dark eyes, revealing the successful businesswoman beneath the coveralls and outrageous flirtations. "I've been searching for a good bookkeeper for months. You're hired."

Karen choked on her beer. "Sounds like a solid plan, hiring with no interview or references. Didn't I just mention my crappy construction skills? My sources say you require even accountants to fill in if necessary."

Harlan waved a dismissive hand. "Hughes trusted you enough to hire you. That's enough for me."

"He didn't hire me." The needles in her heart sharpened and grew fangs. "I volunteered."

"Dammit." Her full, pink-glossed lips pursed in a pout. "I was hoping you'd screw up and confirm he paid you, which would eliminate him from the competition. A girl uses what she can to get ahead in a man's world." She winked.

"Like messing with a competitor's parquetry?" Karen narrowed her eyes.

The smile Cooper flashed was all sugar and spice. "If I'm going to mess with wood, it wouldn't be of the forest tree species, if you know what I mean."

Ew. "Or renting all the tri-planetary sanders in the immediate area so there wouldn't be one available for a rival?"

Harlan threw her head back and laughed, long and throaty. "I wish I'd been that clever." Her dark eyes twinkled, not an ounce of regret or pity. "What a coincidence, though, right? I discovered the sander shortage because my own equipment broke down, and I needed one for a client. That job doesn't have a deadline of today." She propped her chin on a fist and sighed. "What I wouldn't pay to see Leo Hughes throw a hissy fit."

"It wasn't very exciting. He found a sander in time, not that you need any edge." Sawdust filled her throat. "If he loses the city hall contract competition, it's on me."

"I admit I was surprised by his choices. Renovating the ballroom at Granton Hall is ambitious. Would've been a challenge even for me and my best, most experienced guy." Harlan took the tumbler Jed set on the counter and swirled the amber liquid. "Then he picked an assistant with zero experience. I thought the golden era of Hughes & Sons Construction might finally be at an end."

Karen stared at the glittering line of colorful bottles behind the bar and willed her eyes to stay dry. Of all the people to show up at Seven Devils, why did it have to be Cooper, reminding her of all the reasons she came here to forget?

"But as much as Hughes is grumpy as hell and annoyingly immune to my charms, he's a pro. He doesn't do anything halfway. If he chose you to help him, he knew what he was doing." Harlan clinked her glass against the bottle in Karen's limp hold. "Cheer up, honey. He'd never let shoddy workmanship stand under his watch. When he loses to me tomorrow, it will be because I'm better."

If only. Cooper's words twisted that dagger in her heart deeper. Karen took a swig of her beer. Leo would have been better off not telling her anything about Granton Hall until after the competition. The renovation would have been done to perfection. He'd have no worries about winning the contract and gaining the publicity he needed to make his dream for the antique estate reality. Not only had she ruined it for him, she'd ruined it for all the women and children he wanted to help. She'd ruined the legacy he wanted to leave in memory of his father.

She drained the bottle. Jed slid a basket of wings and tots in front of her, too late. Her appetite had taken a hike.

"Speaking of grumpy, I'd be all for climbing that tree if he even looked at me twice. He knows how to keep a girl humble." Harlan snagged a tot from the basket and popped it into her mouth. "I suspected that all those lickable muscles were being wasted on another man, a true tragedy for women everywhere. But that night, before you kissed him, the way he looked at you nearly smoked me alive. I wasn't about to stop you, not with those sparks." She winked. "I'm a bit wicked that way."

Thinking about that night, Leo's mouth on hers, the fantasies invading reality, threatened to pull her deeper into the well she'd found herself in. Leo was her own personal tragedy, and she had no intention of sharing that with Cooper. "Why aren't you celebrating your upcoming win somewhere?"

"I am." Harlan lifted a chicken wing. "Do you mind?" She pulled it apart before Karen answered and ripped a hunk of meat free with her teeth. "Want to start on Monday?"

Cooper celebrating by hanging out alone at Seven Devils hit too close to home. Karen couldn't decide which of them was more pathetic. "You're not going to interview me, check my references, discuss what I can bring to Cooper Homes? Confirm my construction skills or lack thereof?"

"I do have a question, off the record." Cooper wiped her mouth with a white napkin, the gesture so prim and proper it bordered on comical. "Are you and Leo still a thing? Together? Swapping body fluids?"

After tomorrow, she'd be lucky if they remained acquaintances.

"Actually, that doesn't matter." Cooper swirled her whiskey glass. "He's so into you he can't see straight. Unless you royally screwed the pooch at Granton Hall, that won't change overnight. I'd wait my turn, but patience has never been one of my numerous virtues."

Karen lifted her bottle, remembered it was empty. Hell, her heart ached.

"I like you, Ives." She laid a business card on the counter, finished her drink and stood. "Give me a call. I think we can figure out a proposal that will satisfy us both."

If she wanted to stay in her chosen field and in Graywood, Cooper's job offer was the lone oasis in an endless desert. But did she want to work for Leo's competitor, someone who took every opportunity to make him uncomfortable? Best friend or not, even if he put her in the enemy category, she had too much respect for Leo to do that to him.

"Harlan." She pivoted in the stool as Cooper struggled into her denim jacket. "I appreciate your blind faith in my abilities." The chuckle coming from Cooper seemed sincere. "But after the last few weeks, it's clear that me being anywhere near unfinished construction projects isn't good for anyone."

"Karen, Karen, Karen." Cooper rested her elbows on the back of the empty bar stool. "Leo is yummy on an unchartable level, I get that. I'd commit any number of sins to keep him. I tease him because it's fun to ruffle his sleek feathers. We don't see eye to eye, which is okay." Memories shadowed her eyes, and every ounce of humor and pretense faded into a woman who had endured a war and walked off the battlefield victorious. "But don't let any man, even Leo Hughes, keep you from what you want—not his opinion, what he does or doesn't offer, whether or not he supports you. If you want it, go for it. Life is too short to let whatever makes you happy and free slip away."

The wisdom in her words took Karen by surprise. "You should be a bartender."

"Too boring." Cooper winked. "Think about it. Keep my card." With a swish of denim, she swept for the door. "I hope you call."

Karen turned back around and thanked Jed as he opened another beer for her. No matter what she chose to do, it would be without Leo.

Chapter Thirty-Two

Halloween morning, Leo stood in the city hall parking lot with a crowd of hometown busybodies and cameras. He kept his expression serene and pretended to listen to the mayor's speech as she huddled beneath a hastily erected awning. The rain predicted for later in the afternoon had arrived early, and everyone showed up in coats and boots, umbrellas held tight.

He'd left his umbrella behind and slouched beneath his rain jacket hood. The tip of his nose regretted his decision—wet, cold and miserable. Liam stood beside him, looking comfortable in his Bermuda shorts and slicker. Within gloating range, Cooper vibrated with anticipation, bright-eyed and dry beneath an umbrella patterned with screws, nails and hammers.

The empty space where Ren should be felt like an arctic sky, endless and icy. After she'd gone, he'd texted her at every break, all delivered, none read. He'd left a dozen messages, asking her to attend today, hoping for a response that never came. When she decided on a certain path, changing her mind took a mountain of patience and an eternity of waiting.

He could handle the wait, would let her know every day that he wasn't going anywhere. It was the uncertainty that eroded his confidence, minute by minute. What if she never returned to him?

A win today would erase that worry. He'd noted Liam's harsh observations and analyzed every detail. Beyond an extra polish here, a touch-up there, the repairs had been flawless. The ballroom was a restored masterpiece, bringing back an era of elegant candlelight dances, when guests arrived by carriages wearing their best gowns and suits.

When they won today, Ren would have no reason to doubt, no excuse to avoid him. While her distrust hurt, he understood her fear of repeating the past. Only she could decide to fight it. He'd prefer to stand back-to-back with her on that battlefield.

"Dude, are you listening?" Liam elbowed him in the side. "The mayor's announcing the winner."

Cooper grinned from beneath her oversized umbrella, looking presentable in calf-high boots that met the hem of a belted raincoat. "The big moment, Hughes. Can't wait to see how sore of a loser you are."

Ignoring Harlan as much as possible, Leo focused on the mayor.

"I'd like to thank all the other judges who invested their time. Each and every site was inspected multiple times and the final decision based on the results of our talented competitors." The mayor stepped aside and gave the limelight to the people lined up behind her. Cameras clicked and flashed. The audience clapped as the judges waved.

Leo skipped over the local judges and landed on Jared Summers, the writer from *Renovation & Remodel*, the one judge he hadn't met before the competition. He'd made a point not to do more than shake hands with the man. To avoid any accusations of hometown favoritism, he'd been carefully neutral in any interaction, letting the renovation itself do the entire work of winning.

Jared waved at the crowd when the mayor introduced him, and when his gaze found Cooper, his smile widened. Leo cursed under his breath. Maybe staying aloof had been a mistake.

The applause settled and the mayor gestured to someone in the crowd to come up front. "And an extra thank you to Graywood's newest local landscaper, Oliver Hunter of Hunter Horticulture and Garden Design. He agreed to be our secret judge." Looking dapper in a fedora, overcoat and brogue boots, Oliver joined the mayor. He flashed a winning smile. "Over the past month, Mr. Hunter wore all manners of disguises and played parts both small and large to keep the contestants honest."

"Sonuvabitch." Leo scowled. "I paid him to tame the grounds around the ballroom. I suspected him of foul play but not being the secret judge. That ruins my foul play theory."

"Foul play?" Liam looked at him askance.

"Not by me." Cooper batted her eyelashes as the audience quieted.

Leo shifted to block Cooper from his conversation and lowered his voice. "Someone broke into the ballroom and messed with Ren's parquet while we were out one night. Tried to scare us by arranging the loose pieces into the shape of a spider."

"Oh…that."

The lightness in Liam's tone, the way he focused on the stage as if by ignoring his big brother he might escape in one piece clicked into place. Leo narrowed his eyes. *Liam* had messed with the parquetry and hadn't said a word about it, waiting for him to figure it out.

"After the crowd clears and all witnesses are gone," he growled, "we're having a chat, long and violent."

"Bygones," Liam said from the corner of his mouth. "Not my fault you lost your sense of humor and involved the authorities over a harmless prank."

"Harmless?" Leo ground his teeth together until he could control his fury. The spider and tobacco pouch, music and letters, relocated equipment and minor repairs—how much of it was Liam responsible for? Liam knew how important this project was to him, how losing could ruin him. The stress, lost sleep, near heart attacks went far beyond fun and games.

"The votes are in, collected and counted by an independent source." The mayor dragged his attention away from Liam. His brother owed Mayor Evans his life. She lifted a white, sealed envelope. "The winner will be awarded the contract to renovate Graywood's city hall building and be offered a sought-after spotlight in the nationally acclaimed *Renovation & Remodel* magazine."

"Open it already," Cooper muttered, her fingers tight and bloodless around the handle of her umbrella.

For once, Leo agreed with Cooper.

The mayor ripped open the envelope as rain drummed on umbrellas, pavement, and the tip of Leo's icy nose. Leo held his breath as she freed the card inside. "And the winner is…"

"Dammit, woman," Cooper said through clenched teeth. "Spit it out."

At Cooper's outburst, both Leo and Liam looked at her. She looked like she was ready to stab the mayor in the eye with the point of her umbrella.

"The winner is," the mayor continued, her smile bright, "Graywood Grand Homes. Congratulations."

A knot of men and women hooted in celebration and the crowd erupted in applause. Leo stared at the mayor, numb, waiting for some sign that she'd read the name wrong, made a mistake or confessed Liam played another sick joke.

I lost.

He could recover—eventually—but this loss reached far deeper than his pockets. His dream to turn Granton into a safe place for single mothers and their children would take years longer, maybe decades, to complete. He'd have to make it a spare time project rather than his sole focus. On top of that, Ren would blame herself for the loss. As long as she believed it, there would be no convincing her otherwise.

He'd lost everything.

"Graywood Grand Homes?" Cooper scoffed, her voice sounding far away. "They can't hammer two boards together without cracking a hard hat. This is an outrage. I'd believe it if Hughes beat me, but them? No way in hell." She snapped her umbrella shut, and raindrops glistened in her pale hair. "I'm speaking to the mayor." She stomped through the crowd, on a war path toward the unlucky mayor.

"Tough luck, Leo." Liam squeezed his shoulder. "I'm at your disposal for however long you want to spend in the ring. I'll bring pizza, too—"

He shrugged off Liam's hand and forced himself to the people surrounding Graywood Grand Homes. Woodenly, unable to remember names or faces, he shook hands, offered congratulations, acted the gentleman he'd been taught to be and escaped into the rain.

Alone.

* * * *

Halloween had sucked big time. Karen kept all the lights in her apartment off and huddled on the floor in the dark while the laughter and chattering of trick-or-treating children flowed by like the underworld river Lethe. She wished she could take a sip of its waters as the dead did so she could forget her earthly existence, too.

The local evening news had covered the competition results, and the slim hope that Leo would win despite her interference, that their friendship could be resurrected from the ashes, had disappeared in a *poof* of sawdust. It had been bad enough leaving him, sacrificing the privilege of being swept away by his magic, but knowing she'd been responsible for the destruction of his dream to honor his father? Her own broken heart was one thing. Breaking his was too much to bear. She sank into a black hole and didn't bother struggling for the surface.

November morning shimmered into existence and drifted into evening over and over, a blurred, endless cycle—two days passing? Three? She couldn't bring herself to care.

Rain pattered sullenly on the roof. Night held her apartment in gloom, perfect for her mood. Curled on the couch, she pulled the *Dark Shadows* pillow Leo had given her last Halloween over her face, a suffocation attempt with feathers and embroidery, at least enough to pass out for a few moments of peace. When that failed, she groaned and threw the pillow across the room. It smacked into a lamp. The lamp teetered, then toppled into a chair, its shade caved in, defeated in the cushions.

The doorbell buzzed as if alerted by the lamp's demise. Karen blearily looked at the door. The drumming rain outside and stillness of her apartment had become so familiar, the noise seemed out of place.

A knock vibrated the door, followed by a voice. "Miss Karen? Are you home?"

She recognized that English accent. Why would Oliver be here? She pushed herself to a sit, which took far too much energy, and raked her fingers through her hair. Yoga pants and the ratty, oversized sweatshirt from her high school Shakespeare club had been her wardrobe choice of the week. If Oliver dared to disturb her wallowing, he deserved the fright he'd get. On bare feet, she trudged to the door and opened it.

Oliver's eyes widened as he took her in, but he wisely made no comment. Raindrops glistened in his dark hair and gray wool sweater. He held a bottle of wine. With outdated civility, he sketched a bow. "I regret intruding on your solitude, but I must speak with you."

Conversation wasn't anywhere in her wheelhouse at the moment. She'd be lucky if she could string two sentences together, let alone have an intelligent discussion about…anything. Add wine to the mix, and she'd be a drunken fool in two sips.

He must have sensed her hesitance because he added, "It's of utmost importance, Miss Karen. The wine is not for tonight, more an apologetic gesture for imposing without invitation." His eyebrows rose. "Although, I did attempt to phone you."

Yeah, she hadn't wanted to see what tragic news her cell phone might hold for her. Keeping it off made it easier to pretend the world outside her apartment remained in limbo, like her.

"Please?"

She sighed and opened the door wider. "Fine."

Oliver's gaze skipped over her apartment, the box of crackers lying askew on the coffee table, several mugs and cups of varying size, the half-full cereal bowl and its colorful sugar crisps floating in milk that had turned pink. Nothing but health food for her. He flicked on a lamp, and light chased away her new friends, the shadows. After settling the bottle of wine on an empty spot between the glassware, he got comfortable in the chair across from the couch.

Dammit. She was hoping for a quick conversation before kicking him out and resuming her date with darkness and gloom. Karen picked up her pillow along the way and slumped onto the couch, one leg tucked under her.

"What's up, Oliver?" She pulled the pillow close. Nothing better than stuffing to shield her from reality. "I'm quite busy."

"I see that." He flicked a glance at the toppled lamp. "I promise I won't keep you from your critical labors long."

She narrowed her eyes. "Watch your tone, sir."

His mouth quirked, and the hint of humor faded. Leaning forward, he clasped his hands. "I hope you don't bear me any ill will for acting as the secret judge."

"Why would I?" She shrugged one shoulder. "Of the acts you were suspected, the secret judge wasn't one. Sounds like a job well done."

His expression darkened. "My only deceit was hiding my role from both you and Mr. Hughes, as required." He paused. "However, I do have a confession to make."

"I knew it." Curiosity dragged her from the melancholy for a moment. "You murdered an innocent passerby with your pruners and buried the body beneath the rosebushes."

His eyebrows rose, then a smile came to full life, sharp and shiny as any pruners. "Not quite so thrilling as that, I fear. I suppose I should count myself fortunate for only being suspected of foul play with spiders and parquetry."

"Everyone knows to be on guard with the gardener, especially if he's English and shows up unexpectedly, offering convenient groundskeeping services."

"Thank you. I am now aware of the conditions I must aspire to."

The tiniest of grins found its way to her mouth.

His shoulders lifted and fell as he drew a long breath and released it. "I am a descendant of Greta Lockwood, Edwin's sister."

Karen sat up straight. "No way."

"It's true, I'm afraid."

"And you didn't mention it right away because...?"

"Mr. Hughes was already hesitant to hire me. Informing him of my personal attachment to his new real estate investment wouldn't have helped my cause."

She nodded. He had her there.

"I always knew, deep down, that my ancestral history would bring me here, to Graywood and Granton Hall. The timing of the competition and my arrival was nothing short of serendipitous. I took being offered the role of secret judge as a good omen." Shadows seemed to gather around him as he lowered his voice to a hush. "Tales of Granton Hall have passed down through our family for generations, of the tragedies that befell my great-uncle Edwin and his childhood friend Elizabeth there."

Frozen, Karen clutched her pillow tight on her lap. For a moment, the sorrow she'd clung to the last few days ceased to exist.

"I'd always been fascinated by the legend, of love forbidden and whispers of murder, wicked deeds never made right, restless spirits and haunted halls." A sparkle entered his eyes. "You see why I might share your same interests in the supernatural?"

"Totally." If she'd switched places with Oliver, she'd be all over it. At least he had a valid excuse for his infatuation. She only had her natural quirkiness to blame.

"A year ago, I inherited my great-grandmother's house when she passed on. As I went through the process of cleaning it out, I discovered an old trunk in the attic."

"Family secrets," Karen whispered.

"I daresay. Old portraits, drawings, baubles, poems and letters, a journal handwritten by Greta Lockwood herself." He shook his head, memories in his eyes. "I sat in that attic for hours, poring over my ancestral history, reading Greta's faded words."

Oliver stared at his hands for a long moment, as if he'd slipped back in time, back to that attic and the discoveries he'd made. At last, he cleared his throat and continued. "After the deaths of Edwin then Elizabeth soon after, Greta had no desire to remain at Granton Hall as its housekeeper. She fled as fast and as far as she could and landed in England—married, settled down, had children. But no matter the distance, she never forgot what happened at Granton Hall, to her beloved brother and her dear friend Elizabeth."

"What happened?" Her voice shook in time with her pounding heart, the truth of Elizabeth and Edwin's fates so close she couldn't stand it.

"Greta believed Edwin's death wasn't natural, that he was murdered...poisoned."

"By Arthur Granton?" Karen grabbed a random mug from the coffee table, took a sip of days-old, room-temperature coffee and blanched. Her coffee, even when fresh from the pot, never tasted like the ones Leo made for her.

"Indeed, at least to Greta's mind. Due to Edwin's lowly position, the local authorities refused to investigate his death. Arthur had the status and clout to push the issue if he desired. The fact that he chose not to, even after Greta's request, deepened her suspicion."

If Arthur had read any of the letters she'd found in the grandfather clock, penned by Edwin with such obvious love for Elizabeth, it wasn't hard to imagine what might have happened.

"A jealous, cuckolded husband eliminating the competition." Karen nodded, feeling giddy, like an investigator discovering unexpected clues to an ancient mystery. "Makes total sense."

"There was no competition, according to Greta. Elizabeth never demonstrated any affection toward Edwin beyond friendship. Edwin's love remained unreciprocated." Oliver leaned back in the armchair and stretched out his legs. "Until after his death."

Her heart spasmed, trapping all the breath in her lungs. Rain slashed against the windows, pounding with the tempo of her pulse. The darkness crept closer, daring her to acknowledge the terrible truth, a truth that hit so close to home it felt like a physical blow. Elizabeth and Edwin had been best friends since childhood. She'd believed he would always be there for her. She'd taken Edwin's love for granted, marginalized their relationship, pushed it into the background for reasons Karen could easily imagine — comfort, boundaries...fear.

And lost him forever.

"Elizabeth realized she loved Edwin after he was gone." Her mouth went dry as sand. "Too late."

"Indeed." Oliver fiddled with a snag in his sweater, as if needing something to do without a garden tool in his hands. "Greta and Elizabeth mourned Edwin together. Elizabeth became inconsolable, despondent, then disappeared. An investigation was launched, of course, without answers. Once again, no foul play was discovered, and as Mr. Granton did not pursue the matter, her disappearance remained a mystery."

"And Greta believed Arthur killed Elizabeth for loving Edwin?" When she'd read Edwin's sappy letters by the glow of her cell phone, huddled on the floor in Leo's bedroom, she'd felt his pain at losing Elizabeth's friendship. But the agony Elizabeth must have endured, losing Edwin forever? Maybe, with her best friend gone, she hadn't been afraid to die.

"Greta's journal makes no mention of it. My guess is Elizabeth became more of a nuisance than the proper wife Mr. Granton wanted, and he remedied the problem."

Cold skittered down her arms. "Do you think her bones are buried in Granton's walls?"

"I don't believe anyone will know for certain until the house falls into rubble." His smile held a bittersweet edge. "That won't happen in the near future, thanks to our determined Mr. Hughes."

Her stomach dropped at the mention of Leo's name, and reality crashed like a cold, ocean wave salting her wounds. She hunched into her pillow. "Why are you telling me instead of Leo? It's his property."

"I attempted to. After the gathering at city hall, I intended to speak to him, to explain." Oliver spread his hands in a helpless gesture. "He didn't linger long enough for me to do so."

All the guilt she'd been holding inside boiled up from the depths of her gut.

"Later that day, I returned to Granton Hall. Mr. Hughes was most distraught. Before I uttered a greeting, he trespassed me from the premises. I dared not attempt to change his mind. He appeared quite ready to forcibly drag me. He followed me to the end of the drive and locked the gate behind me. I am certain he would have run his sword through me at the slightest provocation."

Oh, Leo. She blinked back the tears that sprang to her eyes. Imagining him wandering alone at Granton Hall, mourning the loss of his dreams...

All my fault.

"I intended to give him these." Oliver slipped a paper from his pocket and pulled a chain from around his neck. A silver key swung on the chain. He'd worn that key at Seven Devils.

"I found them inside Greta's journal. Call it intuition, but I believe they belong at Granton Hall." He stood and pressed both items into her hands. "I trust you will know what to do with them."

She snorted. "I don't even know what to do with myself at the moment."

"I'm confident you'll figure it out, Miss Karen. I assume Mr. Hughes provided you with a gate key, and you're far prettier than me." He turned for the door. "I suspect you have less odds of being trespassed from the premises by its surly owner."

"Wait! What about the curse? Or the rumor that Elizabeth was a witch?" Tossing the pillow aside, she clutched the paper and key close and stood.

He paused and held her gaze. "Greta never mentioned any witchery. Those rumors rose from another source. She did, however, claim to have seen Elizabeth's spirit as she departed Granton Hall, a sad, wee wisp of white wandering the conservatory."

The memory of the darkness stirring between statues when she'd made the blood vow with Leo whispered over her neck, reminding her of the irrevocable pact made between two best friends.

"And the curse?" Her voice cracked.

"Whether or not the curse is real, history has proven that tragedy occurs every fifty years since Arthur's death. If the cycle runs true, another one is expected soon." He dropped his chin, and the shadows dipped into the hollows of his eyes, as if he was a child telling a ghost story with a flashlight. "Avoiding Granton Hall for another week or two is advisable."

Leo. He was there, alone. Her hands trembled. "Did Greta happen to mention if Edwin smoked a pipe?"

"Yes." He cocked his head, eyes narrowed. "Greta groused often in her journal about Edwin's bad habit, how the smoke and cloves clung to her dresses and the drapes. She nagged him incessantly, even went so far as to hide his matches and tobacco. There was a mention of a lazy afternoon in the woods, Edwin with his pipe, Greta with her needlework and Elizabeth with her black kitten."

"Black kitten?" She could barely get the words out.

"Edwin found a stray kitten wandering in the woods." Oliver watched her as if she was a puzzle missing a piece. "Elizabeth convinced Arthur to let her keep it and doted on the poor creature. When it disappeared, she was so distraught that she imagined she heard it crying within the walls."

Frost shivered down her spine. For an endless minute, only the mechanical tick-tick of the clock pendulum in her kitchen broke the silence.

Oliver opened the door, and the cold, wet night slithered inside. He looked at her one last time. "I'd ask again about that discussion over a bottle of wine, but it has become increasingly obvious that you are beyond my influence, head over heels for Mr. Hughes. Good night, Miss Karen."

The door closed behind him, leaving Karen alone with the key, letter and more questions that only the dead could answer.

Chapter Thirty-Three

Damn if I won't get this monster up in its proper place at last. Gritting his teeth, Leo pulled on the rope and lifted the iron chandelier another foot into the air. Even through his thick leather gloves, the rope cut into his palms. He shouldn't be doing this alone, but he was done tripping over the thing, done being reminded of the fateful night it had fallen when he'd made his play for Ren with blood vows and sinful kisses.

And lost her.

He shoved the thought away, anchored the rope to the hook he'd drilled into the concrete floor and heaved again. Losing drove him to stand up, dust off the debris and work even harder, no surrender. He might have lost the city hall contract to an unexpected contender, but he'd be damned before relinquishing his dream for Granton...or Ren.

"Get back to your home, you vexing, massive bastard." He grunted through clenched teeth, beads of perspiration forming on his brow. With a mighty tug that strained his shoulders, he hoisted the chandelier another few inches. The iron monstrosity swayed gently as if a fragile, delicate thing, the rope creaking beneath its weight. The higher it got, the heavier it seemed.

Rain pelted the roof in an angry rhythm, adding chaos to the constant chill of the corridors, the shadows that never left the corners, even in daylight. At least the pipe smoke had vanished. With the ballroom done, he could focus on more necessary repairs — the fallen section of the second floor, the rooms where people would live, heal and laugh on a regular basis. Maybe he should have been working on those from the start.

Sir Snugglebottom hopped down the stairs, done with his evening nap. He'd taken to nesting in Ren's empty bed and had looked so adorable there that Leo hadn't the heart to move him. He'd curled up beside the kitten and slept in Ren's bed, too, wrapped in the reminders of her until he had the real thing in his arms again. Her lingering presence was as much of a ghost as the other spirits haunting Granton Hall.

Sir looked up at him and mewed, long and plaintive.

Leo anchored the chandelier and crouched. He waited for the kitten to climb up his arm and settle into his favorite perch on his shoulder. "I know, buddy," he murmured between scritches behind Sir's ear. "I miss her, too."

His cell phone buzzed in the back pocket of his jeans, and his heart jackhammered. *Ren.* He stood, one hand steadying the kitten on his shoulder, and answered without looking.

"Hughes." *Please be Ren.*

"Mr. Hughes." The male voice wasn't the one he hoped to hear. "This is Jared Summers from *Renovation*

& *Remodel* magazine. I was one of the judges in the recent Graywood city hall competition."

"Of course." He wasn't likely to forget that dark day any time soon.

"I apologize for the late call but didn't want to delay telling you the news."

"News?" He couldn't take any more bad news without something breaking — and it wouldn't be him.

"I spoke to my editor about the work you did at Granton Hall, showed him the before and after photos. The renovations you made on that decaying ballroom?" A whistle. "From the replastered ceiling to the pristinely repaired parquet floor and every detail in between, nothing short of construction magic. I was outvoted, but mine went your way."

"I appreciate that." His stomach twisted, as if he relived that day all over again. The morning of the final judging, he'd looked over the ballroom with pride. Then the world as he knew it had flushed down the loo.

"I know it's not the same as winning, but my editor agreed to spotlight Granton Hall in a later issue of *Renovation & Remodel*, if you're still interested."

Leo paused, frozen in time, his heart hammering. Interested? This could change everything. He'd never cared about the city hall contract, only the publicity he'd receive from the magazine, what it would mean for the charity he planned for Granton Hall. Suddenly, the world didn't seem so dark.

"Mr. Hughes? You still there?"

"I would be honored, Mr. Summers." He cleared the gruffness in his voice. "You have no idea."

"Excellent, and please, call me Jared." Jared chuckled. "I'll let my editor know the good news."

The second Jared hung up, Leo set Sir on the floor, sprang into the air almost high enough to touch the dangling chandelier and whooped. The startled kitten launched down the corridor as Leo's laughter echoed to the rafters. He had to tell Ren.

He started to text her and nixed that. She hadn't read any of his texts since she'd left. As soon as he dialed the first digit of her number, he canceled that, too. Even if she answered, this news was too big, too life changing. He had to tell her face to face. It was a few minutes before nine o'clock. Fifteen minutes would put him at Ren's apartment. He couldn't wait until tomorrow.

As he headed for the door, the lights flickered and went out altogether. The hum of electricity died, leaving the drumming rain to fill the emptiness.

"Wonderful," he muttered. But even the generator failing — again — couldn't kill his mood. He kicked on his cell phone light and tugged open the front door, not bothering to grab a jacket. Imagining the expression on Ren's face when he told her everything coiled inside him like a spring, uncontainable. He rushed down the steps.

Crack!

At the second step down, the rotten wood under his boot collapsed. His cell phone flew from his hand. As he stumbled, the rest of the steps broke beneath his weight, and he plunged backward, landing in a bone-jarring thud. Before he cursed, the ground gave way, and he fell for another few terrifying seconds.

Leo hit a hard surface with enough force to knock the breath from his lungs. Pain ricocheted through his entire body, echoing in his ankle, head and back. Wood and dirt showered him from above. For a minute, he lay there, struggling to breathe, staring up at the black hole he'd plummeted through at least a dozen feet above.

He'd assumed nothing rested beneath the porch but solid earth and grass, not a false floor. Blindly, he felt the surface beneath him as his body throbbed. Bruised and beaten up as he was, at least he could move his arms. Smooth, hard concrete spread on either side. The blueprints hadn't indicated that the basement extended this far. What had his fall uncovered?

Groaning, he lifted onto his elbows, and new pain shot up his leg. His right foot remained stuck. He fumbled in the dark. Something metal and heavy—a pipe?—wedged his boot tight, and from the aching blaze in his ankle, it was either sprained or broken.

Perfect. No phone, no light and stuck beneath the house in the dark. He should have fixed the stairs first, but that stupid chandelier had been an enemy he needed to defeat, a symbol of his fallen relationship with Ren. Righting the iron monstrosity, returning it to its proper place would have at least made him feel as if he could fix one thing in his life.

The glow of his watch showed the time. Straight up nine. A shiver coasted down his spine, and the grandfather clock in the ballroom came to mind. When Ren had got it going again, it had stopped again—at nine.

Pipe smoke and cloves overpowered the scent of earth, rain and dust. In the darkness, a violin moaned to life, and every hair on his body rose as recognition struck him like a wrecking ball.

Danse Macabre. The shadows shifted, fluttering, as if coming to life.

Leo struggled to free his ankle, his blood colder than ice. He hadn't fallen into an undocumented cellar or a section of the basement he hadn't yet discovered.

He'd fallen into a grave.

* * * *

Karen's hands shook as she unfolded the onion-skin letter Oliver had given her with the key, so similar to all the notes she'd found inside the music box. The handwriting wasn't at all like Edwin's familiar, spidery letters, but elegant and flowing.

My dearest Edwin. She sucked in a breath as she skipped to the signature at the end. *Yours now and always, Elizabeth.*

"Holy hell," she murmured, sinking onto the couch.

My dearest Edwin,

It is far too late to share with you the undying affection I have always held in my soul for you alone, my love. Far too late to express how dearly I held every moment spent with you in the gardens, how I held my breath each time I received your letters. The words you wrote were my life blood, a song to my deafened ears. Without your undying friendship, your sweet sentiments and daily smiles, the joy you alone awoke in my soul, I would have perished ages ago.

And now that day has come. You are gone, and I cannot bear that I never told you the secrets of my heart. Instead, I lived with the sure knowledge you would always be there to greet me. I lived for you, yet did not have the strength, nay, the courage to speak the truth. Instead, I allowed fear to rob me of the life I should have had with you. I acted in haste, and you departed this world fully believing I had betrayed both our friendship and the love that had blossomed between us through the years.

I wish you had not left me with such unexpected haste. I wish I had imparted you with the truth before my opportunity was stolen. I wish I could rescind all the wasted days and spend them with you. I wish I had been stronger than my fear. I know now that wishes possess no power to set matters right or bring you back to me. Wishes are naught but smoke and fantasies for foolish, fainthearted girls who were not wise enough to act while it mattered.

No longer will my courage fail me. No longer will I be the weak coward, timid and afraid. I will not bear this existence alone, without the other half of my soul. Tonight, we shall be together again, never to part. Friends eternal, love everlasting.

Yours now and always,
Elizabeth

"Holy hell," she repeated. Elizabeth had loved Edwin all along and never told him. He'd died believing their friendship was broken beyond repair. It sounded as if Elizabeth had taken her own life to be with her beloved Edwin again in death.

The ache in her heart expanded, threatening to crack open her ribs and spill out, red and flowing. She ran her finger over the key Oliver had given her with the letter, tracing the knots of vines. Her relationship with Leo wasn't the same as the fateful lovers at all. Nope, no way. Not at all. She'd told Leo how she felt, her fears and failures. He knew she loved him, knew why she couldn't love him the way he wanted.

Poor Elizabeth. Karen wasn't sure which regret would be worse—never knowing Leo loved her or losing him forever, living alone with only her regrets. If anything ever happened to him...

The clock in her kitchen sang, announcing the hour. Nine o'clock. An icy finger tapped down her neck in rhythm with the chimes, and as the scent of pipe smoke and cloves laced the air, a sense of dread curled around her.

Karen closed her eyes and pressed her hand on her abdomen as her stomach rolled. Something was terribly wrong.

Don't be ridiculous. Psychic abilities didn't run in her blood. No curse could take Leo down. He was too strong and stubborn. All he had to do was frown while carrying his sword and any ghost would run in terror. She pulled her *Dark Shadows* pillow onto her lap and hugged it tight. Leo was fine, safe in Granton.

Alone.

The rain increased in intensity, hammering the roof like hundreds of cloven hooves, dancing, dancing, dancing.

She jumped from the couch, scrambled for her phone on the end table, and turned it on. Message after message scrolled by. Leo, Leo, Leo. Gia. Leo. Mom. Leo, Leo, Leo. Liam.

Liam? She didn't know he even had her number, and it wasn't a text, but an actual telephone message. She bit her lip. It could be a trick to get her to respond, a trap that, once sprung, she couldn't escape without looking like a bumbling, graceless loser. But Liam wasn't one to sugarcoat. He'd never coddle her or call to apologize, no matter how many times Leo thrashed him in the ring. If he took an effort to call her, it had to be important.

The chill in her neck scampered down her back, and before she reconsidered, she listened to Liam's message.

Ren. Stop being an idgit and go see Leo. He's being even more of an idgit than you. Get your ass to Granton and talk to him before I have to crack both of your skulls in the ring. I don't care if you don't have a proper weapon. He's locked the gate, won't answer his phone and needs his best friend right now. That will always be you.

Pull up your Goth-girl tights, stop being a wimp and talk to him – or prepare to face the consequences, Hughes-style. Oh, and that parquet spider in the ballroom? An exasperated sigh. *All me. No one appreciates my sense of humor.*

The call ended, and Karen blinked. *What the hell?* Why would Liam pull a prank like that? She pushed that mystery aside for later, her heart thumping in time with the rain.

She wasn't like Elizabeth. Cowardice had never been her deal. After Hank had dumped her, she'd held her chin high through the apologetic comments and pitying looks. For frick sake, she'd even managed not to snap at the news of Hank and Hanna eloping. She'd shut down the black, mean voice in her head and given them her blessing with a fake smile sweet enough to rot both of their teeth.

Moving to Graywood had been for a fresh start where she could be just Karen Ives, not the hometown girl who'd lost her future. Quitting her fantastic job at Hamilton & Associates had been a desire for new job scenery. Keeping Leo in the friend box had been to maintain their amazing friendship without ruining it with romance.

Hadn't it?

Maybe she *was* a coward. She didn't want a future without Leo, and as long as she avoided the discussion awaiting her, she could pretend he would always be there, to love her through anything. Pretending was far safer than seeing the truth in his eyes, that she wasn't worth the effort or trouble.

That I'm not enough.

She sucked in a shaky breath. Maybe Leo needed her there as a verbal punching bag, to have the one responsible for his ruin within sight to purge his pain. It was the least she could do for him. Even if nothing remained of their friendship, she'd endure whatever words he threw, apologize a hundred different ways, and hope he forgave her someday. If he needed her for any reason, she had to go.

At the very least, she needed to collect her things, give Leo the letter and key Oliver had found. She slouched in the cushions, rain slashing at the windows. *Tomorrow.* She'd suck it up and head to Granton Hall in the morning. After all, she'd made a blood vow, dammit.

Cloves infused the air. A wisp of smoke curled through the gloom, there and gone like a puff of breath in winter. Dread answered, a cold, clawing thing in her chest, and she swore the darkness whispered a single word that made all the hair on her arms stand up straight.

Go.

Chapter Thirty-Four

Karen hit the brakes hard as her headlights landed on the closed Granton gate. Her car screeched to a stop and gravel flew. Rain punished the roof and windows. High-speed windshield wipers battled the deluge, losing. She'd hoped Oliver had exaggerated Leo's locking the gate. She didn't want to waste a single second when the voice in her head screamed to hurry.

By the time she unlocked the gate with the spare key and returned to her car, cold numbed her hands. Moisture soaked through her yoga pants from thigh to calf, a clinging chill on her skin. At least she'd been smart enough to grab a raincoat and wear boots before rushing from her apartment.

The driveway had never seemed so long or dark. Branches clawed at the car windows as she barreled toward the house, rain blurring her vision. Between one beat of the wipers and the next, the pointed gables of Granton Hall came into view. Darkness filled every window. A glimpse of chrome flashed in the headlights as she circled around, Leo's motorcycle parked in a cleared spot of the covered walkway. If his truck wasn't beside the cracked fountain, she might have believed the mansion had once again been abandoned to ivy and ghosts.

Leo was inside. She knew it to her bones.

She jumped out of her car, leaving the keys in the ignition, and raced to the ballroom entrance. Leo would probably be there, trying to figure out where he went wrong. Puddles splashed beneath her boots, soaking her legs more. Her cell phone light bounced as she ran, a fleeting spotlight on the garden swallowing her. Statues appeared to weep in the flashes. Moss leaked between stones. Black shapes soared and shrank, one second ordinary shrubs, the next swiping demons. She reached the boxwood hedge and blew out a relieved breath.

The ballroom windows glinted in the rain, a glass sanctuary waiting for her late arrival. She reached the guest entrance and burst inside. Thank God Leo hadn't locked it. As the door shut behind her, silence surrounded her, heavy and throbbing. Rain grumbled on the roof. She tried the light switch by the door, nothing but a dead click.

Great. The power had gone out again. No wonder the alarm system hadn't shrieked.

"Leo?"

Only her voice answered in the corridor emptiness, a vulnerable echo. The memory of the spider image created from broken parquet pieces shivered through her. Even if Liam was responsible for the tasteless prank, that didn't explain the real spider or key. Too much coincidence, too many supernatural elements to dismiss.

A trail of clove-sweet pipe smoke wisped in the gloom. Her breath clouded the air as the perpetual chill of Granton Hall dipped to winter cold. She stuffed her free hand in the pocket of her rain jacket and passed the stained-glass windows leading to the ballroom. Night dulled their colors to fleeting threads of life dancing just out of reach. She stepped onto the landing and peered through the ballroom's glass doors.

Nothing but shadows. The pipe smoke dwindled, as if to say she headed the wrong way.

"Lead on, Casper," she whispered, refusing to name any presence. She'd watched enough movies to know better than to utter a true name. "And if you're not friendly, I've got some iron and salt for your face."

The smoke vanished. A scrabbling came from the corridor, and she whirled, aiming her cell phone into the darkness beyond.

Sir barreled straight at her, his tail puffed to three times its size. His eyes gleamed, iridescent. Several feet away, he clawed to a stop and arched his back, studying her.

After her panic attack settled to somewhere between reasonably alarmed and merely terrified, Karen crouched and wriggled her fingers. "Hello, sweet boy," she crooned. "You're not mad at me, too, are you?" The kitten pranced nearer, his fur still ruffled, tail up straight, keeping his distance. "Where's Leo?"

The second she reached for him, he darted back into the corridor toward the heart of the house.

"Useless furball. Adorable, but useless." She straightened and followed, her pulse motoring. Leo would never leave Sir alone to wander the halls at will. There were too many places for a kitten to get into trouble.

Such as the walls.

A deeper chill rattled her bones, and she wished Oliver had never told her about Elizabeth's black kitten, how it had gone missing and she'd heard it in the walls. Her boots slapped the bare planked floor. Shadows lurched along the floor, skittered up the walls to the ceiling, teasing the edges of light from her phone.

As she reached the vestibule, eyes flashed again. Sir sat in the center of the room. The iron chandelier hung from a rope a dozen feet off the ground, anchored to a hook drilled into the floor. Leave it to Leo to try to suspend the monster by himself.

"Leo?" she called again, aiming her light at the stairs. The quiet amplified the blood in her head to a roar. She texted him.

I'm here to steal your precious saw. A girl needs new hobbies. Where are you?

After their fight, he'd be waiting for her to contact him, his cell phone close. He wouldn't ignore her. The silent treatment wasn't his deal, no matter how annoyed or hurt he might be.

The phone faded and went dark, leaving her in smoke and shadows. Sir meowed and circled her ankles.

"Where is he?" She picked up the kitten. The small, solid warmth of another living being offered a slim comfort. "Have you seen him?"

Sir rubbed his face in her palm, purring.

"Useless," she muttered.

A chilled draft touched her face, carrying familiar, clove-infused smoke. All the hair on her neck prickled.

Slowly, clutching the kitten tighter, she faced the heavy front door.

It wasn't latched. A bare inch of the night beyond gleamed through the gap. Rain glistened on the floor, blown in from the wind. The door creaked as another gust fluttered through.

Maybe she had it wrong and the power had been cut off, the security system deactivated. If a lowlife lurked outside, they were already aware of her presence. Hell, she'd been talking to the cat, thoughtlessly flinging her light around. She'd wasted any element of surprise.

Karen set Sir down and tiptoed to the door. Keeping the kitten back with one foot, she eased the door open wider. At the last instant, she whipped her cell phone light around like a weapon. At least her enemy would be momentarily blinded.

But no one waited on the porch. Rain dripped from the eaves and her breath clouded in the air. The leather pouch with the Lucifer matches found in Edwin's old shack, the one Leo had kept putting in her room in a sad attempt to freak her out, perched in the middle of the porch. A few inches past it, Leo's phone sprawled, its screen cracked, collecting a puddle. A black, ragged hole gaped where the stairs should be.

Ice slivered in her blood as she scrambled to hands and knees next to the hole. Hands shaking, she aimed her cell phone beam into the space beneath the porch. Disturbed soil and sickly plants remained on the ragged edges of what appeared to be either a false floor or the remains of a bomb shelter ceiling. More than a dozen feet down, Leo sprawled in the wreckage, his leg trapped at an awkward angle by a metal pipe. His stern, beautiful face was smudged, skin pale beneath the grime. Runoff trickled down, and his wet-dark hair clung to his head. Blood stained his ear. His eyes were closed. He wasn't moving, as if he were...

Between heartbeats, Karen's entire world stopped and splintered into a thousand jagged pieces. It was as if her soul had been skinned and Leo's blade sliced it in two. Her future spun out before her in an endless spool of thread, a shadow life, deficient and incomplete from what it should have been. Friendship alone could never fulfill the longing of her heart, the space that had been carefully carved out to fit Leo.

"Leo," she gasped. *Please be okay.* If she hadn't been such a coward and walked out, maybe he wouldn't have fallen. *All my fault.* Good God, she couldn't breathe.

Leo's eyelids fluttered, and the world lurched, pulled back into a steady rotation. Her lungs filled with air, and her heart began pumping again.

"Ren?" His voice was the best sound she'd ever heard. He squinted at the light shining in his eyes. "Is that you?"

She smothered a sob of relief behind her hand. Leo was alive. She hadn't lost him. There was still time for her. *Thank God.* Never—no matter how hard or often her doubts crept in, she'd never leave him again. She'd never let a single day pass without showing him how important he was to her. How deeply, endlessly, eternally she loved him. Karen stuffed her phone in her raincoat pocket.

"No!" Frantic movement scraped in the darkness below. "Leave the light on."

"I can't climb down while holding it, Hughes." She perched on the edge of the hole and dangled her legs while getting a good grip on a joist that remained intact. It seemed sturdy enough.

"Don't. It's not safe." The desperation in his voice, the fear, rattled her almost as much as seeing him lying helpless in a hole. Leo was the strongest person she knew, but nothing would stop her from having his back, always.

"All the better not to leave you there alone." She twisted and slid down until she hung in the air, anchored to the surface by her fingertips. The void beneath the porch felt like a black hole tugging at her boots. Already, her arms strained. "Seriously regretting not taking you up on the offers to work out. I'll do my best not to land on you."

"Ren, don't—"

The drop wasn't that far, six feet or so, but her legs crumpled at the impact. She toppled backward in a pile of loose earth and broken boards. Her elbow smacked a hard surface, sending ripples of numbing pain up her arm.

She lay there for a moment, catching her breath. "Ow."

"I'm prepared to accept your deep and undying regret for not listening to me." Leo's voice drifted in the darkness, close. "Ever."

"Just because I do what I want doesn't mean I don't listen." She struggled to a sit, gritting her teeth as she bumped her arm and fumbled for her phone.

"Are you really here or what my imagination spun to life when I hit my head?" He shielded his eyes as she turned on her flashlight app. "Don't answer that. I prefer not to know."

The chilled air sank through her damp clothes and bit her skin as she studied him close up. Blood matted the back of his head and stained the concrete beneath him red. A rusty pipe trapped his boot at an angle that seemed to defy scientific explanation. But even smudged with grime, bruised and bloody, finding him alive and breathing was the most beautiful sight in the world.

Tears stung her eyes. She scrambled to his side and peppered kisses over every inch of his face.

Leo stiffened, then huffed a strained laugh. "Guess I should fall through rotten stairs more often."

"I'm sorry," she said, the words a sob. "So sorry, for everything. Are you okay?"

"Mainly, my pride is bruised." He shifted and winced, the liar. "My uncooperative foot refuses to be dislodged from a pipe that shouldn't even be here. It's going to need to be cut out. My ankle aches like Cooper is pounding nails through it. With no phone, I've been stuck. It's damn embarrassing."

"You're bleeding." She brushed his head. Her fingers came away dry. How long had he been here, in the dark and alone?

"My skull is thicker than most. I'll survive."

She wasn't a crier— She *wasn't*. The tears didn't seem to care. They spilled down her face.

"Aw, Ren." He cupped her cheek with a callused hand. "Don't cry, darling. I hate it when you cry."

"I never cry," she hiccupped.

"I know you don't."

"You're really okay?"

"I've had worse sparring my brothers." He brushed at the tears with his thumb. "I'm fine, Ren. Truly. Trapped like a rat, but fine."

"No rats allowed." She set her phone down, screen up for light. Knuckling her eyes to erase the tears, she swallowed hard. "I don't want to be Elizabeth."

He went still and his eyes sharpened, watchful. "What do you mean?"

"I thought I'd lost you, Leo, and I don't mean right now when I thought you might not come back to the land of the living." Clasping his icy hand between hers, she squeezed tight, anchoring herself to him. "I'm so sorry for not having the strength to trust you with every sliver of my heart, for painting you with the colors of my past when you're a completely different shade of savage perfection, for not being brave enough to tell you how madly I love you. Seeing you down here..." Her voice cracked, but she refused to stop spilling what she'd held inside for so long, pretending it wasn't real or lasting. "I don't want an existence without you. You're the only man who's always made me feel safe, adored, like I matter more than anyone else in the world. I never should have run from you. If you still want me, if you can forgive me, I'll fight any battle necessary to stay with you."

Eyebrows raised, he studied her for a long moment, long enough that her pulse thundered, pounding in her dry throat. What if he didn't want her anymore, had decided over the last few days that life was more peaceful with a cat for company? What if he couldn't get over the fact that she'd lost the competition for him, and all his dreams right along with it?

"Hmm," he said at last.

"Really? That's all you have to say?" She scrambled to get up, but he kept a vise-like grip on her hand, refusing to let her go. "I thought you were too honorable for payback, Hughes. Guess I was wrong."

"When it comes to you, I'll do everything in my power to keep you through any available means, honorable or not." With surprising strength considering he'd fallen into a hole, he jerked her down and wrapped his arms around her, holding her hostage on his chest. He stroked her bangs from her eyes. "But I'd never do anything to hurt you. I questioned whether or not I'm hallucinating since I've waited an eternity to hear those words from your lovely, perfect mouth."

"Oh." The word was hardly more than a breath.

"Yes, *oh*. You can never lose me, Ren. I'm yours, always, in whatever way you'll have me. The love I have for you is so deep and powerful it's become an integral part of my soul. Sometimes it's so intense I think my skin will split to keep it all in." He dragged his knuckles down her cheek, sparking a trail of tingles, and held her gaze with a steadiness that she couldn't doubt. "I don't know how to put it any plainer, how to say it in the right way to get through to both your thick head and your defensive heart."

The tears returned, and she blinked them away. *Oh, this man.* This stubborn, perfect, generous man wrapped up in the form of her best friend who refused to give up on her. How could she have thought that he'd ever walk out on her? He'd be true to their vow until his very last breath, and so would she. She wouldn't throw a life with him away for any reason.

Done with talking, she took his mouth with hers, conveying all the emotions she couldn't express with mere words or blood vows. He was every private fantasy, every broken dream, every hope she hadn't dared to believe she deserved. She'd never get enough of him. Karen poured everything she was into the kiss, into Leo, into them. Every detail of her past, present and future, no more boundaries.

Leo wrapped his arm around her, pulling her tight against the hard length of his body. The tenderness in the kiss heated, ignited, turning feverish. He slid his fingers through her hair and cupped her nape, holding her mouth hostage with his. It didn't seem to matter that he was flat on his back in a forgotten cellar, his ankle lodged and damaged. He kissed her with fierce hunger, as if he could draw her into him, merge them together as one.

She moaned, her blood blazing to life, fire pooling low in her belly. No matter how deep his kiss, it wasn't enough. It would never be enough. She slipped her hands beneath his shirt, desperate for direct contact, her need for him boiling, overflowing. The warmth of his skin seeped into her fingers as she trailed his ribcage. She never wanted to stop touching him, tasting him, filled with a love she never believed possible. *Never again.* She'd never leave him, never doubt his love, never dismiss their future together again.

So slowly she didn't realize it at first, Leo softened the kiss by degrees, lulling her to calm. At last, he nibbled on her lower lip and ended the kiss with a sigh.

"Oh, come on, Hughes." She grinned down at him. "Where's your sense of adventure? You don't want to get it on while bruised and bloody with your foot stuck in a metal pipe? In a dark, dank…whatever this is?"

"Tempting as you are, in case I don't make it out of here, I have a confession to make."

The gravity in his voice set all her alarms on high alert, and the temperature seemed to drop. She cupped his face, the stubble on his jaw rough beneath her palms. "You're getting out of here, Hughes. No deathbed confessions allowed."

"I'm only telling you this now because you're emotional, feeling sorry for me and probably won't kill me. I can't pass up this golden opportunity. You know the coffees I make for you every morning?"

She squinted. Maybe his head injury was worse than he let on. "What about them?"

"I added my spinach protein drink to them." His lazy smile came to life. "Every. Single. One."

"You sneaky bastard. Sabotaging my coffee is —"

"Genius. I know. But that's not all. Before I fell through the steps, I got a call from Jared Summers of *Remodel & Renovation* magazine. They want to publish a spread on Granton Hall. I was running out to tell you in person." He grimaced. "Didn't quite get there. Jared loved the parquet work, by the way."

Karen sank to her knees. "He did?"

"We lost the competition fair and square, darling. It had nothing to do with the quality of the workmanship. And now I'll get the publicity I wanted for the charity." He twined his fingers with hers. "Ren, darling, we won."

Despite her newbie construction skills, they'd won. She couldn't believe it. "Get. Out."

"I want to, trust me. Because, Ren?" Perspiration beaded on his brow. Holding her gaze, Leo dropped his voice to a hoarse whisper. "We're not alone down here."

Chapter Thirty-Five

Leo ignored his throbbing ankle as Ren nabbed her cell phone and flashed its beam at the gloom around them.

His thoughts replayed the blinding light drawing him back to awareness and Ren's descent from above like his guardian angel, making him wonder if he was lucid or dreaming. He still reeled from her confession, the passion in her kiss. For a few precious moments, he'd forgotten what he'd heard and seen before darkness had swallowed him whole—the music, the stirring in the shadows, the undeniable awareness that *something* inhabited the space with him.

"We're alone, unless you count that spider in the far corner. Pretty sure the rain is holding him back from devouring us." Karen peered down at him, lines of concern on her forehead. "Iron skull or not, the fall must have been hard. You were out cold when I got here, maybe lost enough blood to be delusional. I'm getting you out of here."

He grabbed for her hand as she scrambled away, taking her heat and light. "Ren, don't go."

"I've got this, Hughes. There's enough of a slope that I can climb out, no problem." She planted a hand on her cocked hip. "Unless you want me to call Officer Hellman?"

"Hell to the absolute never."

Her grin turned wicked, showcasing the dimple he could never resist. "How about Liam? I'm sure he'd love to play hero to his big brother."

He snorted and glanced at the corner where the music had drifted from. Only the dark stared back at him. Whether imagination, hallucination or the result of his head cracking concrete, he wasn't sure he wanted to know what the shadows held secret. "I'd never hear the end of it."

"Exactly." She crouched beside him and pushed her cell phone into his hand. "Don't worry. I won't let any curse take you from me."

"Curse?" Goosebumps formed on his chilled skin.

"I'll be back faster than Freddy clawing into a favorite nightmare." A peck on his cheek, and she vanished again.

"Wait. Ren." He fumbled with the phone and aimed the light just in time to see her boot heels disappear through the hole in the porch. Her hurried footsteps crossed overhead, followed by the front door slamming. "Dammit."

Careful not to tweak his ankle, he gingerly sat up and inhaled, long and deep, gathering his strength. Hidden eyes seemed to drill into his back. The drum of rain resembled a dozen heartbeats out of sync. With the scent of earth and moisture feeding his lungs fetid, musty air, he had the impression that he sat in a barrow, waiting to die.

He tightened his grip on her cell phone, evidence that his imagination hadn't conjured her. Ren had come back for him. He wasn't alone, and he had a light.

Warmth spread in his chest. Ren had come back to him. She loved him, would fight beside him through any battle instead of running. Together, they could tackle anything. Ren was finally, completely his.

He wanted to laugh to the steepled gables and the clouds beyond until the rain stopped and morning took the sky. Despite falling beneath the house and being helplessly stuck, it was one of the best days of his life.

A tinkling of music invaded the pattering rain, returning to haunt him.

His heart thundering, Leo took a deep breath and released it. *I will not fear.* Another breath, in and out. *I will not fear.* If Ren could be strong enough to break through her past, he could face whatever haunted Granton Hall.

He turned the light to the corner of the house's foundation, where the music drifted from. Uneven pavers scattered with soil, splinters and uprooted weeds stretched around him. Cracked bricks formed the wall, crooked with age, dusted by spiderwebs and husks of insects long ago consumed and abandoned. As if shying away from the light, the music faded.

Leo focused on the solid details. The cellar had to be on the other side, but the distance between the cellar wall and this unexpected pocket had to be more than twenty feet. The bricks, cheap, red clay, were nothing like the solid gray stone the remainder of the structure. Whoever had created this room hadn't been the original builder — or even a good one. It reminded him of the cottage in the woods Ren had dragged him to. The brick shelving where they'd found the tobacco pouch had been similar, collapsing from poor construction and materials.

A gleam of metal shone between the cracks of two crooked bricks, and his heart thundered. Something had been bricked up behind the wall.

A scuffle came from above, and he whipped the light up.

"I'm ba-ack." Ren hefted a heavy-duty flashlight in one hand, a pack strapped to her back. She scrambled to the edge, swung herself onto one jutting board like a trapeze artist, and dropped to the ground with a huff, wildly waving her arms, then regaining her balance before she fell on her perfect ass again.

"I give the dismount a nine point eight. Would've been a ten if not for the flailing."

"You're adorable, Hughes." She kneeled beside him, traded him the flashlight for her phone and swung the backpack free. "Luckily for you, I always keep track of where you keep the tools, especially the saws." Lifting his cordless reciprocating saw, she wriggled her eyebrows. "Guess who finally gets to use the saw? And there's nothing you can do about it."

"God help us all."

A pile began to form beside her as she continued pulling items free. A rope, battery-operated angle grinder, goggles, hammer, gloves, even a water bottle and blanket. No wonder she'd lost her balance when she dropped. That pack must have weighed a ton.

He grabbed the water bottle as she wrapped the blanket around him. "You're proving quite handy, even for an accountant. I might have to keep you around."

"Maybe you don't have a choice anymore." She tweaked his nose and tossed some goggles in his lap. "Sucker. You should've escaped while you had the chance."

"The only escape I've ever wanted is with you."

Her face brightened and the fireworks sparkle in her eyes dimmed the pain, lingering fear and mysteries hidden behind the crumbling brick wall. Only Ren being with him mattered. She kissed him once, quick, before slipping on some gloves and goggles. "I brought the angle grinder and reciprocating saw for choices, but I'm thinking the saw will be faster for a pipe, cut cleaner, less sparks, right?"

"You, my prodigious volunteer, have been paying attention...not that I ever doubted."

"I expect a certificate and ribbon for completing the Hughes Hard-Ass Construction Course for Idiots when this is done."

"I can think of a few more inspiring rewards." He gave her a steady look. "Preferably without clothes." His blood heated as pink stained her cheekbones. Thank God, he affected her as much as she affected him.

Ren shook her head, as if clearing her wicked thoughts. "I'll be sure to remind you of the promised bonuses." She nodded at the rusty pipe trapping his ankle. "Get your gear on, Hughes. I'd hate anything to happen to your pretty eyes."

"If you amputate my ankle by accident, I extend my forgiveness." He aimed the flashlight at the pipe, giving her a full view of the project.

She snorted and set the saw blade on the pipe a safe distance away. "I won't let my boyfriend lose a foot.

You'd never be able to retain the Hughes family champion title, and that would be humiliating."

"Would, too, but more importantly, keep calling me 'boyfriend'. I like how it sounds."

"You're surprisingly soft and pathetic with a head wound." She rolled her eyes, but her mouth twitched, betraying a smile. "Boyfriend."

He grinned.

The saw roared to life, and he lay flat on his back, shutting his eyes against the blinding sparks, not Ren's virgin journey with his saw. The pipe vibrated against his ankle, jolting agony up his leg. He gritted his teeth and counted down the seconds for the blade to cut through metal. He hadn't exactly lied about his injuries — he'd survive both the bump on his head and the twisted ankle — but he wasn't about to let Ren know how much he longed for an ice pack and a few pills to ease the pain. Already, he'd be facing some serious damage control with the Hughes clan. Falling through his own stairs, trapped like a rodent, most likely hobbling around for weeks… His brothers would never let him hear the end of it, and one of them would take advantage of his weakness and steal the title.

Bastards.

And he definitely wasn't shutting out whatever hid behind the brick wall, waiting to be found. *Wanting* to be found. Cold slithered up his neck. He ignored that, too.

The pressure on his boot disappeared, and the saw rumbled to a stop.

"Careful." Ren set the saw down. "Don't move yet." With one gloved hand, she pulled on the broken pipe, offering enough space for her to wiggle his boot loose with her free hand.

He performed the difficult task of lying on the ground, trying not to whimper like a rescued puppy. At last, his foot was free. Getting the boot off his swollen ankle would be a battle for later.

"Victory is ours." Ren popped off her goggles and grinned.

"Grab that hammer and help me up." Stuffing the flashlight in his waistband, he pushed himself to a sit and held out a hand.

"Not your volunteer anymore, bossy." She rummaged for the hammer she'd packed. "You're lucky I kinda like you." She hauled him to his feet and slipped beneath his arm, steadying him. He hissed and wobbled, balancing on one foot as dizziness threatened to take him back down.

I will not fear. He pointed the flashlight at the brick wall, at the metal winking between cracks. "Help me get over there." He gave her slender shoulder a squeeze. "Since you kinda love me."

"You're going to manipulate my weakness for you as much as possible, aren't you?"

"Count on it."

Ren huffed a laugh, and after a few struggling steps that left him gasping for breath, they made it to the crooked brick wall. He removed his arm from the support of her shoulders, handed her the flashlight, and hefted the hammer.

"Might want to stand back for this." Hoping he didn't lose his balance and fall like a graceless imbecile, he swung the hammer at the bricks.

The wall shuddered, and a giant cloud of dust billowed out, blinding him. Coughing, Ren hid her eyes in her sleeve while he pulled his shirt up to cover his face until the silt settled. He turned back as Ren fumbled with the flashlight. The beam bounced and landed on the hole his hammer had made, wide enough for him to walk through. Most of the wall had crumbled, too old and weak to withstand a direct blow. Jagged fragments of clay clung to a wooden frame like broken teeth. Behind the rubble, coated with dust and moss, was an iron door.

"I knew it," Ren breathed. "Granton Hall is too Gothic-creepy not to have a secret room." She bounced up and down, taking the light with her. "I can't wait to see what's inside."

"I'm sure it's locked." *Hopefully*. Whatever mystery rested behind that door could be faced tomorrow in full daylight, with an entire team.

As if in tune with his thoughts, *Danse Macabre* began again, faint and tinny, coming from behind the door.

Ren was instantly at his side, grasping his arm tight, her heat and support all that kept him upright. The fear from earlier, when he'd been alone and helpless, ran cold in his veins. But with her beside him, he could endure it. Having her standing brave with him, he could face any terror, even the one he suspected waited behind that door.

"You okay?"

Clenching his jaw, he nodded. *I will not fear.*

"Excellent, because I have the key." She triumphantly lifted a silver key.

Of course, she has the key. "Do I dare ask where you found that?"

"Oliver gave it to me."

"Hunter." He couldn't help the snide tone.

She grabbed his wrist and looked into his eyes. "Hughes, I have so much to tell you about Oliver and his ties to Granton Hall, the letter and journal he found in his grandmother's attic, but that has to wait." She pointed at the waiting door. "We have to get in there."

"We really don't. Morning would be an excellent time for further exploration."

"Don't you feel it?" she whispered, clenching the key tight. "Like we were brought here, to this very location at this precise moment to open that door?"

Unfortunately, he had to agree. A sense of expectancy, of impending dread, weighed heavy on his chest, as if he turned away now, an invisible noose around his neck would tighten, no escape. As much as he didn't want to know what hid behind that door, not knowing would be even worse.

A whiff of cloves and pipe smoke joined the damp and dust, confirmation — or a warning.

Leo released a long breath. "Open it." As she shoved the flashlight at him and danced forward, he added, "Carefully."

Helpless with his bum ankle, he stood at the edge of the rubble, aimed the light and watched the love of his life get her supernatural thrills, danger be damned. Ren set the key into the lock, a perfect fit. Metal clicked as she twisted. With a push, the door groaned open. Pipe smoke and cloves clouded the air.

"Holy hell." Ren's voice echoed as if she'd stepped into a cave. She moved aside, giving him a full view.

"Holy hell," he murmured. The door led to what appeared to be a cell. A skeleton sat in the corner, its skull bowed, jaw tucked to its sternum, as if it had fallen asleep, waiting. Tatters of a gray dress clung to its frame, no more than a gathering of cobwebs. Wisps of long, black hair clung to the skull. The finger bones remained clasped together around a silver metal cup. The melancholy scene reminded him of an ancient story, a maiden who had sacrificed herself protecting the entrance to a dark realm.

An open music box rested on the floor beside the remains, the miniature skeleton figurine standing at attention harrowingly familiar.

"This has to be Elizabeth." Ren's voice was solemn, quiet, as she crouched beside the skeleton, not touching anything.

For a moment, Leo swore the smoke coalesced, forming the silhouette of a man kneeling at Elizabeth's feet. Between one blink and the next, the image dissolved. The smoke and cloves vanished, as if, after long years of residence, the owner of the pipe had finally departed for good.

Catch you later, Edwin. Much, much later. Leo cleared the lump in his throat. "I think it's time to call Officer Hellman."

Chapter Thirty-Six

As the police car rolled out of Granton Hall's driveway, Karen shut the door and heaved a long breath. Dawn made a silver thread on the horizon, seeping through the windows to melt the shadows. The night had passed in a blur. While the police investigated, stretching warning tape everywhere, taking photos, poking around wearing plastic gloves, she'd huddled in a blanket with Leo on the porch swing and watched as the unexpected space beneath had become an official crime scene.

Elizabeth Granton's bones, found after all these years… Whether she'd locked herself in or someone else — Greta? Arthur? — had trapped her there, it was a lonely, terrible way to die.

Now Leo sat on the stairs, his injured ankle wrapped tight, a temporary fix. In typical manly-man fashion, he'd refused an emergency room visit and insisted on a doctor appointment at a reasonable hour. The neon purple compression tape made a bold statement against his ripped jeans and mussed hair. He hadn't been allowed to sleep due to the possible concussion. Dark circles bruised his eyes, and his skin remained pale.

Her heart fluttered. Holy hell, he was beautiful, alive and all hers. She would never let him go again.

"Ren, darling, if you insist on looking at me like that, you'd better come here." He patted the empty space next to him on the stairwell.

"Look at you like what?" She kept her tone innocent.

"Like you want to take full advantage of an injured man."

"Hmm." She gave him her wicked grin and didn't move.

"Get over here," he growled.

"I suppose, this once, I'll appease the snarly injured man." She crossed the distance and sat beside him. "To crush your hopes straight away, I'm immune to pitiful patients and their demands. You'll get no sympathy from me."

"Don't need it." Faster than she could squeak, he pulled her onto his lap, wrapped her tight in his arms and pressed his mouth to hers.

The kiss stole her senses with its sweetness, warm and melting, so tender she had to surrender. When he took her hand and placed it over his heart, tears stung her eyes. His pulse thrummed, steady and strong beneath her palm, a reminder that he was here, alive, with her. With each passing beat, the love she held for him sank deeper, as if delicately stitching his name on her soul.

Leo leaned his forehead against hers and closed his eyes, his breath drifting over her face. "While I laid there in the darkness, I was sure I'd never leave that place, that no one would come for me. I know it wasn't a rational thought, driven by panic and fear." He twisted his fingers in her hair, gentle, as if he needed to anchor himself to her. "I was terrified you'd never come back to me, Ren."

The desperation haunting his voice knifed her heart. She'd put that doubt there when she'd left. Knowing he'd been alone and trapped, thinking for even a moment she'd abandoned him forever killed her.

"*Leo.*" She cupped his face between her hands. "I will *always* come back for you. You're everything to me. I love you, one hundred percent."

He sucked in a sharp breath and his lashes lifted. "Say it again."

The guarded hope in his eyes hit her square in the chest, and the last remnants of her doubts and boundaries dissolved like mist in the morning sun. He was scared, just like her, afraid of having his heart broken, terrified of losing the one person who mattered most to him—her. Joy boiled up, fierce and sudden, so much that her heart threatened to burst at the seams. *She* was that person to him. Karen, the weird Goth girl who never quite fit in, had finally found exactly where she belonged.

With Leo.

"I love you." Her face hurt from smiling.

"Not that." His throat bobbed. "I know you love me."

"Hell, Hughes." Her voice cracked, no more than a whisper. She slid her arms around his neck and held his gaze. "You hold my heart. I'll always come back to you. Want another blood vow to prove it?"

"Absolutely. Later." His eyes heated as he slipped his fingers beneath her hoodie and up her spine, leaving a trail of goosebumps. "Much later." With his other hand still in her hair, he tilted her head back and pressed hot, open-mouthed, bone-melting kisses from her ear to her throat.

Karen shivered. She closed her eyes, savoring the softness of his lips, the friction of his callused fingertips on her skin, the gentle, sandpaper rub of his stubble. He licked her pulse point and she gasped.

"Let's go upstairs," he murmured. "I'll keep you in bed until next week."

"Wait!" Her breath came fast, rough, as he unzipped her hoodie, brushing her breast along the way. Chilled air caressed her exposed skin. "What about the curse?"

"What curse?" He nibbled along her collarbone.

"This is the fiftieth year since the last Granton tragedy." She swallowed a moan of need as he bit the cord between her shoulder and neck. "If the curse needs blood, I refuse to let it be yours or mine." Before she completely succumbed to his spell, she pushed off his lap. Standing on the bottom step, she clung to the railing, needing the support. Only a few kisses and Leo turned her into mush. She pretended she remained in complete control and stared him down. "I thought I'd lost you, Leo. As much as I love this place, I won't tempt fate."

"Ren, darling." He hauled himself up with the banister, favoring his ankle, and towered over her. Leaning down, he trailed his knuckles over her cheek. "You still don't get it. If there ever was a curse — and I'm neither confirming nor denying — you've clearly broken it."

Heat shimmered along her cheekbone, echoing in all the other places he'd touched, calling her to surrender. "How do you figure?"

"Maybe I was drawn here, led by an encounter with some cemetery phantom. There's no denying Oliver played a part with his familial ties, bringing the key and Greta's journal." He took her hand and tugged her up to the step above him, putting them at eye level. "But without you, nothing would have changed. Without your unrelenting curiosity, the key found in a spider's nest would be tossed in the trash. Without your willingness to brave every fear, both yours and mine, that grandfather clock never would have revealed Edwin's secrets."

Her throat tightened, making it impossible to speak.

"Without your undying friendship, I might still be in that hole, trapped and alone. Without your fascination for the supernatural, Elizabeth may very well have not been found for another century or more. Without you, Edwin wouldn't have his peace."

She blinked back another burn of tears. *Hell.* The combo of Granton and Leo had warped her.

"Ren, it was you all along that Granton Hall needed. From the moment we met, I knew you were the one I need, too." That lazy smile she adored came to life and his eyes gleamed. "My daring curse-destroyer."

"Curse-destroyer." She tapped her chin. "I could get used to that nickname."

"Hmm."

Her humor faded, overrun by deeper, stronger emotions that demanded to be free. "I need you, too, Leo." She leaned in and brushed her lips over his, a promise of forever. "Every day."

He pulled her against him and wrapped his strong, sure arms around her. "Tell me again."

All the events of the last month poured into her with an intensity that shook her. Sharper than any blade, more powerful than any blood vow, whatever words she said in this moment would impact the rest of her life—her future with Leo. She didn't need a whiff of smoke and cloves to connect the dots.

"I need you, love you, don't want to live without you." She eased back enough to study the eyes that had always seen the weft and weave of her soul and wanted her, loved her anyway. The words that Elizabeth wished she'd said to Edwin, words lost behind fear and lives lost too soon spilled free. "Friends eternal, love everlasting." She took his hand and held it over her wildly beating heart. "Yours, now and always, Leo. All of me...forever."

"Now and always, Ren."

The vow shuddered through her like a spell tangling in her blood and bones.

He captured her mouth and kissed her, long and deep, guiding her backward up the stairs, and all concerns of curses faded into the ether. Between an occasional hiss of pain from Leo, they helped each other remove clothing along each stumbling, hobbling step of the way. Between kisses, caresses and the flames building hot between them, she didn't recognize where he'd led her until the backs of her knees hit the mattress in her room. Sir Snugglebottom lifted his head from where he curled on the corner of her bed, clearly unimpressed at being disturbed.

Then she was on her back, Leo's body a heated, welcome weight on her, his mouth bewitching her senses once more. He twined his fingers with hers, and as he slid into her and they moved together, her heart rate adjusted beat by beat until it matched the tempo of his. With every thrust of his hips, each whispered endearment, second by burning second, one word settled deeper into her soul.

Home.

* * * *

Two weeks later…

"I know we're at Granton Hall." Beneath the blindfold Karen had insisted he wear, Leo smirked. The surprise she had waiting for him would *not* be ruined.

"No, we're not," she lied. She waved a hand before his face.

"I'm not peeking." Sniffing as if his honor had been questioned, he hobbled down the ballroom corridor, graceful even with a crutch. "I recognize that particular squeak of the front door and the hallway floor creaks at the second step." His mouth turned down beneath the black blindfold. "The police must have approved fixing the stairs since we didn't fall through."

Dammit. She'd kept him locked in her apartment while his ankle healed. Broken curses and personal revelations had nothing to do with her motives. A smaller space made it easier to keep an eye on him — or pamper him, depending on one's perspective — and while he slept, dealt with the upcoming magazine article, or micromanaged his construction crew from afar, she'd tended to her own doings. Sometimes, it was galling how easily he figured her out.

"I recently learned some useful skills from the best master construction worker ever." She slipped her arm deeper through his, enjoying the softness of his black cashmere sweater on her skin, the brush of his jeans against her flared, velvet skirt. He was way underdressed for the occasion, but telling him to wear a suit would have raised his suspicions even more.

"Master." One side of his mouth twitched. "I like the sound of that."

"Don't get your hopes up." She guided him down the corridor. The carpet and paneling had been replaced, any hint of debris removed. A new paint scent laced the air. Her forest-green dress whispered with each step, and she couldn't wait to see his expression when he saw her in it. Sleeveless, with a black corset and laced-up back, she totally rocked it with buckled boots.

"Why are you being so sneaky, Ren?" His forehead creased. "Whenever you're sneaky, it never bodes well for me."

"Don't you trust me?" she asked sweetly.

"On certain occasions, this not being one of them. How much longer do you intend to torment me?" Leo lifted his nose in the air. "I smell food."

"A leftover hamburger your crew left behind." Another necessary lie.

"This is invalid abuse."

"Suck it up, Hughes." Karen led him by the arm and matched her steps to his. With his casted ankle, keeping up wasn't a problem. "You'll get there when you get there."

With Liam's help, she'd worked on this project all week. He had some making up to do, and she wasn't above manipulating brotherly guilt. She'd needed the assistance for the final touches of her ultimate declaration of love. She bounced up and down. Hughes wouldn't know what hit him.

He paused and faced her, frowning. "Why are you bouncing? Halloween is over. If you're offering me as a sacrifice to a clown with a chainsaw, I'll haunt you for eternity. You've been warned."

"You'll have to wait and see," she sang. She tugged on his arm. "Just a little farther. You can do it."

"You're lucky I love you."

She laughed at the snarl in his voice. "So lucky. Now stop whining and move, Hughes."

He tapped his lips. "Not until you kiss me. You've shorted me on kisses this week, and I'll have my due."

"Fine." She heaved a sigh, as if smooching him was some sort of punishment. Lifting on tiptoes, Karen tugged his head down to her. She kissed him until he fisted her hair and growled into her mouth. If the surprise waiting for him wasn't so epic, she might have saved it for later and dragged him upstairs instead.

"Nice try at distracting me," she gasped, breaking away, "but there's no escaping your fate."

His mouth curved into that lazy half-smile she loved. "It was a valiant effort, though."

Yes, yes, it was. "No comment." She released a long breath, calming her heartbeat, and took him by the hand. "Onward and upward. A few more steps."

Karen led him past the stained-glass windows dulled by night and onto the marble landing, to the closed ballroom doors muffling any noise. She guided him to a stop. "Okay, I'll remove the blindfold now." She unknotted the material. "Gird your loins, Hughes."

As she pulled the blindfold free, his blue eyes went wide. His gaze traveled over her slowly, and every inch of her heated and tingled beneath his approval.

"Good God, Ren." His voice rasped, husky with need. "You're so beautiful I can't breathe and—" At movement in the ballroom, he turned his head and went completely still.

She opened the doors wide and let the final results of her hard work sink in. Vanilla-scented candles filled every chandelier and cast a golden glow over the parquet floor and walls, adding a hint of magic — the good kind. Garlands of rowan berries, holly and white roses draped the rafters, banisters and windows. A suit of armor stood on guard beside a full buffet table, courtesy of Gia's persuasion, since the armor belonged to Ian. A trio of musicians in masks and medieval garb waited for her cue on the stage. Filling the ballroom were family, friends and citizens of Graywood, all in masquerade masks, suits and fancy gowns. Leo's brothers stood in a knot, each one bearing a glowing light saber — and a crutch to even the playing field and keep everyone honest.

Hughes must be affecting her, because she'd surprised herself by inviting her own family. They'd shocked her right back by saying they'd love to come. Her parents smiled from one corner. The pride in their expressions made her heart swell more. Her sister Iris had stayed behind to handle the farm, but Hannah hadn't passed up the opportunity to show off her new husband.

Karen let her grin widen to wicked as Leo pulled her close. Maybe it was petty to be enjoying Hannah's sour expression so much. Gloating was another learned habit courtesy of Leo. But best of all? Seeing Hank again had zero effect on her heart. She might even consider talking Leo out of crushing them.

"Ren...what is this?" Leo tore his focus from the ballroom and fixed it on her.

Her face hurt from smiling. "While you were being prodded, pampered and laid up this week, I was busy."

"*You* did this?"

"Liam helped me — his version of an apology for the spider parquet prank." She looped her arm through his. "And everyone here made a donation to the Granton Hall nonprofit charity."

"What charity?" His voice cracked.

"The one I set up for you last week." She shrugged. "It's not official yet, of course. My accounting skills are exceptional, but the red tape still has to be dealt with. I'm not a witch with supernatural powers."

"Not so sure about that."

She narrowed her eyes at him.

"I mean that in the best of ways." He cupped her face and kissed her softly. "In one week, you organized all this? And you even convinced Cooper to invest?"

She glanced at where Cooper stood among the crowd, grinning slyly at Liam. Her peacock mask matched the aqua rhinestones sparkling on her clinging, low-cut gown, which her prey seemed to be attempting not to appreciate. Harlan cleaned up nice, but Liam had his work cut out for him if he hoped to avoid that train wreck. Odds were, he'd be crashing with her. Harlan was a nigh unstoppable force.

"She's still hoping I'll take the accountant job at Cooper Homes." And if Cooper agreed to her part-time conditions, she'd take it. It all depended on Leo. "But if you have any upcoming need for parquetry, let me know. It's kind of my specialty."

He studied her for a moment. "What are you saying, Ren?"

"If the offer is still open, I'd — "

He took her mouth again, cutting her off with a long kiss, sweet and full of promises. She barely heard the wolf whistles coming from the ballroom. The musicians took it as a sign, and the keen of a violin joined the clear melody of flute and a harp's dreamy strum.

"Always, Ren." He kissed the tip of her nose. "We'll be an unstoppable team. There's nothing I want more than to work and play with you every day, to spend my life and hours with you."

She arched an eyebrow. "Nothing?"

His eyes heated to blue flames, and that lazy smirk she'd loved from the first made her pulse kick up. "Didn't I mention that the offer is all-inclusive? You should always read the fine print before accepting jobs, darling."

"I know exactly what I'm getting into, bestie."

"Hmm. Don't you mean love of your life?"

"Both." Tears blurred her vision. When they had been only friends, she'd hoped to find someone who could match what she felt for him, at least enough to make her forget that he was everything she wanted and thought she couldn't have without losing her best friend. The fact that she had both best friend and soulmate packaged in the man of her dreams was a frickin' miracle that she'd never take for granted. She slipped on her mask. "Ready to meet your people, sir?"

He lifted her hand to his lips and brushed a kiss over her knuckles. "With you beside me, I'm ready for anything."

Karen laced her fingers with his and, together, they entered the room where every piece of her heart had been found and arranged into perfect place.

Epilogue

Leo set the shovel aside and wiped his brow. November morning mist curled over moss and pine needles, keeping the shadows close. The statues and rose bushes watched, forlorn in the gloom. Karen huddled in her jacket and jeans on the stone bench nearby, her caramel-laced coffee in her gloved hands. The matching music boxes, one carrying the tobacco pouch, the other letters written by Edwin and Elizabeth, rested beside her.

The sunrise walk through the darkness to the rose garden with Ren, holding her hand the entire way, had passed in solemn silence. He'd spent the last half hour digging a hole between an iron arbor and a faceless faun statue bearing faded initials at its base, a testament to love found and lost. Now it was time to say goodbye.

"Ready, Ren?" He kept his voice quiet, as if speaking too loudly was disrespectful to any lingering phantoms.

She nodded and set her coffee cup down. A music box in each hand, she made her way to him. Before handing him the music boxes, she lifted on her tiptoes and kissed him. "I love you, Leo."

His heart ached in the best way. He'd never get tired of hearing those words from her lovely mouth. And he understood why she chose to say them now, in this place where a bond forged in friendship and stretched by love had ruined two lives. It was a promise that not all history would be repeated, that their vows to each other would remain strong and true, no matter what trials they faced.

He took the music boxes from her and placed them side by side at the bottom of the hole. "May you both find peace in the next life."

"And each other." She dropped the lock of hair and ribbons she'd found with the letters into the grave. "I wish the police investigation confirmed more than Elizabeth's identity and that she'd died from poisoning."

"Such as?"

"If she locked herself in that room and took the poison herself."

"Or if her husband trapped her in there?"

"Maybe it was neither." Her eyes narrowed. "After all, Greta had the key. Sad that we'll never know."

"Maybe some truths are meant to remain buried."

Her adorable dimple appeared. "You just don't want me to find any more secrets."

He hid a shudder. "Granton Hall has no more secrets."

She patted his arm, her eyes glinting with an evil light. "Don't worry, Hughes. I'll find them for you."

"Wonderful." Leo lifted the shovel. "Want to do the honors?"

"I think it's best if you do the burying." She frowned and focused on the remnants of the past, all humor faded. "It feels like you're closing an old chapter of your life while I'm opening a brand new one."

"But we both conquered our fears." He handed her the shovel. "We'll do it together."

She smiled up at him and grasped the shovel handle with him. "Together."

"Forever."

Together, they buried the past and, hand in hand, returned to Granton Hall to tackle their future, whatever may come.

Want to see more from this author?
Here's a taster for you to enjoy!

Music, Love and Other Miseries: Every Minute
C.J. Burright

Excerpt

Adara never should've made any deathbed promises to her brother. Pebbles cracked like bones beneath her heels as she trudged between the boxwood hedging the country club's parking lot. If she hadn't made a sacred vow to accept all social invites from Gia, her brother's wildly still-alive girlfriend, she wouldn't be facing the torture of another Hamilton & Associates Belated Yule Celebration...in February. Apparently with prestige and power came the ability to reschedule Christmas.

She slipped between two cars too expensive to breathe on, the glowing mansion lights guiding her. While only a few miles out of town, the country club felt another universe away, especially tonight. Over a year had screamed by in a blur, and it felt like no time had passed since she'd walked this same path — same shoes, same black dress.

Different Adara.

She bit her lip. *Nope, not going there.* Especially not tonight when she had to cope in public.

The rolling pebbles gave way to smooth courtyard pavestones. Gia waited beside the gurgling center fountain with one hip cocked, cute as always in an eye-burning red sequin-and-chiffon number.

"Halloween was two months ago." Gia arched one perfectly shaped blonde eyebrow. "What happened to classic winter white?"

Adara slogged the last few steps between them. *No slinking away now.* Gia would send out the SWAT team to track her and was more than willing to take her down at gunpoint. "Black is appropriate for every occasion. Besides, it encompasses all colors."

"So does a black hole." Gia batted her spiked lashes, not at all innocent.

"You're right." Adara spun back toward her car. "I'll go home and change."

"Not even." Gia lunged and latched onto her arm, bringing a breeze of spicy perfume. "I anticipated your usual wardrobe tragedy and came prepared." With her free hand, she dug in her clutch and whipped out a strip of shiny material. "Hold still or I'll smack you."

Adara reluctantly obeyed while Gia wrapped a festive green and red plaid sash around her waist and cinched it tight, Christmas resurrected two months too late. She resisted cringing when Gia's scrutiny lifted from the ribbon to her zero-makeup face.

That blonde eyebrow went up again. Faster than any sharp-shooter, Gia popped open a tube of scarlet lipstick and held it to Adara's mouth like a weapon. "Resistance is futile. Clown or glam, Dar. Your choice."

Resistance was tempting. A circus look might keep people back. Then again, looking deranged would give people even more reason to talk. Some secrets didn't need to be shared. She glared as a matter of principle.

"I knew you could be rational." The makeup session was over in three seconds. Gia smiled, triumphant. "There. You're perfect."

"Perfect for what?" Adara didn't bother hiding the snarl in her voice.

"To be out in the world of the living." The words were teasing but Gia's tone was gentle, understanding.

A single pang pierced her heart, sharp as any arrow, so fierce it threatened to steal her breath. It was an improvement, though. A year ago, the pain had been nonstop, debilitating. She managed a hoarse whisper. "I never should've made that promise to him."

"As if you had a choice." Gia snorted, thankfully ignoring her emotional slip. "Joey could've persuaded a nun to strip—and she'd be the one paying him. He knew you'd stay in your one-person bubble forever unless he coerced your immortal oath to truly live after he"—her throat worked and her smile wobbled for a second—"after he left."

Adara focused on the mansion's pillared entrance. She wanted to think about her brother's death almost as much as she wanted to be at this party. She cleared her throat and the shadow of sorrow with it. "Truly living equals soirées with stuffed suits using liquid cheer as an excuse for lewd behavior? Dance moves my mind can't possibly unsee? Dodging covertly placed mistletoe and any awaiting tongues?"

"Tonight it does." Gia looped her arm through Adara's and tugged her up the brick stairs. "Show me you still know how to smile."

She bared her teeth.

Gia shuddered. "Forget it. Just look pretty and focus on your goal."

"I have a goal?" She thought merely showing up was a victory.

"Yep. Be nice."

"I'm nice."

"To plants and children, not so much to adult humans."

Plants and children were easy. They didn't expect deep conversation or emotional displays. Adara dragged her feet, the mansion close enough to spill hints of the party happening inside. Red and green lights blinked through the windows onto the stone sidewalk, and buzzing chatter filtered free with the occasional laugh. No music yet. Once the band started, she might fake an excuse to leave. Not even General Gia was heartless enough to make her stay and suffer if particular music started playing.

"Cheer up, Dar." Gia squeezed her arm as she opened the great iron door, freeing a wave of warm air. "Ian will be here."

Adara almost growled. Ian, the lawyer with the supersonic smile who'd taken advantage of Gia's grief at last year's party... *Scum-sucking dirtbag shark.* "Perfect. I can castrate him for Christmas. It's never too late for gifts."

Gia paused in the foyer and stared at her. "Honestly, don't smile. I like my job. If you give Mr. Hamilton a heart attack, I'll have to be your teacher's aide, and you know I'm allergic to chalk and children."

Closing the door behind them, Adara drew a long breath laced with pine and cinnamon. "Let the fun begin."

* * * *

Garret dumped his leather jacket over his violin case and straightened his white button-down shirt. He hadn't even changed after the plane had landed, instead loading his luggage and instruments into a rental, confirming Ian's obnoxious email invite a second time and heading here, Millionaire Estates. Ian probably thought he'd flake — and maybe he should — but it had been years since they'd met up, years since he'd been home, and performing a few numbers at a postponed holiday work party was the recharge kickoff he needed.

Hushed laughter drifted into the coat room, the intimate sound easing the last travel tension from his shoulders, whispering he'd made the right choice in returning. Not that he doubted his decision... The second he'd stepped onto pavement, energy had buzzed through his boots like lightning. Three years on the overseas concert circuit and its large audience disconnect had stolen a piece of him.

He was home to take it back — with interest.

Tucking his violin and bow beneath one arm, Garret entered the candlelit hallway draped in clove-laced garlands and followed the soft pulse of '60s music. It had been too long since he'd celebrated Christmas with family or friends, and he didn't mind rewinding a couple of months, another catch-up on things he'd missed while on tour. This particular bash had been going on for at least an hour, long enough for pleasantly toasted guests to miss any latecomers sliding in for the festivities but not so much that the old-timers had taken off.

He wandered through the double-door entrance and the holiday aura washed through him. People were gathered in talking packs, either standing or sitting, most with a bottle or glass in hand. More danced to the Beach Boys song blasting from unseen speakers. Even with Garret's height advantage, Ian would be hard to spot. A medley of glitter and glass dazzled from every direction, dominated by a giant tree with twinkling tinsel and obnoxious ornaments, its pine scent a reminder of Christmases past.

Attention on the crowd, searching for a hint of Ian, Garret eased past chatting people and around tables decorated with cinnamon-scented pinecones. He bumped into something and caught his balance just as a giant plastic reindeer nosedived. Tail in the air, it fell at the feet of a woman leaning against the wall, paying homage from the tip of its blinking red nose. For a brief, searing moment, her gaze met his.

The festival of chaos and colors faded into the background, leaving room for only her. She blended with the shadows, as if hoping to vanish with the night. Sorrow haunted her eyes, a thousand notes trapped.

Garret blinked and the moment passed. *Ben-zonna.* His favorite foreign curse fit the occasion. *A thousand notes trapped?* That was remarkably sappy, even for him.

No smile, no words, she picked up the glittering Rudolph monstrosity and settled all four twinkling hooves solidly on the floor. Without looking at him again, she resumed watching the other people like they were on a carousel revolving around her, moving too fast to touch.

Anyone who could make his world stand still for even a heartbeat demanded at least an introduction. Keeping his violin protectively close, he eased past the reindeer decoration and mimicked her wallflower pose, barely a foot separating them.

She didn't acknowledge him, her laser-point focus set on something or someone in the crowd.

Garret followed her gaze and hid a groan. Of course it had to be Ian. His childhood friend mingled with a cluster of women wearing Santa hats and short skirts.

All smiles and hands, Ian played his part. Interestingly enough, his glances kept straying to the petite blonde in the red dress another conversation group away.

He leaned slightly in the woman's direction. "So is it Ian or the blonde in red?"

The barely-there pursing of her generous crimson lips promised she'd heard, and the following silence went on long enough to mark a protest. She sighed softly, not sparing him a glance. "What?"

No matter the impatience threading her tone, her husky voice held a song all its own, low and heady, hitting him straight in the gut. "I was wondering whether you're plotting to murder Ian or the blonde." He shrugged. "From the fire and brimstone look you're sending that way, one of them is going down."

"Ian's the only one deserving of a pitchfork stab in sensitive places." She uncrossed her arms and dropped them to her sides, still not making eye contact. "I'm just watching Gia's back. And in case you were also wondering, I don't need a drink, I'm not lonely and I loathe dancing. Any mistletoe I find on your person will be promptly stuffed up your nose."

He gave a startled laugh. "Duly noted. For the record, I rarely drink, I don't mind solitude and I keep my dance moves private to prevent public panic. Mistletoe gives me hives, so I'm relatively safe from your anti-vegetation assault."

Her mouth twitched, a mere tremble and nothing close to a smile, but it was a start.

Before he could turn that tic into a true smile or ask her name, the beach music choked and a snow-haired man in a designer suit climbed the stairs to a stage across the room, presumably the esteemed Mr. Hamilton.

The mystery woman beside him straightened and shifted toward the stage. Apparently, the only way to get her to look at him would be if he was there, on display. He tightened his grip on the violin. Becoming the center of attention was one of his super skills.

Mr. Hamilton launched into a speech about success and the justice system, and Garret tuned him out, riveted on the woman so close. Her hair gleamed like obsidian in the twinkling lights, stopping bluntly at the slender line of her neck. She wasn't wearing glitter, eyeliner or powder like the other women, which made her crimson lips all the more sinful.

Polite clapping erupted, the only reason he knew the speech had ended. Old man Hamilton departed the stage and Ian stepped aside, the prince waiting to ascend once his king cleared the way.

Some opportunities couldn't be resisted. Garret tucked his violin beneath his chin and readied the bow. As Ian's polished shoe hit the first step, Darth Vader's theme song marched up from his instrument and into the vaulted ceiling, shaking the crowd into a momentary silence. A few brave souls snickered, and he didn't miss how the woman beside him stiffened. Faces turned his way, but Ian's response was the one he watched for.

The flip of emotions on his friend's face was everything he'd hoped for, annoyance to realization to amusement. It took Ian less than a millisecond to target Garret in the shadows. He grabbed the microphone and said in a heavy-breather voice, "If only you knew the power of the dark side."

Laughter rippled over the crowd, and Garret grinned. Ian hadn't lost his sense of humor over the last three years, a good sign. Lawyering could strangle happiness until only bitterness and jaded opinions remained.

"I came up here to spread cheer through overpriced and frivolous gifts, but that will have to wait a little while longer." Ignoring the good-hearted groans, Ian straightened his slouchy elf hat. "Patience, people."

Garret sawed out a measure of the *Jeopardy* game show theme. He'd perfected musical harassment decades ago, as his older sister London could attest. It was his best self-defense tactic besides quick reflexes.

Ian pointed threateningly at Garret and flashed one of his trademark smiles, white and brilliant with a bite. "If you're going to play, get on stage and do it right."

When he'd accepted Ian's invitation to the party, he knew companionship and conversation weren't all that Ian would expect. Ian liked to impress, and with stodgy lawyers who appreciated fine music in their midst, he probably hoped for an edge when it came to earning the coveted partner title. Being friends with an accomplished musician might be the one—Garret drummed his fingers once on his jeans, right at the frayed hole near his pocket—or not. Not everyone at this particular party would appreciate his rendition of *Thunderstruck*. He didn't possess the concert musician vibe and his tastes weren't always geared to Bach and Mozart, as Ian well knew. He'd never quite fit into the classical musician stereotype, not even in the long years he'd focused on the classics. He straightened from the wall. Classical preferences or not, he could make everyone happy.

His intriguing companion folded her arms and shifted at an even sharper angle toward the stage. She still hadn't looked at him again, as if determined to burn Ian alive with her stare while keeping all intruders — including him, insultingly — outside her personal bubble.

Hooking his thumb in his pocket, Garret strolled into her direct line of vision, resisting the urge to look over his shoulder and capture her gaze. Breaking bubbles was another one of his super skills.

About the Author

C.J. Burright is a native Oregonian and refuses to leave. A member of Romance Writers of America and the Fantasy, Futuristic & Paranormal special interest chapter, while she has worked for years in a law office, she chooses to avoid writing legal thrillers (for now) and instead invades the world of paranormal romance, fantasy, and contemporary romance. C.J. also has her 4th Dan Black Belt in Tae Kwon Do and believes a story isn't complete without at least one fight scene. Her meager spare time is spent working out, refueling with mochas, gardening, gorging on Assassin's Creed, and rooting on the Seattle Mariners…always with music. She shares life with her husband, daughter, and a devoted cat herd.

C.J. Burright loves to hear from readers. You can find her contact information, website details and author profile page at https://www.totallybound.com

Home of Erotic Romance

Sign up for our newsletter and find out about all our
romance book releases, eBook sales and promotions,
sneak peeks and FREE romance books!